PAYBACK

PENNY MICKELBURY

Bywater
BOOKS

2025

Bywater Books

Print ISBN: 978-1-61294-303-9

Bywater Books First Edition: February 2025

Printed in the United States of America
on acid-free paper.

Cover design: TreeHouse Studio

Bywater Books
PO Box 3671
Ann Arbor MI 48106-3671

www.bywaterbooks.com

PROLOGUE

She saw the three boys in the alley as soon as she entered, but they were on her before she could turn and run. They were younger than she was—maybe sixteen or seventeen—and they were drunk, stinking of cigarettes and booze. They grabbed at her, and she was powerless to stop them because they held her arms, pushing and leading her deeper into the alley, into the shadows. She knew what was coming, and when it did, she fought and kicked and screamed. They slapped and punched her in the mouth until she stopped screaming, and smacked her arms and legs every time she landed a punch or a kick. When they pulled off her shoes, she knew what was next. She fought with all the strength she had left, but the group leader punched her hard in the face, momentarily knocking her out. Unfortunately, it wasn't long enough to keep her from feeling what happened. When she was naked from the waist down the attempted rape began.

"Goddamn she's tight! We got ourselves a fuckin' virgin! I ain't never busted a cherry and my first one is a nigger!" But he did not penetrate.

"Get off, Tony, and let a real man with a real dick show you how it's done."

"Yeah, Berto, you show him!"

"What the fuck is wrong wit this bitch! Gimme that bottle!"

And he used the bottle.

"Ye bleedin' eejits! What the feck are ye doin'?"

"Well, if it ain't Officer Irish Whiskey—drunk as usual!"

"What are youse doin' to the lassie? I gotta call this in!" he mumbled drunkenly, fumbling for the walkie-talkie on his belt. But he dropped it, watching it as it fell, then looking down at it, confused.

"Don't let him call nobody!"

"Give him the bottle!"

"I ain't givin' his drunk ass my rum!"

Tony snatched the bottle from Berto and gave it to Officer Swinley. "Enjoy yerself, Officer!"

The three rapists ran out of the alley leaving the drunk cop staring down in horror at the young woman on the ground. "Jesus, Mary, and Joseph," he whispered, crossing himself before unscrewing the top on the bottle of rum and taking a swig. He staggered over to a fruit crate, eased himself into a sitting position, continued sipping the rum, which he found he liked more than the rotgut Irish whiskey that was his mainstay. When the rum was gone, he closed his eyes for a little nap, unaware that the brutalized woman on the ground had tried and failed several times to get up. He was unaware that a young man well-known to him, Denny Williams by name, was cutting through the alley on his way home, saw and recognized the woman on the ground, and ran to tell her family, and was still unaware when William Jackson Senior and Junior ran into the alley ten minutes later and found his drunken ass snoring.

Jackson Senior grabbed the fallen walkie-talkie and began screaming into it, and within minutes cops began streaming into the alley. One look at Jack and the passed-out Officer Swinley led to a call for higher-ranking officers, and an ambulance from Harlem Hospital. By that time an angry crowd had gathered. The police had hoped to have Officer Swinley on his feet and out of

2

sight before the people who suffered from his incompetence saw him, but it was too late for that. The crowd parted only to permit the ambulance to enter the alley, place Jack on the stretcher, load her and her father into the rear, and screech away. Then the anger at the police returned, loudly and fiercely, and the cops were, for once, wise enough to realize that their bullying behavior would have no effect on those who had witnessed the damaged body spread-eagled on the filthy alley ground and the drunken cop who had closed his eyes to her.

CHAPTER ONE

"Stompin' at the Savoy" was more than a song title. Much, much more—even people who had never crossed the storied threshold knew that. How could they possibly know what they'd never experienced? Because from outside, even from several blocks away, the sound of some of the best bands in the world, playing some of the best music ever written for big bands, and the sound of thousands of feet pounding the wooden dance floor keeping time with the music, carried on the night air.

Even people who didn't reside on Lenox Avenue between 140th and 141st Streets in Harlem, New York City—which is where the Savoy Ballroom was located—could hear the sweet sound because they kept their windows open, even in winter, to listen. And to roll back the rugs in their apartments and dance. It was a neighborhood tradition because few in the neighborhood possessed the elegant—or semi-elegant—wardrobe necessary to swing and stomp at the Savoy Ballroom, even if they could manage the 65 cents, 85 cents after 8 p.m., price of admission.

Bobbie Hilliard possessed both the wardrobe and the 85 cents. The new tuxedo and calfskin loafers all but guaranteed that the first date with one of the Savoy hostesses, Florence Brown, would be successful. As it was two weekends before Thanksgiving, a successful night could mean a holiday season celebrated, at least in part, with the very lovely Miss Brown.

"I'll get out here," Bobbie said, opening the car door. Traffic had not moved in at least fifteen minutes. It would be faster to walk the remaining three blocks to the Savoy. "No need to wait for me, Jack. Go home and enjoy yourself—read one of those books you have stacked up or go play chess with Mr. Joe!"

"Take the top hat and the cane!" Jack called to Bobbie. "You'll look like those sharp ofay fellas, those white boys, in those movies where they dance with the elegant ladies."

Bobbie left the top hat where it was on the back seat but reluctantly grabbed the cane because it would please Jack. "You can always leave it with the hat check girl if you don't want to be bothered with it all night. I can see how holding the cane and a girl might be . . ."

Bobbie didn't hear the rest of the sentence because it was drowned out by blaring horns. Everybody—those going to the Savoy and those who were not—were tired of sitting still in traffic and going nowhere. Bobbie gave Jack a backward wave with the hand that held the cane and darted across 141st Street to Lenox Avenue, where the foot traffic was as heavy as the car traffic. A good number of them were white people from downtown coming uptown to, in the words of a writer from one of the sleaziest rags, "rub shoulders with the jungle bunnies while hopping to the jungle beat." Nothing to do but take it slow and easy, which was probably the best thing to do since hot and sweaty was not an elegant look. Or a good smell.

At the entrance, Bobbie gave the ticket taker a buck, waved away the 15 cents change, and headed for the hat check stand. A scene directly ahead turned the phrase "stopped dead in one's tracks" into an ugly and unexpected reality: a group of men, three in tuxedos, two in double-breasted, striped suits, circled a woman in a beautiful rose-colored gown. She looked terrified. The men laughed. Then one man grabbed the hem of the woman's dress and tried to pull it up. Bobbie ran toward them, cane raised and ready to strike if necessary.

"What in the merry mother fuck are you people doing!" Bobbie grabbed the woman's arm and pulled her away from the men, whose grins quickly became snarls.

"This is none of your business," said the one who had tried to lift the woman's dress.

"That's right, buddy! Step aside," said one of the suited jerks who raised a hand to push Bobbie aside. Bobbie cracked him across the wrist—hard—with the cane, and, like bullies everywhere, his buddies took a quick step away from him.

"You don't understand—"

"Why five grown men find it necessary to gang up on a single woman? You're right, I don't understand that at all," Bobbie said coldly.

"That's just it, my friend; this is no woman," said one of the tuxedos with a leering grin. "She's a he. A faggot in women's clothes."

Bobbie swung the cane again, harder this time, at the man's elbow, and the arm went limp and hung at his side as he whimpered.

"What'd you do that for?!" one of the other tuxedos yelled, looking all around, a slight smug grin on his face, causing Bobbie to look all around, too. A crowd had gathered.

"Because I don't like bullies," Bobbie replied calmly. "I don't like it when five grown men gang up on one woman—"

"I told you: that's not a woman, it's a man!"

"Even if that's true, five against one—" Bobbie started to say.

"If that's true, then this ... person ... will have to leave," said a tall, imperious man in tie and tails who seemed to have just materialized. His name was Harold, and Bobbie knew him to be the manager. "I hope you'll be good enough to escort ... her ... out?" It may have been phrased as a question, but it was an order.

Bobbie hesitated only briefly. This person, whether male or female, had been humiliated enough for one night. Leaving her—or him—to deal with the humiliation alone, especially while still surrounded by her tormentors, was not—

"He took my money. I had five dollars in my purse and he took it," the woman said, a perfectly manicured red fingernail pointing at the man who had called the woman a faggot, a man Bobbie was certain was a pot casting aspersions at the kettle.

"Return her money and do it now so we can leave," Bobbie said in a tone causing the manager to take a step toward the man. It was as if he would retrieve the five bucks himself if necessary to restore calm to his ballroom. He feigned disinterest in the gathered crowd, though, while impressed with his nonchalance, Bobbie knew better. Appearance was everything and even a hint of a crack in the legendary Savoy elegance could be disastrous.

With his good arm the man reached inside his jacket pocket, retrieved a five-dollar bill, and threw it to the floor. The manager picked it up and returned it to its owner. Then Bobbie took her arm and steered her through the gathered crowd and out the front door.

"Just a moment please!" they heard behind them, and Bobbie turned to find Harold, the manager, his outstretched hand holding two one-dollar bills toward them. Bobbie wanted to tell him what he could do with his lousy two bucks, but his companion quickly snatched the bills and offered one to Bobbie.

Bobbie didn't give a damn about the dollar. "Will you please tell Florence Brown that Bobbie Hilliard apologizes for standing her up tonight," she said to the manager.

The man nodded, adding, "I'll also tell her what kinda fella you are if she doesn't already know."

Bobbie grinned and thought, she knows exactly what kind of fella I am. Question is, Mr. Manager, do you know what kind of woman the delectable Miss Brown is? Of course he didn't, and he never would, and the thought amused Bobbie for a moment before it caused profound regret at the thought of the lost opportunity. *Please let Florence be the understanding and forgiving kind of woman as well.* Though in truth, Bobbie didn't really care one way or the other. She wasn't after a relationship or any kind of longevity with Florence—or with anyone. She liked elegance and she liked beautiful women, and she liked to dance with elegant, beautiful women. There would be other nights. And other women.

"Thank you for helping me, but you don't have to stand out here on the sidewalk with me. I'll be fine. Go back inside to your date."

Bobbie looked closely at the woman beside him. A man almost certainly. "What made them attack you like that? And I'm Bobbie Hilliard, by the way."

"I know the one who called me a faggot, a case of the pot calling the kettle black. I spoke to him—just nodded, really, nothing to cause any suspicion among his friends—and he lashed out at me, pointing at me and calling me names. I'm a Bobby, too—Bobby Mason, and I'm very pleased to meet you," he said, checking the hurt in his voice and getting himself under control.

They shook hands, then Bobby Mason, insisting that he would be fine, urged Bobbie Hilliard to return to the Savoy and his date. "I'm sure that a taxi will be by any minute."

Bobbie laughed gently, causing Bobby to glance at her, then at the dense traffic, and back at her. She smiled and touched Bobby's shoulder. "You haven't been here very long, have you? In New York? In Harlem?"

Bobby Mason gave a small, wry smile and shook his head. Then, surprising both of them, tears began to spill from his eyes at almost the same moment that the staccato beat of a car horn drew Bobbie's attention. Lots of horns honked and blared, but this one honked with a familiar tune: "Shave and a Haircut." Bobbie looked up and around and—yes! There was Jack, flashing the car's lights! Thank goodness Jack had ignored the directive to go home and relax.

Bobbie grabbed Bobby's hand and pulled him into the street, into the traffic that was going nowhere, between two cars, and across the street into traffic that was moving slowly enough that a tuxedoed man and a gowned woman crossing the street were in no danger of being struck. Skirting the rear of the highly polished beige-and-brown Chevy, Bobbie opened the back door, practically pushed Bobby inside, climbed in behind him, and slammed the door. "I can't tell you how glad I am to see you, Jack!"

"Does that mean you're glad I didn't listen to you and take myself home?"

Instead of answering a question that didn't need answering, Bobbie said, "Jack, please meet my new friend, Bobby Mason."

Jack slammed on the brakes mere inches from the rear bumper of a rusty old Buick and turned to look at the two people in the backseat. Bobbie was grinning like a Halloween pumpkin. "Bobby, meet my old friend, Jack Jackson."

"Pleased to meet you, Bobby," Jack said, wondering why a long-haired woman wearing a pink gown was named Bobby. She turned back to face the traffic. "Where to?"

"Out of this traffic," Bobbie said, "and I don't care what direction you take as long as we're moving." She cranked the window down a few inches, for which Bobby Mason was grateful. The car smelled like a bus station bathroom.

They drove south on Lenox and when they finally reached the corner of Lenox and 137th, Jack took a fast right turn and sped down the block. The car stopped midway in front of a bodega that was doing a brisk business. The establishment door was propped open despite the cold November night air, and the new record by Clyde McPhatter and the Drifters, *Money Honey*, blared from inside the store and a crowd gathered at the door to listen, as if at a concert. Though the song had barely been out a week, folks were singing along, not missing a lyric, and one couple was executing impressive dance moves that would have been right at home at the Savoy—though the couple, in their threadbare clothes and scuffed, worn shoes, they would not have gotten past the front door, even if they'd had the price of admission.

"That's a good song," Bobbie said, cranking the window down a couple more inches.

"Yeah it is," Jack and Bobby said practically in unison. "And I can definitely relate," Bobby said with feeling. "Money is what I need!"

"I wouldn't mind having a woman to dance with on a regular basis," Bobbie said as the dancing man swung his partner out and gathered her in closely on the return.

"I'm sure Miss Brown would be happy to see you—at your convenience, of course," Bobby said almost primly.

"Where to?" Jack asked again, almost snarky.

"How about down to the Paradise?" Bobbie asked. "Since you never got a chance to stomp at the Savoy, Bobby, would Small's Paradise be an acceptable backup? Have you ever been there?"

Bobby shook his head back and forth and Bobbie didn't know whether that meant he'd never been to Small's or that he didn't want to go, but before she could ask she realized that once again tears were streaming down Bobby's face.

"What is it? Is something wrong?" Bobbie asked, concerned, but he was shaking his head. Then he grabbed a handkerchief from his purse, wiped his face and blew his nose, and began to talk, to explain in detail who he was and why he was in Harlem dressed in women's clothes.

He told a long story about his boyfriend being killed when they both served in Korea, then added, "I came here tonight to honor Jerome and to keep the promises we made to each other. I didn't really think it through, didn't think about what could happen if things went wrong. I just wanted to imagine, to pretend, that our dreams really did come true. And what

11

beautiful dreams they were!"

And when he was finished talking, Bobbie and Jack sat in silence for a very long time. Long enough that Bobby began to shiver, causing Bobbie to crank the window back up, with an apology. The night air had become a few degrees colder, especially blowing into the backseat of a moving car.

Jack broke the silence. "So, you're a Korean War veteran, and you just got back from over there where your boyfriend died in combat. That's terrible. And now you came here, to Harlem, because y'all had talked and dreamed about it so much that you came by yourself? To the Savoy to honor your dead boyfriend?"

Bobby nodded. "He said we would go dancing at the Savoy Ballroom. That we could get jobs and a pretty apartment and see the kind of Colored people we never did see at home—educated people, talented people, and that we could be like them if we worked hard and tried hard. And we could be like we wanted to be and not have to be scared that somebody would find out that we were . . . like . . . that there were enough people like us here that we wouldn't get treated like I was at the Savoy tonight."

"But you didn't bring that on yourself, Bobby. You didn't do anything wrong," Bobbie protested, sharing her new friend's hurt and pain.

"I wouldn't have been treated like I was if that fella wasn't a faggot his own self and scared to death somebody would find out he likes boys instead of girls. And when you found out about me, Bobbie Hilliard, you didn't laugh at me and call me names. You want to take me dancing somewhere else even though you know I'm a man in a woman's dress. You're the kind of people Jerome was talking about. And now I know he wasn't just wishing and hoping." Bobby wound down and stopped talking.

"Did you tell him, Bobbie?" Jack asked, turning toward the back seat and locking eyes with her best friend. Jack's eyes were clear and light brown beneath thick brows and lashes, eyes that reflected the constant, intense pain she had endured for more than a year. And when Bobbie didn't reply, Jack slapped the back of the car seat. "You have to tell him! Tell him right now, Bobbie, or I'll tell him." Never a large woman, Jack's constant pain seemed to shrink her small body even as it enlarged the force of her personality.

Bobby turned sideways in the seat and faced Bobbie. "Tell me what?"

"That I'm not a man. My name is Roberta Hilliard and I'm a woman. So is Jack. And I know that we're no substitutes for who and what you've lost, but we will help you, Bobby Mason, in any way we can."

Bobby blew his nose and sighed deeply. "If it's not too far out of your way, I would really appreciate a ride home. I don't feel like dancing or . . . or pretending that just because I'm in Harlem, New York City, I'm gonna have some kind of wonderful life." His shoulders sagged and he slumped into the corner of the back seat. He said he lived in a rooming house on 111th Street near Seventh Avenue, and he closed his eyes.

"Do you have food and booze in your room?" Bobbie asked.

Bobby's eyes opened and he sat up and peered at her. "Half a pint of rotgut rye and a bag of pork skins."

"Then I'd be pleased if you'd come back to my place. I've got a full Frigidaire, a full bar, and a guest bedroom with its own bathroom." She added the last because she knew that bathrooms in rooming houses were in the hall and the line could be long with hot water in short supply.

"Why would you do this for me? You don't know me or anything about me—"

"Where are you from, Bobby Mason?" Jack asked. She turned to face the backseat again and stared daggers at him, her ever-present and sharp pain making the daggers appear sharp and dangerous.

"East St. Louis, Illinois."

"I don't know anything about the place," Jack said, derision dripping from every word, "but have you ever heard anybody in East St. Louis, Illinois, tell you not to look a gift horse in the mouth?"

"It's all right, Jack," Bobbie said.

"No, it's not all right," Bobby said, "and I do truly apologize. To both of you. That was very rude of me and y'all have been nothing but kind to me. I don't know why I was so rude, Miss Hilliard, I can't explain it, but I do know that I would be very pleased to visit your place—and your full bar and full Frigidaire and full bathroom and guest room. How soon can we get there?"

Jack stomped on the gas and the Chevy lurched forward as if it, too, was ready to quit dithering and go home. They were far enough away from Lenox Avenue that traffic was no longer bumper to bumper, but it still was Saturday night in Harlem and despite the dropping temperature, lots of people still were out and about.

Bobby Mason dried his eyes and observed the passing scene with interest. He hadn't often had such an opportunity—he didn't know anyone with a car and taxi rides weren't in his budget—but he had memorized the subway and bus maps so he knew Jack was heading north, toward what the locals called Uptown. He recognized some of the street names from his subway rides but he'd never actually been on the streets, and he most certainly had never been on this one: Convent Avenue. There must not be a subway stop on this street because he'd never heard of it. Was there a convent nearby?

When Jack stopped the car in front of a block of . . . Bobby didn't know what to call them. They didn't look like the apartment buildings he'd become accustomed to seeing, nor were they the familiar brownstones and rowhouses of the Harlem he was getting to know on his exploratory walks. He had already learned a lot on his quest to learn the history of New York City in general and Harlem in particular, the most important lesson being that they—New York City and Harlem—were no one thing. There was nothing matter of fact or run-of-the-mill about the houses here. And this place called Uptown was as varied and different as the people who lived here, from the drag queens who populated the rooming house where he lived to Bobbie Hilliard and Jack Jackson. Whoever they turned out to be, tonight they were women who came to his rescue and for that he was, perhaps always would be, grateful.

Bobbie opened the car door, got out, and extended a hand to the passenger in a gown that uncomfortably restricted his movement. "I don't know how women can stand being bound up in these outfits!" he groused, managing to stand upright. "These damn dresses or the shoes!"

"We don't either!" Bobbie and Jack exclaimed in unison.

Bobbie leaned into the driver's side window to chat with Jack while Bobby walked around the rear of the Chevy. He stepped onto the sidewalk and walked in front of the row of buildings which all appeared to be stone. Were these single-family residences or apartment buildings? He'd know soon enough.

Bobbie Hilliard, top hat and walking stick in one hand, keys in the other, quick-stepped up the walkway and up the three steps to where Bobby Mason stood before a pair of huge, ornately carved wooden doors. Her key turned smoothly in the lock, and one side of the entry swung open to reveal an elegant if dimly lit foyer.

Bobby stepped in, Bobbie following and, after closing the heavy door and ensuring it was locked, led the way to their left where they stood before a gilded gate, which Bobbie opened to reveal the oldest elevator in the world.

"I don't mind taking the stairs," Bobby said, talking fast and thinking he could walk faster than the ancient-looking lift could transport them.

Bobbie laughed, pushed him inside, pulled the gate slowly closed, and tapped on the two-button panel to the right. The ancient elevator rose, slowly, quietly, and smoothly. It made Bobby think of some of the elders in his grandmother's church—seemed like ages ago—who moved with a slow elegance that said they could move faster if they chose to, but what was the hurry? They'd get where they were going when they got there. And when the elevator got where it was going, it stopped with barely a jolt and the door slid open onto a wide expanse of a room that took Bobby's breath away. The room was huge, and its focus was a shimmering black Steinway grand piano. As Bobby gaped, his hostess removed her shoes, placing them on a shelf beside the door. Bobby did the same and followed her into the room.

"If I lived here, I'd never leave home," Bobby exclaimed, his appreciation clear. The room was a work of art filled with objects so glamorous that if they weren't works of art, they easily could have been.

"There are days when I don't," Bobbie replied quietly.

"I've never seen anything so beautiful—not even in a magazine. And even in those photos I didn't think people really lived in those rooms."

Bobbie smiled but with pain. "This is all my mother. It took years for this room to become this room—one object at a time—except the piano. It moved in with us because my father was a musician, but the rest of it . . ." Bobbie looked around at the different sofas and couches and chairs, benches, tables, pillows, ottomans and photographs on every surface, at the walls covered with floor-to-ceiling bookcases and framed artwork where there were no bookcases.

She had made only minor changes in the time she'd lived here alone. After all, why interfere with perfection? Snapping out of her reverie, she aimed for a hallway, beckoning Bobby to follow. "Your room is at the end down here, and the bathroom is here. I'll bring you some clothes to change into, and I'll get changed and then do something about food and drink."

Bobby showered, grateful to be free of the gown and pumps, definitely, but most grateful for the cold cream that would remove the makeup. His dresser for this evening, known throughout the drag community as Queen Esther, had applied it with what seemed like a spatula. And yes, Bobbie said grinning, she had nail polish remover.

Finally, dressed in the Columbia University sweatshirt, pants, and thick socks Bobbie provided, he made his way back toward the living room. He heard music, some really fine jazz piano though he didn't know who it was, but he didn't see Bobbie. He did smell food, though, and followed the scent down a long hallway, rather than follow the sound of the music he loved, because he was ravenous. Bobbie's back was to him when he entered the kitchen. She wore a floor-length, multicolored silk robe tied around the waist with what looked like a velvet scarf, and she swayed ever so gently in time with music.

"Who is that?"

"Oscar Peterson. Do you like it?" Bobbie replied, stirring whatever she was cooking.

"I like it a lot but . . ." He paused: but what? "I don't really know, Bobbie. I just know it's kinda different from other jazz piano music but I know I like it."

"You've got a good ear, Bobby Mason, and very good taste."

"Speaking of which, whatever that is you're moving around in that pan, it smells wonderful," he said, then stared in open-mouthed wonder when Bobbie turned to face him. She started to laugh and couldn't stop. She howled with laughter. She doubled over and held on to the countertop to keep her balance. She pointed to Bobby, then touched her own face where tears of laughter were streaming down.

Gone was the dapper young tuxedoed gent she had been. Bobby began to chuckle, then chortle, then join in the howl, for now he was nothing like the woman in the pink gown he was earlier. It took a few minutes but the table finally got set, the wine finally was poured, the food was served, and only because they both were starving did the laughter finally get under control so they could sit down and eat.

"You know that we must remain friends, Bobby Mason, so that twenty-five or fifty years from now we can tell people about the moment we first saw each other as our true selves despite having spent the evening together."

"You, Bobbie Hilliard, without heavy, black-framed eyeglasses and a mustache, look like a . . . a very, very beautiful girl."

"And you. Bobby Mason, without half a pound of pancake on your face, look like a very, very handsome boy."

Try as he might, Bobby could not control the deep laughter rising within him and spilling out. "I hope there's a heaven and I hope Jerome is in it because he's the one person who can most appreciate the fact that the second best date I've ever had in my life is with a girl." He wiped the tears from his eyes: the happy tears being joined by sad tears for a brief moment. "I think I need to get to know more girls," he said.

"I highly recommend it," Bobbie added. "One cannot know too many girls."

Dinner finished and kitchen cleaned, she expertly made Manhattans and they sat opposite the unlit fireplace, their feet on ottomans. Bobby's feet were grateful to be rid of the pumps even if Queen Esther had deemed them large enough for his feet. They still were women's shoes and his feet still were men's feet and his toes did not appreciate being squeezed into a point. He was thinking that from now on he'd keep his feet where they belonged.

Despite her initial regret, Bobbie now was grateful that this evening was many hours shorter than it would have been had she kept her date with Florence Brown. She'd probably still be at the Savoy, her new tux reeking of cigarette and cigar smoke, her new calfskin loafers bearing the imprints of the shoes of other people, and if the past was prologue, as it usually was, her fascination with Miss Brown would be wearing thin by this time. "Ready for a refill?"

Bobby hoisted his empty glass then pushed himself to his feet. "What was that and how do you make it?"

"A Manhattan and come on, I'll show you," she said, crossing to the bar on the other side of the room, her robe billowing behind her.

"That robe is gorgeous," Bobby said, following the rich, billowing fabric to the bar.

"It's a kaftan, actually, and it belonged to my father."

"Your father wore a woman's robe?"

A bottle of bourbon in one hand and Angostura bitters in the other, Bobbie peered at Bobby. "Men in many countries around the world wear the kaftan, and it can be both a casual garment and a formal one. This one was a birthday gift from my mother."

Bobby straddled the bar stool and watched Bobbie gather the ingredients and mix them to create the perfect Manhattan. She stirred and poured and he tasted. "Damn, that's good! And you make it quickly and expertly. I'm impressed."

"No need to be. I own a bar, and if I can't make a drink quickly and expertly then I should be in another business."

Bobby stared at her, waiting for her to laugh or otherwise signal that she hadn't meant that she actually owned a bar, but her face remained unchanged. She replaced the bottles on the shelves behind the bar, wiped the top, picked up her glass, and returned to her chair.

The Oscar Peterson album ended and one by Billie Holiday dropped down onto the turntable. Bobby had watched as the fingers on Bobbie's right hand played on the arm of the chair what Oscar was playing on the piano. Now he watched as the hand conducted the musicians making the music for Billie. "Can I ask you something?"

Bobbie's hand stilled and she looked at him, knowing what was coming, and very nearly denied the request, but if she was to be friends with Bobby Mason, and that seemed more likely by the minute, then better to get it over with. She sighed and nodded her head.

"Where are your parents, Bobbie?"

"They're dead. They were killed. Murdered, along with my little brother, three years ago."

Bobby didn't know what to say. How could he, since there was nothing to be said, no appropriate, satisfactory, or adequate words. He hung his head, then lifted it and looked at her, to find her still looking at him, her face a closed and unreadable mask. Finally he said, "I am so very sorry, Bobbie. How truly horrible."

"Yes, it is. And thank you. I know you understand how it feels to lose someone you love at the hands of someone you hate."

"Does it matter if it's been three years instead of three months?" Three months since his Jerome was felled by a Korean soldier's bullet.

She shook her head. "Not one damn bit." Three years since Robert, Eleanor, and Eric Hilliard were shot and killed by a deputy sheriff on a two-lane blacktop road seven miles from Atlanta, Georgia, where fifty family members awaited them. Their crime was being Colored and driving a new Packard sedan with New York license plates.

"If you could avenge their murders, would you? Would you hunt down the murderers and do to them what they did to your family?" He was talking fast and looking at her as if he could read her mind and what was written there, but before she could speak he continued. "I fantasize about finding the soldier who killed Jerome. I know that's nuts. It was a war and how would you possibly find one soldier who fired one bullet at another soldier, at an enemy soldier? But that's as far as my fantasy goes because that would mean I'd have to return to Korea and I never want to see that hellhole again! Not even to get payback for

Jerome." And in his mind, where he often heard Jerome's deep yet gentle baritone, *"You better not go back there, Robert Mason!"* Jerome always called him Robert, never Bobby.

Bobbie nodded slowly, a range of emotions playing on her face, until one settled: understanding mixed with agreement. "I think I'm with you on that one." Despite all the relatives pleading and begging for her to "come home for a visit," she would never set foot in Georgia. Robert and Eleanor were Atlanta natives. Harlem was her home. She stood up. "You sit as long as you like. I'm going to bed. Good night, Bobby. And by the way, you were a pretty good date your own self, despite your boy-ness."

"Good night, Bobbie, and thank you for everything—including that compliment."

She was smiling when she left the room. She truly did like Bobby Mason. He sat for a few more moments despite the fact that he could feel sleep about to claim him, but he wasn't ready to capitulate. Bobbie Hilliard was too much on his mind.

That she was the most remarkable woman he had ever met was not in question, even at her young age. And given her reaction and the expression on her face, he thought she probably knew the name of the man who murdered her family and that she had seriously considered seeking retribution, making him pay for what he did to her, for what he took from her. But making him pay meant returning to Georgia, which she would never do.

Her actions earlier proved that she could and would deliver payback—Bobby was certain that the two men she'd struck with her walking stick at the Savoy had suffered broken bones. Bobbie had swung the stick swiftly, accurately, and forcefully, and then walked away as if they already were forgotten. It was Bobby Mason she cared about in that moment even though she didn't know him, because she thought she was protecting a woman being brutalized by men. She would, he knew with certainty, avenge the slaughter of her family with the same focus if she could do that without returning to Georgia. Just as she would avenge her friend, Jack—if Jack needed avenging. It was clear Bobbie cared very deeply about Jack, and the feeling was mutual, Bobby could see that. The woman was prepared to sit in her car waiting for Bobbie Hilliard to leave the Savoy Ballroom and if not for entirely unforeseen circumstances, it would have been a long wait. And yes, Jack's Chevy was practically brand new and clean as a whistle, but it stank of urine, and the odor emanated from the front seat. Bobbie clearly accepted whatever troubled Jack without comment or complaint or apology—she didn't need to say that anyone who objected could find other transport. Bobbie was a woman in whom quick violence and deep compassion lived side by side in luxury and elegance, a woman who would welcome a stranger in need into her home without hesitation.

Bobby rose, took his glass to the kitchen and washed it. Then he extinguished the lights, but the floor-to-ceiling windows across the front of the room admitted light from outside—from streetlights and passing cars and the apartments across the street—so he easily found his way to his room. He was in bed and buried beneath the covers in seconds, his final conscious thoughts being of the unlikely duo of Bobbie Hilliard and Jack Jackson, and their even more unlikely presence as his rescuers and friends.

As for Bobbie, in her room, wishing for sleep that all too often was too elusive, she took stock of herself. She always cared about those who, for whatever reason, could not care for themselves. She had learned that behavior from her parents who always reached out to help those less fortunate than themselves. "Each one, teach one" was a motto they not only quoted but lived by. *So will I,* she promised them again, and slept.

"Jack might have just gotten you a job," were Bobbie's first words to him the following morning, Sunday, when he joined her in the living room. "Coffee and bagels on the counter," she said, pointing, but not looking up from her newspaper. She was on the big sofa that backed up to the wall of windows, and she was surrounded by newspapers and magazines—*The Amsterdam News*, *Pittsburgh Courier*, *Chicago Defender*, *Ebony* and *NAACP Crisis* magazines, the *Negro Digest*, and a stack of books.

He stared at her to be certain she wasn't joking, then went in search of coffee and a bagel, a kind of bread foreign to him until his arrival in New York but as common here as toast and jam back home. When he returned, coffee cup in one hand, plate of bagels and cream cheese in the other, she looked at him over the rim of her cup, smiling.

"Were you serious? About Jack and a job?" Bobby asked.

"She called me with the news half an hour ago."

Bobby did a perfect guppy imitation—lips moving, no words coming out. Finally, he managed to say, "I don't know what to say, Bobbie. I really don't!"

Bobbie gave a disbelieving shake of her head. "I don't either. Jack doesn't like many people. In fact, I can count the number of people Jack actually likes, though she does manage to tolerate a few more. But to go so far as to get someone a job after a single encounter?" Bobbie grinned widely now, shaking her head back and forth. "I am amazed, I truly am, and I've known Jack Jackson since the first day of first grade."

"Do you think you could control your amazement long enough to tell me about the job?"

"Sorry," Bobbie said, and taming her grin, she told Bobby that the super two buildings away from where Jack lived was looking for an assistant to start work immediately. "And the best part of the job is that it comes with a studio apartment, and the super will interview you today."

"But . . . but . . . what could Jack have told him, except how smashing I look in a rose ball gown and a red wig, that would have won me a job?"

"That you're a veteran just home from Korea. The super is a World War II vet so vets always rise to the top of his hiring list. Jack said he wants to meet you in person and see your discharge papers—"

Bobby sprung to his feet. "They're in my room, in a lockbox under the bed."

Bobbie stood. "Then let's go get your stuff." She picked up the phone, dialed, and reported where they were going so Bobby knew the call was to Jack, and as she hung up the phone she looked down at Bobby's feet and groaned.

"You'll have to wear the bedroom slippers. Sorry, your feet are much larger than mine." She gave a worried frown, then her expression changed to thoughtful. "I do have a pair of Converse high tops that are too large so they may fit you quasi-comfortably."

They were close to the same height, as Bobbie was tall for a girl, and at two inches shy of six feet, Bobby was short for a boy. Owing to the rigors of war and his skimpy funds, and ergo skimpy meals, he was skinnier than he'd ever been so he could wear her clothes, though he couldn't fasten the pants at the waist. But no way could he wear her shoes. He had the feet of a man, and after last night he had no desire to stuff them into women's shoes. He hoped they were Converse shoes made for men since he didn't want to go out into the world wearing bedroom slippers.

Bobbie held open a Saks Fifth Avenue shopping bag and Bobby placed the wig, pumps, and tissue paper-wrapped gown inside. The expression on his face said that he was not sorry to be rid of them, especially as his toes spread comfortably in the Converse canvas shoes. He allowed that small victory to give him cause to feel hopeful that his first real job interview in New York City would result in his first real job in the most famous city in America, thanks to the intervention and kindness of his first friends.

Bobbie donned a pea jacket, tossed Bobby a bomber jacket, and led them through the kitchen, out the back door, and down a rear hallway to a second elevator. When he thought about it, he did know that many of the uptown apartment buildings had garages from which cars exited onto the side streets instead of the street in front of the building. And sure enough they exited the elevator in the garage, where Bobbie led them to a shiny, new Buick Special. It was red and gleamed as if it had just come from the dealer.

Bobby whistled his appreciation and was about to ask about the car but he felt Bobbie close off. He knew cars. This was a 1950 model that had not been driven very much—practically not at all. He also knew, without needing to be told, that the vehicle had belonged to her parents.

The drive downtown to 111th Street and Seventh Avenue didn't take very long, primarily because the church crowd was not yet out and about. Bobbie drove quickly and expertly, maneuvering the big car with its big engine down Broadway and turning onto 111th. She drove four blocks past the Hamilton Lodge Ball building, the site of drag balls featuring Colored drag performers since the 1860s, and stopped in front of the house where Bobby rented a room. He was out of the car and up the front steps before Bobbie put the car in park.

Contrary to what Bobby had come to expect, the building was eerily quiet. Then he remembered what day and time it was. On Sunday morning after a Saturday night with the majority of the residents out making merry until daybreak, nobody was moving about but him. He was the only resident who, despite his wardrobe of the previous night, was not a drag queen . . . he was just a boy who liked boys. He ran up the stairs to the top floor and down the hall to the last room on the end—the largest room in the house—and knocked. And knocked. And knocked. Until anger swung it open.

"What in the hell is the matter wit' you, boy, beatin' on my door like it's some kinda drum? Don't you know what time it is?" Even sans wig, makeup, and top dentures, Queen Esther was a formidable presence. Not by accident was she the Mother of the House, and she took her responsibility seriously.

"I'm really sorry, Queen Esther, but I had to return your things before I go—"

"Where you goin' this time of mornin' that you can't wait until noon o'clock, like a normal person to come callin'?"

"I'm leaving. Moving. I got a job—"

He now had the old queen's total attention. "What kinda job? Where?"

"As a handyman in a building on St. Nicholas Avenue, assistant to the super, and the job comes with a studio apartment." It was all true, Bobby told himself—except he didn't have the job. Yet. But at Queen Esther's reaction he was glad he'd lied.

"Good for you, boy! Good for you. Not here in New Yawk but a month and you already walking in high cotton. I'm proud of you. Now, gimme that bag."

Bobby relinquished the Saks shopping bag, and Queen Esther removed and inspected the items one by one: gown, wig, and shoes, nodding satisfactorily. Then her eyes narrowed, and her nose wrinkled. "Is that piss I smell!?" She held every item to her nose and inhaled deeply. "It's faint, but I know I smell piss."

"You know what the bathrooms are like in a public place," Bobby said.

"You got a point." Queen stuffed the items back into the Saks bag and sauntered over to the dresser, red satin mules slapping against her heels. She opened a drawer and withdrew a handful of envelopes. Like a magician—or a card shark—she pulled one from the stack and held it out toward Bobby. The envelope contained the deposit he paid to rent the gown, shoes, and wig for the evening, and he could tell that, minus her fee, his refund was complete. She sauntered back across the room.

"Piece of advice: I bet you were gorgeous in that gown but you ain't made to be a woman. Me, on the other hand—I was born wrong and that's just a fact. I shoulda been born a woman. I AM a woman, goddammit! Lotta people born in the wrong body and cain't do nothin' about it but suffer."

The sadness in Queen's face was the kind Bobby had seen before—in the faces of older women worn down by life and nothing they could do to change their lives. "But you ain't no woman. You a boy what just happens to like other boys and ain't nothin' wrong with that. Good luck, Bobby Mason. Gonna miss you." And the door closed, the lock turned.

Bobby ran down to the second floor, to his room, unlocked the door, and spent less than a minute throwing all of his belongings into his green Army duffel. He pulled the bed away from the wall and there was his metal lockbox, wedged into the corner where he'd left it. He grabbed it up, pushed the bed back, slung the duffel over his shoulder, and ran down the stairs. He dropped his room key into the slot, and by the time he was out the door and down the steps, Bobbie was out of the car with the trunk open.

"That didn't take long." She looked at him. "What happened?" she asked as he threw the duffel in, slammed the trunk shut, and trotted around to open the passenger door.

"Tell you later . . . though I did lie and say I already had the job, and I kinda feel like I do if Jack's in my corner. Is that nuts?"

"You couldn't have a better good luck charm. Let's go shake the hand of your new boss."

"'Afternoon, sir," Bobby said, and saluted Morris Greeneway when he entered the man's office at two thirty that afternoon. Bobby immediately recognized him as not only a veteran but almost certainly an officer, and when the man crisply returned

Bobby's salute his suspicion was confirmed.

The space occupied by the building superintendent of the St. Nicholas Avenue apartment house was enormous—because so was the ten-story building it served. Greeneway stood behind a large wooden desk and waved Bobby into one of the chairs in front of it. Bobby fished his discharge papers from his inside coat pocket and gave them to Greeneway before he was asked, and it didn't take the former Captain long to learn what he needed to know: that Robert Henry Mason the Third was honorably discharged from the US Army having attained the rank of corporal.

"You stayed in Korea—and in the Army—two months longer than necessary. Why?"

"Two months' more pay, sir. I didn't know how long it would take me to get a job here or how much rent would be." He couldn't tell the man that with Jerome dead in Pusan Province, he'd have to fund all his plans and dreams himself.

"And now that you have a job and no rent to pay, what's your first order of business?"

Bobby almost couldn't say the words. Until this moment he hadn't allowed himself to think the thought. "Find out what the tuition is at New York University."

Bobby signed the document making him an employee of the Upper West Side Real Estate Management Company. Morris Greeneway gave him a fully equipped leather tool belt, two khaki-colored pairs of coveralls—his uniform while on the clock— and a ring with three keys. "To this room and your apartment." Bobby took the keys and held them tightly in his hand before dropping them into his pocket. "Let me show you to your quarters so you can get settled in; then you'll meet me here at 0700 tomorrow morning. Welcome aboard, Mr. Mason."

The apartment was much larger and much nicer than Bobby expected. It was also frigid and the super hurried over to the radiator to turn on the heat. Then he lit the burners on the stove to show Bobby that the gas was on, as was the electricity, point proved when the man flipped a wall switch and the ceiling light came on. Then the super left, leaving Bobby free to survey his new circumstances.

There was a very narrow window in the galley kitchen that looked out at St. Nicholas Avenue and let in stingy light through heavy security bars. There was a transom almost to the ceiling in the bathroom, a room that held a toilet, a tub and a shower, and a floor covered in black-and-white tiles. The main room was large and wonderful. Polished hardwood floors gleamed. A barred window faced St. Nicholas Avenue and would require a curtain at night, but during the day it provided good light. Bobby didn't know what he'd expected. Truth be told, he really had no expectations, so thankful was he to have a place to live that wasn't in a run-down rooming house. But this apartment exceeded even the expectations he hadn't had.

There was a chair and table, which the Super said Bobby could keep or return to the storage room, but either way the telephone on the table came with the apartment and would cost Bobby about two dollars a month, which would be deducted from his paycheck. Unless he made long-distance telephone calls, which would be added. Once a month, he thought, he'd call home. But for now, he picked up the receiver and allowed the dial tone to buzz in his ear for several seconds. Then he pulled out a piece of paper from his pocket and dialed Bobbie's number.

"Hello, Bobbie Hilliard! It's me, Bobby Mason, calling you from my very own apartment on St. Nicholas Avenue in Harlem, New York City."

She was almost as excited as he was, which she proved by taking him on a shopping spree, and as grateful as he was for what she bought him, he was more grateful for what she taught him about shopping, about which he knew nothing. When he lived at home his mother and grandmother did all the shopping. When he left home for Lincoln University he didn't need to shop because he lived in the dorm and ate only because his job in the dining hall provided him two meals a day.

So when the first items Bobbie put in the cart were paper towels, toilet paper, paper napkins, cleaning products (different ones for the kitchen and bathroom) and brushes and cloths to do the cleaning (also different ones for kitchen and bathroom), he asked her to explain.

"You do understand that you must clean where you live, don't you, Bobby?"

Actually, that thought had never crossed his mind though he did recall that it seemed his mother and grandmother were always cleaning, especially the kitchen and bathroom. He also recalled that the bathrooms in the dorm were cleaned several times a day though he didn't think that the bathroom in the boarding house had ever been cleaned. His job in the Lincoln University dining hall had been to clean—constantly—and the woman in charge of the maintenance staff watched her charges with an eagle eye, and inspected the premises with the same scrutiny.

"And I have to clean all the time?" he asked.

"If you don't want bugs and if you don't want your home to stink, yes. Every time you use something, clean up behind yourself."

"So I can assume you won't visit me if I have a stinky home with bugs crawling all around?"

She rolled her eyes at him and said to be damn certain that he used the separate brushes to clean the toilet and the shower and tub. They finished shopping, filling the huge trunk of the big Buick. She helped him unload and take everything inside; then she hugged him and danced him all around and congratulated him. "This is a beautiful apartment, Bobby! I'm thinking that Jerome is somewhere looking out for you."

"I was thinking that very same thing, but I wish he was here with me."

Bobbie nodded her understanding. "I'm going home. Call me if you need me."

"Bobbie—I can't thank you enough."

"You're welcome. I'm glad I could help."

"Can I call Jack? Maybe go see her? I owe her—"

"Get settled in first, then the best way to thank Jack? A gallon of vanilla ice cream and jars of butterscotch and caramel syrup. She'll love you forever."

"I already love her forever . . . but no chocolate sauce? I thought everybody loved chocolate."

"Probably best not to use 'Jack' and 'everybody' in the same sentence." She heard Bobby still chuckling when he closed the door behind her.

She was in a hurry to get home because she had work to do; otherwise she'd have stayed to watch him enjoy putting his stamp on his new home. He was like a little boy in his excitement though she could see, could feel, the sadness just beneath the surface. Anyway, he no doubt had tears to shed and he should be able to do that in private.

She also needed her own privacy for the work waiting for her since she had finally, and most reluctantly, agreed to join a group of friends to explore thoughts and ideas about ways to create something like a new Harlem Renaissance.

Harlem was the artistic and cultural center of Negro life despite the fact that many thousands of its residents, new refugees from the Jim Crow South, lived and worked in grinding poverty and possessed little or no formal education. They had even less knowledge of concepts like artistic endeavor, which fueled The Harlem Renaissance of the 1920s and 1930s, and later entities like The American Negro Theatre. That company created and performed award-winning stage events in the basement of the 135th Street Public Library until, after a decade, it was dissolved in 1951. These accomplishments gave the neighborhood a cultural cache that even the newly arrived residents recognized as sources of pride without any real understanding of why. The natives recognized the need to perpetuate the accomplishments and their source for the generations yet to be.

The Harlem Renaissance and the ANT, as the American Negro Theatre was called, offered uplift and hope and proof to the world at large that Negroes could make significant and permanent artistic and intellectual contributions to American culture and society. Successful theater spawned art, music, and dance projects and programs that not only attracted young people but offered them encouragement and instruction. Bobbie's piano prowess was integral to more than one ANT production, and she taught piano and voice in more than one of the programs for Harlem youth. Her involvement grew from that of her parents, who had contributed their time, talent, and money. Her father had been a world-renowned jazz pianist and her mother a painter of note. Bobbie felt she could do no less, especially since their talents were so brutally stilled, and Bobbie wanted to ensure that Eleanor and Robert Hilliard would not be forgotten.

That commitment, however, somehow had become the expectation that she should form, build, and grow a new theater company to fill the void left by the absence of ANT: The Black Mask Theatre Company. It had a name, but that was all. There was no actual theater company. And just because she loved theater didn't mean she knew how to build and grow a theater company—she didn't.

What she did know was that art by, about, and for Negroes, needed to be available and accessible to everyone, and most especially to young people, to teach that its pursuit was a worthwhile endeavor. So, the idea under discussion was how to create and fund an organization that would be a first-rate artistic and cultural entity that would instruct and entertain the entire Harlem community. Bobbie believed this was a worthy endeavor. That belief, and a gorgeous, smooth-talking woman, is how she got roped in.

It happened on a Wednesday night in mid-October. The Slow Drag, Bobbie's bar, was open Wednesday through Saturday nights, 8 p.m. until 2 a.m., and Bobbie was always pleased to be able to say that while Wednesday and Thursday often were slow, they were never dead. So on a slow Wednesday, two women approached her at the bar: the drop-dead gorgeous Eileen McKinley and her very attractive, though not drop-dead gorgeous, companion, Joyce Scott, regulars at the church Bobbie once attended, one she had not returned to since the funerals of her family three years ago. Eileen was very married to a man and Joyce was very not, but they were a couple.

"Hello, Bobbie. Good to see you," Joyce said, extending a hand.

"I'm surprised but pleased to see both of you," Bobbie said, shaking both their hands and wiping down the bar before placing napkins in front of them. "What can I get you?" These were Episcopalians, not Baptists, and Bobbie knew she could offer them something.

"A Gibson for me and a Manhattan for Eileen," Joyce answered as they settled themselves on the bar stools. When their first tastes of the drinks Bobbie set before them elicited surprised delight, Bobbie shook her head, only half feigning dismay.

"Why are people so surprised that I can make a good drink? I own a bar for crying out loud! Mixing a good drink is a prerequisite." She watched them take a second appreciative sip and asked, "What brings you beautiful women to my humble establishment?"

"I've called you several times but never gotten an answer," Eileen said, "and though I assumed that the phone number was the same, I realized I could be mistaken. Joyce was aware of this place—she's been here a few times—and suggested I try you here."

"The phone number is the same though not many people call me, and Joyce is correct about where to find me Wednesday through Saturday nights." Bobbie paused and took a closer look at Joyce to be sure she'd recognize her again. "I'll have your Gibson waiting for you next time I see you."

"I'll remember that," Joyce said. She took her drink, kissed Eileen, and headed for the jukebox. Bobbie watched Eileen watch Joyce. She was a stunner, without a doubt, but without any hint of artifice, as if she had no awareness of her beauty or of its effect on others. Or perhaps she cared only what Joyce Scott thought. She also was Bobbie's sorority sister though that had little meaning, especially since her mother's death. Bobbie had joined her mother's sorority because she adored her mother and she never resented doing things to please her, like attending monthly sorority meetings because it pleased Eleanor. And truth be told, she enjoyed the scenery: Eileen was not the only sorority woman worthy of an admiring glance.

"So, Eileen, pretend that I actually answered the phone."

Eileen swallowed and leaned across the bar, closer to Bobbie. "I need your help. I'm part of a group working to keep artistic expression alive and well in Harlem—across the board artistic expression, open and available to everyone. We do a lot of talking but we have yet to devise or develop a plan to make it happen."

"Or to articulate exactly what it is you want to happen, Eileen. That's the real crux of the problem," Joyce said, sounding like the college professor she was. She'd returned from the jukebox to stand close behind Eileen, who leaned comfortably into the embrace waiting for her.

Eileen sighed, inhaled the last of her Manhattan and looked squarely at Bobbie. "Unfortunately, that is correct."

"And why do you think I can do something, or anything, about that?"

"Because you're an artist, you were raised by artists, you grew up surrounded by artists. You know what a successful artistic endeavor looks and feels like." Eileen was pleading and against her better judgment, Bobbie allowed herself to sympathize. After all, it was not in her makeup to ignore a woman this gorgeous even if her lover was standing right there. Besides, with a woman this gorgeous, Joyce must be used to the response to her by now.

"Yes, but that doesn't mean I know how to create such a thing. I am, however, willing to meet and talk and share thoughts. And if you tell me when you're most likely to call, I'll be sure to answer the phone."

She turned away to make them fresh drinks, aware that Joyce had reclaimed the empty space beside Eileen and that Eileen leaned into her, a natural and comfortable motion, and a momentary stab of pain and wistfulness shook Bobbie. How must it feel to live with that kind of connection? She'd probably never know, and felt the accompanying sadness.

So now, a month later, she was in her former bedroom, which had become her office once she finally made the move to take over her late parents' bedroom. When she turned on the light and entered, it looked as disorganized as she felt. After half a dozen meetings with Eileen and her committee, Bobbie had only the vaguest notion of what might need to happen to lay the groundwork for a cogent artistic plan.

She was cheered only by the fact that she had learned that several of the women were members of sororities, which, like her own, had some form of community service as a mandate, and that all of the women were members of one or the other of the three largest, most influential Negro churches in Harlem: St. Philips Episcopal, Abyssinian Baptist, and The Mother AME Zion Church. Most, like Joyce and Eleanor, were highly competent professionals, and the others, like Eileen, were married to men of means. Clearly this meant that when there was a real plan of action, these women had the push and pull to convert ideas into programs.

Bobbie turned on the desk lamps and turned off the ceiling light, hoping that not illuminating the chaos from above would make it appear less chaotic.

She tilted back in the chair, placed her feet on the desktop, and closed her eyes, letting her thoughts wander. She gazed at her former bedroom. It was two years before Bobbie finally moved into her parents' bedroom. She emptied the closets and drawers of their belongings, and the walls of their art—except her mother's paintings. The room was repainted, the furniture rearranged, different draperies and pictures hung. It was her room now, and her brother's room was the guest room—and Bobby Mason had been the first guest. The large room that was her mother's home studio remained closed and locked. And the expansive living room remained her constant reminder, as if she ever could forget, of the cruel events that made this entire space her home, where she lived alone.

She suddenly dropped her feet to the floor and pulled the three-ring binder notebook toward her, uncapped her pen, and began writing. Every artistic enterprise needed donors and benefactors, and it needed volunteers, the people who toiled behind the scenes to make the art possible. Bobbie made lists: of donors and potential donors, of people who could build sets (Bobby Mason?!) and sew costumes and wigs (Bobby's Queen Esther?!), of people who could get programs designed and printed. She listed who could teach classes: music, painting, dance, voice. Perhaps she knew how to build a theater company after all. Perhaps she was building an arts organization.

Then she closed the notebook and turned her thoughts to The Slow Drag. She usually didn't work on Mondays but because she'd taken Saturday off (God, was that just yesterday?), she'd exchanged off days with her manager, Justine, and tomorrow would be a busy day. She briefly contemplated asking Justine to come in anyway but decided against it. She'd need all the regulars plus the extras on Wednesday through Saturday for Thanksgiving weekend. It was busier than Christmas or any other holiday because so many women in Harlem were without family or, as was the case for many, were banned from their families because they were bulldaggers.

Either they weren't welcome to visit their own families or the families of their girlfriends or, if welcome at all, many of their families were still somewhere down South. So all the new Harlem-ites could do was miss them and drown their sorrows at The Slow Drag. The nightclub wasn't exactly a home away from home but it was better than the cold-water flat with the bathtub in the kitchen that was home until they could do better.

Though Bobbie had stopped serving alcohol at 2 a.m. as usual last year, she had kept the place open all night, serving free coffee and soda. She could not, in good conscience, allow drunk and lonely Negro women out on the street at two in the morning looking for a way to get home. Too many were too drunk to walk, maybe even too drunk to remember where they lived or how to get there. But she'd check stock and inventory tomorrow because she'd need every pourable drop of every kind of whiskey and beer and chaser from 8 p.m. Wednesday through 2 a.m. Sunday, and she would need to have sufficient nickels to keep the jukebox playing, napkins to wipe tears and blow noses, and muscle to maintain order.

Were it not for so many of Harlem's Colored women relying on The Slow Drag as a place of refuge, she'd close Thursday, Friday, and Saturday. The only upside to staying open was that by keeping herself occupied with work she herself could not succumb to sorrow and drink herself into oblivion. So, to protect both herself and her customers from wallowing in sad songs, she would periodically override the jukebox selections and program half a dozen fast-paced, high-energy numbers. Singing, dancing, finger-snapping lesbians don't sing the blues.

Bobbie realized she was hungry, and no wonder—it was almost six o'clock. She stood up just as the phone rang and hurried into the living room to answer it. "You gotta come see the kitchen and the bathroom!"

"How fabulous are they?"

"I don't have words. That's why you gotta come see for yourself!" She could picture Bobby Mason hopping up and down with excitement.

"Why don't you come eat first—unless you've cooked dinner as well in your fabulous kitchen?"

"It ain't that fabulous. I'll see you soon."

"Do you want to spend the night here since your perfect home doesn't have a bed?"

"I appreciate the offer, but I didn't work my no longer perfectly manicured fingers to the bone this afternoon not to wake up to the proof in the morning."

"Then bring that big green carry-all with you."

"Why? You gonna zip me up in there to keep me warm?"

Bobbie hung up on him, chuckling to herself. She realized why she liked Bobby Mason so much so quickly. He reminded her of her baby brother, Eric.

Eric would get so excited about something that he'd stutter trying to talk about it, and he'd hop from foot to foot or run from room to room to tell Dad at the piano, Mom in her studio, or Bobbie in her room, about whatever had excited him. She smiled through her tears.

Bobby was still damp from his shower, but he wrapped her in a bear hug anyway. "And before you ask, yes, I cleaned the shower!" he said.

"Of course you did. I have total faith in you, Bobby Mason."

He left his shoes at the back door and padded into the living room, heading straight for the fireplace. "I knew you'd lit a fire and pulled the drapes closed. It's really cold."

"Yet you're wearing only a sweater, and you're still damp

from the shower."

"I didn't know how cold it was until I got outside, and I didn't want to go back inside to get a jacket. Anyway, I ran here, which warmed me up." He brandished the green duffel. "Though I suppose I could have wrapped myself in this."

"A lesson in New York City living, my friend: always assume at least a ten-degree temperature drop when the sun goes down, especially this close to one of the rivers. And another lesson: wear layers so you'll be warm while you're outside; then you can remove the top layers once you're inside."

He gave her a strange look. "You mean I'll start taking off my clothes—"

"No, silly, not your clothes, but the hat and scarf and gloves and maybe the overcoat, depending on how heavy it is. Which brings me to another lesson. If you haven't already got some, get some long underwear. Several sets."

"Is there a How to Live in New York City handbook I should buy?"

She shook her head. "Just listen to the natives and watch what we do, then do what we do 'cause there's a reason for it."

"Yes, madam," he intoned, and curtsied before asking if he could help with dinner.

She shook her head. "Just warming it up. But you can fix us a drink," and she gave him an ice tray from the freezer.

"I can't make a Manhattan—you know that, right?"

"And I don't want one. Bourbon on the rocks with a splash of orange juice."

"Bourbon and orange juice? Are you serious?"

"It's delicious."

"If I'm gonna drink orange juice without a side of grits and eggs, it'll be with two fingers of vodka," and he took the ice tray and headed for the bar.

They drank and ate with Bobby doing most of the talking and Bobbie most of the listening. She would occasionally comment on something he said or ask a question but she otherwise was lost in her own thoughts.

"Bobbie, you're not listening."

"Oh shit, Bobby! I'm so sorry. My mind was—"

He waved away her apology. "I know you have more on your mind than my life."

"And your life is very important to me, and sharing in your excitement is much more fun than what I've been wrestling with. I'm lost in thoughts of an arts organization I am starting and, well, thoughts of my family come up up all the time." She shook her head as if to banish the thoughts. "Tell me about your life before Harlem, Bobby."

"I met Jerome in the Spring of 1950 when I was a sophomore at Lincoln University and he was a senior. Couple of months later he had graduated and the Korean War started. He'd already told me he was going back to New York and he'd asked me to go with him and I'd said yes. But first he said we should enlist and when the war was over we could go to school on the GI bill— him to graduate school at NYU and me to finish my degree."

"So, when things didn't turn out like you planned, you still came here to make good on your promise to Jerome?"

Bobby nodded, then shrugged, then shook his head. "I came because I didn't know what else to do or where else to go. But yeah, Jerome was a part of it too. He said Harlem was special. He said there were people up here, Colored people, Negroes, who were writers and actors and painters and dancers—artists, he called them—along with the doctors and lawyers and teachers and preachers. And not just two or three but many. People like you, Bobbie."

"There are intelligent, accomplished, creative, professional Negroes everywhere—"

Bobby shook his head. "Not like here, not where they try to make it possible for everybody to do better. That's why so many of us keep running from Jim Crow to get here. Just as broke and broke down up here as they were down there, the difference being hope—the possibility that things could get better, if not for themselves then for their children. Or their grandchildren. Do you understand, Bobbie?"

She nodded. "Yes, I do understand."

"I wanted to see and feel Harlem. Even though I didn't stomp at the Savoy I got to see it—and I met you, the proof that Jerome was right. And the job that Jack got me? Never would or could happen in Pennsylvania or East Saint Louis. I want to finish school at . . . at NYU or . . . or Columbia or . . ."

"Do you know that you live and work within walking distance of City College?"

He knew that he was doing his guppy imitation again—mouth moving, no words coming out. When Bobbie told him exactly where the campus was, the breath caught in his chest. He had walked past it a dozen times. He knew exactly where it was. "Is that where you went?" He finally managed words.

She shook her head. "I went to Hunter, a women's college downtown, though men were admitted to the uptown campus a few years ago, but my mother attended a women's college— Spelman in Atlanta—and she loved the experience and thought that I would, too. Though I doubt she had any idea how much I'd love it."

Bobby watched her remember her mother, then asked, "What did she do? Was she a musician, too, like your father?"

"She was a painter and she taught art. At City College."

Bobby stood up and cleared the table. Then he made Bobbie another Early Times and orange juice and himself another Smirnoff and orange juice and they sat sipping in front of the fire. He told her what Queen Esther had said about being born in the wrong body, and about Bobby not belonging in a dress, and asked her opinion.

"Sounds like Queen Esther is a wise woman."

"Do you think you were born in the wrong body?"

41

Bobbie choked on her drink. "God no! While I wouldn't be caught dead in a dress, I love being a woman because I think that helps me know how to love women, and I love loving women."

"So . . . the tuxedo and the mustache . . .?"

"The only way I'd be able to dance with a woman in public without being humiliated as you were, just as that gown was the only way you'd have been able to dance with Jerome."

"Yeah," he nodded slowly, "you're right, but I think I'm done with women's clothes—especially the shoes. I'm just a boy who likes boys, like Queen Esther said—" Suddenly his eyes lit up. "Can boys dance together at The Slow Drag?"

The sad look and the accompanying slow head shake answered the question, but he waited for her words and wasn't expecting the explanation that came with them. "Too many women have been mistreated by men and so they don't trust men. But they also want a place they know is safe to be their true selves, a place where there are no men."

"I understand, Bobbie, truly I do, which means I need to find a place where boys who like boys can dance together. Do you know if there's a boys' place like The Slow Drag?"

Bobbie shook her head. "I don't, but I'll ask around."

"And I'll do some looking around but if I get lucky, we'll do our mutual liking in our own homes. And speaking of which, I'd better get back to mine." He drained his glass and took it to the kitchen, then after returning the bottles to the shelves behind the bar, took the cloth to wipe the top. Back in the kitchen he noticed the green duffel bag on the floor by the door. "You told me to bring this?"

She sprang to her feet and beckoned him to follow down the hallway to 'his' room. Piled on the bed—blankets, sheets, pillows, towels, and a pair of golden velvet draperies with the rod to hang them. On top of the pile was a radio, a lamp, and an alarm clock.

"You can't keep doing things for me, Bobbie."

"Sure I can. Besides, I now live alone in a place where four people once lived, and everything here sat unused on a shelf in a closet. Better that it serves a purpose than be left to dry rot, don't you think?"

"Well . . . since you put it that way . . . yes, and thank you again, so very much."

"You're very welcome. Now go home, Bobby Mason. I've got work to do."

At the click of the door lock, Bobbie did not go to her office but to her bedroom instead. She stripped, changed into her swimsuit and a set of heavy athletic wear bearing the Hunter College logo, over which she donned a heavy, long overcoat. She added thick socks and boots and grabbed her Hunter College carryall from the closet shelf. It contained her school ID, entry card, and parking permit, and she was out the door and headed for the garage. Traffic was heavy, as usual, even going south on the Henry Hudson Parkway by the river, until she reached the first eastbound street to cross Central Park. Once on the East Side she'd just drive until she got to Hunter's campus at Sixty-Eighth Street and Lexington Avenue.

She parked, put her permit on the dashboard, grabbed her carryall, and hurried into the building. Ignoring the elevator, she took the stairs up to the pool level, thankful to find the locker room almost empty. She stripped off her clothes, grabbed her goggles and swim cap, and entered the womb that was the pool where a familiar peace descended.

Two lanes were occupied. She dove into the fourth lane and rode the water for as long as she could, knowing that its warmth would soothe and loosen her muscles. Then she began stroking, slowly at first, then with progressive speed and power until she achieved the rhythm most comfortable for her. She stroked and breathed and swam and breathed, until her breath was ragged and her muscles rubbery. This was reality: she was on the Hunter College swim team and she was a star. She won medals. This was familiar. She came here every day, and then she went home to Harlem, to her family. She no longer had the family but she had this pool and her skill in it, and she had her Harlem home. Her tears were just water on her face. She took a hot shower, making sure to remove all the chlorine. Then she applied a light layer of Vaseline from head to toe while she was still warm and damp to maintain her skin's suppleness and her hair's moisture. She dressed quickly, heading back out into the cold night, wrapped warmly from head to toe.

Bobbie drove home slowly, enjoying the sights once she was back on the West Side and heading uptown. Lights, bright and blinking, advertised almost everything . . . and sometimes nothing at all, merely lights for the sake of lights. And all kinds of people were out and about—some with a sense of purpose, others with no purpose at all other than to be out and about in Harlem, one of the most famous places in the world. Traffic moved slowly, and sometimes not at all, because not everyone experiencing Harlem was doing so on foot. Thankfully she was not in a hurry.

She opened the doors to The Slow Drag almost two hours early on Wednesday because there was a long line reaching down the sidewalk almost to the corner. Negro women standing in a line in the cold to enter—where? The Slow Drag had never been raided and Bobbie didn't intend for it to happen now. She opened this place to be a safe haven for Negro women and she would do whatever she could to keep it that way. Keeping a low profile was the best way to do that.

It was a well-appointed place and women dressed accordingly. Bobbie offered a range of the best booze and music available. And she employed a staff to maintain both quality and order. She also paid a couple of police lieutenants monthly, more than they made annually, to guarantee that a bunch of white cops would never raid The Slow Drag and brutalize or terrorize her women. She knew that the names of men arrested in raids were printed in the newspaper, a tactic designed to embarrass and humiliate. She would not allow that to happen to her women—some of whom were nurses, teachers, librarians, secretaries, and who most certainly would be fired from their jobs. That's to say nothing of those with husbands and families. Bobbie would not have them herded out of The Slow Drag and shoved into a paddy wagon, newspaper photographers capturing their terrified faces for posterity.

The lines formed on Thursday and Friday, too. Saturday found things back to normal. In fact, the place wasn't even crowded until almost ten, though by eleven it was packed. There was a woman sitting alone at a table. She'd been sitting there for about twenty minutes, and Bobbie thought that no one in her right mind would leave a woman like that sitting alone for even two minutes. She certainly wouldn't. The woman was stunning. And she didn't appear worried. Or angry. Or . . . anything. She seemed totally composed. Her hair was upswept and held in place with a comb. She wore a crimson knit dress fitting like an embrace, and her shoes, nail polish, and lipstick matched the dress. Bobbie kept one eye on the woman as she mixed and served drinks. Finally, when there was a lull, she rushed to the other end of the bar to whisper to Justine.

"Who is that woman? Who brought her here?" Bobbie asked.

"Don't know her name but PJ Bailey brought her."

"Where's PJ?"

"Over in the corner with her pals," Justine answered.

"Is PJ drinking?"

"Oh hell yeah she is!" Justine exclaimed. "On her third G&T. Swallowed the first two like they were ice water."

Bobbie returned to her end of the bar, served everyone there, then unlocked and lifted the bar arm and walked out onto the dance floor and over to the lone woman. "May I have this dance?" she asked, extending her hand.

"With pleasure," the woman replied in a low gentle voice accompanied by a smile. She took Bobbie's extended hand and stood up smoothly, picking up her purse. Looking down at her coat, folded on a chair, she asked, "Is it all right to leave the coat here?"

Still holding the woman's hand, Bobbie picked up the coat with her other hand and headed toward the bar. "You can leave both the coat and, if you wish, the purse on the shelf back here," offered Bobbie, lifting the heavy bar arm and stepping behind the bar. She pointed to the shelf that held her own coat and hat.

"I'm Grace Hannon and thank you," she said, adding her coat and purse to the shelf.

"And I'm Bobbie Hilliard. Shall we dance?"

As if the jukebox were complicit, it segued from "Mama He Treats Your Daughter Mean" to "Money Honey," and Grace and Bobbie eased into a smooth swing, moving as if they'd always danced together. Bobbie swung her out and Grace returned to the circle of Bobbie's arm as if coming home. The record changed to "Pedal Pushin' Papa" and Bobbie and Grace kept the floor. They had an audience. By the third record—"Mercy Mr. Percy"—they had the floor to themselves and a crowd cheering them on.

When the jukebox served up "Tell Me Pretty Baby," Bobbie felt a pang of guilt. The place was packed and she should be behind the bar mixing and serving drinks, not swinging the delectable Grace Hannon around the dance floor as if . . . as if what? And once again the jukebox seemed to provide the answer by slowing the pace dramatically with "Baby It's You."

"You're one hell of a dancer, Dr. Hannon," Bobbie said into Grace's ear. She was holding her as closely as she dared hold a woman she didn't know, though not nearly as closely as she'd like.

Grace leaned her head back just far enough to look at Bobbie without breaking the contact of their bodies. "You know who I am?"

"You were my mother's doctor."

Bobbie heard—and felt—Grace's intake of breath. "Eleanor Hilliard," she whispered, and tightened her arm around Bobbie's neck. "I am so very sorry, Bobbie."

"Thank you, Grace. So am I."

They spoke no more until the record ended. When it did, they released each other reluctantly. Bobbie had to get back to work. But she kept Grace's hand, leading her toward the bar. "There's a stool I can put out here unless you'd like to return to your table—"

"No. I'd much rather sit here."

Bobbie lifted the counter arm, slid behind the bar, and began taking orders almost immediately—almost because she first asked Grace what she wanted to drink. And as she mixed drinks for the customers four-deep at the bar, she grabbed the Early Times from her private stock and mixed Grace a double Manhattan. She placed the drink on a napkin in front of her, beside a glass of ice water on another napkin.

Bobbie quickly dispatched the crowd in front of her—rum or bourbon and coke, and gin or vodka and lime or tonic being the favorite orders and also the quickest to make. And it took practically no time to reach into the cooler for bottles of Pabst or Schlitz, pry off the caps, and place the bottles on napkins.

Bobbie was a good bartender—her eyes constantly in motion—and a fast one, so she was fully aware of PJ Bailey as she approached Grace from behind. PJ looked her usual smooth and smart self in a charcoal gray suit with a vest and a crisp white shirt. Bobbie stood in front of Grace when PJ, standing behind her, reached for the Manhattan. Bobbie's arm shot out, her hand closing around PJ's hand just before it reached the glass.

"What the hell do you think you're doing?" PJ snarled as she tried, and failed, to free her hand from Bobbie's vise-like grip.

"Keeping you from drinking what you didn't buy."

"What I do with my girl is none of your business!"

"Your girl? The one you left sitting at a table alone for half an hour without a drink? Nice suit, by the way. You're looking dapper as always, PJ." Bobbie released PJ's wrist, then slid the Manhattan closer to Grace who picked up the drink and took a deep, appreciative sip.

"This is delicious, Bobbie. It may be the best Manhattan I've ever had."

Bobbie feigned regret. "Then I guess I'll keep trying until I achieve perfection."

Grace grinned and covered Bobbie's hand with her own. "I'm officially volunteering to be your permanent guinea pig."

PJ huffed in disgust, suggested that Grace get home on her own, and stalked away. Bobbie tightened her grip on Grace's hand and assured her that she needn't worry about how she'd get home.

"Do I look worried to you?" Grace said with a big grin that became a full-throated laugh. "I'm not even worried that I'm burning the midnight oil too late." The mirth remained on her face as she studied Bobbie. "And you look rather dapper yourself, Miss Hilliard." Bobbie wore black corduroys, a black turtleneck, and black work boots, one of her behind-the-bar uniforms— everything able to go safely into the wash except the boots which went to the shoe repair shop to be cleaned and shined.

"Even doctors get Sunday off, don't they?" Bobbie asked.

"That depends entirely on sick people, and fortunately I have no sick people on my schedule at the moment. I do, however, have two expectant mothers who have had more than enough of being pregnant and would love to deliver sooner rather than later. Babies, however, come when they're ready to come." She looked at her watch and stood up. "I'm going downstairs to the pay phone to call the hospital, just to be safe."

Bobbie lifted the arm and beckoned Grace behind the bar. "There's a phone all the way down and behind the bar." And suddenly she had a line waiting to order. She made and delivered drinks until Grace returned with the news that while she'd not be helping new little people into the world this night, she herself was ready for sleep. Bobbie gave Grace her coat and purse from the shelf beneath the bar, lifted the arm, and told Grace she'd meet her at the door. Bobbie locked the arm, grabbed her own coat and hat, and hurried to the other end of the bar. She apologized to Justine as she explained that she was seeing Grace home in a taxi—

"You know Jack's outside?"

Bobbie was startled. "Is she all right?" she asked with unexpected urgency.

"She's fine," Justine answered, giving Bobbie an odd look. "Said she had a job up this way and decided to wait for you." She held up bags that Bobbie recognized. "She brought us burgers and fries from Miz Maggie's."

"Best in town," Bobbie said, donning her coat and hat and taking Grace's arm and explaining quickly that her ride home was waiting. "My friend Jack is driving but she won't be able to get out to open the door and see you inside—"

"I can take a taxi, Bobbie."

"I don't want you to take a taxi," Bobbie said as they approached Jack's Chevy. Bobbie opened the back door, and as Grace slid in she introduced them: "Grace Hannon, this is my very best friend, Jack Jackson. Jack, this is my very new friend Grace Hannon whom I hope will become my very good friend."

"Count on it," Grace said, *sotto voce*, and kissed Bobbie on the cheek.

"Jack, when Grace gets home, she'll flash her lights, letting you know she's in the house."

"Good night, Bobbie. See you soon," Grace said, and rolled up her window.

Jack was actually chuckling when she put the car in gear and started to drive sedately away, but the car stopped and Bobbie ran to the driver's side where the window was already down. "I'm picking Bobby Mason up at the drag queens' ballroom at one thirty, then coming to get you," Jack said, and drove away.

Bobbie watched the Chevy's taillights, but her mind was full of Grace Hannon. A woman had never affected her as Grace had, and it wasn't just that she was gorgeous, though she most certainly was that. There also was, Bobbie thought and felt, both a strength and a gentleness . . .

"Get outta the street!" a voice yelled as horns blared, and Bobbie realized both were directed at her. She was standing in the middle of the street. She scurried to the sidewalk and into the door that was held open for her.

"Thanks, Vern," she said to the doorwoman-cum-bouncer, and took the stairs two at a time. She pushed open the door to The Slow Drag, and the sound almost blew her backward. She'd momentarily forgotten the soundproofing work she'd had done to prevent the music from drawing the attention of people who didn't need to know what transpired upstairs.

After a minute or so, though, the sound was completely normal. She thanked Justine, and by the time she reached the other end of the bar her coat was folded and on the shelf, her hat on top of it. She began mixing drinks. Exchanging greetings with familiar faces, she answered questions about the weather: Yes, still cold but no sign of snow so far. She replied in words, but her mind and thoughts were all about Grace. Grace Hannon, whose parting words were "see you soon."

PJ was getting drunker and madder by the minute. Who the hell did Bobbie Hilliard think she was.

"Rich enough and good-looking enough to get any woman she wants," PJ's pal, Von Thompkins answered—salt rubbed into the wound.

"She's got enough women! A new one every week. Why can't she leave mine alone?"

Von, keeping herself hidden within the crowd on the dance floor, eased her way to the end of the bar where she could watch Bobbie without being noticed. She was definitely good-looking, and she had the kind of ease about her that said she didn't have to hustle for a dollar or wonder whether the next meal would happen. Von made her way back to the other end of the bar and PJ. When her friend's feelings weren't so newly wounded, Von would learn everything PJ knew about Bobbie Hilliard. She also wanted to know everything PJ knew about the sexy woman in the sexy crimson dress who PJ claimed was a doctor, because if she was, and if Bobbie Hilliard really had fallen hard for her—and it looked like she had—then maybe Von could collect some payback from the too rich, too good-looking, too lucky bar owner.

The sexy doctor got up and went to church the following morning primarily to see and talk to her best friend and her best friend's girlfriend. They met in the parking lot after the service as usual whenever they wanted to talk without being overheard, and there was sufficient speculation about them in the congregation of St. Philips Episcopal Church that people definitely wanted to overhear any conversation these three women had.

Grace leaned in close and said, "I met the woman I'm going to marry last night."

Eileen and Joyce stared at her as if she were speaking in tongues, decidedly not an Episcopal Church ritual, but every bit as confusing as the words they'd just heard Grace utter. They'd lost count of the number of first—and last—dates Grace had had, and they had watched her lose interest in women after one dance or one conversation. "Who is this

51

woman of wonder?" Eileen asked.

"Bobbie Hilliard," Grace replied softly, and all but swooned.

"I told you," Joyce said in a satisfied almost whisper. "Didn't I tell you that Grace and Bobbie would be perfect together?"

Grace stared in disbelief at them, first at one and then at the other. "I don't believe you," she said, before asking Joyce why she thought so. Joyce told her, then asked Grace when she planned to see her intended again, and Eileen groaned at the look on Grace's face.

"I do sometimes despair of you, Nellie Grace Hannon. Here you are in the church parking lot, practically stripped down to your bra and panties, and you don't know when you're going to see the woman again?" Eileen McKinley, Grace's best friend, was aghast as well as dismayed. How could a woman so beautiful and so brilliant be so ... so ...

"Relax, both of you. Bobbie will call you in the morning, Grace." And the two beauties relaxed and smiled at Joyce Scott, who always was calm and rational—and right.

Grace pulled on her white coat and wrapped the stethoscope around her neck as Nurse Thelma Cooper knocked and entered her office. "A Miss Hilliard is on the phone for you, Grace, and Mrs. Baker is ready to unlock the door and let 'em in when you're ready."

"Please put the call on my private line, Thelma, and I'll meet you in Exam One," Grace said, sounding calmer and more in control than she felt, certain that Thelma could hear her heart thudding in her chest from across the room. She picked up the phone. "Good morning, Miss Hilliard."

"Good morning to you, Dr. Hannon. Grace. Would you like to have dinner with me tonight? At a time and place of your choosing."

"I'd love to, Bobbie. How about my place at seven or better make that seven thirty? And I'm a very good cook, by the way."

Bobbie stood holding the phone receiver, listening to the loud buzz of the dial tone, and thinking she didn't care whether Grace Hannon was a good cook or not. She placed the receiver in the cradle and the phone rang. "Grace?" Bobbie said.

"So sorry to disappoint," Eileen said so drily it sounded like ice cracking.

"You never disappoint, Eileen . . ."

"You lie, Bobbie Hilliard, but you do it so well I'm sorry I'm not Grace. I'd love to hear what was coming out of your mouth next." And when Bobbie told her, Eileen sounded as excited as Bobbie felt about the impending dinner. "Grace is a magnificent cook; take a red and a white, as well as a bottle of champagne—Grace loves champagne. And yes, definitely take flowers. She loves flowers, too—except roses."

Grace's welcoming embrace and kiss, and her equally enthusiastic receipt of the wine, champagne, and flowers, both warmed and confused Bobbie: All of her reactions to Grace Hannon were unfamiliar. She was behaving like, like, she didn't know what. Good thing Grace was in full possession of her faculties. She was at the kitchen sink arranging the flowers, admiring the selection, complimenting Bobbie on her choices, as she placed them in vases of different sizes, while Bobbie managed to gain control of her wits by doing something she did understand: expertly wielding a corkscrew and decanting the Bordeaux. "It will be a perfect complement to the beef bourguignon," Grace said, and suggested they have dessert before dinner.

CHAPTER TWO

Bobby Mason quickly developed a routine: Work, neighborhood exploration, Bobbie Hilliard, Jack Jackson, and completing the transformation of his apartment into his home. And though it was less a routine and more a mission, he was compiling a wardrobe to allow him to be comfortable in New York City winters without fear of freezing to death.

Today was a neighborhood exploration day . . . or more precisely, a day to put into practice some of what he'd learned in the last almost three weeks. With his first paycheck as an assistant building super and his final paycheck as a US Army corporal in hand, he headed out to open a bank account. He wanted to go to the Carver National Bank downtown on 125th Street, but that was too far to walk and he really wanted to stay in the neighborhood, so he accepted his boss's suggestion that he use the company bank. Since the suggestion came with an introduction to the bank manager, Bobby's account was opened in record time and he was back out on the street, bank passbook and some cash in his pocket.

The December day was bright and cold, but there was not much wind coming off the river, so he was walking briskly. Anyway, he was properly dressed and smiled to himself recalling how both Jack and Bobbie had complimented him on his expanding wardrobe. "You look like a real New Yorker," Jack told him with an up-and-down scrutiny, "especially the feet. Smart."

He wore thick-soled Army-issue combat boots with two pairs of socks. He had noticed that many men wore the same boots, but now he knew it wasn't because they didn't have or couldn't afford others. With the proper socks inside, the Army boots kept his feet from becoming icicles. Unless they were in North Korea in the winter . . .

Bobby quickly banished that thought. There were other, better, things to think about, like the almost unfathomable variety of items and food for sale on Broadway. Window shopping, window wishing, was one of his favorite ways to spend time, and he loved hearing his grandma's surprised and amazed exclamations as he related it all to her. Though he was a frequent pedestrian on this block, he always seemed to find something new and different to catch his attention. He was about to cross the street to Broadway when he saw a crowd suddenly form. And grow, and continue to grow. He didn't know whether to join in or walk the other way. Then the crowd surged forward and women began to scream, and Bobby hurried toward whatever was happening, as the screams were not ones of terror or fear.

Pushing his way in, he saw that the crowd surrounded a black Cadillac sedan. Somebody famous. There were always famous people in Harlem. Just last week Jackie and Rachel Robinson had to fight their way through a crowd into the Hotel Theresa for dinner in The Penthouse Restaurant on the top floor. But the man who stepped out of the back of this Cadillac was no baseball player—he was the most beautiful man Bobby had ever seen. His smile would have lit a dark room. He was shaking hands and allowing himself to be hugged. Then he raised his arms, and the crowd silenced and gazed at him, as if they could see the words flowing from his mouth. And what a sound it was. Bobby had never heard such a voice or seen such a man. This was Congressman Adam Clayton Powell Jr. On his next free afternoon, Bobby would register to vote. This was reason enough to be in New York.

"He really is something special," Bobbie agreed later that evening as they sat before a roaring fire listening to a jazz pianist Bobby had never heard of, a woman named Mary Lou Williams. A woman jazz pianist! The things Bobbie Hilliard knew and took in her stride, as if everyone should know these things. And perhaps everyone should.

"You could hear the congressman every Sunday—his church is within walking distance for you, on 138th, though I'd recommend taking a taxi so you're not breathless and sweaty when you arrive."

"Thinking about the good reverend makes me breathless and sweaty," Bobby said.

"Easing toward sacrilegious territory, though you're certainly not the first person, male or female, to harbor such thoughts about Rev. Powell. And you do know, don't you, that his wife, Hazel Scott, is one of the best jazz pianists in the world?"

"I do now; thank you, Professor Hilliard, repository of all things musical."

"Yes," she said, deflated by the sadness descending upon her. "Though my mother was the professor and my father was the repository of all things musical." Her voice was flat and Bobby could have kicked himself, though to be fair, he had no way to know what would trigger a sad, painful memory of her family. And then he watched as she got herself under control, smiled away the sadness, hugged him, and congratulated him on achieving his goal of not looking like a country bumpkin in the big city.

"Just following your suggestions, yours and Jack's," Bobby said, still hugging her tightly. "I feel like I've always lived here. Except when something totally new and unexpected happens, like Congressman Reverend Powell." He gave a rueful shake of his head. "No way I could claim to be a native and not know about him." He released her and took a pad and pencil from his pocket. "So, where do I register to vote?"

When she told him, he realized he could have registered to vote when he applied for his veterans benefits. He hadn't known that the huge building on Broadway housed federal, state, and local government offices.

"Just another bit of information to file in your knowledge bank, Mr. Mason."

He acknowledged the compliment but his face fell, and when Bobbie asked the reason, he told her that while surrounded by the admirers of Congressman Powell at least two people tried to pick his pockets.

"I don't keep anything important or valuable in the overcoat pockets but it still pissed me off. I gave one guy a hard elbow to the gut and he doubled over and slunk away. I'm pretty sure he followed me from the bank and that pissed me off, too—that I didn't notice him until almost too late."

Bobbie studied him, really, and he was growing uncomfortable. "Why are you looking at me like that, like I'm doing something wrong?"

"I don't know if it's wrong, Bobby, but I don't think you beating yourself up over what seems like a minor mistake is very helpful."

He was angry now. "If that fella saw me in the bank, saw me get cash, and I didn't notice, that was a major mistake, Bobbie—nothing minor about it. And if it was dark and he caught me on a side street—"

"How much cash did he see you get?"

"What difference does that make?"

"How much, Bobby?"

"Twenty bucks. A ten and two fives. So what?"

"So that was your major mistake. Twenty dollars is a lot of money in Harlem—"

"Damn right it is. Having that twenty dollars in my pocket is the first time in my life I didn't feel poor. I've been poor all my life, Bobbie, and I hated it. You don't know what it feels like but it's spirit killing. Knowing that no matter what you do, it will never be enough. I watched my ma and grandma work themselves to the bone for never enough money. This twenty dollars is going to them—ten to each of them. I just wanted to feel what having it in my possession felt like for a couple of days, to feel one of those weights lifted just a little, for just a short time."

"What weights, Bobby?"

"Being Colored and poor. One should be enough, don't you think?"

"Yes. Yes, I do." She frowned. "But I wouldn't want to not be Colored. I just want them to stop treating us like we did something wrong by being born like we are. But I don't want to change it. I could listen to Mary Lou Williams play the piano all night or watch Jackie Robinson play baseball or listen to Marian Anderson sing. We're not the problem, Bobby. You being poor is not the problem. Having a boot on your neck every time you try to stand up—that's the problem."

He reached over and took her hand. "You have the same view of life and living Jerome had. How do you do it?"

She squeezed his hand. "I find the good, Bobby, and the truth. They're there."

"After what happened to your family? You can't still believe that?"

"I can and I do. I must. It's the good I find that keeps me from curling up into a ball and dying, which I wanted to do for a long time. Or murdering people who look like the ones who murdered my family. Finding what's good prevents those things."

"Give me an example. Please."

"You are a good thing that came into my life, Bobby Mason.

You remind me of my sweet little Eric. I miss him so much. And when you get excited about something and you dance and hop around—this is the kind of man my little brother would have become, and although I no longer have him, I have you as my friend."

"Do I really dance and hop around when I'm excited?"

"You most certainly do, just like Eric did."

"Then I must always be the kind of man Eric would approve of."

"He would have liked you."

"Oh!" Bobby jumped to his feet. "A good thing *did* happen today. I was so focused on the bad. Okay, here's the good." And he told her about his visit to a secondhand store on Broadway he'd visited before where he'd seen a bookcase and an ottoman he liked. He had returned there today to ask how much it would cost to have them delivered. "The owner told me the store didn't deliver. Then he pointed to the ottoman and said that I should be able to carry the footstool. He emphasized *footstool,* like I shouldn't know what an ottoman is. I left the store feeling lousy."

"I hope you're not planning to spend any of your hard-earned money there."

"Mr. Greeneway took one look at my face and asked what was wrong, and when I told him, he said the store owner lied about not delivering. Then he said the same thing about not spending my money where it's not appreciated."

Bobby's face lit up like Eric's would have as he told Bobbie how the super took him to a space at the end of the cavernous workroom. Behind a padlocked gate were half a dozen bookshelves, a pile of rugs, and three ottomans, furniture left behind by people who had moved out of the building. "Greeneway told me to take what I wanted because the people who left it had received letters telling them to come get it or else. Now the only thing I need to buy is the sofa bed. And some pots and pans so I can cook dinner for you and Jack. And is Grace included?"

"Oh mais oui!" Bobbie answered fervently.

Bobby laughed. "The woman has got you speaking in tongues. Jack said she had your number."

"She has my complete, total, and undivided attention."

"And that's how intrigued I am to meet the good doctor, but . . ."

Bobbie sat up straight. "But what?"

"You're already burning the candle at both ends and the middle. Where will all that attention for Grace come from?"

And with a wide, self-satisfied grin she told him that she and Grace were officially together. Then she told him to zip his lip because she hadn't yet told Jack this news. Bobby smiled and promised to keep the news to himself.

Bobbie thoroughly enjoyed being inside The Slow Drag on a Monday afternoon, seated at one of the tables, eating lunch with Justine, the jukebox playing softly.

She'd known Justine almost as long as she'd known Jack, and she had the same level of trust in her. Justine swallowed the last of her Nehi grape soda, wiped her mouth, and sat back in her chair, her gaze steady on Bobbie.

"You're putting a lot of trust in me, Bobbie, and I appreciate it. But are you really sure you want to walk away?"

"Does it feel like too much pressure, too much weight, Justine? I won't want to weigh you down. If it's too much, just say the word."

She grinned and shook her head. Justine was a fireplug of a woman, built low to the ground, strong and immovable, just like a fireplug. These traits had served her well on the high school track and basketball teams, but she was deemed too short for college athletics. She took the news the way she took everything—with a grin, a shrug, and an eye toward what would come next, and something always did.

If Jack were healthy, the two of them together could really run the place, but Jack was not healthy, so onward.

"We need to hire several more people," Bobbie said. "I can do that, you can do it, or we can do it together, and at least two of them need to be professionally trained bartenders."

"I'll do it—might as well learn how—and you can review the paperwork before we decide who to hire, okay?"

"Fine." Bobbie nodded, adding "I know your heart, Justine, so I'll just say no alcoholics and no cons or thieves. Anybody caught drinking or stealing is out the door. Gone. No discussion, no conversation." And she slapped her palms together up and down several times.

Justine inhaled, then released the breath. "I don't know if I can be that tough, Bobbie."

"Sure you can. How much you earn every week depends on how much you take in. If employees are drinking the booze or pocketing the proceeds, well—"

"Well, when you put it like that, Bobbie. Damn. And about Jack: She . . . can't anybody do anything to help her?"

"I think for the first time there might just be an answer to that question."

"The lovely Grace Hannon wouldn't have anything to do with that, would she?"

"The lovely Grace Hannon has something to do with everything," Bobbie replied, and Justine about fell off her chair, and only part of the reaction was exaggeration. Everyone they knew, and a few people they didn't, soon would be privy to the fact that Bobbie Hilliard was no longer on the market. Hearts would be broken. Justine sat up and looked at her friend. "Are you really, finally, a one-woman woman?"

Bobbie, a wide smile on her face, nodded happily and acknowledged that she was as taken by surprise as everyone else. Her legendary dating habits—a new woman every other week, each more gorgeous than the one before—never was about conquest. It wasn't that she didn't want to settle down with one woman, as much as she had never before met a woman who all but wore a sign proclaiming "I'm the one." They were smitten after their first dance and head-over-heels by the last one. "I didn't expect it but I certainly do like it. Now get up, Justine, so we can finish planning."

"But I want to talk about Grace Hannon," Justine whined, reluctantly resuming her seated position in the chair.

"Not happening."

"Oh come on, Bobbie. Toss me a bone. Is she from up here in Harlem?"

"She's from Queens," Bobbie answered, watching as Justine wondered if she knew anyone from Queens, or knew anyone who knew anyone from Queens. Natives of one of the five boroughs of Manhattan may as well have been born in five different states.

"What year did she finish high school?" Justine asked. "Where did she go to college?" And Bobbie changed the subject. She didn't know when Grace finished high school. She didn't know how old Grace was and didn't care. Of all the things they'd asked and told each other, their ages were never part of the discussion.

Bobbie received the desired reaction when she said, "You do know that Christmas and New Year's fall on weekends?"

"Oh shit!" Maybe she'd been too quick to embrace management of The Slow Drag. How was she expected to know when Christmas and New Year would take place when she was just four days removed from the nonstop work of the Thanksgiving weekend? And she hadn't even recovered yet from that.

"Does this mean our dancing days are over?" Grace asked when Bobbie told her of the plan to step away from The Slow Drag.

"Not a chance, Twinkle Toes," Bobbie replied, massaging those toes and the feet they belonged to. Grace had set a Harlem Hospital record by a private physician today, delivering three babies, the first at 6 a.m., the last at 4 p.m. All the mothers were bursting with pride, and the babies—two girls and a boy—were well and healthy. Their exhausted doctor was famished, but had wanted to go to her office first.

Bobbie had picked her up from the hospital and taken her to the office, where, after determining that Nurse Lewis had kept things running smoothly, the doctor sent the nurse home. The next stop was Miz Maggie's to pick up their dinner, and finally to Grace's where a long, hot bath was the first order of business for the weary doctor. It was followed by a dinner of roast chicken, rice and gravy, string beans, and cornbread.

"This is so good!" Grace said between bites. "I ate half a cheese sandwich between babies one and two, and the second half while baby number three, the boy of course, was deciding whether he really wanted to be born. But his mother finally told him, and I quote, "if you don't get yourself outta me, I'ma reach down there and snatch you out myself!" Grace howled telling the tale.

Bobbie made the mistake of trying to visualize the exhausted mother reaching down to grab the recalcitrant boy and pull him out of his dark, warm, safe space into the bright, noisy light of the world and laughed so hard she choked on a mouthful of iced tea. Grace pounded on her back. "I had no idea that a delivery room could be such an entertaining place."

"Today was an especially good day," Grace said with satisfaction.

"Do the new little people have names?" Bobbie asked.

"Peggy, Cynthia, and Arthur Jr."

Bobbie raised her glass and toasted the new arrivals with a wish for long and healthy lives. Grace closed her eyes and said a silent prayer echoing that sentiment; then she stretched luxuriously. "Shall I continue the massage?" Bobbie asked.

Grace shook her head. "But I'd be really happy if you mixed me another bourbon and coke, and before you ask, yes I'm certain that I don't want to try it with orange juice."

"Philistine," Bobbie muttered *sotto voce*, and padded into the kitchen to fix the drinks. When she returned to the bedroom, Grace was sitting up, wrapped in her robe, and looking remarkably wide awake. "She lives!" Bobbie exclaimed.

"You restored me," Grace replied, adding, "and to prove that I'm no philistine, you may put me down for a sizable contribution to whatever you're calling the artistic endeavor you're spearheading. And I am so very proud of you for undertaking the challenge to keep the arts alive in Harlem and making damn certain that artistic pursuit is available to every adult and child who is so inclined."

"Hear, hear!" Bobbie cheered and bowed. "Can I add you to the publicity committee?"

"Good God no," Grace said, and meant it. "Money is what you get from me, and my presence at every event, newly arriving babies permitting."

Bobbie hugged and kissed her, assuring her that those two things, "along with your continued presence in my life, are more than sufficient." Then she sobered. "There is something I want to discuss with you."

Grace sat up straight. "I'm listening."

"It's about Jack . . ."

Grace had wondered about Bobbie's friend's circumstances. Why she never got out of the car when she was around, or why the front seat had the odor of urine. Of course she was curious, but she had never asked. She suspected that Bobbie could not or would not divulge aspects of Jack's personal, private life without her permission.

"Jack said it was all right for me to tell you what happened to her. She likes you, Grace."

Grace took her hands and held them tightly. Clearly whatever was coming was painful if not traumatic, and quite possibly both.

"A little over a year ago Jack was walking home from class. She was in grad school at City College. Did you know that?"

"No, I didn't," Grace said."

"Getting a master's in education. First in her family to go to college..." Grace watched her struggle to continue. Whatever had happened to Jack was as painful for Bobbie as if it had happened yesterday. Grace squeezed her hands until she could continue talking. She realized that the trauma to Jack had occurred just a year and a half after the murders of Bobbie's parents and brother. A lifetime's tragedy quota fulfilled in eighteen months.

"She was walking home after class. Her family lived—still lives—in a building on 140th off Broadway—"

"She was walking by herself?"

Bobbie nodded, smiling sadly. "She always did unless it was too hot, too cold, or raining. She really liked the walk. I had a class that night, too, and I was supposed to meet her for dinner at—"

"If you're about to say that whatever happened to Jack is your fault because you didn't meet her as planned, don't you dare speak those words!"

"But it *is* my fault, Grace. I was late because I dared to challenge the proficiency of two male students in my composition workshop—"

"Does Jack blame you? Does she hold you responsible for whatever happened?"

Bobbie shook her head. "No, of course not."

"Then neither should you blame yourself." Grace inhaled deeply. "What did happen, Bobbie? Tell me."

And as Bobbie told her, told her all of it, Grace wept and Bobbie held her until the tears subsided. Then she tightened her arms and said, "There's more, Gracie, and it's worse in a way."

Grace pushed herself out of Bobbie's embrace and looked at her in horrified disbelief. "What on earth could be worse than what Jack endured in that alley?"

"What she endured after surgery at Harlem Hospital."

> *She lay on her back, her legs held up in the air, suspended by chains and pulleys of some kind, and spread open and resting on some kind of platform. The pain was excruciating, more than she could bear. She sent her mother to find the nurse, to ask for more pain medication. The nurse came quickly and said she would ask the doctor to prescribe more. Hours went by. Jack's father, who had come after work to replace her mother, went in search of a nurse to request more pain medication. It was a different nurse since the previous one had gone off duty, but the response was the same: she would ask the doctor to prescribe more pain medication when he made his rounds.*
>
> *"You shouldn't need additional pain control. What I've given you should suffice."*
>
> *"But it doesn't, I'm telling you! The pain is excruciating, and I need some relief."*

He gave her an odd look. "Excruciating?" Then he laughed and left without writing an order for additional pain medication. Jack wept through the night. The nurses, even the white ones, took turns holding her hands, wiping her face, and whispering words of encouragement even while cursing the arrogant young doctor.

The following morning an older doctor appeared, followed by half a dozen younger ones, including the one who had laughed at her. Jack asked him for more pain medication, but he ignored her and began explaining to the younger doctors the surgery that Jack had had, omitting an explanation of the reason for the need of such bizarre surgery. The young doctors, all of them male, stared in fascination at the exposed vaginal area of the young Colored female patient, who was weeping and begging for pain relief. Then one of them approached the bed, reached out, and touched Jack's vagina. The final indignity.

"Get your hand off me you fucking stupid, ignorant cracker bastard!" and she hurled a pitcher of water at him with the same strength and accuracy she had once hurled softballs at teammates. The pitcher hit him in the middle of his forehead.

"You black bitch!" he howled. "I'll kill you!"

"No you won't," Nurse Leola Bailey replied calmly, stepping in front of him but addressing the senior physician. "I saw the erection he had when he touched the patient's vagina, and if you or any one of them tries to injure this woman any more than you already have I'll bring charges against him before the medical board. And since I have more seniority than any of you, they will hear my complaint. Now, Doctor: Write the order to increase Miss Jackson's pain medication."

Jack received more pain medication. Nurse Bailey was transferred to the night shift despite her years of seniority. No action was taken against Jack for hurling the water pitcher at the young man who had no business being a doctor. And when she left the hospital a week later, she could hardly walk and she leaked urine constantly.

Grace was rigid with rage and fury. She was up and pacing, first the length, then the width, of the bedroom, fists clenching and unclenching, then pounding on her thighs. She did not utter a sound and Bobbie was glad, for it no doubt would have been a fearsome sound. She had never seen Grace angry and would not have believed that this calm, gentle, giving, and loving woman—a woman who earlier this day had delivered three new souls to other loving women—could possess such anger. So she did the only thing she could do: watch and wait and be there if needed. Finally, Grace came to stand beside her at the bed. She took a pad and pencil from the nightstand drawer and asked for Jack's full name and date of birth.

"When was the surgery, Bobbie? The exact date?" And she knew that Bobbie knew, that she would, could, never forget, any more than she could forget the date of the murder of her family. What Bobbie also knew was that Dr. Grace Hannon would gather every piece of data and information relating to the treatment of Jacqueline Ann Jackson, born 27 February 1925. Bobbie also knew that among the thoughts swirling around Grace's brain was the fact that the awful things that had happened to Jack Jackson happened in the same Harlem Hospital where she delivered three brown babies that day.

"Will Jack let me examine her?"

"In your office, yes. She likes you and trusts you, but she feels the same way about Harlem Hospital as she did the day she left there more than a year ago."

"I can examine her at my office; that's not a problem, and take x-rays, Bobbie, but if what I think is true—and I won't know for certain until I examine the previous x-rays and all the doctors' notes—but I think that corrective surgery may be possible."

"You'll know for certain when you have all the records?"

Grace nodded, adding, "but not until then, so please say nothing to Jack. I don't want to raise false hopes. But if it comes to fruition, I can make a case for being part of the surgical team. In fact, I most probably should have been on the original team."

"I wish to God you had been. Jack would not have suffered as she has." Bobbie wiped away a tear. "When do you want to do the exam?"

"Sunday, when the office is closed. Myrtle will come in to help. And Bobbie—I want the names of all the doctors and nurses that Jack remembers, especially the nurse who was transferred to the night shift."

"Leola Summers," Jack replied almost before Bobbie finished asking the question. "I think about her, remember her, always. She was punished for helping me."

There was no rational response to be made to the idea that someone was punished for doing the right thing so Bobbie collected the other information Grace requested, and Jack remembered everything—every name of every person who attended to her, and not only the nurses and doctors but the kitchen staff who delivered her tray and the housekeeping staff who cleaned her room. "It's good that you remember so much, Jack. Grace will be pleased."

"I wish I could forget it, Bobbie. All of it. God knows I've tried. But, well, when I smell like piss all the time and I hurt like hell all the time . . ." She shrugged, then laughed and gave Bobbie a shrewd grin. "It was really smart of you to find a woman who could save both of us."

"What makes you think I needed saving?" Bobbie asked, and only someone who knew her as well as Jack did would have recognized the effort required to maintain her nonchalant demeanor and she quickly changed the subject. "Will you tell Bobby?"

"I told him last night, and we both boo-hooed like little children. I'm glad you found us a really good brother, too. And I hope," Jack said in a tone of voice that turned hard and cold, "that he finds the ones who did this to me before I find 'em 'cause he'll kill 'em."

The usually bustling office of Dr. Grace Hannon was quiet Sunday morning when Nurse Myrtle Lewis rolled the wheelchair off the elevator, down the empty hallway, and into the equally empty office, Bobbie Hilliard and Bobby Mason following. Jack looked all around with interest. She had never visited Dr. Grace's office, but she didn't believe this first time would be the last. She believed that Grace Hannon would be her doctor for some time to come. Bobby Mason also looked all around, every image already a permanent memory. He'd been devastated when Jack told him what happened to her, though he was relieved to finally have so many questions about his new friend answered. But Jack Jackson was much more than a friend. Like Bobbie Hilliard, she was a sister, and if he could get his hands on the pieces of shit who had damaged her . . .

Bobbie Hilliard was already in the exam room with Grace when Nurse Lewis, with Bobby following, wheeled the patient in. "Hello, Jack," Grace said. "I'm really glad you're here."

"Me, too, Doc," Jack said with a grin, "and I've never in my life said that to a doctor."

"Then let's get you onto the exam table; use that step stool . . . Nurse Lewis on one arm, Bobby, you on the other and turn her around . . . lift gently, bottom up on the table. I'll get the legs, and now let's get you comfortable. Nurse Lewis has a gown for you, Jack, and, Bobby, if you would please excuse us for a few moments?"

Jack was calmed by Grace's quiet recitation of everything that would and did happen: her legs would be elevated and separated so that Grace—and only Grace—could see. When it was time for the x-rays, Nurse Lewis and the x-ray technician would need to see, but the technician, Grace explained, would be in another room. "If anything makes you uncomfortable, Jack, tell me or Nurse Lewis right away and we will do whatever is necessary to correct the problem."

While Jack was being x-rayed, Grace reviewed the documents from the previous surgery. Bobbie had dared not ask how she had obtained them so quickly, though she very much wanted to know. So rather than make a nuisance of herself, she joined Bobby in the waiting room.

"Are you all right?" he asked, taking her hands.

She squeezed his hands. "Jack's all right so I'm all right. And Grace is amazing!"

"Yeah, you've told me that at least a million times, and the hymn 'Amazing Grace' is all you play on the piano these days. Good thing I already knew the words so I could sing along."

"Good thing your ma and your grandma got you to church on a regular basis so you could learn those words!" Bobbie retorted as Bobby sang: "Amazing Grace how sweet the sound that saved a wretch like me. I once was lost but now am found, was blind but now I see."

"I say, you've got a pretty decent voice, Mr. Mason. I need to talk to the music people about you—"

"Oh no you don't, Bobbie Hilliard! I'm very happy to be kept busy constructing sets and hanging lights and organizing all the people involved in the physical aspects of productions, performances, presentations, and whatever else you might get up to. And of course, I'll do my assistant super job and attend classes at CCNY 'cause who needs to eat and sleep?"

"Oh Bobby." She grabbed him and wrapped him in a bear hug. "So you're enrolled for the spring semester?"

"Pending the arrival of my transcript from Lincoln." He beamed and bounced up and down a bit.

"I'm so very happy for you, Mr. Mason, not to mention so very proud of you."

"Me, too, if I do say so myself." And he bounced a bit more.

"Don't you want to get up and do an Eric dance?" Bobbie asked.

"When I'm officially enrolled, me and The Baby Brother will dance up one side of Convent Avenue and down the other."

"And Jack and I will be out there cheering you on."

Bobby quickly sobered. "Do you really think—"

"Grace thinks it's possible, Bobby, and that's good enough for me."

"Jack deserves to be all right." He looked at his watch and stood up. "Gotta go. I'm on call this afternoon. Tell Jack . . ." He couldn't finish the sentence, and he didn't need to. He went wide-eyed when Bobbie gave him the keys to the Buick. "How're you gonna get home?" he asked.

"You know all those yellow things that ride up and down the street and stop when you wave at 'em? I think I'll get home. And anyway, I'm not leaving until Jack leaves and that may not be any time soon."

Bobby hugged her and left, and Bobbie rejoined Grace in the exam room. She was alone as Nurse Lewis had taken Jack to x-ray, and she was no longer reading, though she sat staring at the stack of files and folders.

"Is it as you thought?" Bobbie asked.

Grace didn't reply immediately but Bobbie saw a deep and profound sadness in her face, which was quickly replaced by a return of rage. "I'll be in the administrator's office first thing in the morning." But Bobbie could only imagine that conversation because Nurse Lewis returned with Jack, who looked very tired.

Grace took her hand. "I'm going to examine you now, Jack, but first I'm going to give you a sedative because the exam and the treatment will be extremely painful."

"You're going to put me to sleep?"

"Yes," Grace said.

"Could those other doctors have done that?"

"They could have and should have."

73

"Then why the hell didn't they!" Jack exploded, and when Grace didn't reply, Jack said, "I'm asking you, Dr. Hannon, because I want to know. I really do want to know!"

Grace inhaled, then looked steadily at Jack. "Many people in the medical profession unfortunately and absolutely incorrectly believe that Negroes don't feel pain the same way white people do. They not only believe it, they teach it, which is why so many Colored patients like you suffer unnecessarily."

Jack and Bobbie were speechless. Bobbie regained her voice first.

"Do they also teach that we are something less than human and that's why we don't feel pain?" Bobbie asked and Grace closed her eyes, inhaled deeply, and avoided looking at Bobbie and Bobbie knew why. Grace no doubt was present in classrooms when such racist vitriol was espoused by teachers—by doctors—who no doubt never considered the impact of their words on the young Negro woman hearing them. Grace had to live with not only being taught lies, but being expected to incorporate them in her practice. And Bobbie had just confronted her with that reality. When Grace finally opened her eyes, Bobbie mouthed an apology. Grace nodded her acceptance and returned her total attention to Jack.

"I am going to clean and treat the sores in your vaginal area and on your thighs caused by the constant presence of urine, and that will be quite painful, which is why I will sedate you. Do you understand, and is that all right, Jack?"

"Yes, and yes, and thank you, Dr. Hannon."

Grace raised an eyebrow. "What happened to calling me Grace?"

Jack attempted—and failed—to duplicate the eyebrow move and settled for a smirk. "Grace is my friend, and you're still right here, but Dr. Hannon deserves, and will always get, my respect."

"Thank you, Jack," Grace replied, then asked Bobbie to please leave, but Jack said it was all right if Bobbie stayed. Grace told her to stand near the head of the bed, meaning she'd have no view of Jack's vulnerability or the impending assault upon it. Nurse Lewis stood to one side of the bed and set up an IV pole while Grace did the same thing on the other side. She swabbed Jack's inner arm with a cotton ball and inserted a needle deep into the vein there and taped it in place. She then injected the contents of a syringe into the opening at the top of the needle. Jack's eyes flickered and closed almost immediately and she slowly released her hold on Bobbie's hand.

Grace and Myrtle Lewis lifted Jack's legs and placed her feet into stirrups at the foot of the exam table, donned face masks and rubber gloves, and began to work. It was instantly clear that they had worked together for a long time. The nurse anticipated—knew—what the doctor needed and gave it to her. Over and over and over. Once, Grace cursed loudly and Myrtle touched her shoulder, gripped it really, and Grace took a deep breath, nodded, and the nurse released her and they resumed their work. Finally Grace said, "All right. Now," and Myrtle gave her a plastic bag with tubing attached. Grace inserted the tube and Jack moaned slightly.

"She's coming back," Myrtle said softly, and Grace quickly hung a bag of fluid on one IV pole and inserted its tip into the needle taped to Jack's arm, while the nurse hung a similar bag on the opposite pole and inserted and secured a needle in Jack's arm as Grace had done on the opposite arm. She tested to make certain that the fluid dripped from the bag into the tube, and flowed down and into Jack's arm. Grace took Jack's hand and leaned in to speak as her eyes fluttered.

"You will feel pain as you wake, Jack, but it will only be for a little while, then back to sleep. Do you think you can manage for that little while?" Grace had spoken softly and gently, but urgently.

Jack nodded, then groaned and cried out. "I will sedate you again, Jack, and for a much longer period. The other IV contains nourishment. You are malnourished and dehydrated, and while I understand why you curtailed your food intake, it wasn't good for you. You are now catheterized—"

Jack's eyes opened wide. "No more peeing on myself?"

"No more peeing on yourself."

"Sleep for how long?"

"Until tomorrow."

"Thank you, Grace . . . Aaahhh, oh, oh, oh!" The pain was too much.

Grace opened the valve on the IV tube. The sedative began to flow into Jack's veins and her eyes closed, she sighed, and then slept.

"The child hasn't had a good night's sleep in over a year," Myrtle Lewis said sadly.

"I hope that's merely the first thing we can change," Grace said as Myrtle charted Jack's blood pressure and temperature, noted the time, hung the chart at the end of the bed, and left the room. Bobbie followed.

"She really is amazing, isn't she?" Bobbie was awed by what she'd just witnessed.

"All day, every day," Myrtle said. "She gives as much to patients at the end of the day as she gives to the first patients of the day, and truthfully there are days when I don't know how she does it." Myrtle gave a rueful smile, then added, "But on those days when I feel drained, I tell myself that if she can keep going, then so can I."

Grace stood looking at Jacqueline Jackson for several minutes, watching her eye movements beneath the lids and listening to her breathe. When the eyes stilled and the breathing slowed and deepened, the doctor turned out the light and left the exam room, leaving the door slightly open. She walked down the hall slowly because she suddenly felt exhausted and completely drained. She heard Nurse Lewis in the restroom so she entered her office. Bobbie was there, looking out the window, down at the street five stories below and busy even on a Sunday—it was Harlem, after all—and when she turned to face Grace there were tears in her eyes.

"Bobbie? What's wrong?"

"You are truly my Amazing Grace. And you are wonderful." She crossed the room, wrapping her arms around the doctor, holding her tight and close, allowing the tears to fall freely. Grace returned the hug and they stood in the embrace until Bobbie pulled away and wiped away the tears with the back of her hand. "Watching you work, Grace, is—I don't have words for what it is. Your gentleness with Jack, so much the opposite from her previous experience. And the trust in you I saw in her, And I know that what I saw is how you treat all your patients. I know that you must soothe women and ease their fear and pain through a delivery or a difficult diagnosis, and I know you engender their trust. Watching you should be required coursework for all physicians, especially the men. You leave me speechless and breathless, Dr. Hannon."

Grace chuckled. "I do recall that I have, on occasion, caused that response in you but it was never accompanied by tears," and she laughed out loud as Bobbie tried—and failed—to control her face, remembering those times. "And I am most appreciative of the compliment. Unfortunately, medicine, as it is currently practiced, is not kind to women, so we doctors, of necessity, must be."

Bobbie took her hand and led her to the sofa so she could sit. She clearly was exhausted. "Do you think that will ever change? The way medicine treats women?"

Grace shrugged, gave a slight shake of her head, and shrugged again. "I think in time it will have to, but only when there are more women professors in medical schools and many more women in the classrooms. And given how slowly the profession changes, I expect I'll be much too old to still be practicing if and when that change comes."

"You will never grow old, Grace. Wiser, perhaps, if that's even possible, but never old," Bobbie said, rubbing Grace's back before abruptly stopping. "And since I seem unable to keep my hands off you, would you like a massage?"

"Oh God yes!" And she stretched out on the sofa, on her stomach, and sighed.

"From top to bottom or bottom to top?"

"Bottom up, please. My feet and legs really hurt."

Bobbie pulled a chair close to the foot of the sofa, picked up one of Grace's feet and using both thumbs began to apply pressure the way the team trainers did in college, first to the pads beneath the toes, then to the heels. Grace moaned a mixture of pain and pleasure, which changed to a muttered curse at the light tap on the door.

"Come on in!" she called out.

Myrtle Lewis stuck a wary head in. "Are you sure?" She relaxed at the sight of Grace's foot being massaged by Bobbie, who was sitting in the chair, and came all the way in.

"Is Jack all right?" Grace asked.

The nurse nodded and smiled. "BP and HR are perfect, as is her temp, and her face seems to have relaxed a little, so maybe her body will, too. Eventually. But what I came to tell you is that Bobby Mason called a few minutes ago to say he got home with the car and he's having food delivered—"

"And here it is!" said Nurse Thelma Cooper, bustling in and carrying several bulging bags. "It was delivered by somebody called Any Day Now. I found the young man downstairs in the lobby staring at the open elevator, having forgotten where Bobby told him to go."

"Any Day Now," Bobbie repeated with a gleeful chortle, then said it again. "That's really good, Nurse Cooper. I can't wait to tell Jack and Bobby." And they all followed Nurse Cooper and the food into the kitchen.

"Oh how I do love Bobby Mason," Grace enthused to a

chorus of "me too" as the food emerged. It was enough fried chicken to feed an army, accompanied by mashed potatoes and gravy, collard greens, cornbread, a whole pound cake, and a gallon of iced tea. Harlem was where they were, but some part of the South was where the food was born. Before she sat down Grace said, "I want to call Bobby to say thanks; what's his number?" She went to the phone, picked up the receiver, and dialed the numbers Bobbie recited.

"But he won't be home until later, Grace—he's on call at the apartment building today."

The woman who so forcefully pulled the door open glared at Bobby, yelling "What took you so long? I told you my toilet was overflowing!"

"Good morning, Mrs. Collins," Bobby said, extending his clipboard to the woman. "If you would sign and date the work order please, I can take a look at the toilet."

She pushed the clipboard back toward him. "Why do I have to sign anything? Why can't you just unclog the toilet? Isn't that your job?"

"I can't do any work until you sign and date the work order—"

She snatched the clipboard and scrawled her name, the date, and the time of his arrival as 11:30 a.m., and shoved the clipboard back at him. He looked at what she'd written and marked through the "time of arrival," replacing it with the correct and current time of 10:40. "What do you think you're doing?" she snarled.

"Recording the correct time of my arrival: It is currently 10:40 a.m. and if you want me to look at your toilet you'll initial the correct time and allow me to get to work."

"Talk fancy for a janitor, don't you?" She snatched the

pad, scrawled her initials, shoved the clipboard in his chest, and marched down the hallway, into and through the kitchen, toward the bathroom, where the water met them.

Mrs. Collins stood well back as Bobby and his rubber-booted feet, plunger, mop and bucket in one hand, snake in the other, moved forward. He was willing to bet that flushed sanitary napkins caused the problem, and it didn't take long to prove himself right. He snaked them up and deposited them into the bucket, flushed the toilet to make certain it was flowing, mopped up the water on the bathroom floor, and turned to exit.

"Hey! Where you going? You get back here and mop these floors!"

"You'll have to mop your own floors, Mrs. Collins. And in the future, refrain from flushing sanitary pads and you won't have this problem." He hurried to the front door and out before he could hear her reply. He'd leave it to Mr. G to get her signature for the completed work. And to tell her that clogged toilets and pipes caused by her own negligence would appear as a charge on her rent bill.

Back in the office, he recorded the time of his return from the Collins apartment on the line below where he had recorded the time of her call. Then he wrote a detailed description of the work he'd performed. He included the fact that Mrs. Collins was angry because he had not mopped her floor. He signed and dated his report, noted the time, and picked up the phone to call Bobbie, Grace, and the nurses. Oh how he wished he could be with them, helping to care for Jack. In the short time of their association, they'd become as close as friends of many years.

Bobby had quickly learned not to worry about the hostility directed at him by some of the building's residents. "Like water off a duck's back," his grandma used to say about how she dealt with similar hostilities directed at her because of her color. "You can't waste your time wondering why crazy people act crazy." And Bobby didn't care why Mrs. Collins behaved the way she did because he understood full well that her hatred of Negroes had more to do with who she was than who he was, and he was just a man trying to do the job he got paid to do. He rinsed off the heavy rubber boots in the work sink and returned to the office and the phone. He'd brought a book to keep himself company in case it was a quiet afternoon: *Annie Allen*, Gwendolyn Brooks's book of poetry he'd gotten from the library. It wasn't quiet at all, but fortunately there were no more residents like Mrs. Collins to deal with and the day passed quickly.

Much later, as Bobbie, Myrtle and Thelma washed, rinsed and dried the dishes, the phone rang. "It's Bobby!" Grace called to the room. Into the receiver she said, "and I'm answering my own phone because everyone else is cleaning up after the feast you provided. That was so very wonderful of you, Bobby, and so very appreciated. We were starving."

"I wish I could be there with you. How is Jack?"

"She's sleeping, Bobby, which is good, and she seems to be doing quite well—"

"Better than quite well," Bobbie said, sharing the receiver with Grace. "I wish you could have seen Grace and her fabulous nurses in action. If they'd been responsible for Jack's care in the beginning—"

Grace reclaimed sole possession of the phone and when Bobbie pouted, Grace smacked her on the butt. Myrtle and Thelma laughed so loudly Bobby asked what was happening, then laughed when Grace told him. They were enjoying themselves, no matter that it was Sunday and they all were at work.

Their lightness of spirit was from hoping it just might be possible for Jack Jackson to be restored to something resembling wholeness. Nothing was certain—they all understood that—but until now the only thing that was certain was a future of continued pain and suffering for Jack. So, maybe, just maybe . . .

Grace relinquished the phone after a few minutes and they all got a chance to talk to Bobby, which made his day—and theirs. Then, over cups of coffee and tea, and slices of pound cake, they sat and talked for a while.

"I still want to know how Mr. Any Day Now got his name," Thelma Cooper said, and Bobbie explained how Ennyday was a devotee of Pig Latin.

"Don't know how or why but one day Denny Williams declared that from that moment forward his name was Ennyday, and not Denny, and that his siblings were to be called Ennyjay and Ennybay, not Jenny and Benny—"

"Wait a minute," Grace interrupted, halting the laughter. "Are you saying they're triplets?" And when Bobbie nodded, Grace said slowly, "Ennyday is a bit slow, isn't he?" But it wasn't a question—she knew very well that he was. "And his siblings, how are they?"

"Benny, the oldest, seems fine. He doesn't live at home but he helps out as much as he can because the father is disabled and he drinks. The youngest, Jenny—"

"Is quite slow, isn't she?" Grace interrupted.

Bobbie nodded. "Yes, she is, and she almost never leaves home, which is why we all try our best to look out for Ennyday. He tried being a thief but always got himself caught or beat up and whatever he managed to steal was taken away from him. So we convinced him to stop stealing and in return folks hire him to run errands, and we pay him—"

Thelma Cooper jumped up. "Oh goodness, I didn't give him anything!" she exclaimed as she ran out of the kitchen.

Then Bobbie was on her feet and out the office door, headed for the elevator, followed by Thelma.

"Where are you going?" Grace exclaimed.

"He may still be downstairs waiting."

"But, but, it's been . . ." Grace sputtered.

"If Jack and I are up here, then one of us will pay him. He knows that, and since neither of us did—"

And sure enough Ennyday was sitting on the floor between the front door of the building and the elevator, and he stood up and grinned when he saw Bobbie.

"I'm sorry I didn't come down sooner, Ennyday," Bobbie said.

"That's okay. Bobby told me Jack was sick. Can I go see her?"

Bobbie shook her head. "Not this time, Ennyday. Dr. Grace gave her some medicine that made her sleep." She touched Thelma's shoulder. "This is Nurse Cooper, one of the nurses who helps Dr. Grace take care of Jack."

Thelma extended her hand to Ennyday. He studied it for a moment, then took it and pumped it up and down like someone trying to raise water from a country well. "Thank you for taking care of Jack. She's my friend."

"Thank you for bringing us the food Bobby sent," she said, and gave Ennyday a handful of change, which he promptly deposited into his pocket without looking at it.

"You're welcome, Nurse," he said.

Bobbie held up two dollar bills. "Do you remember what these are, Ennyday?"

He nodded. "One dollar. Two of 'em."

"And what do you do with them?"

He wrinkled his brow in thought, then smiled and took the bills from Bobbie. "I'm supposed to fold 'em up small and put 'em in my pocket so nobody can see 'em and take 'em away from me." And he folded the bills, one at a time, then stuffed them deep into his pocket. "And when I get home I give 'em to my mama and she hides 'em from my daddy so he can't spend 'em."

Bobbie nodded. "Tell your mama I will see her tomorrow or the next day."

Ennyday nodded and was across the lobby and out the front

door like a flash.

"Good heavens!" Thelma Cooper exclaimed as she watched his exit.

"He'll run all the way home," Bobbie said.

"Safely?" Thelma asked

"Most of the time," Bobbie replied, and they rode the elevator up to the fifth floor and the office of Dr. Grace Hannon, Obstetrics and Gynecology.

CHAPTER THREE

Dr. Grace Hannon stood before the two powerful men who were the hospital administrator and chief of staff, even though they, more than once, urged her to sit.

She stood because she wanted them to see that she was calm and would not waver or falter when she told them why she had so urgently requested their presence. And she stood because she wanted to see their faces when they read and heard what she had to say. And she stood because they were seated, relaxed, and comfortable in their power and authority over her no matter what she did.

She had dressed deliberately. Both men were notorious womanizers though her Color saved her from having to endure their unwanted advances or, worse, their retaliation if the advances were rejected. But she also knew they appreciated her appearance this morning.

She wore the crimson knit ensemble that Bobbie liked so much because, she said, the dress looked like it hugged her. She wore a new long, white, stiffly starched coat, fountain pens—one black, one gold—in the breast pocket, and a stethoscope around her neck. She talked, as if giving a lecture, explaining in detail what had happened to Jacqueline Jackson in the alley where she was attacked while taking a shortcut home. She described in detail how a drunken New York City police officer was passed out in that same alley, providing no assistance to the brutalized rape victim. Then she explained, in the same calm detail, what had happened to Jacqueline Jackson while she was a patient at Harlem Hospital. She included what she called the sexual assault by one of the young residents, the carafe of water thrown at him by Jacqueline Jackson, and fact that the nurse who prevented retaliation against Jack for throwing the water was transferred to the night shift.

The chief of staff exploded in anger, denying that any such things had occurred on his watch. The administrator looked closely at the documents and x-rays provided by Grace and told the chief to shut his mouth. As if she hadn't been interrupted, Grace continued, explaining her recent examination and x-rays.

"What do you want from us, from this hospital?" the administrator asked.

"Miss Jackson, her family, and I want this hospital to perform corrective surgery—"

"There is nothing to correct!" the chief shouted, jumping to his feet.

The hospital administrator looked at the chief of staff as if he'd sprouted horns and a tail. "You sound like a complete fool. Sit down and shut up while I think about how best to handle this."

He looked directly at Grace. "There's no question that we must correct any and all mistakes made in the treatment of Miss Jackson, but we must also protect the reputation of this hospital. We cannot have the public thinking, believing, that we . . . that we butcher patients. That we don't give the same care to our Colored patients that we do to everyone else."

"I believe the work the Department of Psychiatry is doing with poor Negroes at St. Philips is speaking to that issue," Grace said, "and that program is going a long way toward changing the negative perception of this hospital." She watched the administrator relax slightly. Grace continued, "Every effort this hospital takes in that direction helps to erase decades of built-up bad feelings."

"And making Miss Jackson whole—"

"This hospital is not responsible for whatever damage that girl suffered!" the chief of staff thundered. He was red-faced and perspiring heavily. "Perhaps if she lived a different kind of life—"

Now Grace released the anger she'd been containing. "I see you're perpetuating the lie your protege told you," Grace said, staring at the man, "that that Miss Jackson is a prostitute and that's why she was in that alley. Only the ones who butchered her ever told that lie out loud. And you were one of them. You were one of the pitiful excuses of surgeons who abandoned his oath to abstain from doing harm," Grace declared, continuing, "Jacqueline Jackson was a graduate student at City College, working on a master's in education. She is not and never was a prostitute, and any reputable physician would understand how unlikely it would be for a prostitute to have an intact hymen. Your protege, however, is a butcher," she practically spat the words, "and has no business practicing medicine, in this hospital or anywhere else."

The administrator raised his hands, palms forward, and inhaled deeply. He stared at his chief of staff and ordered, "Don't you say another word." Then he turned to Grace. "Where is Miss Jackson now?"

"In my office, under sedation."

"I will schedule her surgery for first thing tomorrow morning. Dr. Oliver Crawford will be in charge, assisted by Dr. Arthur Jennings. I want you to scrub in, Dr. Hannon, prepared to assist if there is damage to the young woman's reproductive organs. I want the best surgical nurses we have there as well. I will make all the necessary arrangements, including having Miss Jackson admitted sometime later today." He looked at Grace.

"Can you be available to Drs. Crawford and Jennings?"

"At their convenience," Grace replied.

"What about things at your office?" he asked.

"My nurse has things well in hand and I have no mothers scheduled for imminent delivery, though babies have been known to keep their own schedules," Grace said with a slight smile.

"Speaking of which, Dr. Hannon, you set a hospital record the other day. I will make certain your accomplishment is included in the staff newsletter," the administrator said, managing a slight smile of his own, but it was forced through thin, angry lips.

He looked at his watch. "I'll be in my office. There's a lot to get done in a short time." He turned to the chief of staff and coldly said, "And I want you in your office in case I need you."

"Thank you for your time this morning," Grace said.

"Thank you for coming to me first, before turning the *Amsterdam News* loose on us." He literally shuddered at the thought.

Grace left the administrator's office, not interested in what would transpire between him and the chief of staff. She hurried to the doctors' lounge, grabbed her overcoat and purse from her locker, and was headed toward the elevator when she spied Thelma Cooper. They maintained a professional cordiality until they entered the quiet and empty restroom reserved for the few women physicians.

There, Grace hugged her and whispered, "We won! Jack's surgery is tomorrow morning. Please make certain the administrator knows you're one of the surgical nurses I recommend to scrub in. And Thelma—I can't thank you enough—"

"I owe you my thanks, Grace. Assisting as a surgical nurse where all eyes will be watching—oh my! You'll be scrubbing in, won't you?" And when Grace nodded, she added, "I can hardly believe how many things they're doing right this time."

"I wish they'd done all the right things a year ago and saved that young woman from so much pain and misery," Grace said.

Thelma hugged her tightly. "You're seeing that the right things are done right now, and I'll see you in the morning, Grace, to witness more of the same."

"You're the best surgical nurse I've ever worked with. Now two of this hospital's best surgeons will get to see what a first-class surgical nurse looks like."

It was snowing lightly when Grace got outside, and she hopped into a taxi for the short ride up Broadway to her office. Arriving there, she could tell by the look on Myrtle's face that Thelma had called with the news. Before Grace could ask, the nurse pointed toward the kitchen and said, "She's on the phone."

Bobbie jumped to her feet when Grace entered the kitchen, told whoever was on the other end of the phone call they'd talk later, hung up, and grabbed the good doctor in a huge bear hug. She lifted her, and danced her around the room, ignoring demands and pleas to be put down. Only when Nurse Lewis entered did Bobbie comply. "You truly are one amazing woman, Grace Hannon, and I love you more than words can say!"

"You love me in this dress," Grace said primly, extricating herself from Bobbie's grip.

"Any person with two seeing eyes would love you in that dress, Dr. Hannon," said Bobbie grinning and still holding her around the waist.

Grace freed herself, stepping quickly away from Bobbie and into her white coat. "I'm going to see my patients and let them see me," she said, and left them. They watched her go, beaming with pride and respect and gratitude. They both loved her more than words could say.

"I think I can breathe now," Nurse Lewis said, inhaling and exhaling deeply.

"Am I wrong, or did she just put her entire career on the line?" Bobbie asked.

One more deep breath in and out and Myrtle said, "I only wish you were wrong. She took a great risk. She knew she was right, but we all know how little that matters. I think it was really in her favor—in addition to the proof she had—that the administrator hates the chief of staff, and so does everyone else. That little bastard, pardon my French, has no business wearing a white coat!"

"Then how—"

"Because his very rich daddy pulled the right strings, donated to the right causes, and kissed the right butts."

"So his incompetent son could maim and cripple a young woman?" Bobbie asked incredulously.

"They almost never have to face the consequences of their bad actions. I can't wait to hear how the administrator dealt with it," Nurse Lewis said.

"I'll have to hear about it later. Gotta go. I just hung up in the middle of whatever Justine was saying and I must go make that right; then I've got to go to Jack's parents—" Bobbie stopped talking and looked frightened. "Suppose she says no to the surgery, Myrt? Suppose Jack won't go through with it? She has suffered so much, and not just from the pain but from the embarrassment of the ever-present stench of urine."

"Based on what Thelma told me, I think our Grace can make a convincing case. And Jack trusts her, Bobbie, more than she trusts any other doctor."

Grace had gradually been reducing the amount of the sedative Jack was receiving so she was not so deeply asleep. Grace gently squeezed her hand and softly called her name. Jack's eyes fluttered, closed, then opened, and finally focused. "Hey Doc."

"How're you feeling, Jack? Is the pain better?"

Jack nodded. "It's not gone but it is much better."

"I've got some news and I want you to listen very carefully. Are you awake enough for me to share the news?" When Jack nodded, Grace said, "The hospital has agreed to a corrective surgery—"

Jack tried to sit up. Her expression alternated between frightened and frantic, hopeful and excited. "They're going to fix me?"

Grace nodded, telling Jack everything that happened in the meeting.

"Two new doctors and you and Nurse Cooper will be there? The whole time?"

"Yes."

"And that other one—"

"Will not be allowed in the operating room. That's a promise I will make sure is kept."

"When?"

"Tomorrow morning. We'll check you into the hospital later today."

Jack lay back and wept. Grace and Myrtle watched her closely. When she finally was cried out, Myrtle wiped her face with a wet towel and placed pillows behind her to help her sit up. "Where's Bobbie? Does she know?" asked Jack.

Grace nodded and explained Bobbie's absence. "But she's waiting to hear your decision before going to tell your parents—"

"Can I call and tell them? I want them to hear it from me."

Mr. and Mrs. Jackson were there when Jack checked into the hospital later that day, and they both wept at the sight of their daughter in the bed with her legs separated and suspended in stirrups. However, she was in a private room this time, with a door that closed, and this time there would be no parade of male doctors coming to ogle.

They hugged Bobbie, then turned to hug Grace and Bobby. They tried to hug their daughter, but she pushed them away with a "Not yet!" She still was in a lot of pain, but at least she didn't smell like pee, for which she would be grateful to Grace Hannon for the foreseeable future.

They shook the hands of the two new surgeons, who would, they fervently hoped, restore their daughter to good health. Then the parents and friends of Jack Jackson left the room so the doctors could examine her and learn as much as possible about their patient's condition in the short time available to them.

When the two male doctors left, Grace and Jack talked for a long time. Grace told Jack everything she knew about Drs. Arthur Jennings and Oliver Crawford, including their ready acceptance of Nurse Thelma Cooper scrubbing in as a surgical nurse because Grace vouched for her, and their reputations as excellent surgeons and "really decent fellas," in the words of a trusted doctor friend.

Grace squeezed the hand of the woman who was now more than a patient and took her leave. Returning to their daughter's bedside, the Jacksons bid her good night with a promise to see her first thing the next morning. Then Jack's dearest friend Bobbie Hilliard spoke soothing words to her and left to be with Grace. She had to make certain the good doctor had a healthy meal and a good sleep in preparation for the following day's work.

A short time later, one of the night nurses came in to take Jack's temperature and check her pulse and respiration, to see if she needed anything for pain. She said she would check on Jack throughout the night, dimmed the light and left, leaving the door ajar.

It was then that Bobby Mason entered the darkened room, pulling a chair close to the bed, taking Jack's hand and announcing he would be with her all night.

Later, both Jack and Bobby were startled awake by the loud voice of the night nurse outside the room saying, "You can't be here. Get out!"

"Shut your mouth, you Black bitch!"

"It's him!" Jack screamed, trying to get up.

Bobby was on his feet, his hand grabbing the arm of the man in the white coat like a vise grip before he had managed to get close to the bed and Jack.

"Get your hands off me, you Black bastard!"

Instantly, one of Bobby's hands was around the white-coated man's throat while the other had one of his arms twisted behind his back. "If you say another word, I'll break your arm," he said into the man's ear, pushing him toward and then all the way out the door and into the hall. He met the night nurse and asked, "Who is he?"

"The quack who butchered this girl and he's not supposed to be here."

"Where is the nearest stairwell?" Bobby asked. The nurse pointed and led the way as Bobby pushed the doctor along, maintaining his grip on the squirming man.

"Please stay with her until I get back," Bobby said to the nurse, all but dragging the doctor to the stairwell door, one hand squeezing the man's throat so he couldn't make a sound, the other still twisting his arm behind his back so he couldn't escape. He wanted to ask the man what the hell he thought he was doing, what the hell he intended to do, but the words refused to rise in his throat. Until he went to Korea, he'd never thought about killing another human being, and until this moment he'd never thought he'd kill again.

The nurse opened the stairwell door, then stuck a matchbook under the bottom to prevent it from locking when closed. Then she hurried back to Jack's room where she promised the now terrified patient she would stay with her until her friend returned.

Bobby propelled the cursing, snarling doctor into the

stairwell and onto the landing, then kicked him down the stairs. He followed at a run and on the next landing, pulled the now horrified, fearful man to his feet again, and again kicked him down to the next and bottom level.

Bobby took his time descending the stairs this time, trying to decide what to do next, but the decision was made for him when the doctor wobbled up to a standing position and, spewing curses, tried to hit his assailant. Bobby grabbed the hand that missed him and pried the fist open. "Is this the hand you used to butcher my friend?"

"Your friend the hooker? You one of her customers?" he smirked. It was enough to push Bobby over the edge. He opened the door, placed the doctor's hand on the inside door jamb, making sure it stayed there, and let the heavy door slam. The initial scream became a plea to open the door, and when Bobby did, the weeping doctor cradled his damaged hand in his good one and curled his body into a ball, but Bobby pulled him to his feet.

"Get up and give me the white coat."

"No! Only doctors wear these."

"So why are you wearing it? Take it off!"

But he couldn't manage one-handed, so Bobby snatched it off the whimpering man, opened the door and pushed him out into the cold, then folded the white coat into a pad and placed it in the door jamb to make sure it didn't lock.

From there he force-marched the doctor toward the front of the building. It was a long walk and Bobby wanted to get him close enough so someone would see him. He didn't want the fool to freeze to death. And he didn't want to freeze either, so he ran back the way he'd come, opened the door, and ran up the two flights of stairs to the door kept open by the matchbook. As he came into the hall, the nurse saw him. "Everything all right?"

He nodded, asked about Jack, and was relieved she'd calmed down and was asleep. He saw the look the nurse gave the white coat in his hand. "Do you have a bag I can put this in? And where can I wash up?"

When Bobby woke up it was because Grace was squeezing his shoulder. She pointed to the door and he followed her out of Jack's room and into the hall. "Is it time?"

"Almost, but tell me about last night, Bobby. Was that . . . was he here?"

Bobby nodded. "He was, until he wasn't. I don't know what he could have been thinking, Grace. Walked right into the room like it was okay."

"What must it be like to move through the world knowing that its rules don't apply to you? What freedom!" She intended to sound light but Bobby heard the anger-tinged sadness and frustration.

"The rules do apply to them, Grace, and sooner or later the truth catches up with them, and they have to pay the piper."

"Do you really believe that?" A raised eyebrow accompanied the skepticism.

"Well . . . sometimes a little help is required to make the point," Bobby said.

"Then thank you for the point you made," Grace said.

"Who said I made a point?"

"Go get some sleep, Bobby—and some food—before you report to work."

"Bobbie will call me?"

"As soon as Jack is out of surgery." She hugged him and headed to the doctors' lounge to wait for Drs. Crawford and Jennings.

Bobby quickly returned to Jack's room, briefly squeezed her hand, grabbed the Gristedes grocery bag holding the white medical coat, grabbed his own coat and hat, and headed to the elevator. He'd take a taxi home and follow Grace's order to eat and get some sleep before reporting to work.

He wondered, without actually looking to see, whether the battered doctor had been rescued and only hoped that the man's hand could not be repaired sufficiently to allow him to practice surgery ever again. And with that hope, he realized he had no remorse for his actions, nor was there sorrow for that lack of remorse. Perhaps someday, if the preachers his ma and grandma listened to and believed in were right, his payment to the piper would come due. But he'd only worry about that if the piece-of-shit doctor had to worry about his actions, too, and pay whatever piper people like him owed.

Once in the operating room, masked and gowned, Grace stood near the doctor who administered the anesthesia and spoke so Jack would know she was there before sleep took her. Then she took her place across from Crawford and Jennings and Nurse Cooper and another nurse unknown to Grace.

"Good morning, everyone," Oliver Crawford said. "I believe all of you know why we are here but just in case someone doesn't—"

"I'm the chief surgical nurse and I was present the first time this woman was operated on, and there was no problem with that surgery."

Without responding to her, Dr. Crawford said, "Nurse Cooper will be the chief surgical nurse today—"

"That's my job!"

"You will move away from the table and stay away unless you are called for, and if you can't do that you will leave this surgery. Am I clear? And I expect an answer, Nurse."

Without speaking, the nurse backed away from the table, but not far away.

"Get the nursing supervisor in here," Crawford said. "And Nurse Cooper, assume the correct position, please."

"Yes, Doctor," Thelma said, moving to stand beside him. "Would you prefer that I anticipate the instrument you require or wait for your request?"

"Let's anticipate for starters. And if everybody is ready—"

Thelma picked up a scalpel and placed it firmly in Crawford's outstretched palm. On the opposite side of the table—and Jack's body—Grace irrigated and suctioned, keeping the area clean and visible to the surgeons. They worked so well together that Grace knew they did it often. And Thelma worked so well with them that Grace knew she would soon, if not already, be part of their surgical team. She was glad she was masked so no one could see her satisfied grin.

The surgeons quickly found and repaired the problem of the constantly leaking urine. There was a tear in the urethra, a likely result of the damage and trauma to the vagina not previously repaired, though it should have been. Oliver Crawford muttered curses under his breath as he sutured, and he and Arthur Jennings shared meaningful glances. They no doubt would have much to discuss later, as would Grace and Thelma.

Dr. Crawford watched Grace as closely as she watched him, and he saw her expression change. "Is something wrong, Dr. Hannon?" Never raising her eyes, she reported that small drops of blood reappeared after every irrigation and suction, but where was it coming from?

Both surgeons looked closely and saw what Grace saw: tiny, minuscule drops of blood that kept slowly appearing. Crawford held up a hand to stop Grace from irrigating and suctioning, and the blood puddle gradually grew. Jack had complained of constant blood that wasn't menstrual blood. "Somebody get me some light in here! Now!"

"Oh dear Lord," Grace said. The blood was coming from a small tear in the abdominal aorta. "She said she was kicked in

97

the stomach several times—"

"Those sons of a bitches!" Oliver Crawford exclaimed.

"I'd like to kick their asses around the block!" Arthur Jennings exclaimed.

The three doctors were dumbstruck at the sight. Perplexed. Terrified. If the small tear had, for any reason, become larger, become a rupture, Jacqueline Jackson would be dead.

"Dr. Hannon, do you want to make the repair?" Crawford asked.

Grace nodded. Jennings took over irrigation and suction duties as Thelma pressed the smallest clamp into Grace's outstretched hand, followed by the smallest suture needle and the thinnest thread. The tiny tear was repaired with two sutures but Grace added a third and quickly cut and tied off the thin thread. They all kept watching, barely breathing, as the seconds ticked by. Not a single drop of blood appeared, not the tiniest of drops. Normal breathing returned to the medical team around the table.

"All right," Crawford said. "I've seen no evidence of any bone damage. Has anyone else?"

"Look at the inside of the right groin area," Grace said. "Miss Jackson said two of the rapists grabbed her legs and held them open, pulled them wide open and held them open, pulling. She said it was very painful. I'm no orthopedic expert but those striations—"

"How fast can we get an orthopedic consult in here?" Crawford yelled.

"In a few minutes, Doctor!" someone yelled back, and in a few minutes the head of the orthopedic surgery department burst in, a nurse trailing in his wake still tying his gown and mask.

"So, what's all this? Ollie Crawford, is that you?"

"This is Dr. James Gordon, everyone," Crawford said, explaining to Gordon quickly but succinctly why his expertise was needed. The orthopedic specialist quickly got himself to the foot of the table and without a second glance touched Jack's right leg.

"Looks like somebody tried to pull this poor girl's leg right out of its socket." He lifted the leg and gently rotated it, bent it at the knee and rotated again, finally straightening it and gently placing it down.

"No wonder she couldn't walk. However, this is a problem of tendons and ligaments, not bones. I think I can help without resorting to surgery. A lot of progress in the field of orthopedics, thank goodness." He looked closely at Jack, then gave her a gentle pat on the shoulder. "Most of it aimed at getting big, bruiser jocks back on the field, not getting little ladies like this back on her feet and walking normally. But good medicine is good medicine and good doctors practice good medicine."

He outlined a process involving medication and strapping the leg in place for a couple of months. "The medication is painful; it's injected directly into the joint and hurts like hell. Since she's already under, I'll inject her. But in the future, I'd advise intravenous introduction. It hurts going in, and it burns and stings for a couple of hours afterward."

"Can you explain how to strap the leg?" Grace asked.

Gordon reached over his shoulder and a long length of canvas appeared in his hand. It was about eight inches wide and several feet long with a buckle at one end. "This will make at least two straps for her since she's such a small girl." He reached over his shoulder again and a syringe appeared in his hand. He showed it to Drs. Crawford, Hannon, and Jennings, then injected the contents into the interior groin joint of Jack Jackson's right leg, and she groaned.

He showed them where and how to place the strap that would immobilize Jack's hip. "Between this and the medication, whatever is damaged inside there will eventually heal. This is a very powerful anti-inflammatory that works quickly and lasts forever—unless the area is damaged again. And even though she doesn't look like a football or ice hockey player, she'll need to take it slow and easy for a few months." He took his time showing the doctors how it was done and then prepared to leave. "Don't hesitate to call if you need me." Then he thanked them for inviting him to consult, they thanked him for coming, and he left.

"I'd like to keep her catheterized," Grace said, "especially since she won't be moving around for a while," and when the catheter was in place, Drs. Hannon, Crawford and Jennings and Nurse Cooper began to put an end to Jack Jackson's surgery.

"Dr. Grace Hannon, please call the operator. Dr. Grace Hannon, please call the operator. Dr. Grace Hannon, please call the operator."

"Does that mean a new life needs your help joining us in this sometimes-ugly old world?" Crawford asked.

"Most likely," Grace said, stepping away from the table. "But a most considerate new life, and I'll be sure to give him or her an extra hug for kindly waiting until I was free. I'll find you later," she said and was gone.

"Does anyone ever call her Amazing Grace?" Arthur Jennings asked Thelma Cooper.

"Everyone who knows her," came the reply.

"Well, add my name to the list," he said.

"Mine, too!" Oliver Crawford added.

Baby Girl Savannah's mother, Mavis, beat them to it, by hollering, "Amazing!" when Dr. Grace Hannon delivered her six-pound, eight-ounce girl a mere seven hours after her first contraction. The baby came so quickly and easily that Mavis didn't have time to be nervous or fearful about giving birth to her first child. And, as promised, Grace was with her the entire time, talking to her and encouraging her in a voice that was both calm and soothing, even when giving orders: "Push. Stop. Gentle breaths. One more big push right now! And here she is, Mavis, your baby girl."

"You really are amazing, Dr. Hannon!" The new mother wept with joy when the doctor placed the baby girl in her arms, "and if she didn't already have a name, I'd call her Grace after you. But she's the first girl in my family not to be born in Savannah, so she will be called Savannah."

"Can't argue with that," Thelma Cooper said when she met Grace coming into the recovery suite and asked about the delivery. Looking into the room, Grace saw Drs. Crawford and Jennings standing on either side of Jack's bed.

"Is everything all right?"

"I think so," Nurse Cooper said. "Vitals are all in the normal range, but The Boys are concerned that she seems to be experiencing some discomfort at that injection site."

Still smiling at Thelma's calling Crawford and Jennings "The Boys," Grace hurriedly tied on a mask and took Jack's hand when she reached the bed. She knew the anesthesia would be wearing off, that some level of consciousness would be returning, and that Jack would know someone was holding her hand, and that it would be Grace or Bobbie. Jack's eyes fluttered but didn't fix.

"Boy or girl," Jennings asked.

"Six and a half pounds of beautiful baby girl named Savannah," Grace replied.

"What a beautiful name," Crawford said. "And did you give her a hug?"

"You bet I did," Grace said, turning her attention to Jack who was stirring. She tightened her grip on Jack's hand and felt the pressure returned. "She's coming around."

On the other side of the bed Oliver Crawford took the other hand. "Welcome back, Miss Jackson. I'm Dr. Crawford and you came through your surgery with flying colors. We think you'll be very pleased with the results."

"How's the pain?" Grace asked, and Jack pointed to her right groin. "Anywhere else?" Jack lay still for a long moment. The issue of pain now was a relative thing given what she had endured for more than a year. She managed a small smile, a one-shouldered shrug, and then whispered something. Grace leaned in to hear her ask about the catheter. Grace whispered back that the catheter was in place but only until Jack could get up and get to the toilet on her own. "But there's no more leaking, Jack."

Then Grace leaned in for a closer look at the site of the anti-inflammatory injection and noticed some redness and a little swelling. She wondered whether an ice pack would be helpful.

Dr. Jennings gave her a hard clap on the shoulder—she now was, she guessed, one of The Boys—and ran to call Dr. Gordon. While they waited for his return, she and Dr. Crawford gave Jack a thorough head-to-toe exam and concluded that she truly had come through the surgery almost better than expected. The elimination of the constant excruciating pain transformed her. Her face and her body had relaxed, and she once again was the pretty girl Bobbie had always known.

Dr. Jennings sped back into the room with the response that Dr. Gordon also thought Dr. Hannon was a genius. Crawford took the chart and wrote an order for pain medication and ice packs to be administered as needed, and the three doctors went to the lounge. Grace was about to speak but stopped herself. Something about The Boys put her on alert so she sat down and waited for them to speak. When they didn't sit, she knew her instincts were correct.

"I assume you heard what happened last night," Crawford finally said.

"Yes, I heard that despite being ordered to stay away, the man responsible for Miss Jackson's condition showed up in her room."

"I was referring to the beating he took."

Grace sat up straight. "The . . . beating?"

"You didn't know?" Jennings asked, sounding surprised.

"How would I? Why would I?"

"Someone said you knew the man who—" Crawford began.

Grace swiftly stood up and did not attempt to control the anger that rose with her. "I spoke with the man this morning who was hired to keep Miss Jackson safe, and given what transpired last night, I believe it's a good thing he was there or who knows what would have happened to her."

"The hospital is trying to find out what happened to Dr.—" Crawford tried again.

"By 'the hospital' you mean 'the administrator'?" Grace said, and when Jennings nodded, she said, "and did he happen to say why it was all right for a staff member of this hospital to ignore his direct order?" And if she weren't so angry she'd have laughed at the confused looks The Boys wore. "Surely you both recall that the same fella you both are feeling so sorry for right now was ordered to stay away from Miss Jackson? I was in the room with you."

"Yes, but nobody thought he'd get beaten so badly for disobeying."

"Did anyone think what he planned to do to Jacqueline Jackson alone in her hospital room late at night? What do you two think he planned to do? Has anyone asked him?"

They looked ready to run from the room. "The administrator just thought that you might know who the man was since you know Miss Jackson's friends and family, and he also thought you might want to know that the man—whoever he is—slammed a door on a doctor's hand, making almost certain that his days as a surgeon are over."

Grace unconsciously flexed her right hand, then massaged it with her left hand. "If he had followed orders, he wouldn't be in this situation. But perhaps he already knew what I'm just learning to be the case—that the administrator doesn't always mean what he says. And since it seems that I can't take the administrator at his word, he should know that he can no longer take me at mine."

Jennings understood first. "But you promised that you wouldn't talk to the newspaper about what happened to Miss Jackson."

"And the administrator promised that the man who damaged Miss Jackson would be kept away from her." She watched them wrestle with her words and their intent. These were good doctors. She'd watched them work, had watched them put all their knowledge and skill to work to heal Jacqueline Jackson. "Do you two believe that because a person is a white, male doctor, his life has more value than a Negro female?"

Both men wore identical looks of horror and they sputtered their denials before they could get the words out. When they finally did, Grace was inclined to believe them. And yet . . . "Yet you seem unwilling to hold your friend even just a little bit responsible for what happened to him. If he had followed orders, he'd still have use of his hand and it would be up to someone else to decide whether he could still be a doctor."

"I do see your point," Jennings said. "I had never thought about it until now, but I do see it. And I think I understand why you're so angry."

"Me, too," Crawford said in a near whisper. "And . . . and I'm sorry, Dr. Hannon."

She wanted to tell them they had no idea why she was angry, but since she had no wish to explain, she asked instead, "Do you both wish to continue with Miss Jackson's care, and with Nurse Cooper as your surgical nurse?"

"Yes, of course!"

"Definitely!"

"We've already requested that Nurse Cooper be assigned to us."

"We've already requested that she receive a raise."

Later that evening, after dinner at Bobbie's, they sat with drinks in hand relaxing before a roaring fire. There was much to discuss and celebrate as they raised glasses and toasted friends present and absent. Bobby Mason began singing "Amazing Grace" and everybody joined in. Bobbie suggested they create lyrics to an Amazing Thelma hymn.

"You should've seen their faces when I asked if they wanted to keep Thelma."

"I wish I could've seen their faces when they said I was getting a raise."

Grace looked sad but only for a moment. She had tried more than once to get a raise for Thelma and was rejected each time. But no matter who had asked, the important thing was that Nurse Thelma Cooper was getting a raise. "I don't think they'll let her out of their sight."

"Oh hell yes they will! She'll be working for'em, not marrying 'em," Nurse Myrtle Lewis stated emphatically, followed by a very quiet, "Oops. Well, I guess that cat's outta the bag."

"Did I just hear what I think I just heard?" Bobbie queried with pointed and demanding looks back and forth at the two nurses.

"And when did this happen?" Grace asked. "And why didn't you tell us?"

"So many other things were happening—"

"Important things—"

"Everybody already had a full plate—"

"And you two are as important as anything else we've had on the serving tray," Grace said, "and it would have been a joy to take time to celebrate the two of you."

"Well let's do it now," Bobbie said, reluctantly extricating herself from Grace's embrace and jumping to her feet. "There's a bottle of champagne in the fridge waiting for something to celebrate."

"I'll get some glasses," Bobby said, hurrying over to the bar and quickly returning with champagne glasses as Bobbie returned with champagne and a linen towel.

"You can open that without spilling any, right?" Thelma asked with mild skepticism.

"Watch and learn," Bobbie said, and proved her point. She quickly removed the foil wrapper down the neck of the bottle and the wire and metal covering over the cork, then used the towel to gently push and rock the cork back and forth, up and down, until there was a gentle pop. Then the bubbly was poured, and the toasts were made—from the loving to the risqué to the ribald and the bawdy. It didn't take long for five celebrants to empty a bottle of champagne.

Grace rose quickly, hurried into the bedroom and just as quickly came back out, dangling a key ring. "Unfortunately, not the keys to the honeymoon suite at the Ritz, just to my apartment, but yours for as long as you like."

Quickly on her feet, Thelma grabbed them, proclaimed them better than keys to the Ritz, pulled Myrtle to her feet, bade them all good night, and headed for the door. Bobby followed, saying they could drop him off on the way down the hill. Grace had final words before they were out of the door: "Don't forget to make certain Jack does not remember Bobby or anything about him!"

"My first order of business tomorrow morning," Thelma replied.

"You don't have to worry about me," Bobby called out.

"We can if we want to," came a quick reply.

"And you can't stop us," came another.

"I can take care of myself!" Bobby yelled.

"Get him out of here, please" were the last words Bobby

Mason heard before the door slammed shut and Bobbie Hilliard hurried through the kitchen to lock it. When she returned to the living room, she pulled Grace to her feet and into a hug. "Go get ready for bed, love. I'll clean up out here and bank the fire and be with you before you have time to miss me."

"Promise?"

By the time Bobbie completed her tasks, washed her face and teeth, and joined Grace in the bedroom, she expected the good doctor to be fast asleep, but she was not. She was sitting up pretending to watch something on television, but without audio, so she couldn't have been very interested. Though her open eyes were aimed at the TV screen they were focused inward. Bobbie turned off the television and walked over to sit on the bed beside Grace and took her hands. "You've had a very difficult couple of days, my lovely, brilliant doctor, and I'm very proud of you. Yet you are troubled. May I ask why?"

Grace managed a small smile. "I hope I can provide a lovely and brilliant answer." But she said nothing, leaving Bobbie unsure about how or even whether to proceed. Better to leave her alone and allow her to reckon with what was troubling her, or attempt to help her get through it? They'd learned a lot about each other in a short time and they learned more each day, but Bobbie didn't yet know enough about this woman she knew she loved to know what to do now.

"What's troubling me," Grace finally said, "is that I can find no sorrow or pity inside myself for a hand that may now be useless, especially on a man who is supposed to be a surgeon. How can I, who am supposed to be a healer, have no feeling at all?"

"Perhaps because all of your feelings are exhausted," Bobbie answered.

"I don't understand."

"It seemed that you literally felt Jack's pain—the pain she endured in that alley, the pain and humiliation she endured in the hospital as men who were supposed to be healers gawked. Worse, the pain and misery she endured for more than a year since that travesty—I believe you felt that pain, Gracie. I also believe that your promise to help Jack heal was such a heavy weight that the possibility of failure was painful to you."

Bobbie winced because she had never fully allowed the possibility of failure to heal Jack and end her suffering to take hold.

"But you did not fail. Jack Jackson's pain and suffering are over, thanks to you, and you have the right to take the time you need to restore yourself."

Bobbie had been speaking softly, gently, but her tone suddenly changed to edgy anger. "I'm not worried if you can't find it within yourself to feel sorry for the idiot who caused such pain for two women that I love. He can go fuck himself!"

Grace relaxed and fell asleep smiling. She woke up in the morning feeling pleased and fully rested and restored. The feeling intensified when she entered Jack Jackson's room to find her bed cranked upright with a breakfast tray across her lap. She hastily picked up the chart at the foot of the bed and saw that Dr. Crawford had ordered a breakfast of soft food and a regular lunch if the breakfast was well tolerated.

"Do you like soft-boiled eggs, Jell-O, and pudding?" Grace asked the patient.

"More than I ever thought I would!" Jack said happily, hugging Grace when she was close enough. "I will spend the rest of my life thanking you."

"I think you might find a few other things to do with your life, Miss Jackson."

"Hmmm, maybe. Where's Bobbie?"

"She'll be here soon. She picked up Justine first—"

"Excuse me, Dr. Hannon." A nurse unfamiliar to Grace stood in the doorway. "The hospital administrator is in the doctors' lounge asking to see you."

Grace hesitated. She didn't want to leave Jack alone—and she didn't have to. She saw Bobbie and Justine coming down the hall. She waved to them, beckoned them forward, and headed to the doctors' lounge, expecting a gathering. The administrator was alone.

"Good morning, Dr. Hannon, and congratulations on what I understand is an excellent outcome for Miss Jackson."

"Drs. Crawford and Jennings were excellent choices. I appreciated the opportunity to work with them."

"They, it appears, appreciated the opportunity to work with you, Dr. Hannon. They told me how it was you who recognized a potentially dangerous if not deadly tear in the abdominal aorta and repaired it, and it was you who recognized the striated—"

She interrupted him. He hadn't come here to praise her and she knew it. "We worked well as a team, ably assisted by Nurse Thelma Cooper. But that isn't what you want to say to me, is it?"

To his credit he bowed his head in acknowledgement. "I have a grave concern, Doctor, about a man who was a visitor in this hospital last night."

Grace nodded and quickly changed the subject.

"Would you agree, sir, that institutions are only as strong, only as good, as the people who work for them, and that an institution is larger than one person?"

He was thrown off balance, but he was interested. "Yes, I would."

"So what would it say about an institution—about a hospital—if the family of a patient felt it necessary to hire a guard to ensure the safety of that patient? Don't most of us believe that institutions like hospitals and churches are places of refuge and safety? Places where we are safe, always, no matter who we are? No one would feel endangered in a church. Why should anyone feel endangered in a hospital?"

He turned away from her with a sharp intake of breath. Turning back to face her and looking almost peaceful, he said,

"Drs. Crawford and Jennings said you made them think about things they'd never considered in a way they'd never considered. You have done the same thing for me." He extended his hand, and she took it. "I'm very proud to have you practicing medicine at this hospital—at this institution—Dr. Hannon." And he left.

She stood still and quiet for a long moment, relieved that the administrator had dropped the topic of the previous night so she could focus on planning a visit to Mavis and Savannah, one more check on Jack (with the hope that Bobbie was there), and then to her office where she had a full schedule. But when she got to Jack's room, Jack's parents and brother were there, so she left, with Bobbie and Justine following her to the parking garage.

"You know we've got The Slow Drag all decorated for the holidays, Dr. Hannon," Justine said, "and it's beautiful. Sparkly lights and even a little tree over next to the jukebox. You'll come to see, won't you?"

"If I can have a dance or two with my favorite partner," Grace answered with a nod and a smile.

Justine cut Bobbie a look. "If she won't step up, I'll be happy to do my best Sammy Davis imitation for you, Doc!" she said with a from-the-waist bow.

"She does not want you stepping all over her feet and ruining her shoes," Bobbie said, taking Grace by the hand and walking her to her car. Then she quickly released her hand and moved a foot away. They were in the parking garage of the hospital where Grace worked. It wouldn't do for Dr. Hannon to be seen holding a woman's hand.

"Everything all right, love?" Grace asked.

"Everything will be wonderful when I can hold your hand whenever and wherever I wish to and this dream sustains me. Otherwise, I think so, dearest."

Bobbie heaved a sigh of relief as she watched Grace drive away, and she was relaxed on the short drive to Bobby's. Since he certainly couldn't go back to the hospital to visit Jack, they'd agreed to visit him and tell him how she was.

And he had a bit of good news of his own. Ennybay had located a front seat in perfect condition, if in a different color, to replace the one in Jack's Chevy, and he and Bobby had removed the old one. The car windows were left open to air out the car to rid it of the scent of urine. The car would be ready for Jack when she was ready to drive again. Until then, Bobby would drive the Chevy and Bobbie's Buick would return to its parking place in the garage.

With both Grace and Jack now breathing a bit easier, Bobbie could turn her full attention to The Slow Drag and The Black Mask Artistic Project, both of which she had neglected. Justine and her new hires seemed both ready and able to handle what most certainly would be eight nights of nonstop holiday action and activity.

Bobbie had already told Justine that she'd no longer work Wednesday through Saturday nights unless Justine needed her, but that she would work Mondays and some Tuesdays so that Justine and the others could have two full days off. On those days she would handle the bookkeeping and locate a reputable cleaning service so the place would be ready for customers on Wednesday night.

Making amends to Eileen and her committee was going satisfactorily as well. Black Mask Artistic and Cultural Center was sponsoring holiday events on both the Christmas and New Year's weekends—fundraising events—and Bobbie's job was to be present, accompanied by Grace and as many of Harlem Hospital's deep-pocket doctors as possible, to help ensure their financial success.

When Christmas Eve arrived, it was clear that Grace had not disappointed. Inside, tuxedoed Tuxedoed physicians and their ball-gowned wives mingled in awestruck pleasure with Negro actors, singers, painters, musicians, politicians and preachers.

111

All the tickets were sold for the Thursday night event, and a few dozen more were sold at the door. Because it was Christmas Eve, it was scheduled early so people could get home to family and friends, and to church for Christmas Eve services. But it was still a formal event and beautiful gowns and jewels and tuxedos were de rigueur, and their elegance complemented the beautifully decorated ballroom.

The live orchestra, led by Billy Strayhorn, masterfully blended contemporary jazz with holiday standards. He was Bobbie's friend, her father's student, and one of the reasons the event was sold out. Another guest responsible for drawing the crowd was writer Dorothy West who was the Mistress of Ceremonies. She wasn't the most famous writer of the Harlem Renaissance, but she was well known and respected, and her presence brought many notables of that period to the Christmas Eve event—even some who hadn't been seen publicly for some time, especially Langston Hughes, Zora Neale Hurston, and Aaron Douglas. The room went quiet when Dorothy West took the stage. Even those who didn't know who she was or why she was important quieted reverently. She had that effect on people. The softness of her voice demanded that the crowd listen. "The person who planned and organized this event, indeed the driving force behind The Black Mask Artistic Project, is Miss Roberta Hilliard, known as Bobbie to her friends. And yes," said the diminutive writer with something resembling a smirk, "I call her Bobbie." Everyone in the room appreciated the bit of humor coming from the little woman with the huge talent. "She is the daughter of the late Robert Hilliard, an extraordinary pianist, and Eleanor Hilliard, one of the most beautiful and elegant women I've ever known, and a painter of enormous talent. So, you will not be surprised to learn that Bobbie Hilliard inherited great beauty and enormous talent. I'm asking her to come to the piano and play for us. Mr. Strayhorn won't mind because those two played duets when Bobbie was a little girl under the watchful eye of Bob Hilliard. Not a concert, Bobbie—relax! Just come up here to the bandstand and strut your stuff for a few moments, please."

"Did you know about this?" Bobby whispered to Grace, but she just shook her head and kept her eyes on Bobbie. When the crowd parted and Bobbie finally made her way to the bandstand, the drumroll that accompanied her along with Billy's from-the-waist bow and bear hug drew wild applause. But not as wild as when they took turns coaxing red hot jazz from the piano and conducting the orchestra that kept the crowd on its feet. Though only they could hear the words they spoke to each other at the end of their performance, it was clear to all that Bobbie Hilliard and Billy Strayhorn had only words of love and respect for each other.

Dorothy West had the final words of the evening: "Not much I can say after that, except to ask that all of you remember this is a fundraiser for the Black Mask Artistic Project and there are people somewhere—there they are at the back of the room waving their arms—to take your generous contributions. Merry Christmas and Happy New Year to all of you and thank you for being here tonight!"

Things were in full swing at The Slow Drag when Bobbie and Grace arrived, and they received a hearty round of applause, most of it, including more than a few wolf whistles, directed at Grace who was gorgeous beyond words. They danced to a few records, had a drink each, and left with Bobbie's promise to work the following night—Christmas. She didn't mind working because she and Grace would have all of Christmas day to open gifts and enjoy each other and visit with Jack. And when Bobbie left for work, Myrtle, Thelma, and Bobby would be there to keep Grace company.

It was a busy night at the club, a good night. The unexpectedly huge crowd was in a wildly festive mood, no doubt helped by the sparkly lights all around the bar and hanging from the ceiling. Bobbie and the other bartenders were kept busy all night long, barely having time to take a break. If the jukebox had been a person, it would have been crying uncle because it never stopped until Bobbie literally pulled the plug, wished everyone Merry Christmas, and sent them home.

The only sour note played on the entire Christmas weekend was Grace's visit to her family. She refused to tell Bobbie everything that was said and done, but the fact that she spent barely an hour in her parents' home spoke volumes, even though she spoke not at all about her family. By the following day, Sunday, she was ready to talk and tell all though it was clear that the memory remained painful.

She had arrived at her parents' home wearing some of Bobbie's Christmas presents: white boatneck cashmere sweater, white wool slacks, a wide raw silk crimson shawl shot through with gold strands, and a long diamond and ruby necklace that had belonged to Bobbie's mother. Grace had learned from past experience to leave her purse and coat locked in the car because some member of the family always wanted to borrow a few dollars or take her car for a spin. The car was locked and the key was in the pocket of her slacks.

Her sister wanted to try on the shawl and made a grab for it. Grace blocked the attempt—twice. Her mother wanted to try on the necklace, which Grace wouldn't allow, so then she wanted to get a closer look, to see if the stones were real or fake. When assured by her father that the stones were indeed "the real thing," her mother demanded to know who had given Grace such gifts. And when Grace refused to answer any questions, their anger intensified until she proffered the large shopping bags containing Christmas presents for all of them, along with the hospital newsletter with her photo on the cover.

"What's this about you?" her brother asked, gazing at the newsletter, but the others were busy opening presents, their enthusiasm muted when there was no cashmere or precious stones in sight. There also were no thank-yous to be heard, all of which made Grace both sorry and annoyed that she'd left the joy of being with Bobbie to come here, to her family, where there was no joy at all, not to mention no gifts for her.

She was out the kitchen door and into the driveway before her mother realized the exit and ran to open the door in time to see Grace unlock the Caddy's trunk and remove and put on the full-length mink with the initials ERH engraved on the silk lining. "Nellie Grace Hannon, where did you get that coat? You answer me! Who's giving you expensive gifts like these?"

"Merry Christmas, Ma. You have a nice day," Grace answered. *She got into the car, backed out of the driveway, and got out of Queens and back to Harlem as quickly as possible.*

"I know they're my family and I love them. At least I think I do, though I'm not sure I like them. I never know what they want or expect from me," she said to Bobbie as they sat before a roaring fire drinking champagne and eating the fruit and nuts out of a fruitcake because they were too full of turkey, dressing, rice and gravy, to eat the cake itself.

"Aren't they proud that you earned a PhD *and* an MD? I think I'll start calling you Dr. Dr. just for the hell of it," Bobbie responded. And just like that Grace's mood lightened. Her family was her family. They weren't bad people or good people; they were just people. Her mother was a secretary, her father a union electrician with a good job, and her brother an apprentice in the electrician's union with the possibility of a good job ahead of him. Her sister was a student at Queens Community College working on her third major with no degree in sight. Two other, older siblings, another brother and sister, lived out of state somewhere and did not keep in touch and Grace knew nothing about them—not where they were or what they were doing. She barely remembered their names or what they looked like, they'd been gone for so long. What she did know and remember, though, and her mood darkened again as she spoke the memory, was that her mother and two sisters were the family beauties, and it was well-known at church and school, in the neighborhood, at social gatherings. Grace's father grinned if a man made a pass at his wife or oldest daughter instead of taking offense.

"Like he had something to do with how they looked, and he

definitely claimed pride of ownership: they were his, and I was invisible."

"But your beauty, Grace—"

"I was smart, Bobbie, not beautiful, and I was constantly reminded that men didn't like smart women."

"Good thing then that you didn't need to be liked by men," was Bobbie's response.

Mother Nature saved them the following weekend—New Year's Eve and Day. It started snowing early Thursday afternoon, coming down thick and heavy by dusk. Not a white Christmas but the New Year would be buried under the stuff. Weather forecasters began urging people to stay home at six, which was when the wind began to gust. By eight when The Slow Drag opened, blowing and drifting snow made it difficult to get into the building because the snow was a foot-deep drift against the door. People trickled in but the kind of crowd Bobbie expected on New Year's Eve did not materialize and she didn't expect that it would. City officials contemplated canceling the ball drop in Times Square so dire were the predictions of the gathering storm.

Justine kept going downstairs to look at the street, coming back upstairs with ever more ominous reports. The weather forecasters said the heaviest of the snow would not begin to taper off until the early hours of New Year's Day. Justine called Bobbie to the phone and it was Bobby. He was downstairs waiting to drive them home and he almost hadn't made it. If they didn't leave soon, it would not be possible to get home.

"That's it, let's call it," Bobbie said to Justine. They shut down the jukebox and turned on the lights. Bobbie stood on top of the bar. "The weather is getting worse by the minute, and I don't want any of you to get stranded tonight and not be able to get home. Leave now, please, and travel in groups. Nobody tries to go it alone, please. Spend the night with whoever lives the closest. And take the train or a bus—cars aren't getting through the snow."

"Can we stay here, like we did Thanksgiving?" somebody asked.

Bobbie shook her head. "Whoever stays here will be snowed in for a couple of days—"

"And that sexy woman at home waiting for you won't like that!"

Bobbie gave her a laugh and a thumbs-up and jumped off the bar, but instead of going to the front to talk to Justine, she stayed where she was, putting empty glasses in the sink and wiping down the counter. When the last customer left, Bobbie followed the bartenders toward the exit where Justine was standing. Bobbie could see Laverne, the bouncer, behind Justine.

"Empty your pockets. All of them. And turn down your socks," Bobbie yelled to the bartender standing just in front of her. Bobbie didn't remember her name.

The woman whipped around. "Say what? Who the fuck you talking to?"

Suddenly Laverne was in the bartender's face. "Talkin' to you. Do it. Now," Laverne spit.

The belligerence never left the bartender's face but she complied with Bobbie's order, withdrawing cash from several pockets and both socks.

"Down the front of your pants," Laverne ordered, "and you better get it all or I'll reach down there myself."

More money. Bobbie pointed to the overcoat slung across the young woman's arm, and the look of pissed-off resignation on her face was that question answered. When they finally let her leave, Justine told her not to come back and not to seek a reference.

"You gotta pay me for tonight!"

"You tried to steal from me and you think I owe you money? Get outta here."

Bobbie turned down the heat, set the light timers and the alarms, and The Slow Drag was closed for the last time in 1953.

CHAPTER FOUR

"We need to reprise our gender-switching identities to put some things right."

Jack and Bobbie were at Bobby's finishing up the tomato soup and grilled cheese sandwiches that were Jack's favorite meal since beginning her recuperation at home. She never tired of the combo though Bobbie and Bobby were beginning to. The fact that dessert never varied from big bowls of vanilla ice cream with butterscotch or caramel sauce made the main course palatable.

They had Grace's permission to bring Jack to Bobby's from her parents' if they promised to guard every movement of her right hip. Walking was still difficult and somewhat painful, though, as she was quick to point out, "nowhere near as awful as it was before Grace and The Boys repaired me."

She was heeding doctors' orders but she was chafing at her parents' desire to have her remain with them and to return to graduate school. Jack wanted to return to her own apartment, which had been cleaned and aired out and no longer smelled unpleasant. She didn't yet know if she was ready to return to graduate school. She knew that eventually she would, but not when and not whether she would continue in education, though she had absolutely no idea what she would study if not education. Nothing else interested her.

Bobby's call to action piqued their interest, and Jack was eager to be away from her parents for a while. They were relaxed and comfortable at Bobby's. He had made his home as warm and welcoming as Bobbie's. The two Bs drank bourbon. Jack didn't drink anything. She never wanted the bag of urine to be emptied by anyone but herself, anywhere but in her own bathroom.

"I hope this won't be too hard for you to hear, Jack," Bobby said, explaining that the incidents he planned to tell them about happened in the area of Broadway, near where she was attacked, and one resembled the attack on her.

"Don't worry about it, Bobby. Everything either happens on Broadway or just off Broadway. You'd think it was the only street in New York."

"You make a good point," Bobby said, telling them about a market on Broadway, not far from The Slow Drag, where the owner had a sign in the window that he didn't want Negro customers. Except it didn't read 'negro.'

"Say what?!" Jack exclaimed. "What exactly does it read?"

"A badly misspelled version of 'Colored.'" Bobby explained that he asked his boss to visit the market and inquire about the sign. "Seems the proprietor misses the way things used to be, when the neighborhood was Italian and Jewish, and so were most of his customers," Bobby said.

"Well, since the Italians and the Jews have all moved away, and since the whole neighborhood is mostly Negroes and some Puerto Ricans, who does he think his customers will be?" Bobbie asked even though she knew there was no rational answer. "Like my grandma says—" said Bobby.

"Don't waste time wondering why crazy people talk crazy," Bobbie finished for him.

"I told Grandma about you," Bobby said, then dropped the

hammer on the mood that had begun to lighten a bit. "This grocer demands to see proof that customers can afford to pay before he rings up purchases, and when elderly or handicapped people open their purses he snatches them away, takes the money, then pushes them and their now empty purses out of the store, yelling loudly that they were trying to cheat him."

"Hold on!" Bobbie raised a palm to stop Bobby. "He's done this more than once?"

"A few times, but this time, last weekend, the old woman he pushed out of the market fell and hit her head on the sidewalk and is in a coma."

Bobbie and Jack observed him in stunned silence for a moment before Jack demanded to know why the hell people still shopped there if they knew how the owner treated people.

"I asked the same question and as I understand it, it's the best market within three or four blocks—well-stocked, fruits, vegetables and bread are always fresh, and it opens early and closes late," Bobby explained.

"None of which matters if people end up in comas if they shop there," Jack said.

"And we shouldn't have to beg someone to take our hard-earned money," Bobbie said. "He's not giving food away. He needs to learn better behavior."

Then Bobby said, "I want to be the last old Negro he steals from and throws out of his store." Bobbie and Jack nodded their acquiescence, but Bobby wasn't finished. "The other thing happened in an alley off 139th Street. Three ofays tried to rape someone they thought was a woman—"

Bobbie groaned. She knew what was coming. "I hope it wasn't your friend Queen Esther, and I hope whoever it was—"

"It was Miz Maggie's grandson, and they beat him into a coma. An old Negro woman and a young Negro drag queen, both beat into comas by ofays in the same week and within shouting distance of the most famous street in America."

"What do you think we can do about it, Bobby?" Jack asked, and both The Bs heard the pain in her voice and saw it in her body. They quickly got to their feet and stood in front of Jack who was seated on the sofa, her feet on an ottoman. Bobbie carefully lifted her feet and when Bobby moved the ottoman, placed them on the floor. Then they took her extended hands and very carefully and slowly pulled her into a standing position, continuing to hold her hands until she was steady on her feet. Bobbie put an arm around her waist and took the weight as Jack leaned into her and gripped her arms. The Bs watched her as her breathing finally slowed and her grip on Bobbie's arm relaxed. Then Bobby answered her question.

"I'm thinking two things, one short term, one long term," he said.

Bobbie nodded. "The short-term solution involves us exacting some payback."

"Damn straight!" Bobby said. "After I mimic my grandma and become an old woman in that market, then strut my stuff as a sweet young thing in that alley, I'm thinking I'll be ready for acting lessons in one of your Black Mask projects, Bobbie."

"Normally, my friend, the acting classes precede the performances, but I'm always open to new and different approaches," Bobbie said.

"Not me," Jack said, giving Bobby an up-and-down scrutiny. "I want to see you in some acting classes first, and then maybe in some performances."

Bobby hugged Jack and said he wanted to do the payback performances right away, while those events were fresh in everyone's memory. Then they could determine and plan a long-term strategy. "But believe me, there will be payback," he said.

"What do you think that could be?" Jack asked.

"Whatever it is, it will require the participation of lots of people," said Bobbie.

"I agree," said Bobby, "but don't count on those just up

from Down South. Most of them won't do anything that could bring the wolf to their door. They understand better than most what payback can look like." Jack and Bobbie nodded their understanding.

"It's time to get you home, Jack," Bobbie announced.

The next day, Bobbie and Bobby spent the morning visiting theater wardrobe and prop shops so the budding actor would be properly attired and equipped to morph into an elderly woman shopping for groceries from the despicable store owner.

On their route, all of a sudden Bobbie screamed, then pointed. "Stop the car, Bobby! Stop! That's the cop! That's the drunk son of a bitch who was passed out in the alley where Jack was attacked!"

Bobby screeched to a halt, threw the gear into park, and turned sideways in the seat to face Bobbie. "I thought the police department moved him to another beat?"

"That's what they said. He's not supposed to be in this neighborhood."

"Bastards! I guess they thought we wouldn't notice." He opened his door. "Let's go make his acquaintance."

Bobbie grabbed his arm and pulled him back, shaking her head. "Even a drunk would recognize this car—a red and black Buick with enough chrome to build a battleship. I've got to get rid of it. What was my father thinking when he bought this thing?"

"That he'd probably look really smooth driving it."

Bobbie snorted. "Really silly is more like it. I wish I'd sold it right after . . . So many of his musician pals wanted to buy it and I was just holding on to it along with everything else." She struggled, refusing to allow the sadness to take over.

"Where do they hang out?"

"Who?"

"Musicians. Your dad's pals."

"Quite a few of them live full-time in Europe these days, and quite a few others live in a drug-induced haze. Couldn't sober up long enough to drive a car if a record contract hung in the balance. But what I really do want to do is sell this monstrosity of a car and I don't care who to!"

"I wish you already had so I could haul ass outta here and across the street to give that drunk piece-of-shit cop a piece of my mind—look at him. Weaving and stumbling and it's the middle of the day. How the hell does he keep his job?"

"I may have an idea about where to sell it," Grace said that evening when Bobbie told her about the conversation with Bobby. They were enjoying a weekend at Grace's and were relaxing on the living room sofa following one of Grace's eat-until-you-burst meals, which always were cooked here because Bobbie's kitchen "didn't contain the necessary or suitable" pots and pans for the delicacies Grace conjured. It was the end of an especially difficult week for Grace and she was exhausted. Bobbie had offered to take her to dinner, or to bring dinner from Miz Maggie's Kitchen, but Grace said cooking helped her unwind. This evening, though, she did seem especially thoughtful, withdrawn even. She hadn't held Bobbie's hand or placed her feet in Bobbie's lap to be massaged or opened a single one of the medical journals on the sofa beside her. What was wrong?

"Are you all right, Grace? Is something bothering you?"

"I'm fine, Bobbie."

"Are you certain?"

"I'm all right, Bobbie. Tired, exhausted, but all right."

"Well, if you're sure . . . where? And when can we go there?"

Grace gave her a strange look and asked, "Go where, Bobbie?"

"You said you know someone who might want to buy the Buick."

"Oh!" Grace brought her mind and thoughts back to the present with a sheepish and lopsided grin at Bobbie. "I'll make a call tomorrow—"

"I'm sorry, Gracie. I shouldn't have been so pushy. It's just . . ." Bobbie sighed. Why was she all of a sudden in such a rush to get rid of that damned car? Because she suddenly realized that she'd always disliked the car because her mother had disliked it. And why was she remembering those side-by-side facts for the first time? She knew the answer: because she had buried all thoughts and remembrances of her family because letting them surface would be much too painful. Except that now some memories were beginning to surface.

"Grace? Was my mother happy?"

Grace had been watching her with an expression Bobbie didn't recognize, but it changed with Bobbie's question. Grace now appeared almost angry though Bobbie wasn't certain because she'd never seen Grace angry. "Your mother was my patient, Bobbie, and you know I cannot discuss patients with anyone, and I would think you'd know better than to ask."

"I'm very sorry, Grace, if I . . . I certainly didn't intend to insult you, and certainly not to anger you or impugn your integrity."

Grace closed her eyes and shook her head back and forth. "I'm sorry, Bobbie, but please don't ask me for any information regarding your mother. But here's something to think about: Perhaps you're finally ready and able to remember things you may have put away, buried, in your grief?"

Bobbie looked at her but didn't respond so Grace continued: "I'm just thinking that since the matter of the car came up, there may be other memories ready to surface?" Grace suddenly stood up, pushing aside the pile of medical journals untouched on the sofa beside her, and headed to the kitchen, but Bobbie barely noticed.

Was she really ready to remember? Perhaps it was time. More than three years had passed. Wasn't that enough time to be able to view the past with clear sight? But did she really want to remember if what she remembered contradicted what she thought she knew about her parents and their relationship? And could she really coax memories to the surface? Or was it better to let them rise on their own? Perhaps they were better buried, because if there was unhappiness or sadness to be revealed, how much of it did she really want to know, to remember? Wasn't she better off in the long run with happy memories of happy parents?

And what was bothering Grace? She had seen something in Grace's face when she asked if her mother was happy, something strange just before her face went blank. Was Grace worried about something? She understood that Grace—that no doctor—could discuss private patient conversations and interactions. She hadn't seen a doctor since she was a child, hadn't needed to, but she knew they had rules. She'd once asked Grace if she would be her doctor and Grace quickly said no, that it would be inappropriate, and Bobbie knew why. "Have I upset you, Grace? Or angered you? Because if I have—"

"I'm more interested in what's been on your mind lately, Bobbie. Something has you distracted." Grace was up and uncharacteristically pacing from one end of the living room to the other. Bobbie watched her intently and spoke slowly.

"I suppose it's the Black Mask business that is pushing and pulling me in too many different directions, all at the same time it seems. And decisions are required when I've had no time to think. I often wish I hadn't agreed to take on the responsibility."

"But it gives you the opportunity to see, to interact, with many different people."

Bobbie shrugged and nodded. "I suppose."

"At places like The Teresa Hotel?"

She gave Grace a strange look. "Yes."

"A place you're very familiar with, I understand."

127

Now she was confused, and a bit wary. "What are you talking about, Grace?"

"Do you still take your dates, your women, there? To your apartment there?"

Bobbie was shocked speechless. She had given up the Teresa apartment the week after she met Grace. She knew she'd no longer need it. "I don't understand, Grace—"

"It's really quite simple, Bobbie. I have a friend who knows you and knows how popular you are with the ladies, which, of course, I understand very well. You swept me off my feet quite literally in a matter of seconds."

Bobbie's head was spinning. "Who is this friend, Grace, who's feeding you all these lies? Why would someone do this, and why would you listen to such foolishness?"

"Lies? Really, Bobbie?"

"Yes, dammit, Grace! Lies." Bobbie released the anger that had been slowly building, wishing that she had some other place than Grace to direct it.

"Do you deny the apartment at the Teresa and all the women? A different one each week? Beautiful, elegant women?"

"No, I don't deny that I once lived like that, but I do deny the existence of that life in the present."

"And, of course, you retain your love of beautiful women." Looking steadily at Bobbie, Grace made a statement; she did not ask a question."

"Indeed I do retain my love of beautiful women, Grace. Your presence in my life is proof of that." Bobbie was becoming angry though she wasn't entirely sure why. She also was becoming a bit afraid, and she really didn't understand the reason for that, either.

"And I thought you loved me for my brilliant mind," Grace said drily, with no hint of sarcasm or humor. "You like your women glamorous and I'm not the least bit glamorous, and you don't need my brilliance because you have your own. So what do you want with me, Bobbie? Should I just play along until your next trip to the Savoy?"

Bobbie was shocked speechless and becoming angrier by the second. She could not respond, and Grace seemed to have run out of words, so they stood looking at each other. "Who is telling you these things, Grace?"

Grace didn't answer immediately. She leaned against the sofa back and closed her eyes. She seemed to be thinking. Or remembering.

PJ asked to meet her at the Theresa and she reluctantly agreed after initially refusing several previous overtures. She hadn't seen PJ since the night at The Slow Drag when Bobbie rescued her after PJ ditched her and PJ had been attempting to—what? She'd called several times asking to meet but she'd never apologized for that night. So what did she want? And when Grace finally agreed to meet she'd been surprised when PJ set the Theresa as the meeting place though she shouldn't have been. The always broke PJ would expect Grace to pay for whatever they ate and drank. Grace's anger intensified when someone was with PJ.

"This is my friend Von Thompkins. Von, this is my friend Nellie G."

"The one who's the doctor? I thought you said her name was Grace."

Grace looked at her watch. "Why am I here?"

Von controlled the anger that rose in her face. "I asked to meet you. Let's have a seat. I reserved a table." Grace watched the tall, rangy woman stride off, closely followed by PJ. Grace brought up the rear and seated herself at a table near the kitchen across from PJ and Von, who sat side by side.

"I wanted to meet you because PJ said you were hooked up with Bobbie Hilliard who I happen to know very well, and when I told her what I knew she asked me to tell you 'cause she really likes you, Nellie. Or Grace. Or whatever your name is, and she thinks you deserve better."

Grace listened, astounded, and when Von finally stopped talking she stood up quickly and strode away, PJ on her heels.

"Don't be mad, Nellie G. I'm only trying to help you!"

"You've never tried to help anyone but yourself, PJ. Don't call me again."

But Grace couldn't erase from her memory the images of Bobbie and the glamorous, elegant women she squired around the Savoy Ballroom. So she'd gone to the Savoy herself. She wondered if she'd see Bobbie, but whether or not Bobbie appeared Grace knew she was no match for the Savoy Ballroom hostesses. And no matter what she thought of PJ and Von, she didn't doubt for a moment that these were Bobbie's women.

"Does it matter, Bobbie, who tells me if the words are the truth?"

"Of course it matters, Grace, especially if those words don't come from me." Bobbie inhaled so deeply she almost choked as an awful thought crossed her mind: Suppose Grace was interested in the person who had gotten into her head? "Are you interested in someone else, Grace? Is there someone else you want to date?" Bobbie regretted the words the instant they left her mouth, but it was too late. Grace inhaled and her breathing grew shallow as she turned away from Bobbie, but she didn't speak. "If that's what you want, Grace, then say that and do that but don't turn your back on me as if . . . Is there someone else, Grace? Someone you wish to date?"

"It's all right for you to date multiple people but not for me?"

"That's a lie. I don't! It's true that I once dated many different people, but since I met you I've only been with you, Grace, and that's what I intend to continue doing."

"Don't say that, Bobbie, because you think it's what I want to hear."

Bobbie raised her voice a bit. "I say that, Grace, because it is the truth. I don't want to see anyone else. Do you? Is that what this is all about?"

"This is about me not understanding what you want with Plain Jane Nellie Grace when you could have—when you have had—some of the most gorgeous women in Harlem."

"You're one of the most beautiful women I've ever seen, Grace. What is happening with you? If I've done or said something to—"

Grace turned away from her, and Bobbie could see her shoulders rising and falling as she took some deep breaths. Then Grace turned to face her and Bobbie stopped breathing herself. She knew what was coming. *Nonooooooooono* she thought, as if thinking the word could, would, translate into a reality she could accept.

"Yes, Bobbie, there is someone that I wish to date."

There. The words were out and Grace turned away again, unable to bear the pain she saw in Bobbie's face. And the disbelief. She watched as Bobbie struggled to find some words to say, ones that would make Grace change her mind. But Bobbie did not speak. She could not speak. Words would not come. Thoughts would not come. And anyway, if Grace wanted to date someone else, didn't she have the right to do that? And did Bobbie have the right to ask her, to beg her, to reconsider? To change her mind?

Grace's back was still to Bobbie and she hadn't spoken again. She had not retracted her statement that she wished to date someone else. Stunned, Bobbie went to leave without saying a word, tripping on the way out, catching her foot on the leg of the coffee table and going down on one knee. But she bounced up and hurried to the door, where she stopped. She had one hand on the doorknob, but she didn't turn it. She stood there feeling afraid and empty and lost. She wanted to look at Grace, but what if this was the last time she would see her? She turned the knob and hurried into the hall, closing the door softly behind her. Had she remained at the door and listened she would have heard an anguished cry that was more of a howl, and had she been able to see through the door she would have seen her beautiful Grace crumpled on the floor beating on, and covering her face with, the pillows from the sofa.

Without Grace at the beginning or the end of every day Bobbie didn't know how to manage, how to maneuver through them, and she was only one day and night without Grace. But this was not unfamiliar territory. This was what had happened when her family was snatched away. How had she managed?

The memories from that time were never far from her

consciousness: music and booze. She drank a lot, ate very little, hardly slept, and listened to all kinds of music. So that's what she did now, with one useful difference. She committed to completing the task of finally sorting through her parents' belongings, no matter how painful. And she struggled to make decisions about Black Mask projects but found that to be an exercise in futility because she didn't care about Black Mask. Inhaling deeply, she unlocked the door to the room that once was her mother's studio and where her parents' belongings now were stored.

Her mother's sketch pads also had served as her journals and diaries. She wrote on the same side as what she was sketching, then on the back side. Sometimes it was about what she was sketching, sometimes about someone who had entered the room or walked past the door. She sketched her children often and wrote how much she loved them, wrote how wonderful and brilliant and beautiful they were, wrote how they were the best part of herself.

And she wrote that her children would never know that the almost seven-year gap in their ages was due to the two babies she'd lost between Bobbie and Eric. Another girl and another boy. She wrote how the miscarriages had weakened her physically and emotionally. She wrote how her husband kept demanding—the word she wrote—another child, a son. After that entry Bobbie had to stop reading. Her mother's pain was so great she felt it as her own. So she turned her attention to her father's belongings and invited Bobby to participate. Bob Hilliard was a much larger man than Bobby Mason but, like his wife, he had many beautiful things—from suspenders and ties and socks to cufflinks and tie clasps to watches and rings. "Don't you want to keep some of this?" Bobby asked.

"For what? My only brother, his only son, is dead. I did keep the fountain pens but the rest of it is yours if you want it."

"I can't imagine how difficult this must be for you, Bobbie."

133

"I can't wait another three years to get it done. So please, Bobby."

Bobby winced at the hurt and pain and anger. This was worse than he imagined. He didn't know if she, or anyone, should have to handle the aftermath of the loss of their entire family alone, along with the loss of someone as important to her being as Grace.

He didn't think Bobbie could get through this without Grace. Would not get through it. He had no idea what had happened between the two of them, but he did know Bobbie was suffering. Since he was fairly certain she would not discuss with him whatever the issue was with Grace, he would have to call the good doctor and hope she would be more forthcoming.

"I am very grateful for these things, Bobbie. I only wish I were bigger and taller."

"Do you think a good tailor could alter the suits to fit you? Nothing you can do about the shoes and shirts but the suits and jackets and slacks?"

"Hmmm . . . that might be possible," he replied. "Can you give me a couple of days to find a good tailor and ask?"

"Of course, Bobby. Take your time. Everything will be in this trunk, which will be in this room."

He gave her a long, tight hug and she returned the embrace, but did not speak. He exited through the kitchen door, and he heard her lock it behind him, heard her engaging the security latch.

He tried to run home, but the bags of Robert Hilliard's personal belongings were heavy and slowed him down, which was a good thing. His heart was as heavy as the bags. Receiving items such as these as the result of a terrible tragedy . . . tears pricked his eyes and ran down his cheeks while his heart broke for Bobbie. Arriving home, he dialed Grace immediately and a voice he did not know answered. "This is Robert Mason. May I please speak to Grace?"

"She's busy," said the unknown female voice who hung up. He called again immediately and before he could say a word the same unknown voice said, "I told you she's busy. Don't call here again."

"Oh fuck!" was Jack's response when Bobby called and told her. "Who is this woman?"

"Grace didn't tell you?" Bobby asked.

"Whatever would make you think Grace would tell me she was leaving Bobbie for another woman, Robert Mason!" The non-question singed his eardrums.

"Then how are we going to know what's going on? How can we find out?" Bobby felt himself on the verge of hysteria, but some inner thing told him he couldn't afford to lose control. Not when the happiness of Bobbie Hilliard and Grace Hannon was at stake.

Jack was quiet for a moment, then said, "I'm going to call the office tomorrow and make an appointment to see her. If I tell Myrt I don't feel well she'll get me in right away. You can take me, and we can both talk to her."

"You are a brilliant woman, Jack Jackson."

"Nice of you to notice, Bobby Mason," and he didn't need to be with her to see the smirk.

Then he was stunned by a thought: "Do you think Bobbie has called there and—"

"Oh dear God, I hope not!" Jack's heart hurt at the thought of Bobbie hearing another woman answer Grace's phone.

"Tomorrow can't come soon enough. Call first thing, Jack, please."

But first thing was too late because the night before, Von Thompkins had moved into Grace's apartment. "It's only for a little while," Von said, looking all around, "and looks like you've got plenty of room."

"You can't be serious," Grace said in a futile attempt to push Von out and slam the door. The woman was as strong as a man and a frisson of fear ran through Grace as she backed away. Von grinned through straight and even, though yellow, teeth.

"Don't worry, Doc. You're not my type. PJ is welcome to you."

"What do you want?"

"Whatever you got," Von replied as she pushed Grace aside and began to explore.

Bobbie sat on the floor with her mother's sketch pads spread out in front of her. As much as she didn't want to read any more of her mother's pain and sadness, she knew she needed to. She had tried to argue herself into not reading more. If her mother were alive, certainly she would not share these painful events with her daughter. But her mother was not alive, and her daughter was, and she needed to figure out how to live—not only without her mother but now without the only other woman she had loved.

She continued to read her mother's journal entries, learning much about her adored father, who, it seemed, may not have been worthy of her adoration. She learned he was a husband who left his wife after the second miscarriage and remained in various places in Europe for a year before returning with one objective: implanting another baby in the wife, a baby who would become the desired son. The baby boy beloved by his mother—and his big sister—and prized by the father who now was able to call someone Robert Eric Hilliard Junior.

The revelations shocked and saddened Bobbie but she continued to read. She learned that Eleanor Hilliard had defied her husband and refused to see the doctor who had told her there was no medical reason for two miscarriages. The husband never knew that in his yearlong absence, his wife had consulted another doctor, a woman, who believed that Eleanor's constant inhalation of the oil-based paints she used in her work had most likely caused the miscarriages because it was toxic, perhaps even poisonous.

While in the new pregnancy, under the care of Dr. Hannon, Eric was carried to term, but he was small, and for the first two years of his life, not very strong. Though the woman doctor was not a pediatrician, she worked very closely with Eleanor to help Eric grow and thrive and to help Eleanor regain her health. But this was against the wishes of the husband who didn't believe in "lady doctors." When he ordered his wife to return to the male doctor who was his friend and fraternity brother, Eleanor asked Dr. Grace Hannon to perform a tubal ligation. When Bobbie's father found out, he left again, this time for two years, and when he returned his son didn't know who he was, his wife didn't care, and his daughter was ambivalent.

Bobbie tried to recall with some clarity how she had felt during these times: Was she ever aware of her mother's pain and sadness? Did Eleanor Hilliard ever let her guard down, did she ever break? If she did, Bobbie didn't remember it. Nor did she remember missing her father for a year, for two years at a time. Tall, handsome, gregarious Bob Hilliard. He filled a room with his presence. Wouldn't his absence be just as noticeable? Wouldn't the absence of such a big personality leave a big hole? But Bobbie didn't recall it. Of course she'd been a child then, and though she had vivid memories of the great Robert Hilliard playing the piano, and of his teaching her to play, his absences had no resonance in her memory. Nor was she aware of her mother's emotional or physical pain during those absences.

Bobbie put the sketch pads in the bottom of the trunk, with everything else on top. The clothes and jewelry—there was so much of it, and all of it beautiful, like the woman who wore it. Bobbie had planned to ask Grace to go through it and keep what she wanted, but now that wouldn't happen.

Bobbie would sort through the jewelry and—and then what? She closed her mother's trunk and turned to the trunk of her father's things, which Bobby would decide about very soon. She was about to place everything back inside the trunk when she noticed a rather small suitcase in the bottom. More of an overnight case, she supposed it was, but whatever it was she didn't remember ever having seen it. And yet she must have—she had purchased the two huge steamer trunks specifically to store her parents' belongings, to create an "out of sight, out of mind" storage place to make it easier to deal with their absence. So if this case was in the steamer trunk, she had put it there.

She lifted the case out of the trunk and placed it on the floor. It was heavier than she expected. She pressed the latches—unlocked—and lifted the top to find a thick stack of music charts, all in her father's hand. She riffled through them, making out the melodies, and recognized not a single one.

Had her father composed all of this music but she knew none of it? She picked up the other thing in the case—a solid metal box about ten inches long and perhaps six inches wide and at least that deep. She opened the top and gasped, glad she was already on the floor. The box was stuffed with cash. Literally stuffed. All tens and twenties—no singles—and the bottom layer, two inches thick, were all one-hundred-dollar bills. *There must be thousands of dollars here, maybe even more like tens of thousands of dollars. Was this money payment for music? Or something else?*

Hands shaking, she closed the box and put it back in the sheet music-filled case, closing the case and returning it to the bottom of the steamer trunk. Then she took it out again. She wanted to study the music, to play it, to understand why it was locked away. And she wanted to count the money. There were things she could take a head-in-the-sand approach about, but this wasn't one of them. She closed the steamer trunk, then picked up the case of music and money and took it to her office.

Now what? Her mind and emotions jumped up and down and bounced back and forth as she wished she'd never read her mother's sketch pad journal entries. She willed herself to sit down for a moment. Her entire self was exhausted. She hadn't had a full meal or a full night's sleep since Grace had left her life, so those weren't options. Her stomach wouldn't hold food, and her mind wouldn't embrace sleep. Music was not an option either, not listening to it or playing it.

Before this night her mind was too full of missing Grace. Tonight it was too full of missing parents she thought she knew but apparently did not. And how would she ever square the knowledge that her mother had not been the happy, joyful woman of her childhood memories?

She put on a hat, coat, boots, and gloves, wrapped a scarf around her neck, and opened the kitchen door. She grabbed the keys hanging on a board there, and closed and locked the door. She'd left lights on in every room. Coming home to an empty apartment was one thing. Coming home to an empty and dark place, an empty life, with so many secrets revealed was another.

She initially walked quickly to retain some of the warmth her body held when she left home. It was a cold night with a little wind off the river—not enough to send her scurrying back inside but enough to have her pull the wool cap down over her ears and wrap the scarf tighter around her neck. She stopped to button the top button on her coat. When she got to Broadway, her reason for taking the walk was clear. The sidewalks on both sides of the wide avenue were alive with people just as the avenue itself was alive with cars. Bobbie stood in the doorway of a closed business and watched the street and the sidewalks. She watched people's faces as they passed her and wondered whether the fast walkers really were in a hurry to get somewhere or, like her, were moving quickly to keep warm.

Because she was shivering with cold Bobbie stepped out of the doorway of the gated jewelry store and joined the fast walkers north on Broadway. She did have a destination of sorts. Stopping in front of Grace's building, she looked up. The heavy draperies were tightly closed, but light leaked around the edges.

That didn't mean, of course, that Grace was home or that her—whatever she was to Grace—was inside. Bobbie closed her eyes, envisioning the living room she knew as well as her own. But she didn't know this living room. Not if Grace was in it with another woman.

Not even two whole days without Grace and she was losing her mind. She hurried home though there was no need to hurry. The long night that stretched ahead of her would be fueled by bourbon, music, and headache-producing lamentations. So why hurry? Why not let the cold numb her until she could not feel it? But she hurried anyway and called Eileen before she removed her coat or poured a shot of bourbon.

"Why doesn't Grace know how beautiful she is?" Bobbie asked when Eileen answered.

"Are you drunk, Bobbie?"

"Not yet."

"Where's Grace, Bobbie?"

"Don't know. She left a couple of days ago."

"Brew a pot of coffee. I'll see you shortly." And she was as good as her word, arriving as the coffee finished brewing and Bobbie finished her shower. She added a toasted English muffin to her cup of coffee then sat at the counter and watched Bobbie study the half dozen photos Eileen had placed before her.

"These women are gorgeous, Eileen. Who are they and why are you showing me their photos?"

"Grace's mother and sisters and I'm showing them to you in answer to your question: This is why Grace doesn't think she's beautiful. She lives in the shadow of these women. She's the ugly duckling of the family. People have been gawking at and drooling over them all her life, barely noticing her. Until you did—"

"And I haven't looked at another woman since."

"Women—girls—have been gawking at and drooling over you since you were fifteen, Bobbie, and all you've ever had to do is choose one."

"I did choose one. I chose Nellie Grace Hannon!"

"And why did you choose her, Bobbie?" Eileen asked softly, almost gently.

"Because she is the most beautiful, brilliant, gentle, loving, funny—"

Tears ran down Eileen's face. "Then tell Grace that, Bobbie, and keep telling her until she believes it, until she tells you to stop telling her. Because yes, Grace is all of those things and so much more but she doesn't know it—except for the brilliant part—she knows how smart she is. But she believes that's all she is, and quite frankly, Bobbie, she has no reason to believe that someone like you would want her—"

"Bullshit, Eileen!" Bobbie exploded in anger. "I've heard from both you and Joyce how many women have pursued Grace—"

"For her title, her position: she's a doctor. And doctors have money. Capturing Dr. Nellie Grace Hannon would be a major coup. For anyone but you. The wealthy, gorgeous, brilliant Dr. Roberta Hilliard."

Grace stared in dismay and revulsion at what once was her living room, at what once was a warm, elegant, but comfortable and welcoming place. It looked worse than it had when she left that morning, and if she hadn't seen it she wouldn't have believed it possible. How could three people wreak such unspeakable havoc in a few days' time? But what she really didn't understand was why? Why would Von and the two girls she'd brought with her into Grace's home willfully and wantonly destroy a place of luxury and comfort?

And why in the world had she listened to the damnable Von Thompkins talk about Bobbie? She looked at the destruction before her and wished she'd stayed at her office and slept on the couch. Coming home was a mistake though this no longer was home. This was hell, and it was a hell of her own making, and she knew she could not stay here. But where would she go? Even if she possessed a magic wand and could wave Von and her friends away she would not want to remain here.

"'Bout time you brought your sorry ass back!" Von snarled when opening the door to admit Grace, who had to knock to enter because she no longer had keys. "You left here before seven o'clock this morning and it's almost midnight. Where the hell you been?" Von's fists were balled up as she strode back and forth in front of Grace.

"I told you that I had two surgeries scheduled today—"

"You said they was this morning, bitch! What the hell was you doing the rest of that time to be gettin' back here this time of night?"

Grace sighed and inhaled. "Patients must be monitored for several hours following major surgery—"

"What the hell does that mean?"

"It means I have to keep watching them to make sure they're all right, that nothing went wrong, either during the surgery or afterward. And one woman experienced unexpected bleeding and the other spiked a fever that we had trouble getting under control—"

"You ain't the only doctor in that hospital. What about all them nurses? Why you had to be the one to do all that?"

"Those women are my patients and my responsibility, and I couldn't leave them until they were stabilized, until they were safe. That's my job. MY job, not another doctor's or a nurse's. Why can't you see that?"

Von raised her balled-up fist and punched Grace in the eye, and then in the mouth. "How much do you see right now, bitch?" Then she turned away, stalked into the bedroom—Grace's bedroom—and slammed the door.

Grace reeled and went dizzy. She could see nothing for

several moments. She held on to the table beside the couch until the dizziness passed, then went into the bathroom and closed the door, but she didn't sit down. It was too filthy. Nor were any of the washcloths or towels clean enough to put on her face. Holding her purse in one hand and her medical bag in the other hand, she realized that Von hadn't checked them. Von was too angry about Grace's late arrival to search her bags and pockets for cash or keys. Grace put both bags in one hand so she could hold on to furniture on the way to the front door. This was her living room, and she knew the way, could find the way, with one eye swollen shut and blood running down the front of her from her split lip. She opened the door slowly and silently, sidled into the hallway, closing the door with the same deliberate silence. She hobbled to the elevator and pressed the down button, immediately regretting it as the motor came to life in the quiet building and the car began to ascend. Von would hear it. No, she wouldn't, not in the bedroom with the door closed and the television at full blast. But soon she would look for Grace with the demand for something to eat and drink. She would hear the water running in the bathroom and would pound on the door and yell and scream and curse before finally, angrily, turning the knob and seeing the door open on an empty bathroom.

The elevator door opened and Grace gratefully stepped in. She could not have walked down the five flights to the ground floor, not even to escape Von. Now if she could get to the street and find a taxi, but she couldn't raise her arm—

"Lady, you all right?"

A young couple stared at Grace. Their arms were wrapped around each other, but as if hearing and heeding a cosmic order, they released each other and reached toward Grace. "I . . . I'm a doctor and I need to get to my office. I need a taxi." She knew that she sounded as weak as she felt.

They looked at Grace, up and down, and when they recognized the medical bag she gripped in her right hand for what it was, the young man stepped into the street, waved his arms, and released two shrill whistles. A northbound taxi on the other side of the street made an impossible U-turn across all the lanes of traffic and screeched to a stop right in front of them. The couple led Grace to the taxi, opened the back door, and helped her in.

"This lady is a doctor, and she was mugged trying to get to her office."

Grace gave the cabbie the address, thanked the two young people for coming to her aid, and in her mind began her apology to Bobbie, praying that Bobbie would want to listen, to hear, and above all to forgive.

The following morning, when Grace had not arrived at the office by eight, Myrtle Lewis called her at home. A snarling voice answered. "Who the fuck is this?"

"This is Nurse Myrtle Lewis in Dr. Hannon's office. I need to speak with her, please."

"She's not here so she better be in that damn office!" came the snarled reply and next thing Myrtle Lewis was listening to a dial tone. Just then, Grace Hannon opened the door and came out of her office and Myrtle noticed she was wearing the same clothes as yesterday and looked as if she hadn't slept. Or had slept in them. "The coffee is made, Doctor. Would you like me to bring you a cup?"

"Yes, Myrtle, please," said a voice that didn't sound at all like Grace Hannon. Her body didn't even move like Grace Hannon. As she slowly lowered herself into the chair behind the desk, the face that didn't look like Grace Hannon winced at the effort.

Grace was still seated in the same position when Myrtle returned with a cup of coffee and one of the changes of clothes that Grace kept in the office. "Do you want me to help you get changed?"

"No," Grace said quickly and too loudly. Then, in a more moderate tone, she thanked the nurse, said she could manage—after coffee.

Bobbie opened one eye and peered groggily at the clock on the nightstand. Who the hell was calling her after 8 a.m.? It had been after two when Eileen left and after three before she could fall asleep after their talk, Eileen's final words ricocheting in her brain: *"You get Grace back no matter what you have to do, Bobbie."* She'd fallen asleep wondering what she'd do if Grace didn't want to come back after several shots of bourbon failed to provide an answer.

"Yes, hello?"

"I apologize for the early hour, Bobbie. This is Myrtle—"

Bobbie sat up straight, fully awake, fully recognizing the voice. "Is Grace all right?"

"No," Myrtle Lewis said quietly, "she's not."

Bobbie was on her feet. "I'm on my way, Myrt. Tell her I'm coming." She ran into the bathroom, turned on the shower, and stood beneath the hot-as-she-could-stand-it water until she felt almost awake if not entirely sober. She brushed her teeth and threw on clothes, socks and shoes, stuffing money in her pocket, grabbing her keys, and running out the door and down the hall before stopping suddenly and returning to lock the apartment door. Out on the street she looked both ways for a taxi and for the downtown bus—she'd take whichever came first—and if neither came quickly enough she'd begin walking. She saw the uptown taxi and stepped into the street to stop it, climbed in before the cabbie came to a full stop, and told him to turn around. She gave him Grace's office address and added, "I'll pay double the fare if you burn rubber getting there." He earned triple fare, and Bobbie ran into the office building and up the stairs to the second floor, ignoring the slowpoke elevator and its old-as-Methuselah operator.

Nurse Lewis opened the office door before Bobbie knocked, then closed and relocked the door and led the way to one of the exam rooms. The door was open, and Bobbie gasped at the sight before her. Grace sat on the exam table in an exam gown, one eye swollen shut, lips broken, swollen, bleeding. Where the gown had slid down to her shoulders bruises and scratches were evident. Bobbie walked to the table and gently took Grace into her arms. She wanted to hold her tightly but knew it was better not to. Grace clearly was in a lot of pain.

"Who did this to you, Gracie? Who hurt you like this?" Bobbie whispered. Grace began to make keening noises and buried her face in Bobbie's chest. Nurse Lewis put her arms around Grace and gently pushed her down on the table, then applied ice packs to her face and chest. Bobbie helped to keep them in place, especially the one covering her eye. She certainly could not work looking like this. "Who did this, Myrtle?"

"That damn Von Thompkins!" The usually soft-spoken, gentle nurse snarled, and her stiffly starched white uniform seemed to bristle in anger, too. "Grace didn't tell me what was happening to her until I found her here this morning—"

"What do you mean you found her here!?"

The nurse sighed deeply and sadly. "She had fallen asleep on the couch in her office. I don't know if she couldn't get in when she got home—she was at the hospital until late—or if she just didn't want to stay there."

"How long—" Bobbie started to ask, but realized she knew the answer. Three days ago, on that terrible day when Grace said she had met someone who knew of Bobbie as a womanizer, someone who had a different woman every week, and an apartment in the Hotel Theresa where she entertained her women. Bobbie at first had been shocked, but then she became worried when she saw that Grace believed that the behavior had continued during their time together. She and Grace had not been together for very long, just a few months, but they were good together. They were strong together, strong enough, Bobbie would have thought, to withstand ugly interference from an outsider. Bobbie would never forget that conversation, or the look on Grace's face.

"Do you know where she lives, this Von Thompkins?" Bobbie asked, still incredulous and almost disbelieving at Grace's condition. Such a gentle and loving woman. Only a monster could inflict this kind of damage.

"In Grace's apartment. She and her friends are staying there."

Fury rose in Bobbie. "Where's Gracie's purse? Where are her keys? Get them for me please—"The words backed up in her throat at the look on Myrtle's face. "What is it?"

"Bobbie—she no longer has keys to her own apartment—" And at the look of total confusion on Bobbie's face Myrt explained that Von Thompkins had decided that she and her friends would live there with Grace.

Bobbie was out the office door and down the stairs and running the ten blocks that separated Grace's office from her apartment, dodging the pedestrians who didn't dodge her. She took the elevator this time since Grace lived on the fifth floor and Bobbie didn't want to be breathless when she encountered Von Thompkins. She rattled the doorknob and was surprised when the door swung open to reveal a leering face. "I knew your sorry ass would be back—"

Bobbie grabbed the woman by the throat, forcing her back into the apartment, and kicked the door shut with her foot, only vaguely aware of the total disorder within. She first slapped, then punched, then slapped again until the recipient of her blows no longer leered. Then, using her fists, she pounded Von

147

Thompkins in the chest—on both sides. She wanted her to look, and preferably to feel, the way Grace looked and felt. Then she knocked her down and kicked her in the ribs—on both sides. Then she pummeled her with fists that flurried like Joe Louis punches, hoping they landed as hard and did as much damage.

Bobbie's three years' worth of simmering rage over the murders of her family and the recent loss of Grace boiled over and out and she didn't try to contain it. It took a while, but the woman began to wail and scream and Bobbie grabbed a sofa pillow from the floor and stuffed as much of it as she could into the woman's mouth because she didn't want to hear the noise. The wailing stopped but then two women emerged from the bedroom, both of them wearing nightgowns that Bobbie knew belonged to Grace.

"What in the merry mother fuck!" she yelled, and the two women turned to run back to the bedroom but Bobbie caught them by the hair, one in each hand, and yanked them back into the living room and, one by one, she threw them on top of the sniveling heap of bully on the floor. She figured they would be too scared to get up and the woman splayed on the floor wouldn't be able to get up. "Don't you move!"

Bobbie gave the order, then hurried into Grace's bedroom and wanted to weep. She'd have to get this place cleaned up before she could ever allow Grace to return to it. She emptied the purses, which were Grace's, and pored through what she found. Grace's jewelry and hair combs. The things she thought belonged to the women she gathered into a pile and dumped it all into a pillowcase—she would dispose of all the bed linens as soon as these people were gone. Then she looked into the wallet on the dresser, the one she was certain belonged to Von. She closed it and put it into her pocket—she'd go through it later. She also pocketed the ring of keys. Right now, she just wanted the three of them gone.

"Get up and get out, all of you," she said, returning to the living room where the three interlopers were huddled together, not looking at her. "Did you hear me?" she yelled. "I said get up and get out of here!"

The two women, whose names she did not know, still wearing Grace's nightgowns, struggled to their feet and pulled their—whatever she was to them—to her feet. Her face was swelling and her lip was split and bleeding. If looks could kill, Bobbie would be dead. Then Bobbie looked more closely and recognized a pair of her own pajamas on this clown, who now felt brave enough to try to shit-talk Bobbie.

"I'm gonna kick your ass—"

Bobbie slapped her hard, then backhanded her even harder. Then she balled up her fist and delivered a solid right to the woman's left eye and she went down. Bobbie had good upper body strength from years of tennis and swimming, but those activities did nothing to strengthen the hands and Bobbie was relatively certain that she may have just cracked a bone. "Get out, all of you, and I won't tell you again."

"What are we supposed to wear?" one of the nightgowns whined.

"I don't give a good goddamn," Bobbie growled. "Go bare-butt naked for all I care. Just get out of here and do it now!"

"We got to get our coats and stuff out of the closet," the bully snarled through her split lips and started toward the coat closet with an intensity that put Bobbie on alert.

"Get your asses back over there and don't move until I say you can. I'll get the coats."

"I'll get my own damn coat!" the bully growled with impressive braggadocio and started toward the closet. Bobbie punched her hard enough in the gut to knock her down, but also hard enough to split the skin on her own knuckles, hard enough that she wanted to scream in pain, but that would never do. She glowered at the heap of whining bully on the floor, directed a hard kick at ribs that no doubt already were throbbing, and started toward the coat closet, keeping the bundle of women in sight.

Grace's things were shoved tightly to one side and the coats of the three interlopers hung in the middle. On the floor beneath the coats were three stuffed pillowcases and Bobbie didn't need to look inside to imagine what they contained, so she ignored them and focused on the three coats. There was nothing in the pockets of the coats—jackets, really—of the two girls, because after taking hard looks at them, looking at what lived beneath the too heavily applied makeup and the too large silk nightgowns, she realized that these indeed were girls, not women, and she didn't want to think too long or hard about why they were with Von Thompkins.

She turned her attention to the man's overcoat. The pockets bulged and Bobbie emptied them, one by one. Grace's things. Bobbie kept her temper in check, primarily because her hand throbbed and pulsed with every movement, and she almost cried out when she reached down into the inside pocket of the big overcoat. Good Christ that hurt!

But what she found overrode the pain: a huge wad of cash and Grace's bank book. It was clear Von was getting ready to run, almost certainly because Grace had run last night. Bobbie had gotten here just in time.

She stuffed everything from Von's coat into her own pockets and grabbed the three coats, one at a time, and tossed them across the room to their owners. With clear space in the closet Bobbie saw the baseball bat leaning against the wall and almost smiled. Grace had said it was for protection and Bobbie had teased her. *"Do you plan to ask the burglar to please stand still while you get your baseball bat out of the closet?"* But she knew Grace really had the bat because it was a Willie Mays bat bearing his image and signature. Bobbie grabbed it, closed the closet door, and opened the front door. Then she took a few practice swings, hoping the throbbing, burning pain in her hand didn't show on her face.

150

"Out, all of you, right now."

The three women moved slowly toward the front door. The two young girls eyed the bat sideways and scurried the last few steps, and into the hall. Badass bully girl tried for a saunter but stepped lively when Bobbie raised the bat.

"I need some money for a taxi."

"Then get a job, asshole, instead of beating women and stealing their money."

"How am I supposed to get all the way home to Brooklyn?"

"Don't know, don't care. Walk or crawl—don't care. Just get out of here!"

Bully girl Von did a slow, sullen stroll to the front door, stopping on the threshold, but before she could turn around to say whatever she'd been thinking about saying, Bobbie slammed the end of the bat into her back, propelling her into the hallway, and slammed the door.

She hurriedly turned the locks and slid the chain into place, then ran into the kitchen to make certain the back door was locked with the chain on. She tried not to look, not to see, the destruction all around her.

She turned on the cold water in the sink and let it run over her throbbing right hand. She stood there, trying to promise herself that she'd never again be angry enough to hit someone. However, unless people stopped their evil ways, she knew it was a promise she could never keep, especially if the evil was directed at someone she loved. She could not avenge the murder of her family, but those who hurt Grace would feel the payback for a while.

Bobbie turned off the water and took her now frozen right hand into the bathroom to look for a towel, but she didn't get past the door. In only a few days, three people, two of them children, had transformed a beautiful, peaceful space into . . . Bobbie didn't have words to describe the destruction done to Grace's home. It looked and felt planned and deliberate. This wasn't a case of a towel or a glass forgotten about and left in the wrong room, or the dinner dishes left in the sink overnight. This was every drawer and cabinet open, every glass and plate piled in the sink or left on the dresser in the bedroom or on the floor. Food cartons in the bed, on the floor, in the bathtub, for the love of Christ. They ate in the bathtub!

Grace had two telephones, one in the living room and one in the bedroom. Bobbie found the living room phone first and called Bobby. She apologized for waking him and then let the words tumble out, telling him everything. It had been less than two hours ago since her own phone had rung, Nurse Myrtle Lewis on the other end summoning her. It felt like days ago. Now here she was, delivering the same blow to Bobby.

He was silent for several long moments. She could picture his face as he heard the words, then tried to make them make sense, and when no sense could be made, his shock turned to sorrow. Then to anger. Finally, he knew he would do whatever he needed to do to help his friend.

"What can I do, Bobbie?"

"I've got to get this place cleaned up. Can you ask the super what cleaning service he uses, and then call in whatever favor is required to get people here immediately? I don't care what it costs. And the same goes for a locksmith—"

"You're talking to the locksmith! Don't forget what I do for a living! After I talk to the super, I'll strap on my tool belt and come your way."

Bobbie's next call was to Grace's office. Myrtle answered on the second ring and told Bobbie everything she desperately needed to know. Grace's injuries were not life-threatening, and she would heal relatively quickly. "She'll be sore for a few days, but she'll get back to her old self. Her old physical self," Myrtle said.

"You worried about her mental health?" Bobbie asked, afraid of the answer.

"She's already blaming herself for allowing what happened."

"But it's not her fault!" Bobbie exclaimed.

"I know that," Myrtle snapped, "and so does Grace. But every woman, especially the smart ones, think they should have recognized the danger before it struck. We have a file drawer full of the same circumstances, just different women."

Bobbie gasped. "Same circumstances. You mean where women have done this to other women?"

"It's not just men who brutalize women," the nurse said wearily, "though thankfully the entire drawer is not woman-on-woman violence. That would be too much."

Bobbie found her voice. "I'll call when this place is cleaned up and the locks are changed; then I'll come get Grace—"

"We'll bring her home, Bobbie. Thelma is off today, and she's been helping me handle the patients here. Other than Grace herself, no real emergencies in the office so far."

Knowing that Grace was in the care of two of the best nurses in the business, people who loved her, helped ease some of Bobbie's tension and worry. But not all. She hadn't known that women did to other women what Von Thompkins had done to Grace. But Myrtle had that file drawer full of evidence to the contrary—and that was just one doctor's office, and a woman doctor at that. Based on what she'd read in her mother's writings, male doctors probably wouldn't see it as a problem if men beat their women. As if being a Negro woman wasn't hard enough, did they now have to fear others like themselves? Bobbie didn't understand it, didn't want to understand it, couldn't bear to understand it.

"I'll call you when Grace's home looks like Grace's home again," Bobbie said, hanging up. She went into the kitchen to get an ice tray but was disgusted by the sight inside the refrigerator, so she merely turned on the cold water and let it run over her hand. It hurt like hell. On the plus side the water was as cold as ice, and while her hand didn't hurt any less, perhaps—

hopefully—the swelling would be controlled.

Just then a familiar staccato knock sounded at the door. She expected it was Bobby but hurried across the room and slid open the peephole cover to peer into the hallway to make certain.

They hugged like the old friends they had become in such a short time. Bobbie pulled him inside, closed the door, and put the chain on. Then she watched Bobby's eyes roam the living room, and the dismay and disgust on his face was an exact replica of what she had felt. "How—" he began, then shook his head and switched gears.

"The cleaning crew will be here in about an hour, by which time I'll have the new locks installed," he said, adding what he'd stopped himself from saying just seconds ago. "What the hell kind of people would do this kind of damage on purpose to Grace's beautiful home?"

Bobbie shook her head, trying to control the tears welling up and threatening to spill over and out. "I don't know, Bobby. I don't know who they were or why Grace would allow them to stay here." The tears came. Then the sobs. Bobbie wept as she had at the loss of her mother, her family.

"Grace left me, Bobby, because she didn't trust what I thought about her."

"What the hell does that mean? Who told you that?"

"Eileen, and she knows Grace better than anyone." Bobby gave her a look that demanded an explanation. "I assumed that Grace knew how much I cared for her and why I did, but I didn't really spell it out so she thought I was like her other suitors who wanted to be the one to win Dr. Grace Hannon."

Bobby held his wonderful, loving friend close and let her cry for a bit. Then he pushed her away gently, just far enough away so they faced each other.

"She left, Bobbie, because she thought you wanted her to go," he said calmly and gently but directly. He watched her face, still filled with considerable hurt and pain, but also now with shock and confusion.

"Why would she ever think that?"

"When she gets here, ask her."

"Ask her what?" Bobbie demanded, jumping to her feet. She felt like the ball in a bolo bat toy: swung this way and hit, then swung another way and hit, but always hit.

"Ask her why she thought that you no longer wanted her," he replied calmly, "because that's the only reason she left. She believed you wanted her to go, that you wanted to be free of her so you could see other women."

"How the hell do you know that, Bobby Mason? Did she tell you that? 'Cause she didn't tell me that. If she had—"

Bobby grabbed his friend's hands and held them tightly, holding her eyes with his own. "I told her she was wrong, and I'm wrong to tell you this because she and I were having a trusted conversation between friends. I asked her where she got such crazy information and she said from someone who knows you, and who has known you for a long time."

"Anyone who has known me for a long time—"

"Knows that you haven't looked at another woman since you met Grace Hannon. Jack and Justine already told me, Bobbie, and that's what I told Grace."

"And what did she say?"

Bobby shook his head and at first refused to meet Bobbie's eyes, but he finally looked at her and said, "She wondered what someone like you, who could have a different drop-dead gorgeous woman every week, and who used to have a different drop-dead gorgeous woman every week, could want with someone like her, who wasn't drop-dead gorgeous and who hadn't been with a woman in almost a year."

"Did you tell her, Bobby, that I adore her?"

"And she adores you—"

The ringing of the downstairs door buzzer halted Bobby's words about Grace's feelings for Bobbie, to be replaced with,

"That'll be the cleaners," and he hurried to buzz them in until Bobbie stopped him.

"Make certain that's who it is before you open the door," Bobbie said.

"You don't think . . . She wouldn't be stupid enough to come back here, would she?"

"I almost wish she would." Bobbie's words were icy cold and grim, and she meant them. Her hurt and sadness, not to mention the throbbing pain in her hand, had not diminished her rage.

"It's the cleaners," Bobby said, opening the door to admit three uniformed employees of the Westside Apartment Maintenance Service.

Bobbie gave him the money to pay their fee, told him to please keep the doors closed and locked, and left to return to Grace's office. She went out the kitchen door because she wanted to go to the basement, to the garage. She hadn't seen Grace's car keys among the items retrieved from Thompkins' coat pocket and she wanted to be certain the car was in its parking space. It wasn't.

She hurried out to the street and hailed a taxi. Traffic was as dense as it always was on Broadway on a weekday morning at—she checked her watch—eleven thirty, past the morning rush hour, preparing for the lunch rush hour. Bobbie felt as if she'd already put in a full day at work. But she didn't feel nearly as exhausted as Myrtle Lewis looked.

"How is she?"

"We had to sedate her. She kept trying to get up—"

"And do what?" Bobbie demanded.

Myrtle hesitated for a moment, then said, "She wanted to find you."

Bobbie didn't know how to reply so she said, "I didn't find the keys to Grace's car or the car—"

"It's in the garage here," the nurse said, explaining that Von Thompkins had asked to drive the car and had become angry

156

when Grace refused. "Then, when she realized that Grace had brought it here rather than allow her to drive it, she became furious. That's the first time she hit Grace."

Bobbie started to make an angry fist and cried out in pain. The nurse took one look at her hand and called for reinforcements. Thelma came running. She took one look at the hand that Myrtle held and started to laugh.

"Whipped her ass, did you?"

"Tried my good god-damnedest to kill her."

Still chuckling, Thelma took her arm, told Myrtle she was going to x-ray the hand, and led Bobbie away. "I hope you and Grace can fix whatever went wrong between the two of you," she said as she led the way down the hall to the x-ray room that Grace shared with two other doctors.

"If it's within my power to fix, believe me I'll fix it," Bobbie responded.

"Well, as far as I'm concerned, you're off to a great start." And she held Bobbie's very bruised and painful right hand up in the air the way the ring announcer holds up the hand of the winning boxer.

"Ow, oh damn, Thelma!"

"Oh good gracious, Bobbie. I'm so sorry. I know better, truly I do." The chagrined nurse lowered Bobbie's hand, gently cradling the damaged fist between her own two hands. "Let's get an ice pack on there to stem the swelling and ease the pain a bit. Then we'll get an x-ray to see what kind of damage you may have done."

"Not too much, I hope. I can't take care of Grace with one hand. My left hand gives a useful performance only on a piano keyboard."

"I think being with you will be all the healing she needs, Bobbie."

"Can't tell you how much I hope you're right."

Three hours later Bobby arrived with the new keys to

Grace's apartment and news that it was restored pretty much to its former glory. The cleaners had thrown away what was broken beyond repair or destroyed. The security latch was on the kitchen door, Bobby said, so no entry was possible from the garage, and the front door was double-locked, and the locks could not be picked.

"Nobody can get into that apartment without these keys," Bobby said, giving two sets of them to Myrtle, who gave them to Thelma. They thanked and hugged him, and Bobbie walked him to the elevator.

"Thank you for being my true friend, Bobby Mason. I don't know what I did before you."

"But we know what you did before Grace—"

"And I stopped doing it the night I met her!"

"Then make damn certain she knows that, Bobbie." The elevator door slid open and Bobby got on as the ancient attendant pulled the gate closed. The last thing Bobby Mason saw was the resolve on Bobbie Hilliard's face, and he smiled.

"He really is a very special guy," Thelma said.

"The best," Bobbie agreed. "It's hard to believe he's so new to our lives."

"My minister grandfather would have called it providential," Myrtle said.

"He wouldn't have been wrong," answered Bobbie. "The man is a gift, no doubt. He said the cleaners did an excellent job of restoring Grace's home."

"Except she probably won't see it," Myrtle said.

Bobbie gave her a look. "Only one of her eyes is swollen shut. The other one sees just fine."

"She's refusing to go home, Bobbie," Thelma said calmly as if what she just said made perfect sense.

"But she can't stay here," Bobbie said. "Can she?"

"It's her office so, yes, I suppose she can if she wants to," Thelma said. "But she wants to go home with you."

"Oh. Well. In that case—" Bobbie wiped away tears. "Can we leave now? Can she walk? Are you sure she's all right? Isn't she in pain?"

Myrtle put an arm around Bobbie and pulled her close. "Yes, she is in pain, Bobbie, but most of the hurt she's feeling is from what the headshrinkers call mental anguish. She blames herself for everything that has happened in the last few days, and it feels like it's been for a hell of a lot longer than that."

"Somebody targeted her, lied to her, and took advantage of her. How is that her fault? If she can be blamed for anything— and I'm not saying that she should be—it would be for being too trusting, too scared, and too horrified to tell us what was happening," Bobbie said.

"One thing you should know: I hope you hurt Von really badly because she hurt Grace really badly—hard punches directly to the muscles," and Thelma. "With the exception of the eye, none of this damage is visible to anyone but you and us. And, of course, Grace. Von knew exactly what she was doing, Bobbie, which makes me believe this isn't the first time she's done it."

"What should I do? How do I help Grace?" But as a college athlete Bobbie knew the answer: ice packs and anti-inflammatories. She could hear her coaches when the pain began to subside: get those muscles moving. And get into the whirlpool to keep them warm and flexible.

"Sounds like you know what to do," Myrtle said, more of a question than a statement and Bobbie explained. "Swim and tennis teams at Hunter, and Grace was on the swim team too, you know."

"No, we did not know." Myrtle looked sad.

"Can I take her home now?"

Then she had a horrible thought. A couple of them, actually. First, her place was a mess and second, there was no food. "Okay if I call Bobby?"

When Thelma nodded, Bobbie opened the door to Grace's office and was appalled at the sight. It was as much of a mess as Bobbie's own apartment. The two of them clearly did not do well when not together.

The other B-person, the one ending in Y, would finish work in half an hour and go to Bobbie's and restore order there.

"And please order lots of food from Miz Maggie's and have it delivered by a taxi. Grace can eat anything, right?" she called out to whichever nurse could hear her.

"Nothing that requires lots of chewing," Thelma called back, and Bobbie recommended he order black-eyed peas, sweet potatoes, and banana pudding for Grace.

In an examining room, Grace was cranked to an almost upright position on the exam table instead of lying almost flat as she'd been when Bobbie first saw her early that morning. A blanket was pulled up to her chin. Her eyes were closed, but she didn't look relaxed or rested. Bobbie walked to the table and took Grace's hand, and her eyes flew open. She began to sob, all the while trying to speak.

Bobbie pulled her into an embrace that probably was too tight, but she wanted Grace to feel it, to feel that she was safe and protected and being held by arms that would never harm her. Bobbie whispered over and over how much Grace was loved and how that was all that mattered, and she begged her to stop trying to talk. She heard the wheelchair being pushed into the room. "Are you ready to go home now, Gracie?"

"Home with you, Bobbie?" The words were slurred, as much from the sedatives and pain relievers delivered by the nurses as from the punches to the face and mouth delivered by the evil Von Thompkins.

"Yes, Grace. Home with me."

Myrtle and Thelma got Grace settled into the wheelchair. Myrtle added another blanket and Grace's overcoat on top, with a wool scarf on her head tied under her neck. Clearly the nurses wanted to keep her warm, and Bobbie wondered why. Was there a problem she didn't know about? Yes, it was cold, but it was January in New York, and it was supposed to be cold.

Downstairs in the garage Thelma pushed the chair over to Grace's Caddy and tossed Bobbie the keys. She immediately unlocked the doors, got in and turned the key in the ignition, wondering how long it would take the big engine to warm up. Probably as long as the Buick took, and on very cold days it felt like an eternity.

Thelma and Myrtle helped Grace into the backseat. They were gentle and careful, but it was a painful process. Bobbie tried not to think how much more pain she wished she had inflicted on Von Thompkins. There could never be enough pain for that evil piece of shit.

Bobbie pressed the gas pedal and the engine growled, then hummed, and warm air began to enter through the vents. Grace would be warm in a moment. When she and Myrtle were settled, Thelma closed the back seat door, tapped twice, and rolled the wheelchair across the garage to her own car where she placed it in the trunk. Then she got in the car and led the way out of the garage and, after a wait of several minutes, into the heavy traffic on Broadway. Dusk became night with red brake lights on Broadway stretching into the far distance as the caravan headed to Bobbie's home.

Bobbie parked the Caddy next to the Buick in her own garage. She and Myrtle helped get Grace out of the car and had her standing up by the time Thelma parked and got the wheelchair. Bobby met them at the kitchen door as the percolator was finishing its work, and the smell of fresh coffee was a wonderful welcome home. While Thelma got Grace unwrapped Myrtle beckoned her toward the bathroom. "She needs a shower. Or a bath. But she can't stand for a shower or sit for a bath. Any suggestions or ideas?"

Again, Bobbie bit back the question she was burning to ask,

but because she had so recently spent so much time in the locked room where her parents' things were stored, she knew exactly where to find the stool her mother used to sit on sometimes to paint, and the waxed tablecloth she used to protect whatever was nearby from paint spatter.

"Perfect," Myrtle said, placing the stool in the tub and covering it with the cloth. She turned on the water and tested the temperature while Bobbie undressed Grace and tried not to react to the purple and green bruises covering her body. Then she undressed herself down to her underwear and stepped into the tub to help Grace get in, one leg at a time, then to sit. Grace began to visibly relax as soon as the warm water began to flow over her. She sighed and whispered her thanks.

"Call me when she's ready to get out," Myrtle said, starting to leave. Bobbie called her back, stepping out of the tub and over to the nurse.

"She's not . . . She wasn't . . . Von didn't . . ." She couldn't make herself say the words. Myrtle heard the unspoken question and grabbed Bobbie and hugged her tightly, whispering that Grace had not been sexually violated. That apparently sex had not been part of Von's plan. She wanted to hurt Bobbie, and hurting Grace was how she accomplished that. Myrtle left then, softly closing the door, and Bobbie rejoined Grace under the soothing water, not thinking about why someone she didn't know wanted to hurt her but thinking hard about how that someone knew that to hurt Grace was to hurt her. She soaped a cloth and began to gently wash Grace's back and shoulders, which began heaving. Bobbie realized she was weeping, trying to talk, and choking on the words.

"I've been such a fool! I was blaming you for my own failures, I suppose."

"Stop, Grace. Stop it now, please. We can talk later."

"I should have talked to you before I did something so stupid."

"We'll talk later, and yes, we definitely do need to talk. Right now, though, you need to relax your body, you need to feed it, and you need to sleep."

"You won't make me . . . I won't have to go back there."

Bobbie held her as closely as the damaged, yet still beautiful body would permit. "I would be very happy, Gracie, if you stayed here with me."

"For how long, Bobbie?"

"For as long as you like, Gracie. Forever, if you're so inclined."

Grace's face, despite the damage inflicted by Von Thompkins' fist, somehow managed one of its beatific yet impish grins. "Despite the fact that you sound more like a literature major than a music major, I am so inclined, and I am so very happy."

"And what happens to your place? Do you think Thelma and Myrtle—"

"They'll have me packed up and out the door before God gets the news!" And she explained that Thelma lived in a studio apartment much like Bobby Mason's and Myrtle shared an apartment with her mother.

So, Bobbie thought, a couple of things settled, but certainly not everything. "How about we get you out of here, get you dressed, and assuming you're hungry, may I remind you that Bobby Mason is out there with the food and how dangerous it can be to leave him unattended in the face of too much temptation."

Jack was with him, helping Thelma and Myrtle get the food arranged on the stove and plates, bowls, and silverware for serving and eating. Bobby had brought large containers of iced tea and lemonade, and Bobbie was behind the bar taking drink orders. Then they did what they always did when they were together: they ate and laughed and talked and ate and drank and laughed and talked. No one asked Grace anything. However, everyone managed to touch or hug or kiss her more than once, and each time she shed tears of joy and gratitude. And more than once each of them silently wished for time alone with that damnable Von Thompkins, wanting to add to whatever pain Bobbie had already inflicted, wanting to pay her back triple the pain she had caused their wonderful, loving friend.

"I thank all of you for your love and care," Grace said when she had finished eating.

"You will never know how—" She leaned back into Bobbie's embrace and wiped away tears. "I now live here with Bobbie, so Myrt and Thelma, if you're interested—" She didn't need to complete the sentence.

"You know we are!" They carefully hugged Grace and started to say that they could work out the details later, but Grace insisted there was nothing to work out. She wanted to take nothing but her medical books and journals and the bookcases that held them, her clothes and toiletries, and her favorite roasting pots and frying skillets. Everything else she needed to live already existed in this place, she said.

"Roasting pots and skillets?" Bobbie asked, full of confusion and skepticism.

"Heck yeah!" Bobby, who had been sitting by quietly, explained. "My grandma would've walked away and left me *and* my ma before she'd have parted with her favorite roasting pots and frying skillets."

"Welcome home, roasting pots!" Bobbie exclaimed with arms open wide. She told Grace that she'd clear out her office in time for it to become the home office of Dr. Hannon. Then she asked Bobby to meet her in said office.

"I know it's short notice and I apologize for that, but can you rent or borrow a truck and hire some guys—maybe Ennyday and Ennybay—to—" and she waved her arm around the room as if a wand would appear in her hand and empty the room. Oh, how she wished that kind of magic was possible!

"I'm actually considering buying a truck, Bobbie, since I'll need it for my Black Mask duties. I know where there's a pretty good one for sale."

"That's wonderful. Do it, Bobby. I'll pay for it, and having your own truck will make it possible for Black Mask to pay you for using it when the time comes."

"I thought Black Mask work was of a voluntary nature. You know, because we're such lovers of the arts and all."

"It is volunteer work for those like me who don't need the money. People who do need to get paid will get paid."

"Not many Negroes can say that, Bobbie—that they don't need the money."

"I'd gladly give the insurance companies every penny of their money back if I could have my family back, Bobby."

He pulled her into a tight embrace. "Of course you would, my friend! I wasn't thinking and I apologize. I guess I never . . . well, that's not entirely true. I did wonder, but the only insurance payments I know about are those that barely pay for the funeral. And that's after people like my grandma pay a nickel or a dime or a quarter every week for years and years to the Insurance Man who dutifully comes to collect it. Life insurance policies that pay for all this—" He shrugged and shook his head. Uncharted territory in his experience though he was glad to know that it was possible.

Bobbie got him to agree to tell her the cost of the truck and the cost to hire the number of men he thought necessary to move the contents of her office to an empty room in the building where The Slow Drag was located. She made sure it would cover the transport of Grace's things to their new home as well.

"And I know you have a job, Bobby, so do all of this when it's convenient." When he left the room, she opened the box of cash and withdrew the amount of money he'd specified, adding an extra hundred, just in case.

She returned to the living room to find Grace nodding peacefully under a pile of blankets, Jack closely watching over her, while Thelma and Myrtle were almost finished cleaning up what little remained of their dinner. They looked happy and more than a little ready to go home—for now to their own homes, but shortly to what previously was Grace's home.

But first they wanted Bobbie's approval for a plan to tell patients, other doctors in the building, and business and professional associates that Grace had been attacked and battered when she refused to release her medical bag to a would-be robber. "If I tell this story to building management, they'll put a security guard in the lobby and one in the garage—"

"You're worried that Von Thompkins will return," Bobbie said, and it was a statement and not a question.

"I fear that she will," Myrtle responded. "And we also have to be able to respond to questions because we all know Dr. Hannon well enough to know she will not stay home until she heals, though we all know she should."

Yes, they all knew that, and Bobbie approved the plan. "But we also all know who else must approve the plan." When they woke Grace and explained to her, she understood. Seemed she, too, was concerned about the possibility that she could still be in danger.

Bobbie had already promised herself to learn more about Von and where she lived. And somehow make sure she would want to stay well away from Grace Hannon. Forever.

They got Grace into bed and Myrtle gave Bobbie two pill bottles, one for pain, the other an anti-inflammatory. "She's had one of each in the last hour, so you can follow the instructions from now on."

Bobbie nodded, following her out of the bedroom to find Thelma waiting at the kitchen door. She thanked them both for everything. "Is tomorrow too soon to get her into the whirlpool?"

The nurses looked at each other, telegraphing a message the way only the closest of confidants can.

Myrt said, "If Grace feels like going in, it would be good for her as long as she doesn't stay in the water too long."

And after Bobbie elicited from Thelma and Myrtle their promise to call for help getting moved and settled into their new home, they left and she locked the door. She returned to Grace, whom she expected to find deeply asleep, not wide awake, sitting up waiting for her. "You should be asleep, you know."

"I can't sleep, Bobbie, until I tell you why I was so stupid, and I know I was stupid to send you away, but that was more about me than it was about you. I never wanted to be separated from you." She was breathing heavily, hyperventilating almost.

"It can wait until morning, Grace—"

"No, Bobbie, it can't, so please listen."

"All right, Gracie, I'm listening." She sat on the bed close beside Grace and held her hands.

"She told me all these things about you, Bobbie. Von did. About all the women you dated, and your apartment at the Theresa where you took the women."

"What I don't understand, Grace, is why it mattered. I was with you, and if I ever did or said anything to make you doubt my commitment to you—"

"Oh my dear Bobbie, you never did. What I did was all my fault. Yes, I believed Von and was stupid enough to believe what she said, but the real problem was that I believed you preferred those glamorous women to mousy old Grace Hannon—"

"To mous—what in the merry mother fuck, Grace! Please do not ever let me hear you refer to yourself that way."

"You won't, Bobbie, I promise. How I could have been so damn stupid is the real question, and I've asked myself over and over until I think I found an answer."

"We can talk about all this tomorrow, Grace, after you've rested—"

"Now, Bobbie, please. I need you to understand—"

"All right, Grace. All right. Calm down and tell me."

"Because she treated me like my family treated me, Bobbie, like who and what and how I was didn't matter. She ignored me when I tried talking to her, and she was a slob, and I hated every moment of her presence, but it was familiar. It's your treatment of me that was different and unfamiliar, and I wasn't sure I deserved it." Grace started sobbing and talking about growing up in a home where all the women were pretty. Except her. She was the smart one. Too smart to ever catch a husband, her father said, because men didn't like smart women.

"But you didn't even like men," Bobbie interjected, and Grace giggled, agreed, kissed her, and continued with her story, promising that she was almost finished.

"So I studied harder, got better grades than anyone, including the boys in my classes. But until you, Bobbie, a woman I wanted never wanted me. Never. And suddenly, listening to Von, I didn't know why you did. When Von described those glamorous women you dated, she told me I was stupid to think you wanted me."

Grace stopped talking for a moment and smiled. "Now I can see for certain I actually was a fool, because while I may not be beautiful, I've most certainly never been stupid." Bobbie started to laugh and couldn't stop. She grabbed Grace and held her too tightly, but Grace didn't complain. She grabbed Bobbie and held on. They both were crying.

"Please forgive me, Bobbie. For sending you away, certainly, but primarily for not knowing and trusting myself, and for listening to someone as stupid as Von Thompkins who lied and had the nerve to call me stupid."

"If you'll forgive me, Gracie."

Grace frowned, winced, touched the side of her face where her eye and cheek were a very ugly shade of purple, and asked, "Whatever for, Bobbie?"

"For being stupid enough to allow you to send me away. I'll never do that again." And after a moment she said, "I can't imagine a woman you wanted who was dumb enough not to want you. You're one of the most beautiful women I've ever seen, and without a doubt the most brilliant, and you dance like an angel."

"So…" A drowsy Grace struggled to articulate her thoughts. "If you've forgiven me, Bobbie, my love, can we sleep now?" And Grace Hannon was fast asleep while Bobbie Hilliard lay awake pondering how she could manage a suitable Von Thompkins payback.

CHAPTER FIVE

Bobby Mason's "new" truck was a seven-year-old black-and-purple Chevy pickup, and he loved it as if it were his new boyfriend. In fact, that's what he named it: The Boyfriend.

"And what happens when the real boyfriend comes into your life, and he learns that you've named your truck The Boyfriend?"

Bobby gave a sly grin and said he'd tell the new boyfriend the truck's name was The Girlfriend. But girl or boy, he treated the truck like royalty and learned in the process that Ennybay really was learning to be a good mechanic. He gave The Girl/Boyfriend a complete check and found that every working part, from tires and brakes to light bulbs to the battery, needed to be replaced, and then he did the work himself. Bobby constructed a wooden frame inside the bed of the truck, four feet high across the back window and up both sides, with a detachable piece for the bed to let the gate go up and down. Then he attached metal hooks every six inches at the top and bottom of the frame to attach waterproof oilskin cloth to protect whatever he carried in bad weather. He needed it. It snowed the day he and Ennybay moved Bobbie's home office to the vacant space on the ground floor of The Slow Drag building, and Grace's old home office and its contents, clothes, and cooking utensils to her new home at Bobbie's.

Ennybay was a good worker—fast, focused, and efficient—but Bobby still wished he'd hired another man because weather slowed everything down. When he and Bobby finally finished the moving, and after burgers and fries at Miz Maggie's, Bobby hurried to his job and Ennybay hurried to help Bobbie set up her new office. He found her sitting on a box of books looking glum. Nothing had been opened or unpacked. Was she waiting for him before she started? She saw his confusion. "I'm sorry, Ennyday, but I'm really not certain why I need an office since I'm not certain I even wish to continue organizing the Black Mask project." She saw his confusion increase and she smiled, apologized for wasting his time, thanked him, and tried to pay him.

He shook his head, refusing to accept the bills Bobbie proffered. "Boy Bobby already paid me. You don't have to give me no more money, Girl Bobby."

She realized that Ennybay had, in his own way, differentiated between Bobby and Bobbie, the Girl and the Boy with the same name. "Any time you work, Ennybay, you should be paid, even if you do work for your friends."

"And I don't like that name. I like my real name. Benny."

"Of course, Benny, I'm sorry. I meant no disrespect to you. And paying you for the work you helped me do is respect, Benny. Okay?"

He sighed in mild exasperation and explained he had never been paid so many times in the same day—by Boy Bobby and by the nurse lady and now by herself. He'd never had so much money at one time and he didn't know what to do with it. When she told him to save it and told him why—rattling off half a dozen potential scenarios in which saved money would be useful—he accepted the payment she offered, stuffed it into his pockets with his other payments for that day, thanked her, and headed for the door. But he halted abruptly and turned to face her.

"Where do I put it, my saving money? Where can I keep it safe? I can't let somebody find it and take it." That clearly was a possibility that worried him, and most probably with good reason. She thought for a moment.

"Boy Bobby has a lockbox where he keeps his important papers, and it has a key. Is it all right if I ask him to get a box like that for you?"

Benny gave her a wide grin, pumped her hand in thanks, and they left. Benny went his way, pulling his knit cap down over his ears against the cold darkness, and she went hers—a block away, around the corner, and half a block to the front door of The Slow Drag to talk to Laverne the bouncer, who was totally surprised to see her. Laverne was impeccably dressed as always in a tweed jacket, starched white shirt, solid color knit tie (dark green today) over blue jeans and black work boots. "Are you back?"

"Only on Mondays, Verne, and other days as needed, but nobody sent for me and I don't want Justine to think I'm checking up on her. I came to ask you something and then I'm gone."

"Sure, Bobbie," Laverne said, with her head in a constant swivel—watching the street in front of her, and whoever might be leaving the club behind her.

"Do you know Von Thompkins?"

Verne's head stopped its swivel. "That piece of shit! What do you want with her?"

"Do I know her, Verne? Has she ever been here?" Bobbie asked urgently.

Verne shook her head back and forth. The scowl on her face would be a sufficient deterrent to anyone with bad intentions climbing the stairs to The Slow Drag. "No reason you would or should know her, Bobbie, though come to think about it, the only time I remember her being here was the night you met

Grace, and the only reason I remember is because she kept buying PJ drinks, and Von's not the kind to buy people drinks."

Bobbie was shocked to hear this. "Did she come into contact with Grace?"

Verne shook her head. "She pretty much stayed in the corner by the bar bending PJ's ear. Von likes to talk, and thinks she knows what she's talking about, which she never does. And she's always calling somebody stupid."

"Sounds like you know her, Verne," Bobbie said quietly, which caused Verne to give her a close, steady look.

"I used to bus tables and wash dishes at The Theresa a couple of years back—and yes, I remember seeing you. I got to know Von a little, but when she came in here that night, she either didn't remember me or pretended not to, which was fine with me. But knowing the kind of person she is made me keep an eye on her. She wasn't here for long, Bobbie, I'm sure about that."

"And she was talking to PJ the whole time?"

"I kept a watch on her except for a few moments when I had to, ah, escort a couple of rowdies down the steps and out the door."

"Kept a watch on her, why, Verne?"

"Because she's a thief. A pickpocket—that's her specialty. Didn't want her bumping into people in a close crowd. If you get my drift."

A thief. That fits, Bobbie thought, recalling everything that lowlife would have stolen from Grace had she not prevented it.

"Verne, can you think of any reason why she would come after me? I'm pretty sure I don't know her—"

"You probably won't remember it, but you might have gotten her fired a couple of years ago."

That suggestion stumped her. If she didn't know Von Thompkins, how could she have gotten her fired? At Grace's place she'd been close to the woman, in her face, had seen her powerful anger and fury, and had not recognized her. Had she ever seen that face before and just didn't remember? She didn't think so, and she would have if she'd gotten the woman fired.

"Fired from where, Verne? And why?"

"The Theresa. She used to bus tables there in the grill, when she wasn't washing dishes in the penthouse restaurant. She kept trying to work her way up to being a waiter, but her shitty personality always got in the way. That fool wouldn't know good manners if they slapped her ugly mug and kicked her ass."

"But how would I have gotten her fired from a job bussing tables, even if I had ever remembered seeing her?" Bobbie asked, perplexed, and now a bit worried. "She never bussed a table I ate at, I'm certain of that, Verne. If I'd ever seen her before the other day I'd remember." Was it possible to botch a job bussing tables so badly it would warrant being fired? "Anyway, people are gone before tables are bussed. And what do I have to do with Von's table bussing duties?"

Verne told about a time Bobbie and a date had finished a late supper in the grill and were in the lobby when Bobbie ran back to retrieve the jacket her date had left on the back of her chair—to find Von rifling through the pockets.

"You reported it and your date's lipstick, comb, and cigarette lighter were in Von's pocket, and adios Von." Verne's bushy eyebrows rose and wiggled a bit. "What other day did you see Von Thompkins?"

Ah shit. "Verne—"

Verne placed the palm of her right hand against her chest. "Stays right here."

"She hurt Grace and I made her wish she hadn't."

"A thief and a bully. That's all she's ever been," Verne said, frowning. "And also a . . . a . . . what do you call those pieces of shit who like little children? I'm talking about the sick kind of like, not the good kind." The distaste that curdled Verne's face drained the saliva from Bobbie's mouth.

"You mean pedophile?"

174

"That's it. She's one of those pieces of shit! Von Thompkins always has a group of young girls living with her, girls who are barely teenagers." Before Bobbie could ask, Verne said, "She paid their parents for them—parents who are drug addicts or alcoholics, people not able to or interested in raising children and who would do almost anything for a dollar."

Bobbie thought of the two young girls with Von at Grace's and was nauseated. "How do you know so much about her? In fact, didn't I once hear you say you didn't know anybody who lived south of Columbia University? Von lives in Brooklyn—"

"Who told you that? That sorry piece of shit lives up in The Bronx. Always has and probably always will, and I know lots of people who live up there and who know the Thompkins bitch."

"She told me she lived in Brooklyn."

"A thief, a bully, a liar, and a . . . whatever that word was," Verne said, adding, "You shoulda killed her when you had the chance."

Bobbie gave Verne a steady look. "Sounds like you mean that."

"Damn right I do," Verne said, staring directly at Bobbie. "You know I have every respect for you, Bobbie, but not everybody can afford to look at the world the way you do, and I'm not talking about money, I'm talking about giving people the benefit of the doubt. People like Von Thompkins don't deserve the benefit of the doubt."

"But to kill her, Verne?"

"You best believe she'll kill you if she gets the chance, and she won't do it up-front and honest. She'll come at you sneaky and sideways 'cause that's who and how she is. And Bobbie? She'll probably come after Grace again 'cause she knows that's the way to hurt you."

"In that case I will kill her," Bobbie said.

"That's the only kinda payback for somebody like her," Verne said.

Bobbie pulled her knit cap down over her ears, tightened her scarf around her neck, pulled her gloves from her coat pocket, and put them on. The frigid wind from the Hudson River howling up and down Broadway wasn't the only reason: Verne's parting words about Von Thompkins, both chilling and frightening, still rang in her ears.

She walked fast, her tangled thoughts keeping pace with her booted feet. The sight of a pay phone through the front window of a Duane Reade drug store brought order to some of her thoughts and she all but ran into the store.

She called Eileen and invited her and Joyce to dinner, then called Grace to say what she'd done, realizing after the fact that she should have consulted Grace first, but her only comment was that she wouldn't have time to prepare a "satisfactory meal" on such short notice. Stifling a chuckle Bobbie said she'd call Miz Maggie and order dinner and dessert for four, which gave her a chance to inquire about the woman's grandson: was he still in a coma? Unfortunately he was but Miz Maggie said she prayed for him daily, and said she'd add Bobbie to her prayers. Bobbie picked up the bulging, aromatic dinner bags on the way home, one of which was a burger and fries for the driver who got her home in record time. The four friends shed copious tears over what had happened to Grace and the reason for it, though not a single one for Von Thompkins who rated almost no discussion. Nor did Eileen want to discuss Black Mask "when we have so much more important matters before us." She met no resistance.

"I know why we were brought together, Girl Bobbie."

"Oh please tell us why, Boy Bobby!"

"What are you two talking about? Do you need reminding which one of you is which?" Jack looked from one to the other, looking for signs of a spoof or a joke of some kind, but when all she found were their quasi-serious faces she asked for an explanation. They told her about Benny's names for them, and she enjoyed a lengthy belly laugh. "I like it. From now on that's who you two are: Girl Bobbie and Boy Bobby. It's much better than what I call you."

"You call us something?" Bobbie asked.

"Why didn't we know that?" asked Bobby.

"Well, are you going to tell us?" Bobbie asked.

"The Bs. I just call you The Bs."

"But suppose you want one of us," Bobbie asked, "and you're in the kitchen, and you call out: Bobbie, will you come here, please? How will we know which of us you want?"

"I want you both to come when I call," Jack replied with an impudent smirk, and they knew for certain that she was back to her healthy self.

Boy Bobby had prepared a delicious dinner of spaghetti and meatballs, followed, as always, by vanilla ice cream and whatever was Jack's preferred topping that day. Then he proudly displayed his new collection of books. None of the books were new, but they were new to him, and he was gradually filling his bookshelves with books he owned instead of books he checked out of the library. He'd discovered used bookstores, and the college bookstores selling students' books from classes they'd completed. Add the fact that everyone knew any gift for him should be a book and the bookcase would soon be full. He was so proud that he called his grandmother every time he added another book to the shelves, and she was justifiably proud of him. He was the first in the family not only to attend college but to have graduated high school. For a woman who could not read to have raised a grandson who could—she told everyone she knew, and more than a few strangers, about his accomplishments, and they shared her pride, especially those who had known Little Bobby Mason his entire life and who, like his grandmother, could neither read nor write. It was their children and grandchildren, they believed, who would make the world better for all of them.

The Bs and Jack Jackson had another reason for celebrating that evening, and after dinner and dessert Jack told them what it was. Her New Future is what she called it, a future that was, in fact, her present. She no longer was required to wear the strap that bound her damaged hip, and as a result she no longer required the catheter. She still declined liquid refreshment but a large bowl of vanilla ice cream topped with caramel sauce made her happier than just about anything else. It also took her mind off her most recent argument with her parents.

Jack viewed her release from the strap binding and the catheter as proof that she was ready and able to return to her apartment, that she no longer needed to live at home. True, the orthopedic specialist had ordered a cane and twice-weekly sessions with a physical therapist to help her relearn a normal walking gait, but he said there was no reason she couldn't live alone.

"I was shocked and hurt and furious when I learned my parents gave up the lease on my home. I have nowhere to go back to."

"Truth be told, Jack, I expected it. I think your parents were thinking that if you didn't have anywhere else to go, you'd stay at home with them." Bobbie tried in vain to soften the blow, but Jack only became angrier.

"Well, I'm not and I won't. I'm an adult, not a child."

"I've got an idea," Bobby said, dialing the phone. "Sorry to disturb you," he said to the person who answered, "but I've got a question. Is your apartment already rented? Because if not, I've got the perfect tenant for you. She's a Miss Jacqueline Marie Jackson, and she comes with the highest possible recommendations." He gave the phone to Jack and Bobbie, who heard Thelma and Myrtle laughing and celebrating.

"But I can't rent that apartment," Jack said sadly after they hung up the phone. "I don't have a job. You know my parents rented that apartment for me because they didn't want the urine odor in their place, but I can't pay rent because I don't have a job."

"Sure you can," Bobbie said, "because you and Justine are now the co-managers at The Slow Drag—"

"No way! That's her job; you can't just take it away from her like that, Bobbie. That would be so unfair."

"And I would never do that, Jack, but we have talked about how great it would be if you could share the duties and responsibilities with her. Justine is the first to admit that running the place is too much work for one person, and she was waiting for you to get well."

"It wasn't too much for you."

"Justine and I shared the load, but I've taken a step away and she needs you."

Jack's face was a mixture of excitement and worry. "I don't think I can get up the steps. Not yet anyway."

Bobbie's face was all smiles. "You won't have to."

It took a moment, but Jack worked it out. The dumbwaiter that took the booze from the basement storeroom up to the bar would do the same for her since she didn't weigh nearly as much as a load of beer or whiskey.

"This is the happiest I've been since I wondered if I'd ever be happy again. Thank you, Bobbie. For all of it. And for finding Boy Bobby. What did we do without him?"

"He is kind of all right, isn't he, especially for a boy," Bobbie said, giving him a look that contained a smirk that turned into a grin.

"But we need to find him a boyfriend that's not a motor vehicle so he won't forget what he's supposed to do when the real thing—" Jack began.

Bobby threw a potato chip at her. Jack saw it coming, caught it, and popped it into her mouth.

Boy Bobby spoke up. "I've been surrounded by women all

my life. I love women. But I assure you that when I met Jerome, I knew exactly what I was supposed to do." He smiled sadly at some secret memory. "He was impressed, too, considering that I was, in his words, a backwater country boy."

"You mean East St. Louis isn't a big city like Harlem, New York?" Jack asked.

"It's not a big place like New York City, but it is a place with jobs, which is why all my people went up there from Mississippi and never looked back. Like I don't look back there, because I'd never have the job I have or the place I live if I was still back there."

"But we have our own problems right here, even with all the good things that happen, and we need to do something about what happened to that old woman in the market and that young man in the alley—" Bobbie took a breath and Jack's hand— "and what happened to you, too, Jack," Bobbie said. "I haven't forgotten, and I never will."

She paused and took a breath. Remembering what had happened to Jack punched her in the gut like remembering what had happened to Grace. But she continued.

"Bobby and I have a plan—both short-term and long-term—and we will, naturally, tell you all about it. But you can't be involved, Jack, and I think you'll understand why. I also think you and Justine should meet and discuss how the two of you will run The Slow Drag."

"Does this mean you don't think I should return to school?"

Bobbie held up her hands, palms facing out, and shook her head. "No, it absolutely does not mean that, Jack. It means that I know how much you want to live on your own. I want to help you do that and the job is how I can help."

Jack's facial expressions were all over the place—happy, frightened, sad, resigned, and eventually something resembling excitement with a tinge of trepidation. Of course, her parents would be furious. She had always done as they asked and as they wished, primarily because their wishes coincided with hers. But at the moment, she did not know if she still wanted a master's degree in elementary education though she did know that she didn't want it immediately.

"I'm not sure about school right now," Jack said," not while the pain and misery that controlled my body and mind for so long is still fresh. And I still think you should be part of any decisions anybody makes about what happens in and to The Slow Drag, Bobbie. That bar is your baby—"

"If I think you're making a wrong turn, I'll tell you. Otherwise, I'll steer clear. But if you're short-staffed one night, or five hundred of our favorite kind of women show up and you need another bartender, call me. I will always care what happens there, and I will always be available to you."

"You sure Grace'll let you?" Jack drawled with impudent bravado.

"If I ask her nicely," Bobbie answered sweetly.

Grace enjoyed the good news about Jack before Dr. Hannon took over, wondering whether Jack was really ready to be back at work in such a high-pressure job. "Perhaps a return to school might be the best course?" She made it a question rather than a pronouncement.

"I believe Jack ultimately will return to school because she believes that education is the true path for Negroes," Bobbie said, "but I also think she needs to demonstrate her self-sufficiency, and she needs the job to do that."

But Grace's characterization of work at The Slow Drag as high-pressure was definitely accurate. Bobbie was so exhausted when she got home some nights that she fell asleep in the shower. And the fear of a police raid was never far from her mind despite the healthy bribes she paid to two lieutenants to keep the patrol cops away. Only a fool would trust a New York City cop—of any rank—but she didn't have a choice because without those cash envelopes passing from her palm to the lieutenants' hands, The Slow Drag surely would have been raided by now.

Grace listened and, though not totally convinced, agreed to take a wait-and-see posture. "I still see her for checkups every two weeks, but if I see any signs of regression in her health status—"

"We'll all be lined up and executed at dawn," Bobbie intoned.

Grace threw her a mock salute, then returned her attention to the medical journal open on her lap. But she wasn't reading it. She hadn't been reading it before Bobbie entered the room; she'd been staring so intently into the fire she hadn't heard Bobbie enter.

"What's troubling you, Gracie? Other than possibly having to execute me at dawn?"

"And that would trouble me no end," Grace replied, but what she really wanted to say lay just beneath the surface, so Bobbie waited for Grace to tell her.

"I'm going to see my parents tomorrow."

Bobbie, taken completely by surprise, said, "Tomorrow is Saturday. You're changing your visiting day?"

"I want to spend Sundays with you, Bobbie—in bed all day making love, or having brunch with friends, or sitting in front of the fire reading and listening to music and talking. I'm tired of spending Sundays with people who really don't like me. And I need to tell them that I've moved."

Bobbie let all that sink in, especially the "people who don't like me" part, before asking what her parents would have to say about the bruises to her face.

"They probably won't notice." Grace's shrug and offhanded tone belied the sorrow and pain in her voice.

"Is there something you haven't told me, Gracie, about your parents?"

Grace heaved a big sigh and gave a small, sad smile. "I didn't tell you the whole truth about why I believed the stories Von told. I didn't care then and still don't care that you dated other women before you met me—of course you did. What I didn't understand was what you saw in me, why you chose me over all those beautiful women."

"You're one of the most beautiful women I've ever seen, Grace, and I'll always wish I'd told you more often so you could have told Von where to stuff her stupidity."

Grace gave her a crooked grin, then said, "My parents still see me as the ugly duckling of their three daughters."

"Then they're idiots," Bobbie snapped. "And I don't need to see your sisters to know that you don't take a backseat in the beauty department to anyone. And you did tell me some of this, if not most of it, and I don't care about any of it, Grace. Unless you plan to leave me again—"

Grace jumped up from the sofa, scattering her books and papers. She ran to Bobbie who caught her mid-stride and lifted her and swung her around before putting her down. "I'm so sorry that I had to hurt you before I could accept that you really do see me as worthy of your love and believe you when you say I am brilliant and beautiful and that you really do love me. *Me*, Nellie Grace Hannon."

"Dr. Dr. Nellie Grace Hannon—a woman with a PhD and an MD, and I adore you."

"A woman who, according to my parents, wasn't smart enough to know when enough education was enough."

"I'm sorry to have to say this, Gracie, but I don't think I want to meet your parents," Bobbie said, "so please don't ask me to."

"And I'm sorry to have to say this, but I don't think I care whether you meet them or not. I'm just so grateful to be able to realize that for the first time in my life I'm loved for who I am. For the first time in my life I'm truly happy. So happy I even stopped thinking about how much older I am than you—"

"Stop right there," Bobbie yelled. "What in the merry mother fuck are you talking about, Grace?"

Grace was shocked for only a second, then laughed until her eyes watered, and even when she could finally talk she continued to chuckle between words. "I'm almost ten years older than you are—" She stopped talking at the look Bobbie gave her, and when she felt Bobbie trying to stand up, she began kissing her, with the intended and desired result. "I know it doesn't matter and I don't care. Please accept that truth and promise me that you do."

"Then why mention it, Grace? First, you are only six years older than I am, not almost ten, and it obviously is a matter of concern to you though I don't give a tinker's damn."

Grace shook her head. "Not a concern as much as it was a fear, Bobbie, another reason to wonder why you'd want me. But I no longer fear that you don't want me or wonder why you do, and that's the truth, I promise."

With a speculative look Bobbie asked, "So why do I want you?"

With a shrewd look Grace replied, "Because I'm brilliant and beautiful and damn good in bed!"

Both cars were in the garage and the door was down, signaling that both parents were at home and not intending to venture out. Must have been a rough week at work for them, Grace thought. The kitchen door was unlocked, signaling that one or both of her siblings had stayed out all night. Grace smelled fresh-brewed coffee but nothing else and was glad she'd stopped for the bag of pastries she usually brought on Sunday. She placed it on the kitchen table.

Her parents sat in their usual places in the den, her father stretched out on the sofa, the book he'd been reading on his chest. Her mother was in the recliner chair, glasses low on her nose and the book open in her lap, giving the appearance she was reading. Grace knew better.

"Hi, Mama," she said softly, and her mother jerked upright.

"Grace! What are you doing here?" she demanded, not so softly, startling her father into wakefulness. He sat up quickly, his book hitting the floor.

"When did you get here?" he asked, peering at Grace.

"Just now. Hello, Dad."

"You didn't come empty-handed, did you?" he asked.

"No, Dad. There's a bag in the kitchen—"

He didn't wait to hear the end of the sentence. He was on his feet, out the door, and into the kitchen in a flash. She could hear the rustle of the bag as he withdrew the contents and opened the boxes. At her mother's query, Grace said she'd brought a pie, a cake, and a dozen doughnuts.

"But what did you bring me?"

"That's for everyone, Mom—"

"But I told you I wanted one of those cashmere sweaters, Grace." Grace looked startled, so her mother reminded her daughter in detail about her desire to have the kind of cashmere sweater Grace wore on her Christmas visit. "And I told you I wanted one just like it. I know you remember."

Grace remembered. She also remembered her admonition to herself not to be upset or hurt by anything her parents said or did. "Have you ever been proud of me?" Grace asked her mother.

"Been proud of you for what?" her father asked, returning with a plate containing cake, pie, and doughnuts in one hand, a mug of steaming hot coffee in the other.

"For anything, Dad. For anything I've ever done or accomplished."

They both looked at her, puzzled, though she wasn't sure about what. They both surely understood the question. Were they puzzled by the question or unable to think of an answer?

"I'll ask again. Have you ever been proud of me?"

"What does that have to do with my sweater?" her mother demanded.

"Maybe everything," Grace replied.

"And why are you here on Saturday, anyway, dressed like . . . like . . ."

"Like a woman out on Saturday afternoon, shopping and running errands?"

Grace wore deep green wool slacks with a matching sweater and chocolate fleece-lined boots. She had a camel hair shawl around her shoulders, the same color as the swing coat in the trunk of the car.

"Where are you going shopping?"

Ah hell! Stepped in that one, didn't I? "Since I'm here in Queens I'm going to some of the ethnic markets for seasonings and spices. Then I'll visit some in Harlem—and by the way, I've moved."

She fished a piece of paper from the pocket of her slacks and put it on the table. "My new address. The phone number is the same, not that you've ever called it. Maybe I should write it down in case you've lost it?"

"Oh good! You can let your brother and sister have your old apartment," her mother said, reading the address on the paper.

"It's not available," Grace said, moving toward the back door.

"What do you mean it's not available? Why not?"

"Because I've sublet it," Grace said wearily.

"Did you think to ask your brother and sister first?" her mother snapped.

"I most certainly did not," Grace snapped back. "They don't have a job between them. How do you think they'd pay the rent?" Grace's parents eyed her as if she'd spoken in tongues. "Surely you don't think I'd pay the rent for them."

"You can afford it, Grace. Why wouldn't you help them out?" This from her father whose tone and facial expression proclaimed him a reasonable man.

"Why don't *you* help them out," Grace replied, "since you're so worried about them, or are you tired of them doing nothing to help you out? Did you ever care or worry about me the way you worry about them?" She stood there, looking from one to the other, making it clear that she expected answers, but it was clear from the looks on their faces that no answers would be forthcoming.

Her parents seemed too confused by the questions to formulate answers, and by the time they realized that answers were, in fact, expected, she was making her way out of the house and into the yard. Keys already in hand, she opened the trunk to retrieve her coat and purse, quickly donning the coat and unlocking the car. It was cold and windy, and while there was no sign of the snow that was forecast, the scent of it was in the air. She didn't wait for the car to warm up or take the time to turn around. She just backed out, thankful that the residential street was free of the normal Queens Saturday afternoon traffic.

Heading toward the shopping district several blocks away, she pulled to the curb and put the gear in park, leaving the car running for warmth. She had been in her parents' house for only a few minutes, yet it felt like an eternity.

Sitting in the warm car, she had to acknowledge that's how it had always felt, and how, in truth, she had known it would feel today. She was sad but not upset. Or angry. And definitely not surprised, though she did wish there had been more feeling, more of any emotion, from her parents about whether they ever felt proud of her. Was it such a hard question? Clearly it was not a thought they'd ever had or discussed.

She was, however, truly angry that the still visible bruises on her face, especially around her eye, had elicited no response either. They simply didn't see her. They saw her clothes, her jewelry, her car, and whatever she brought into the house for them. *But where was their care for her?* It was always there for the younger siblings who did nothing and contributed nothing. *Am I jealous?*

She quickly answered in the negative. She wasn't the problem, nor, in truth, were her younger siblings, nor were the two older ones who had cut themselves out of the family totally. The problem was the parents. The sooner she accepted them as they were and decided how best to interact with them, the better. She put the car in gear and headed to her favorite shopping district.

Boy Bobby called up every memory of his grandmother to create the elderly woman he would portray for his revenge scheme in the market. Girl Bobbie said he completely looked the part— except that his body movements didn't say "old" the same way that his wardrobe did. But Boy Bobby made an excellent point. "That guy is going to see white hair and a cane and a pair of spectacles riding low on my nose. He's going to see what he expects to see—an old Negro woman, walking slowly and carefully." They set off for the market, taking a taxi almost to the front door.

The sidewalk was crowded—it was, after all, Saturday afternoon—and music came from everywhere, infusing the shoppers and walkers and errand runners with happy energy. The density of the crowd helped to mitigate the frigid wind that roamed Broadway as if it, too, was window shopping.

The Bs stood on the curb where they'd exited the taxi, watching the crowd, but really keeping their eyes on the front door of the market Bobby would enter. They saw a closed front door. Every other business on both sides of the busy avenue had left the front doors open in spite of the cold, windy weather to invite and entice people to enter. They wanted customers to have a look around, to chat with friends and neighbors, and most certainly to purchase goods. The open shop doors were welcoming. The closed door was telling locals they were not welcome.

"I wonder if there's anyone in there with him," Bobby said as they made their way through the crowd to the closed front door of the American Veg and Fruit Market.

Bobbie shook her head. The market was three blocks from her Black Mask office, and she walked past there a couple of times every day. "He's always been here alone."

"How can he afford to stay open without customers?"

"Fueled by hate," Bobbie answered, separating from Bobby so he could enter the store alone.

No welcome bell jingled when he opened the door. The man behind the counter to the left looked up from the paper he was reading and scowled. "What do you want in my store?" he demanded in the heavily accented English of the Italian immigrant just off the boat in the America for which he'd named his market.

"Groceries," Bobby replied quietly. "Where are your baskets?" he asked, looking all around.

"Where is your money?" the man demanded, finally looking directly at Bobby. He was older than Bobby was pretending to be.

Bobby met his gaze. "I beg your pardon?"

"You don't hear so good? I ask can you afford to shop here. I got no time for you people who got no money."

Bobby shook his head dismissively and walked away from the man. "I'm not confused about where I am."

"What you mean about where you are?"

"I mean this isn't Bergdorf Goodman," Bobby said, studying a display of detergent.

The man came from behind the counter faster than his apparent age would have suggested was possible. Bobby didn't turn around, but he was fully aware of the man's every move.

Bobby turned suddenly, facing the furious shopkeeper, who stumbled a bit as he suddenly halted his forward movement. "I want to see what money you got!" he yelled angrily, spittle flying from his lips.

"You'll see it when it's time to pay," Bobby said, holding up the kind of black change purse so many elderly women carried. It was in his left hand and the man grabbed for it, as Bobby raised the cane in his right hand and swung it at the shopkeeper's knees. The whack sent the man to the floor, releasing a furious stream of Italian. Bobby understood him though he knew not a word of the man's language. Bobby backed away a few steps and watched while the man's anger receded, and he climbed to his feet. He was still breathing heavily though his face was losing the dangerous-looking brick red color. He glared at Bobby. Then he stared harder at him, eyes narrowed to slits, and Bobby knew he was thinking that this was no old woman.

"I don't want your people in my store."

"I don't see your people lined up to come in. In fact, I don't see your people in this neighborhood at all."

Another stream of angry Italian and the man pushed Bobby toward the front door, hard enough that he almost lost his footing. "You think you can throw me out on the sidewalk like you did that old woman last week? You know she's still in the hospital?"

"I don't care," the man said, grabbing Bobby's arm, pulling him toward the door. Bobby pried the man's fingers from his arm, bending them back with force until the man howled, and Bobby released them.

"Make this the last time you try to steal money from an old Negro woman. Do you hear me? The last time."

"What can you do? Nothing. This is my store."

"And it can burn to the ground," Bobby said menacingly. "How much insurance do you have, old man?"

The fear in the old man's eyes was the answer Bobby sought.

Bobby left the shop, and as he waited outside for Bobbie to arrive, he remembered the conversation with his boss from a few nights before.

"I've been up here in Harlem for a long time, young Mr. Mason. Most of my life, in fact," Bobby's boss said as they shared a beer. Bobby's workday was over but Mr. G hadn't yet switched the phone over to the emergency number.

"It was mostly Jewish up here, and a lot of other Europeans. Then, over in East Harlem, where the Puerto Ricans are now, that's where all the Italians were. Lots of the businesses up here are still owned by those people; they just don't live here anymore. Some of 'em treat their customers the right way and some don't."

Bobby looked pensive as his boss continued. *"Like the one who wouldn't deliver the furniture you wanted to buy, remember? A lot of the Italians—those that are left— are angry and taking it out on your people and the Puerto Ricans, and it's not your fault. People are taking care of their own, like they should, and the Italians have a problem."*

"What do you mean?"

"If I had a business, I would get insurance from a Jewish insurance company. If you had a business, you could get insurance from a Negro insurance company. Same

*with the Puerto Ricans. The problems
the Italians have is that most of them left
Harlem, especially the businessmen—the
insurance companies and the undertakers
and the dry cleaners and the shoe repair
places. Those who are left can't get their
buddies to give them insurance here."*

He felt Bobbie arrive to stand beside him and told her what happened when he was inside, including his implied threat of arson.

"Do you think he's seen the light and had a conversion?" she asked.

"Hell no. That evil old man will die full of anger and hate." He looked at the store and its closed door, and at that moment he heard the lock turn and saw the "closed" sign go up in the window.

"Thank goodness you had the insurance card to play," Bobbie said, "or we would have had no leverage."

"I hope they believe all the lies they invented about us so they'll believe we would really burn down their stores," Bobby replied.

"One day we just might. We can't continue to beg them for fair treatment. We've been doing that for too long, and it's getting real old and tired," Bobbie said, sounding as weary as her words.

"Yeah. Makes Methuselah look like a baby boy."

They walked two blocks up the street for part two of their plan. There were two markets, and both stores were known for rotten produce, sour milk and orange juice, moldy bread, and barely stocked shelves. Yet people still shopped in these markets because these were the closest, without the need to pay for a subway, or bus or taxi ride to and from a better market.

A dozen or so young people stood outside each of the markets waiting for The Bs to arrive and get them started on their mission. They'd distribute hundreds of leaflets to passers-by informing them of the markets' continued disrespect of their Negro customers—and *all* of their customers were Negroes. The rotten vegetables and fruit, the bugs in the flour and cornmeal, the sour milk and orange juice, would no longer be tolerated.

The young people watched as the would-be shoppers read and discussed the information printed on the leaflets. They stood by ready to answer questions. Then The Bs were back, each taking a handful of leaflets and entering the first market. They'd give the shopkeeper a leaflet and tell him that the sale of substandard products to Negro customers would no longer be tolerated or accepted. The store owner responded as expected. But they did not expect The Bs' upcoming response.

Armed with knives they sliced open bags of flour and sugar over which they poured sour milk and juice, and into the soggy, smelly mess they smashed rotten tomatoes and bananas and lettuce and cabbage, finally tossing hard, moldy bread into the putrid pile. They moved so quickly the dumbfounded store owner, paralyzed and speechless, did and said nothing.

Finally, the enraged shopkeeper made the mistake of attacking. Bobby, young, strong, and trained by the US Army to defend himself, deftly deposited the store owner into the fetid, soggy mess on his floor. They left a handful of flyers on the counter and suggested the owner read and understand. Then they told him he had forty-eight hours to clean up and restock.

He looked terrified and something resembling ashamed, nodding his head up and down like a bouncing ball, trying and failing to speak. His bouncing head led The Bs to believe he acquiesced.

They ran to the second market where the actions were repeated. The merchant reminded Bobby of the one down the street: He yelled and snarled and shook his fist at them. He pointed at the mess they'd made and cursed them. He threw their flyers into the mess on the floor, still screaming and cursing. The Bs, motionless and silent, watched and prepared to defend themselves if necessary. When he finally ran out of steam, Bobby asked, "How much insurance do you have?" Bobbie placed a few fresh flyers on the counter, and they left, running into an alleyway out of sight.

Exhaling sighs of relief because they knew things could easily have gone very badly, they exchanged weary grins. Girl Bobbie told Boy Bobby to go home and get out of his costume while she helped hand out more flyers that urged Negroes not to shop where they were disrespected while also asking shopkeepers to respect all their customers or be prepared for the consequences.

The flyer, with the words "Attention Please Read" in large block letters at the top, didn't specify the nature of the consequences but Bobbie knew word would spread quickly about what had happened in the two markets with the worst reputations. She told the young people to deny all knowledge of recent events.

Bobbie walked away slowly, paying close and careful attention to every kind of store she passed. She entered a combination dry cleaner-shoe shop that she hadn't noticed before. It was a corner shop with its window facing Broadway and the entrance on 143rd Street. The bell tinkled when she opened the door and the proprietors looked up, then away. A man was behind the counter to the left, repairing what appeared to be a work boot, and a woman was behind the counter directly facing Bobbie, sewing a button on a blouse.

"Good day," Bobbie said, receiving no response. She walked toward the woman and placed a flyer on the counter, then approached the counter in front of the man and did the same thing. She left without another word, turning the corner and standing out of their field of vision. She saw them read the flyer, then look up, as if looking for her. They looked at each other, worried, then angry.

Bobbie used a dry cleaner on 150th and Grace used one near the hospital, both owned by Negroes. This one, not owned by Negroes, was called Pietro's. She'd have to find out if there was another dry cleaner nearby, owned by someone who would at least acknowledge a greeting when a customer entered.

She walked back to the market where Saturday shoppers still mingled on the sidewalk and where the young people were still handing out flyers, encouraged that people were reading and discussing them. She had written "Don't Do Business at Pietro's Dry Cleaners and Shoe Repair" on a flyer beneath the heading. She approached the young man who appeared to be the student leader and showed it to him. "Is it all right that I added this?" She told him why. He grabbed the flyer from her and sprinted over to a young woman. He showed her Bobbie's flyer and, after an animated discussion, the two of them hurried over to Bobbie.

"Where exactly is this store?" the young woman asked. Bobbie told her and she jotted the information in a small notebook. She thanked Bobbie and hurried back to her friends, immediately engaging them in a discussion involving the name and address of Pietro's.

Bobbie said to the young man, "May I take some of these flyers with me?"

"Where's this Pietro's?" Joyce asked, her brow wrinkling as she tried to picture it. A Harlem native, there wasn't much she wasn't familiar with, but a slight head shake indicated no knowledge of the dry cleaners/tailor.

"Are you telling us there's an effort afoot to do something about these markets?" Eileen asked, "and you have a list of them; you know where they are?"

"Yep, and Pietro's will be added to the list of targets by the end of the day." She explained how Bobby had met and allied with a group of students at City College to actively advocate for and pursue change for the treatment of Negroes in Harlem.

"I've heard about these students," Joyce said. "People are talking about them and they're attracting a good bit of attention. From what I can gather this isn't a seat-of-their-pants endeavor."

"Bobby says they're well-organized," Bobbie said. "One of them has a relative down South somewhere that's part of an organization—"

"I think I may have heard something about this." Joyce explained that a friend of hers, a professor in the History Department, had taken a sabbatical to go South with another professor to teach the principles of nonviolent resistance to people looking to put an end to Jim Crow segregation. "From what I hear they've not been welcomed with open arms by the powers that be—the Colored ones or the white ones," she said, "and though I completely support the intent, I quite frankly fear for him, for all of them."

"As well you should," Bobbie said. She inhaled deeply as Eileen and Joyce each took and held one of her hands. Neither of them needed to say anything, so Bobbie said to Joyce, "Please let me know if I can help," and Joyce knew she meant financially because they both knew she would keep her pledge never to venture into the Southern United States. Then she gave each of them a sheaf of papers clipped together and stood up to get lunch to the table. She had, after all, promised to feed them, but she wanted to give them time to read her Black Mask report, so she dawdled a bit in the kitchen before bringing in the food.

"Wonderful, fabulous!" Eileen enthused as Joyce capped her pen and added applause to the verbal praise, along with a suggestion:

"You really should be the Executive Director—"

"Not happening, not ever." Bobbie slapped her hands together in the up-and-down motion that meant hell no. "I did what you asked me to do and I'm done, finished."

"But you really did crystallize all of the thoughts and ideas and hopes and wishful thinking of everyone into a concise, understandable—" Eileen began.

"And doable!" Joyce chimed in.

"...document that really is a blueprint," Eileen said, blowing a kiss to Joyce.

"I just listened to the concerns and desires of your committee members. In the three or four meetings I attended, not once did the focus change, not once did people disagree about what the objective was, which made my job easy—"

"Ha!" Eileen scoffed. "Grace said you described the Black Mask job as a pain in the ass that you wished you'd never agreed to do and which you continued only out of love and friendship."

"So you consider us friends?" Joyce feigned disbelief while controlling a grin.

"And do you really love us?" Eileen asked. "I want to hear you say it."

"I love you a bushel and a peck," Bobbie sang.

"But are you really and truly finished with Black Mask?" Eileen asked. "And if so, Bobbie, what's the real reason?"

Tears welled in Bobbie's eyes. "What happened to Grace—"

"Was out of your control, Bobbie. You know that." Joyce's voice was gentle but adamant.

"If I had been more available to her, maybe there wouldn't have been space for anyone to get inside her head and fill it with crap."

Eileen held her hands. "That may or may not be true, but this is: you never again need worry that Grace doubts you, Bobbie."

"You can't know that, Eileen."

"I can, Bobbie, and I do. And I think you know it, too. And I know you know how important her work is to her. She can't do it if she's worried about you, and you can't do your work effectively if you're worried about her."

"You and Joyce worry about each other."

"Actually, Bobbie, we don't. The love, the care and concern, are always there, but there's no worry," Joyce said gently with a smile to match. "We each have full, busy days, and knowing that we will be together with the children at the end of those days is what gets us through them, not worrying about what could happen to us."

Bobbie sat quietly. How had she known these women for so long—for years—and failed to recognize them as friends, for that's what they were? "Thank you," she said. "Now maybe I can figure out what my work is so it can keep my mind busy and not worrying about Grace."

"Your work is The Slow Drag, whatever it is you're doing with Bobby to improve conditions for the people unable to leave the neighborhood, your music, and Black Mask."

Bobbie pointed to the document: "There's your Black Mask."

"And it needs you to see it up and running."

"Your ideas and insights are so direct and clear."

"And the money you raised at the Christmas ball makes it possible to get started," Joyce added, enumerating on her fingers the ideas and suggestions from Bobbie's report. "I agree that we should hire the three people you suggest right away."

"And where will they do the Black Mask work? At their dining room tables? Don't we need to locate space first before we hire people?"

Bobbie sighed. She should have known better than to think she could deliver a report and walk away. "Would you like to see the space I've been calling The Black Mask Office?"

—m— —m— —m—

When a taxi swerved across two lanes of traffic and screeched to a halt in front of her, she threw open the door and barely had sufficient time to fling herself in and slam the door before the cabbie drove off. He'd have her home in no time.

Bobbie had the key in the lock when a paralyzing shock surged through her. Music and talking and laughing was coming from within. It sounded like her family, parents and brother, but that couldn't . . . *But who the hell? Wait! That IS my family. My new family. Grace is in there.*

She turned the key, and the door opened to the sound of happiness and the scent of food cooking to welcome her home.

"Hey, Girl Bobbie, 'bout time you got yourself home!" Boy Bobby called out as he hurried to meet her at the door.

"Grace, Bobbie's home!" Myrtle called out, and Grace emerged from the kitchen, a chef's hat flopping to the left and an apron wrapped around her, arms outstretched in welcome. Jack and Thelma joined them in welcoming her home. This really was her family.

"As cold and dark as it is, I knew you'd be home soon," Grace said, hugging and kissing her in welcome, as if she'd been away for a long time. The reality was that Grace, that they all, were just happy she was home. With them. Where she belonged.

Grace hurried back to the kitchen, Bobby took her coat, Thelma handed her a drink, and she followed Jack to the sofa facing the fireplace. "You playing hooky?" she asked quietly as they sat.

Jack shook her head and explained that she was at the bar at nine o'clock that morning, setting up for the night, after which she went home and took a nap. "Justine and me alternate on this schedule, which means we alternate long work nights with short work nights, and so far we like it." Bobbie gave her a one-armed hug and changed the subject as Bobby, Thelma and Myrtle joined them in front of the fire.

"I'm going to the kitchen to make certain Grace isn't lonesome," Bobbie said, "and to find out what smells so good."

"She won't tell us," Thelma said with a pout. "Whenever I go into the kitchen she puts the top back on the pots. Dinner is to be a surprise."

Bobbie hurried across the living room and into the kitchen, just in time to see Grace put the top on the biggest kettle she'd ever seen outside of a restaurant. "Whatever that is, it smells heavenly," she said. "What is it?"

"A surprise," Grace said, taking her hand and leading her out of the kitchen.

"When do we get to eat this surprise?" Bobby demanded, meeting them at the kitchen door with a drink for Grace and an audible abdominal rumble from him. "We are all starving, and continuing to inhale those fabulous aromas isn't helping."

"Then let's eat." Grace beckoned them forward. She had bought new bowls, cutlery, wine glasses, and napkins.

"This is as beautiful as the food smells," Bobbie whispered to her. "Is this a special occasion?"

"Every day with you is a special occasion," Grace whispered, then told them that the dish was a West African stew, from a recipe she'd obtained years ago from a med school classmate. "But this is the first time I've made it, and I made it today because all of you are so special to me."

Bobbie poured wine and raised her glass. "To Amazing Grace with all the love in our hearts."

"To Amazing Grace!"

They drank three bottles of wine and ate all the stew, which annoyed Bobby no end because he had planned to take some home. Jack went off to work, and Grace was sent to stoke the fire while everyone else cleaned the kitchen.

"Y'all could've left me some stew," Bobby groused, up to

his elbows in soapy dishwater. "What am I supposed to eat for dinner tomorrow?"

"You are welcome to come eat with us any time," Myrtle told him. "You know that."

"And you're always welcome to eat with us," Bobbie said, "and you know that as well. You and Jack Jackson will never go hungry, not as long as we have pots, pans, and a stove."

Soothed and mollified, Bobby gave the final washed pot to Thelma to dry and for Myrtle to put away. He looked all around the clean kitchen. "Where's the cake? I know we didn't eat the cake, too."

"What cake?" Bobbie asked.

Myrtle ran from the kitchen into the living room, calling Grace. "Where's the cake?"

Grace hurried back into the kitchen to reassure them. "I can't believe I forgot about the cake. It's on the shelf behind the bar. The kitchen was too hot, and I didn't want the frosting to melt."

The three-layer chocolate cake was pounced upon and devoured as if a whole pot of West African peanut stew served over rice hadn't been consumed. A second pot of coffee was made, the fire was stoked, and with everyone sated and relaxed the conversation flowed.

It began with the flyers. The Bs decided to keep their involvement in "certain activities" to themselves, primarily because of Grace. She would be furious to learn that they had engaged in acts of violence, no matter what the reason. She still was slightly angry with Bobbie for beating Von Thompkins, and with Bobby for whatever he did to the doctor who hurt Jack. He never discussed with Grace what he did that night—he refused to—but Bobbie would never get Grace's words out of her head about what she did to Von. *I understand, my love, why you did what you did. Von Thompkins is a vile and disgusting person, but if you behave as she did, that makes you what she is, and you're not that, Bobbie Hilliard. I'd hate to see you become that because you love me. That would transform our love and would make it something less than beautiful.*

Bobbie didn't think further violence would flow from the morning's demonstrations at the markets. Yes, there was anger. People were tired of the humiliation of constantly being mistreated in shops and stores, and tired of being polite and accepting, either excusing the nasty behavior or pretending that it didn't matter. Tired past the point of exhaustion for the humiliating mistreatment that was for no reason other than the color of their skin.

"Part of the problem is," Thelma said, "most of those people don't have anywhere else to go. I know you all have noticed how many Negroes in Harlem are recent arrivals from down home where this kind of treatment is the norm—"

"That doesn't make it all right," Bobby challenged.

"No, that's not what I'm saying." She raised a hand to calm him, and he blew her a kiss of apology and calmed himself. She continued. "If the store owners and shopkeepers can make money being rude and selling spoiled milk and rotten produce, they have no incentive to change anything."

"So how do we effect any change?" Grace asked. "How do we give them incentives to change?"

"Thanks to Joyce, I've been reading the writings of a man named Bayard Rustin. He's a scholar and a civil rights activist—and a not-so-secret homosexual—" Bobbie began.

"What? How does he get away with that?" Thelma exclaimed.

"He is apparently so brilliant that people focus more on what he writes and says than on the fact that he doesn't have—or want—a wife," Bobbie replied, adding that he also taught at City College, which is how Joyce knew about him.

"And what does he say or write that will tell us how to change the behavior of white merchants in Harlem?" Grace repeated.

"We boycott them," Bobbie replied, and the silence of

confusion reigned. She elaborated. "As I understand it, one store is chosen and no Negroes shop there for a period of time—a week or a month—however long it takes for the owner to feel the pinch in his purse and cry uncle. The hope is that the lesson will spread and that other merchants will fall in line. If not, then another store will be targeted. And, if necessary, another."

"It could work," Myrtle said slowly, and thoughtfully.

Grace held up a flyer. "Who's in charge of this? Where did these come from?"

"We got them from some young people who looked like college students," Bobby said. "They were in the block between 139th and 140th—"

"And if these boycotts take place, who will suffer if there are repercussions?" Grace asked. "These college students?"

"What are you asking, Grace?" Bobbie asked. "Or what are you saying?"

Grace expelled a sad sigh. "Whenever we fight back, we get knocked down harder. If the boycott is successful, they will look for someone to blame—"

"And they will find no one," Bobby snarled. He held up a flyer. "Nobody's name is on this. What can they do? Walk up and down Broadway, asking every Negro in sight if they know who's responsible?"

"I just don't want any harm to come to any one of us for standing up for ourselves." Grace shook her head, angry now instead of sad. "Enough of us have suffered at the hands of those people for no reason other than the fact of our existence. We cannot, we must not, give them something they can perceive as cause for more violence against us."

Bobbie took one of Grace's hands, Bobby the other, and the five friends sat in contemplative silence for several moments. They didn't need to speak their thoughts. Each of them knew, firsthand, the horrible truth of Grace's statement, none more than Bobbie. Her whole family had been slaughtered by a white

Georgia highway patrol deputy for the crime of being Colored and driving a brand-new Packard with New York license plates. But they were discussing the here and now, the reality of being Colored and living in New York City. And Grace was saying what exactly?

That it was best to do nothing? To wait until the store owners and landlords were ready to change? No. Not Grace. Not possible. Yes, she was gentle and generous and kind and compassionate, but she was not a coward. They all knew how she had stood up for Jack against the hospital administrator, putting her career on the line.

"Look," Bobbie said, "I don't profess to know everything about what Mr. Rustin believes, and I definitely will do more research, but I do know that he advocates social change through nonviolent action. He studied it in India beside Gandhi—"

"India?" Grace said.

"Gandhi?" Bobby said.

"So the boycotts definitely would be nonviolent?" Myrtle asked.

"If I were in charge—and I'm not—but if I were, I would call for select boycotts and they most certainly would be nonviolent," Bobbie said, Verne's parting words about Von ringing in her ears. *You shoulda killed her when you had the chance.*

Grace knew full well that The Bs had some involvement in the effort to force more respectful treatment of Negroes in the markets that fed the community—many hundreds, thousands, of people who lived on and off Broadway and Seventh Avenue from 120th Street up to 150th Street.

"When you find those young people, advise them to put the name of an organization on the flyers. Something like 'Negro Citizens of Harlem for Just Treatment,'" said Grace.

"Why?" Thelma asked. "Are you saying they should invent an organization?"

"Not an organization, a name. So those who don't like what

we're doing—and there will be those who won't like it at all—will look for someone to blame instead of taking out their anger on helpless citizens." Grace smiled inwardly at the thought of the police and the city council and the New York City version of a southern white citizens council searching for an organization called Negro Citizens of Harlem for Just Treatment.

"You think they'll be looking for payback?" Myrt asked, and Grace's shrug said not only didn't she care what "they" might do, but she was tired of talking about them. "I think I'd like a drink," she said. Both Bs said they would, too, heading for the bar.

"What can I fix for you two?" Bobbie asked Myrt and Thelma. They looked at each other with uncertainty.

"We were thinking of meeting friends at The Slow Drag, but we're so comfortable here," said Thelma.

"Besides I hear you make a Manhattan to die for," Myrtle said, "and I want another piece of cake before I leave."

Bobbie made the drinks, and then she put more music on the record player and sat on the ottoman at Grace's feet as they drank and talked more.

"So," Myrt said slowly, "Bobbie, you really won't be returning to The Drag?"

Bobbie shook her head. "Not as long as Jack and Justine are keeping to the schedule they're doing now, and the way they're doing it. I'll go in on Mondays and do the books and supervise the cleanup, and of course I'll go in to work the bar if I'm really needed, but otherwise, no."

Though Grace had never spoken to Bobbie about it—and never would have—she was pleased and relieved that she'd no longer be working until two and three o'clock in the morning. She was also saddened there would be no more fast or slow dancing with Bobbie at The Drag. But she would always remember that one time.

Later, when they were getting ready for bed, Bobbie said "Thank you for tonight, Grace. And by the way, you should add

Chef Extraordinaire to your list of superlatives." She waited for the half a second it took Grace to grasp the reference. She felt sleep about to take over but wanted to say again how much she enjoyed and appreciated the evening. "What made you think to do a dinner party?"

"I suppose I have my parents to thank." Grace sighed. "I was angry and hurt and sad when I left their house. I pulled over, parked, and really and truly thought—about them and who and how they are, and about me and who and how I am. I knew I needed to let go—maybe not of them entirely but of my expectations of them. Then I had the most spectacular revelation: I have another family. I have you. I have Boy Bobby and I have Jack and I have Myrt and Thelma. People who love me for who and how I am, not for the things I have or can give. These are people I love, and I love to cook, so why not feed the people I love?" She yawned. "And that's how dinner happened."

"I had the same thought," Bobbie said, telling Grace what had happened at the front door: hearing voices, then panicking that somehow Von was back. "No, it was just my family."

"You and me against the world, kid," Grace said, grinning and brandishing her fists like Jersey Joe Walcott or Sugar Ray Robinson.

"I'll bring you Sunday brunch in bed, Gracie." When there was no response, Bobbie thought she'd drifted into sleep. She had not.

"What will you have Miz Maggie send?" a very awake Grace asked.

Doing her best to stifle the laugh in her throat, Bobbie asked, "What's your preference? Fried chicken wings and grits, or salmon croquettes and grits?"

Grace made no attempt to stifle her own laughter. "I've unearthed the waffle iron, and I bought salmon at the market. So, salmon croquettes and waffles tomorrow morning?"

"Are you really sleepy, Gracie?" She wasn't. She also wasn't finished talking.

"I want to remodel the kitchen."

"Fine," Bobbie said, her attention already focused elsewhere.

CHAPTER SIX

Grace grabbed the phone in the middle of the second ring. It was 4:35 a.m. "Dr. Hannon," she answered, no hint of sleep in her voice, her tone as warm and gentle as always. She listened, asked two questions, listened a few seconds more, said, "I'll be right there," and was out of bed and heading for the bathroom so fast Bobbie would have missed it had she not been watching. The doctor had years of practice waking, rising, and dressing in the dark, and going where she was needed on the run.

Bobbie quickly rose as well and pulled a sweatshirt and pants on top of the flannel pajamas, added thick socks, and hurried to the hall closet for boots, a knit cap, and heavy jacket. She was in the kitchen at the back door, keys in hand, when Grace hurried in.

"Thanks, love," she said, rushing out of the door that Bobbie held open. Then they were down the steps, into the garage, in the car, and speeding into a traffic-free street in less than a minute.

"What is it?" Bobbie asked.

"A woman in bad shape. I don't know the details." They hit traffic on Broadway. It was Broadway, after all. Bobbie maneuvered in and out, expertly changing lanes, and turned into the driveway of Harlem Hospital used by doctors and ambulances. Grace was out of the car before it stopped.

"I'll leave the car in the garage—"

Grace shook her head. "I may well be here all day. I'll call you." And she was gone.

Bobbie drove home much more slowly, pondering Grace's words: *I may well be here all day.* A woman was in dire straits. Someone's mother, wife, sister, lover, best friend, daughter. Her own mother had been all those things and was beyond help when she reached the Colored hospital in Atlanta. If the woman upstairs in Harlem Hospital could be helped this morning, Dr. Grace Hannon would help her. If it were humanly possible, Grace Hannon would be the physician to every Negro woman and girl in Harlem. But right now she would content herself with bringing all of her knowledge, skill, and compassion to the operating room where a woman in bad shape awaited her. And if she couldn't be helped, couldn't be saved, by Dr. Grace Hannon, then all the hands of all the doctors within the Harlem Hospital could not have changed that outcome, but at least she would have been assisted into that other place by someone who looked like her.

Bobbie wiped away tears, her still-unhealed heart aching with the knowledge of what must have been the final sights, sounds, knowledge of her murdered family members, of her murdered mother.

Bobbie returned home and slept for another couple of hours. She was washing her breakfast dishes when she remembered what Grace had said last night: *I want to remodel the kitchen.*

Bobbie looked all around, realizing she wasn't familiar with many kitchens. Perhaps if she cooked, she would have paid more attention to the places where cooking happened. Perhaps if her mother had been more interested in cooking, or if her father had been more interested in eating at home instead of in restaurants. Grace was a fabulous cook, and she enjoyed cooking. Loved it in fact. So from now on she would pay attention to what Grace did in the kitchen.

Bobbie looked around the kitchen smiling, but suddenly stopped. The kitchen would be a construction site disaster area—for how long? Plaster dust . . .

Ennyday came running when she pulled into the garage where he worked. "Hello, Girl Bobbie!" he called out, extending a greasy palm to her. She shook it with a greeting as warm and enthusiastic as his had been. Boy Bobby had taught him that it was considered good manners to shake the hand of a person you haven't seen in a long time.

"I'm glad to see you, Ennyday. How are you?"

"I am very good, Girl Bobbie. Can I help you?"

"Do you have time to wash Grace's car right now? I have to take it to her at the hospital."

Bobbie looked at the boy's grease-stained hands. He looked at his hands, front and back. He looked at Grace's not very dirty white Caddy, then back at his hands. He ran to the sink on the other side of the garage as a man who was under a Pontiac hood emerged, wiped his hands on a cloth, and came toward Bobbie.

"'Morning, Miss Hilliard," he said.

"Good morning, Mr. Turner. Nice to see you. It's been a while."

"Yes it has. Not since . . ." He didn't finish his sentence, and he didn't need to—Bobbie knew. "Anyway, I was wondering if you got any interest in selling that Buick?"

"I've got every interest in selling that Buick, Mr. Turner. You have any interest in buying it?" And after absolutely no haggling, they struck a deal and he agreed to pick up the car that evening.

Ninety minutes later Bobbie parked Grace's sparkling clean car in the doctors' parking lot at the Hospital. The guard watched her closely. He didn't know her, but he did know Grace's car. She nodded at him and hurried back home. The phone rang before she had a chance to remove her coat and hat. It was Eileen, wondering if she could stop by before heading home, and of course Bobbie said yes. She liked Eileen and Joyce more each time she saw them.

While she waited, she called Grace's office. "Have you heard anything?" she asked Myrtle as soon as she answered the phone.

"Indirectly," came the response. "I understand that the woman was so badly injured Grace had to summon The Boys for assistance repairing all the internal damage, and of course they brought Thelma who, thankfully, is able to make quick update phone calls."

"Will the woman survive?" Bobbie asked, nearly whispering. Perhaps if she didn't speak the question aloud the answer wouldn't be bad news.

Myrt shrugged, which of course Bobbie couldn't see, so she said, "There is no way to know."

"Well," Bobbie said, remembering the other reason for her call, "please tell Grace that her car is in the doctors' lot in the hospital garage. I dropped her off this morning."

"Thanks, Bobbie. I'll tell her."

"And Myrt?"

"I'll call as soon as I know something, I promise."

"And Myrt?"

Nurse Myrtle Lewis laughed and hung up on her. She didn't need to be told to take care of Grace. She'd been taking care of Grace Hannon since long before there was a Bobbie Hilliard to take care of Grace.

Eileen arrived at Bobbie's home, gave her a one-arm hug and dangled a bag with the other. "I brought coffee and beignets."

"Wherever did you find beignets?! The New Orleans variety

or the Paris variety? Not that I care because I will eat as many as you brought. How many did you bring?"

"Enough for us to adequately indulge ourselves and have enough to share with the two lucky women with whom we share everything," Eileen replied and gave Bobbie a piece of paper. "These are two people who want to get started immediately. Is it all right if they call you—"

Bobbie cut her off with a negative head shake. "You have the keys, Eileen; they can come and go as they please. I had a metal door hung at the street entrance so the office is safe and secure from the outside, and nobody from The Drag can get into the Black Mask office and nobody from Black Mask can get into The Drag. There's no cause for worry."

"You're not really going to leave us to our own devices." Eileen didn't ask a question; she made a statement, looking directly at Bobbie and causing momentary consternation. She knew that look. Grace used the same one. Bobbie laughed and hugged her. "You have my congratulations and my sympathy," Joyce Scott had told her when she and Grace were back on solid ground, and when Bobbie asked for an explanation Joyce had grinned and said, "You'll see." And now Bobbie was beginning to.

"I'm happy to help Black Mask whenever they need me, but why would they, Eileen?"

"Because that document you gave us, that blueprint for action someone called it, lives in your head, and people periodically want to pick your brain," Eileen said, and changed the subject almost faster than Bobbie could keep up, something else Grace did, too. "So now that we've got that out of the way, we're having a party Saturday night and of course you and Grace are invited."

"I don't really like parties, Eileen."

"But Grace does, Bobbie, and she especially loves our parties—we give good parties. And since she can no longer dance with you at The Slow Drag, you can dance with her at

212

our party. And anyway, everyone is dying to see the two of you together."

Bobbie had just been had and she knew it. Eileen knew she knew it and could barely control a triumphant smirk. "Who is the everyone you're talking about? And why would anyone be interested in seeing Grace and me together?"

"Oh for crying out loud, Bobbie Hilliard. You are hopeless as well as clueless. More than a few single women have indulged wishful and hopeful thoughts about you both. The fact that you're now together, well, hopes and fantasies have been dashed. I'm surprised you didn't hear the broken dreams crashing to the floor." She chuckled. "Though I expect Grace did." Eileen stood up, pulled on her coat and hat, and headed through the kitchen to the back door because her car was in the garage. But she stopped so suddenly Bobbie almost bumped into her. Eileen turned to face her.

"Is something wrong, Eileen?" Bobbie asked.

"Grace is transformed, Bobbie. Happiness bubbles out of every pore. And you look more at peace than . . . Grace loves you, Bobbie, like your mother loved you, and you have allowed it. You two have rescued each other. Joyce said that would happen." And with a hug and a kiss Eileen was out the door, leaving Bobbie frozen in amazement. She knew that Grace was close with both Eileen and Joyce—closer than sisters, Grace had said—but she didn't know they were her friends, too. Tears filled her eyes but she surprised herself by not weeping. And by feeling happiness rather than sadness. How and why had she deprived herself of the friendship of two such wonderful women for so long?

She was deciding whether to brew a pot of coffee or heat water for tea when she was startled by a knock on the door. Eileen returning? She hurried to unlock and open it to find Bobby Mason and a young woman shivering. She quickly let them in as a frigid wind pushed them forward and slammed the door shut. "Why didn't you come in the front door?"

"We got off the train at … Who's that very gorgeous woman who just left? You stepping out on Grace? Because I'll never forgive you if you are."

"Neither would Grace. That was her best friend, Eileen McKinley."

"Miss McKinley is a dish of vanilla ice cream with chocolate syrup."

Bobbie laughed, told herself to remember to repeat that to Jack, and said, "Actually she's Mrs. McKinley and I'll explain later." She turned her attention to the young woman whose name she did not know. After introducing herself, she learned that Patricia Carter was a student at City College. She looked familiar.

Clearly distraught, Patricia blurted "Did you hear what happened this morning? It was awful!" Bobbie looked to Boy Bobby for an explanation.

"We think a woman was pushed down the stairs in the 135th Street Station early this morning—"

"She had our flyers in her pocket! They fell out as she tumbled down the stairs and scattered all over. And she definitely was pushed; that's exactly what happened, Bobby."

"We don't know that for certain, Pat," Bobby said, striving to maintain calm, hoping it would rub off on Patricia.

"Several people saw her get pushed," Patricia insisted, nothing having rubbed off, "and they saw the son of a bitch who pushed her and saw him grab some flyers before he ran away."

Bobbie raised her hands, palms out, hoping to instill calm in Patricia and retrieve information from Bobby. If he had any. "Do we know what time this happened? Whether the woman was alone? Where she was going or coming from—"

"She was coming from her night job cleaning at the Museum of Natural History," Bobby said, "going home to 135th Street. Her husband was waiting for her—he always met her upstairs on the sidewalk, not down on the platform. It happened at about three thirty in the morning, an ambulance was called, and she was taken to Harlem Hospital."

"Were the police called?" Bobbie asked.

"Why would anyone call them?" Patricia snarled. "They never do us any good. They'd probably have arrested her instead of the piece of shit who pushed her down the steps."

"If someone pushed that woman down the stairs, and if someone saw it happen—"

"They would do nothing," Patricia exclaimed, anger and frustration pushing her to the door.

"Patricia!" Bobbie called out. "Please, just a moment," she said, and the girl came back, still looking angry enough to chew nails and spit out tacks. "If that woman was pushed down those steps," Bobbie said, "and if the flyers are the reason, you should be very careful about asking questions. Yes?"

The girl nodded. "Yes, you're right."

"And you should also be very careful about when and where you distribute flyers. Yes?"

Patricia nodded assent despite her anger. "But we can't let them stop us. We won't!"

"What 'them'?" Bobbie asked and Patricia had no answer, and the tea kettle whistled in the silence. Both Patricia and Boy Bobby declined tea or coffee or anything to eat, so Bobbie grabbed a notepad from one of the drawers. She wrote down her telephone number and gave it to the seething young woman. "Please call me if you learn anything, Patricia. And if you're interested, I have some thoughts about ways to proceed with distributing the flyers without people being harmed." Patricia gave her a speculative look, nodded, and headed for the door. She stopped Bobby when he started to follow.

"I know where I am and I can get home from here," Patricia told him. To Bobbie she said, "I always knew these were nice places, but I had no idea how nice." She opened the door and dashed out before too much frosty air could rush in.

Bobbie brewed them both a cup of her mother's favorite Constant Comment tea and told Boy Bobby about the 4:30 a.m. call summoning Grace to the hospital. "I'm wondering—"

"If it's the woman who was pushed down the subway stairs," Bobby stated.

"Myrt promised to call, and I've heard nothing, so whatever it was, it's serious, and it's still happening," Bobbie said.

"I hope to God she'll be all right," Boy Bobby prayed. "And a part of me really hopes she fell down those steps 'cause it would be too awful to think that somebody pushed her."

"I agree. So I'm changing the subject until I hear from Myrt. You hungry? Shall we go to Miz Maggie's?"

Boy Bobby shook his head and hurried out to the living room where Bobbie's telephone was on the sofa, and grabbed the receiver. "We should call Miz Maggie and have her send food. I didn't realize how hungry I was until this cup of tea told me."

Not only was the idea a good one but Benny was there ordering his lunch. He hopped a taxi, and they were all eating the best burgers and fries in Harlem in less than half an hour. Boy Bobby also learned that Miz Maggie's beloved nephew, who had been so brutally beaten several weeks ago, was out of the coma he'd been in since the beating. The bad news was that he remembered nothing of the attack that almost killed him.

"Might be a blessing," Boy Bobby said. Girl Bobbie nodded her agreement.

"A blessing how?" a confused Benny asked.

"Sometimes when we remember something awful that happened—" Bobbie began but when she didn't complete the thought, couldn't complete it, Bobby did it for her.

"It's like living the awful thing over and over again."

"You mean it keeps happening, the awful thing?" a perplexed, then worried, Benny asked, ducking his head and concentrating on his hamburger and fries, the thoughts coursing through his brain practically visible on his face. More relieved than either of them would admit at having the painful discussion concluded, the two friends talked about Mr. Turner coming over later to buy the Buick, and about Bobbie's conversation with Eileen—about her relationship with Grace being the subject of talk among certain of their friends, and how annoying Bobbie found it.

"Why are you annoyed?" Bobby asked. "Do you really think some woman—maybe many women—hadn't tried to win Grace? You took one look and claimed that prize for yourself. Of course that would be the talk at sorority meetings and bridge clubs. And I'll bet my paycheck that those who weren't eyeing Grace had their eyes on you, only you were too busy with Savoy Ballroom glamour girls to notice."

"Oh shut up, Bobby" was the only thing she could think to say, so they talked about Jack and gave thanks for her continued healing. And they talked about the weather, as New Yorkers did, and how much they wished it would finally stop snowing and being so freezing-ass cold.

"So, when does spring come to Harlem?" Boy Bobby asked.

"Usually not before about the middle of April," Bobbie replied.

"My mama read in the almanac—what's a almanac anyway?" Benny asked as the phone rang, and Bobbie hurried over to answer it, one part of her silent prayer answered: Grace was on the phone, but Bobbie knew immediately that it was not good news.

"We couldn't save the baby—"

"Oh fuck!" The words were out before Bobbie could control them. The woman was pregnant. She quickly apologized—for the woman's plight and for her language. "I'm so sorry, Gracie."

"Not necessary, my love, since that was my response, too, only I didn't say it out loud."

"And the woman?"

"Alive, just barely, though enough for me to leave her and go

217

to the office. When we've seen the last patient here, I'll go back to the hospital. She is in a precarious condition, and it could go bad in an instant. Add to that the two patients with little ones who could decide to make their entrance at any time, which their mothers fervently wish them to do. All of which means I have no idea when I'll be home."

"I'll be waiting for you whenever that is, Grace."

"That brings me great joy and comfort, Bobbie—oh! Thanks for having the car cleaned and delivered. I truly was grateful not to have to look for a taxi after six hours of surgery."

"I probably already know the answer, but has Myrt fed you?"

Grace chuckled, told Bobbie she was deeply loved, and hung up. Bobbie sat for a moment, feeling deeply loved herself—a feeling she had believed was lost to her forever. She allowed herself to sit and feel happiness and joy for a moment.

Then she grabbed a copy of the report she'd prepared for Eileen's committee and hurried to rejoin Bobby and Benny at the table. She gave Bobby the document and set about finishing her burger and fries. Mid-chew she had a thought and envisioned it so completely it shocked her. She would convert her mother's at-home studio to her own home office. The room was practically empty save for the two steamer trunks containing her parents' belongings and her mother's paintings in various stages of completion. She could bring back some of her important office things and completely release her Black Mask office to the Black Mask Artistic Project people to use as they wished.

"Benny," she said suddenly, causing the boy to choke on his food. Boy Bobby clapped him hard on the back while Girl Bobbie apologized profusely for startling him. Then she asked Benny and Bobby if they would be available to move some of her things back to her home office, apologizing for having them do double duty.

"But isn't that Grace's office?" Bobby asked, sounding confused.

"There's another room being used for storage," she began, and saw that he understood which room she meant. He squeezed her hand.

"Whenever you're ready," he said, holding up the report. "And it's no wonder people want to start work right away. This is really quite wonderful, Bobbie. You will have my support and help."

She finally gave in to the relief she felt every time there was a positive reaction to the Black Mask report. She had initially resisted and resented being tasked with the responsibility for coming up with such an important document. She questioned her ability to get it done until finally, after she was fully committed and engaged, she began to realize what was possible, and that's when she began to enjoy herself.

The reaction of Joyce and Eileen and their committee members, and now Bobby's validation, filled her with a sense of satisfaction achieved previously only at a piano keyboard. Her efforts could benefit untold numbers of Negroes for generations. Her parents would be proud. She looked a question at Boy Bobby and he had an answer.

"What do you think, Benny? Should we go get Girl Bobbie's things and bring them back here?"

"Yes, Boy Bobby, I think we should do that," Benny said with an emphatic nod.

They all piled into Bobby's truck and went to pick up her personal items from the basement storeroom of The Slow Drag building. She gave Bobby her keys and asked to be dropped off before they got there so she could walk a few blocks to see and hear and feel—to take the pulse of the avenue in the wake of the events of the morning, because there was no question in her mind that a white man throwing a Colored woman down the subway steps would be the conversation of the day.

If a street could suffer cardiac arrest, Broadway between 130th and 140th would be in danger of stroking out. Despite the fast-moving arctic wind that dropped the already frigid sidewalk temperature by at least ten degrees, nobody talked about the weather.

Most of the conversation groups were on the Uptown side of the street near the 132nd Street station where the woman had been thrown down the steps. People hunched into their coats and scarves. Bobbie easily fit in. Her cap was pulled down low almost to her eyebrows and covering her ears, her overcoat was buttoned to the top and the collar was pulled up, and her scarf was wrapped around the collar; her gloved hands were stuffed into her coat pockets. She walked slowly with her head down, listening. She didn't expect to be recognized or to recognize anyone. She should have known better. Patricia Carter stepped away from one of the groups and walked toward her. Her scarf was wrapped around the bottom of her face as was Bobbie's, but her speech was not impaired and her anger was not diminished.

"How is she? Do you know?"

"She survived the surgery, but she's still in very serious condition," Bobbie replied.

"Will you let me know? Is it all right if I call you later—"

Her question was overridden by another one at a fairly close range: "Can anybody tell me how to get in touch with the man in charge of this group?" The speaker, a man, raised a handful of flyers over his head, the kind of flyers carried by the morning's victim. A hand without a glove. Bobbie scrutinized the stranger: not just gloveless but without hat or scarf and wearing regular shoes, not in boots accommodating a couple of pairs of socks to keep feet warm and dry. He seemed to be waiting for an answer. The expectant look he wore wavered slightly. "I want to give him some money, to make a donation. Can somebody tell me his name, please?"

"Who the hell are you?" Patricia called out.

"Just somebody who wants to help your cause," he said loudly, and brandished the handful of flyers. "Who do I give the money to?" He grinned confidently when he said this.

"Where did he come from?" Patricia muttered, looking all around.

"He got out of a car," Bobbie said grimly. Angrily. "Look at him: no hat or coat."

"We know a traitor when we see one." Patricia took a step forward to point at the stranger. "This one works for Mr. Charlie. Remember his face, and if you see him again—"

"If I see him again I'ma whip his ass." A man stepped out of a group of people and, hands balled into fists, moved menacingly toward the stranger.

"I'm gon' help him!" another man called out, running toward the interloper, and the crowd surged. The stranger threw the flyers into the air and darted into traffic inches ahead of the front bumper of a taxi. The cabbie leaned angrily on his horn, but the man continued to dart in and out of traffic as horns continued to blare at him. He didn't pause long enough to look behind him to see that he wasn't being chased. To see that the people on the sidewalk were laughing, glad to have a reason for even a small, brief respite from the pain and sorrow of the morning.

Several people stooped to pick up the flyers before the wind scattered them, and though they knew what was printed on them, read them again, nodded grimly, folded them, and consigned them to a coat pocket. To share later, Bobbie hoped.

"I wish some motherfucker would try to throw me down some steps just 'cause I got some of these in my pocket!" a thin woman wearing an even thinner overcoat shouted, brandishing a few flyers. But the fierce, frigid wind tore the words from her chattering teeth and the flyers from her frozen fingers and she huddled into herself. Hatless and gloveless and scarfless, only her burning anger kept her upright.

"I'll call you later, all right?" Patricia asked again as Bobbie turned to leave.

"Sure," Bobbie answered, walking away, half a block in

the wrong direction because she was following the woman who had tried to speak out. Bobbie tried to ignore the cold as she gave her own hat, scarf, and gloves to the woman. Then, struggling to control her thoughts and emotions, shivering badly, she continued to walk the wrong way, stepping into the street to hail a cab. She wanted at least the external appearance of calm before she saw Grace. Crossing the street at the light, she finally got a taxi, and by the time she reached Grace's office she felt almost calm.

"Your timing is perfect," Myrtle said, opening the door to the reception area to let Bobbie cross the hallway to Grace's office. "She was about to call you until she realized she didn't know where you were, and I was of no assistance." She looked closely at Bobbie. "Where were you? And why don't you have on a scarf and a hat?"

Bobbie told her and they shared a moment of sad encouragement for the courageous woman. Bobbie put a hand on Myrt's arm to stop her from opening the door to Grace's office. "How is she?"

Myrt hesitated briefly. "Drained. Completely drained."

"Can I take her home?"

"You can try," Myrt replied, "but I don't think she'll go, not until she's visited the patient at least once more."

Grace was stretched out on the couch, her eyes closed, but Bobbie knew she was awake and aware. She pulled a chair over to the couch and as she sat, Grace, eyes still closed, extended a hand. Bobbie took and held the hand, and kissed it, as tears began leaking from Grace's eyes.

A hymn she hadn't thought of in many years came to mind, and though she didn't recall all the words, she began to sing:

"There is a balm in Gilead, to make the wounded whole."

Then Boy Bobby was singing, and he knew the words!

222

Where did he come from?

"Sometimes I feel discouraged, and deep I feel the pain.
In prayers the holy spirit revives my soul again.
There is a balm in Gilead, to make the wounded whole.
There is a balm in Gilead, to heal the wounded soul."

Grace sat up smiling and opened her arms to both of them, an embrace they were only too happy to receive, and they remained that way, the three of them holding each other for a little while longer.

When Grace released them, she said, "I hope our plans for the evening include dinner, because after I visit my patient once more, I want lots of food, including dessert, and at least a pitcher of Manhattans."

The Bs promised to deliver. "We're going to get some of everything Miz Maggie has cooked," Boy Bobby told Myrt, "so what would you and Thelma like for dinner? And dessert?"

"And I'll be making Manhattans by the pitcher-full," Bobbie added. Then she asked Myrt if she could use the telephone to call Jack and invite her.

A short time later, sitting in the truck waiting for the heater to blow out something close to hot air, Girl Bobbie thanked the Boy for the surprise of his presence, for his really lovely tenor voice, and for knowing the words to the hymn. Then, she told him what had happened at the 132nd Street subway station a little more than an hour before, and he went still and quiet, remaining that way for so long that Bobbie began to worry.

"Patricia will call you later tonight, is that right?" he finally asked.

"That's what she said," Bobbie answered.

"Will you help me convince her to stay home—"

"I already tried that. It didn't work. Anyway," and Bobbie turned sideways in the seat to face him, "she's an extremely intelligent young woman who seems capable of taking care of herself."

He shook his head. "I don't know, Bobbie—"

"What don't you know? Whether a woman can take care of herself? Whether a woman can make the kinds of decisions required to help her people and take care of herself at the same time? Have you ever heard of Harriet Tubman? Sojourner Truth? Mary McLeod Bethune? Dorothy Height? Constance Baker Motley?" Bobbie was getting angry. Bobby tried to tamp it down.

"You're right and I apologize." He raised his hands before he reached out and took her hands. "I guess I'm thinking of her as a college kid—"

"Which is what you were when you joined the army and went to Korea."

He dropped his head, sighing deeply. "I keep thinking about that woman being thrown down those filthy stairs: Did she know what was happening to her or why? Did she think of her husband and children? Do you know her name, Bobbie? Did Grace tell you? Somebody loved that woman, and all she did wrong in the eyes of her almost murderer was have some pieces of paper telling her to stand up for herself."

"Fear will kill us faster and deader than those who hate us, Bobby, and I think you know that. I'm sure both you and Jerome felt fear at the thought of going to Korea, and yet you went."

"But Patricia walks around with those same pieces of paper that anybody can see—"

"And we can't stop her, but we can support her."

Bobby looked at her like she had taken leave of her senses. "And what are we supposed to do, Bobbie, when they show us how much they don't like what we do? Pray?"

"Oh hell no! We should do the one thing we know they hate: continue to do and be our best selves, proving to them how stupid they are to try and stop us. Throwing ourselves up in their faces and demonstrating our excellence." Girl Bobbie and her words burned hot, and Boy Bobby felt the heat. He also got the message.

"Black Mask! That's how we show them. This is just a beginning, isn't it? And it's not the only one, is it? It's just the opening salvo!" He was bouncing up and down like her baby brother the more excited he became.

"Just as Patricia isn't the only young person standing against violence done to us, yes, I think there are probably many more, and I think we'll be hearing more from and about them, especially if we continue to be unwitting and undeserving targets of their hatred." Bobbie now spoke coolly and calmly, the heat of just a moment ago barely an ember now. She had been thinking these things for three years, first as a deep need for something to help her believe that the murders of her family were more than one senseless event that occurred in a vacuum. Then she saw and knew that a bigger picture existed. It was still in a small frame, but it grew larger every day, and Patricia and her friends, and Bobbie herself, along with Eileen and Joyce and the Black Mask committee members, were proof of that.

"I'll do my part by finishing my degree, sooner rather than later, and that's a promise." Bobby placed his right hand over his heart, then raised it as if swearing an oath. "Does City College offer a degree in rabble-rousing?"

"I think that falls into the Extracurricular Activity category," Bobbie said with a grin.

"But I want to do something that matters, something that helps."

"All the Patricias will need lawyers to defend them, and the families of women thrown down the subway stairs will need lawyers to file suits against the criminals."

Boy Bobby was silent and thoughtful for a long time. "I don't know if I'm cut out to be a lawyer, but rabble-rousing definitely could be a good fit. Let's go see what's happening at the 132nd Street subway stop, and then let's go get the food," he finally said.

"You don't have to work tonight?" she asked.

"Nope," he replied.

"You didn't work yesterday, Bobby—"

"I know that!" he snapped, cutting her off.

Her stomach lurched and dropped. "Bobby, is something wrong?"

"We can talk about it later."

"Talk about what, my friend?"

"Not right now, Bobbie, please."

"I wish you could have caught him and . . ."

"And what, Jack?" Grace prompted. "Surely you're not suggesting that Bobbie should have chased a stranger into the street and—"

"And taught him what happens to a traitor who betrays his own people. He shouldn't live to see another day. She should have shown him the error of his ways."

"Surely you don't mean that, Jack!" Grace sounded as appalled as she looked. "Bobbie doesn't go around showing people the error of their ways. And certainly not through violent means." She was adamant and certain she knew what she was talking about. Boy Bobby held his breath, recalling not only the incident with Von Thompkins but also the night he met her at the Savoy Ballroom and, with him in drag, how she used expert manipulation of the walking cane to easily break bones in the hand and arm of the man menacing him.

Nurses Myrtle Lewis and Thelma Cooper, who had known Grace longer and knew her better than anyone in the room, were the first to see the gentle, kind, and loving doctor after she'd been beaten almost senseless by Von Thompkins. And they also were the first to see Bobbie Hilliard after she beat Von worse than that despicable character had beaten Grace. Of course Bobbie would show a man who was a traitor to his people the error of his ways, and she'd do it in the middle of Broadway, traffic be damned, employing whatever violence was necessary.

Jack stood up and walked to stand behind Bobbie, put her arms around her friend, and rested her chin on the top of her head. Then she kissed the top of her head and hugged her even more tightly. The new people in their lives watched the two old friends who knew each other so well and who had loved each other for most of their lives and who had shared unspeakable suffering.

"I'm glad you recognized the piece of crap for who and what he was, and I'm glad you told people to be aware of him," Jack said to Bobbie. She turned to Bobby and Grace and Myrt and Thelma. What words could she use to explain to them that Bobbie felt the pain of the woman who was thrown down the subway stairs because she was Colored and dared to contemplate a way to improve her life?

"Bobbie was not good after everything that happened with her family. Who would be? And no matter how hard we try to understand, there is no way to understand what you haven't endured. Healing is a process, and it takes time. I helped her heal and she helped me heal, and Grace and Bobby—you have helped us both heal." Jack again rested her chin on top of Bobbie's head and wrapped her arms around Bobbie's shoulders.

Grace and Bobby and Myrt and Thelma stared at Jack. They'd never heard her speak so many words at one time, and Bobbie hadn't heard it for a long time—not since Jack's injury when she stopped talking altogether for a while. Maybe they both were on the road to recovery. Jack planted another kiss on the top of Bobbie's head and returned to her place on the sofa next to Boy Bobby, who pulled her into a one-armed hug.

Then he turned serious. "But we still have to figure out how to handle all the shit that's sure to come our way when we stand up for ourselves." He spoke to Bobbie but looked at each of the others in turn. He saw they understood his meaning and shared his concern, as well as knowing with absolute certainty that there would hell to pay if they continued to stand up for themselves and that the payback most likely would be brutal.

Bobbie took a deep breath. "Joyce and Eileen have been telling me about a fella named Bayard Rustin who used to teach at City College, which is how Joyce knows about him. He talks of the principles of nonviolent resistance that he learned in India from a lawyer named Mohandas Gandhi, who taught his people to resist the often-violent control the British exercised over them. He taught that their resistance had to be nonviolent because, unlike the British, they had no guns, nothing to fight with. Except their bodies," Bobbie explained.

"But the British could beat the shit out of them, could kill them!" Jack exclaimed.

"Could and did," Bobbie said, "but they kept coming and laying their brown bodies down in protest, and it finally occurred to somebody in charge that they couldn't kill them all. And they eventually stopped trying."

"How many of 'em died before that happened," Bobby asked, "and how long did it take?"

Bobbie shrugged. "How many died? Who knows? And it took many, many years. Decades. But they prevailed. They eventually won their independence from England."

"So some of us will die?" Jack asked.

Bobbie shrugged again, but before she could reply Thelma spoke up: "Do you remember the 1943 riot? A white policeman killed a Colored soldier who tried to keep him from beating a Colored woman—"

"Indeed I do remember that!" Grace exclaimed, but before she could say more Bobby jumped to his feet.

"Was he in uniform?" the soldier queried, and they all had to help calm him before Thelma could continue.

"The US military uniform was only one thing they resented,

hated. They hated our presence. By that time most of the people who lived up here were Colored, and just like it is today, most of the businesses were owned by those who didn't want to keep them nice for us Colored people, and when people complained we paid the price," Thelma said, a mixture of sad and mad.

"Meaning—" the still angry Boy Bobby began before Girl Bobbie interrupted.

"Meaning we need to learn a new way to articulate our displeasure," Bobbie said.

"By this nonviolent resistance?" Myrt asked, her face a mask of skepticism.

"Which won't work anywhere down South," Jack said darkly. "Both of my parents are from down there, and they still have people down there who know firsthand how Jim Crow operates. You wouldn't know from their behavior that the damn Civil War has been over for almost a hundred years."

"Which means that down there or up here in Harlem, a lot of us are about to be dead for standing up—or sitting down—for our rights," Thelma said.

"Well, we can't just wait for them to decide to do the right thing," Myrt said.

"Do they even know what that is?" Jack asked.

"Somebody needs to tell 'em how many Colored soldiers just got through dying for them in Korea, not to mention in World Wars I and II," Boy Bobby said, "so they could have their democracy while we get the same nothing we always had. I, for one, have had e-damn-nuff!" And with that, Boy Bobby stood at attention and saluted all the women looking up at him. Girl Bobbie stood and saluted him back, then hugged her friend who was trying not to cry.

"Tell us about the look on Turner's face when you gave him the keys to the Buick," Boy Bobby said, shifting the mood from serious and reflective to time for eating, drinking, and making merry. And when, after a while, Grace failed to stifle a huge yawn, Bobbie stood up.

"I need to put her to bed. The phone rang at four thirty this morning and she's been up and moving at her normal 100 mph ever since."

"You'll let us know how the patient is?" Bobby asked, getting to his feet, and added, "If you can. And maybe what her name is and if she has family?"

"I will," Grace said. "I am guardedly hopeful though she's a long way from being well."

"If anyone can help her heal and get well, it's you, Grace," Jack said as the group exited.

"I truly and deeply like Jack Jackson," Grace said, closing and locking the door. "And she really does appear to be healing nicely."

"To not be healing nicely would mean disappointing you, Grace, and that she would never do. She loves and idolizes you."

Grace nodded, tears springing to her eyes. "She calls me every week, Bobbie, to thank me and to tell me she loves me." Grace wiped her eyes and Bobbie hugged her tightly. She guessed that many of Grace's patients harbored similar feelings, but didn't know her well enough to call and tell her as much.

"The woman from this morning . . .?"

Grace shook her head in anger and sadness. "So many injuries and so much damage. I had to summon The Boys, and even with the three of us, and Thelma and two other nurses, we could barely control all the bleeding long enough to repair the damage. And the baby! I told The Boys they'd have to handle everything else while Thelma and I focused on the baby, but there was nothing we could do except deliver it and get it out of the way so we could see all the other problems, and there were so many of them." She stopped talking and closed her eyes, either seeing it all again or trying not to. Then she looked hard at Bobbie.

"Someone pushed—or kicked—that woman down those

steps, Bobbie! She tumbled too fast and too hard to have merely lost her balance or missed a step. She literally had head-to-toe injuries—broken bones and lacerations—and she's not a large or heavy woman. Some son of a bitch kicked and pushed that woman, Bobbie. I'm sure of it."

"Do The Boys agree?"

Grace nodded, adding that they'd discussed it in the doctors' lounge after the six hours of surgery. How, they wondered, could a normal fall have resulted in so many dangerous and devastating injuries? And they all concluded, Grace said, that there was nothing normal about what had happened to that woman. Bobbie winced and thought of how they always underestimated how much and how deeply they were hated!

Getting ready for bed, Grace struggled to keep her eyes open, the weight of the day now taking its heavy toll. But her eyes widened when Bobbie crawled into bed beside her and put a paper bag in her hands.

"Whatever is this?"

"Open it and see."

Her eyes popped open even wider at the sight of a brown paper bag full of cash. "Bobbie?"

"Mr. Turner's payment for the Buick, my contribution to the kitchen remodel."

Grace folded the bag closed and put it in her nightstand drawer. "Thank you, love."

"Do you have a contractor in mind, or do you want to retain the original one? I now have his number—I got it from Mr. Turner."

When there was no response, she reached across Grace and turned off the lamp on her nightstand. Then she turned off the one on her own nightstand, and as she closed her eyes and drifted into sleep, she thought she heard Grace mutter "new bedroom furniture."

"Goddammit, I wish we could find the piece of dog shit who did it! Somebody has to know who he is." Bobby was so angry he hadn't once mentioned the frigid temperature that was hovering in the low twenties. It was the next morning, and Bobbie had just told him what Grace had said about the woman's condition. He was so angry he was quivering, yelling and pacing, all of which caused her to regret sharing the news of the woman's injuries.

"No doubt somebody knows who did it but they're sure as hell not going to tell us. We may as well all go fly off the Empire State Building or lay down on Broadway and let the buses run over us, instead of waiting for them to pick us off one by one. Dammit, Bobbie, Patricia said someone saw the guy who pushed her."

"Can the person describe him, say what he was wearing? How tall he was—"

He shook his head, the anger sloughing off like water. "So we have to live the rest of our lives, and our children's lives, and their children's lives, letting them do whatever they want to us, and we do what? Keep turning the other cheek and forgiving them? I'm about out of cheeks, and forgiveness, too." His eyes burned into hers as he said those words. "It will be years before Black Mask delivers a result."

She took both of his hands in hers holding them tightly, her eyes burning as hotly as his. "I have forgotten nothing, and I have forgiven nothing and I never will. But what I will do is always seek a way forward for us, all of us. And right now, today, that way is one grocery market at a time on a street called Broadway in a city called Harlem."

He gave her a shrewd look. "You have a plan, don't you?"

"More like thoughts, ideas. There are a couple of people I need to talk to, people who've been watching and feeling the pulse of Harlem for a very long time." She peered at him. "People like your boss. Will you ask him something?"

"Sure. What?"

"What he knows about the gangs of Harlem."

"Gangs?"

"Every group had one—the Italians, the Irish, the Jews, the Puerto Ricans, and the Negroes. If most of the white people left, did their gangs leave, too? And other than fight and kill, what do they do?"

"I'll ask," Bobby said quietly, getting up to leave.

"You and he are still talking to each other, right, Bobby?"

"Who else would I talk to—when I'm away from my family?" But he had to work hard to keep his smile in place and his farewell salute crisp.

She locked the door behind him, made a pot of coffee, and called Grace, who, Myrt said, was with a patient, and then was going to the hospital. "Nothing urgent, Myrt. I'm home and she can call whenever she has time. Oh, Myrt! Do you have time to answer a question, or can you call me back?"

"If we don't have patients waiting, I'll talk to you after you talk to Grace." And she kept her promise, calling Bobbie a couple of hours later.

"I'm seeking information from as many Harlem natives as possible, Myrt, about the gangs—"

"The gangs? What for, Bobbie?"

"I want to know if they ever had any interest or involvement in what was happening to the people of Harlem."

A suspicious-sounding Myrt asked her to explain what she meant, and Bobbie complied. "Did they care about landlords not providing heat or water or repairing holes in roofs, or about grocers selling rotten and spoiled food, or about someone who would kick a pregnant woman down the subway stairs?"

Bobbie heard the nurse inhale. She could picture Myrt's closed eyes and wrinkled brow. Finally the nurse said, "We didn't have organized gangs like the Italians and the Jews, gangs that had been around since the 1920s and '30s. Then, when the Puerto Ricans moved into East Harlem, they formed their own gangs to keep the Italians from kicking their asses on their way out because they were running away fast—"

"Running away from what?" Bobbie asked.

Myrt chuckled. "From whom: the Puerto Ricans—like the Italians and the Jews ran away from us. Anyway, my oldest brother hung around with some of the numbers runners who worked for Madame Queen, but he wasn't smart enough or tough enough to live that life and he got himself killed . . . and that's who you should talk to, Bobbie. Stephanie St. Clair, the Queen of Harlem. She lives near you, on Edgecombe Avenue."

"I would never have thought of her," Bobbie said, "though I should have." Madame St. Clair possessed more wealth than any other Negro in Harlem, and more than most whites. It was money earned from all the years of owning and running the largest numbers operation in Harlem, and she successfully fought a bloody war to keep the downtown Italian and Jewish mobsters out of her business—a war she waged almost every day, against both the white gangsters and the gangsters in blue, the police. So while she was elegant and rich and smart and fearless, she was not respectable. Not only did she consort with criminals, but she'd been in prison.

"And you know how we Negroes are about respectability," Grace said over a Sunday brunch of waffles, fried chicken wings, and mimosas. Bobbie was all for making waffles an every Sunday thing, Grace not so much. In fact, the only thing she was willing to make a Sunday routine was spending it with Bobbie. What they ate, with whom they ate, what they did—if anything—was all open to spontaneity, a concept Grace's mother was not open to. She'd proved it earlier that morning when she called to ask what time Grace was making her usual Sunday visit.

It was an unpleasant but brief conversation, overheard by

Bobbie at 7:15 a.m. when they were still trying to sleep after a long night of eating, drinking, dancing, and general merriment, compliments of Joyce and Eileen.

Grace ended the conversation, replaced the receiver with an exaggerated gentleness, muttered something *sotto voce*, turned over, buried herself in Bobbie's chest, and was deeply asleep in seconds.

"Should we seek input on respectability from the crowd at Joyce's last night?" Bobbie asked, laughing before Grace could respond. Respectable women all, most of them members of the same sorority, about half of them members in good standing of the very respectable St. Philips Episcopal Church or the very respectable Abyssinian Baptist Church or the very respectable Mother African AME Zion church, and about half of them, including one of the hostesses, respectably married to respectable men. The other half, married not quite so respectably to very respectable women, partied until the wee hours of Sunday morning. But not one of them had ever run numbers, been jailed, or consorted regularly with gamblers, killers or ladies of the evening, as had Madame St. Clair.

"I'm glad you enjoyed yourself, Bobbie—right up to the moment Joyce asked if you cared to join her and Elaine at church this morning." Grace giggled. "The horrified amazement on your face was priceless."

"Why didn't they ask you?" Bobbie whined, almost pouting.

"Because they don't get points for returning me to the fold," Grace said, adding that, unlike Bobbie, she wasn't a life-long Saint Philips member whose parents had been members. "And anyway, I go at least once a month, but why don't you return, Bobbie? I can only imagine how difficult it would have been after you lost your entire family, but you don't think you can return now?"

"I never told you why I left St. Philips, Grace. I've never told anyone but Jack. The good Reverend Father blessed me and told me that the murders of my parents and baby brother were God's will. At which point I told him what I thought of him and his God."

"How awful!" Grace rose so quickly she knocked over her mimosa, and when she reached for Bobbie she knocked over her glass, too. "It's no wonder you haven't returned. I wouldn't have, either. Even if he believes that, it isn't what you say to comfort someone who has lost her entire family." She sat in Bobbie's lap and held her tightly. "I confess I'm no fan of the man, but I never thought he was a fool."

They sat holding each other until they became aware of the sound of liquid dripping onto the kitchen floor. They cleaned up the mess, cleaned up the kitchen, and with a freshly made pitcher of mimosas got comfortable in the living room. Grace chose the records and Bobbie made the fire, then pulled the phones as close to the living room as the cords would allow.

"Do you think your mother will call back? You dismissed her rather . . . harshly."

Grace shrugged. She was still angry. "She never should have called. I went to see them yesterday after leaving the hospital, but nobody was home. I left the usual bag of pastries and a note saying I'd call during the week. And in typical fashion—which is ignoring everything I say— she calls early this morning." Grace shook her head in angry dismay. "The headshrinkers have a name for that kind of behavior."

They sat quietly for a while, listening to music, watching the fire, and sipping mimosas, relaxed and comfortable, both destined for a nap later unless interrupted. But conversation found them first. "I didn't think I would but I really enjoyed last night. I should call Joyce and thank her."

"Yes, you should," Grace said. "She's convinced you don't like them."

"I'm just getting to know them," Bobbie protested. "Until they drafted me to work on Black Mask, I only vaguely remember seeing them in church but—"

"You don't remember seeing them at sorority meetings?"

"Really?" Bobbie was totally surprised. "I went to sorority meetings because it made Mama happy to have me there with her. Kinda like why I went to church with them." She stopped, grinned at some long-forgotten memory, and continued. "I provided entertainment and distraction for baby brother Eric until his giggles became too loud, which is when he was pulled into Dad's lap, and eventually into a nap. But sorority meetings were just . . . they were something I did because it made Mama happy. And anyway, she was always surrounded by women who wanted to talk to her about one thing or another."

"Will you go to sorority meetings with me for the same reason?"

"You know that I will, love of my life."

"Thank you, so please put every fourth Saturday afternoon on your calendar."

Bobbie grinned. She'd been had. Suddenly excited and animated, Grace darted back into her office, grabbed what looked like a sketch pad from her desk, and hurried into the kitchen, beckoning Bobbie to follow. She withdrew four expertly rendered sketches of their new kitchen, drawn to scale and most impressive. Would the woman ever cease to amaze her? Bobbie thought, fervently hoping not. "So, you were originally planning to become an architect or an engineer but switched to medicine?"

Grace grinned. "You like the sketches?"

"They're marvelous. I can actually visualize the new kitchen, Grace, and me eating so much good food. Have you found a contractor?"

"I meet with Eileen's contractor at seven tomorrow

morning." And at Bobbie's surprised look she explained about Eileen's huge house in Queens and her husband's construction and real estate connections. "So if I like him—"

"I can't wait to see the refrigerator in the pantry. And a dishwasher? Does Eileen even have a dishwasher?" Bobbie was thoroughly enjoying the moment. She kept studying the sketches and finding new areas of excitement. "And finally, a formal dining room." She grabbed Grace and did a quick two-step, laughing, but Grace turned serious.

"Are you sure you're all right with this, Bobbie? You don't feel . . ."

"Grace, this is your home, and you're free to make it as comfortable as you need it to be."

"But it was your home first, Bobbie, the home that your parents created—"

"And it's *our* home now, Gracie, but I do have one question—"

"Uh oh." Grace's happy face crumpled. Bobbie grabbed the face in both hands and kissed the cheeks, eyes, and nose until the happy face returned, accompanied by a Grace giggle.

"That's better, and the question is only about the late-night sharing, when you're practically asleep. You were talking about the kitchen remodel, but then last night you mumbled something about new bedroom furniture, and then you were fast asleep."

"I often feel it's the only time we have to talk—just the two of us—at bedtime. I'm busy and you're busy, and I cherish our friends and spending time with them—and by the way, might we include Joyce and Eileen in our gathering of friends to eat and drink?" Bobbie stifled a giggle, readily agreed, and prodded Grace to please continue. "Anyway, I think about things and remind myself to mention them to you; then I forget to mention them and when I do, when my mind is finally clear, it's *really* clear!

"I love you to distraction, Grace Hannon. By all means let's get new bedroom furniture.

"Shall I make another pitcher of Mimosas?"

"Not now, unfortunately. I've got to change and go to the hospital, but I hope not to be engaged for too long."

While she was gone, Bobbie dug out her mother's stationery and wrote a letter to the Queen of Harlem. The thick cream-colored paper bore her mother's initials and address at the top of the page, initials and address shared by the daughter of Eleanor Roberts Hilliard. Bobbie dated the letter, wrote *Dear Mme. St. Clair,* capped the pen, and went in search of ordinary paper on which to draft practice letters. She wasn't exactly certain what to write but she knew it had to be persuasive enough to win her an audience with the Queen.

It was snowing hard when Bobbie got up the next morning. She had slept through Grace's meeting with the contractor. She dressed quickly and hurried into the kitchen. The hastily scribbled "He's perfect" on the top page of the sketches let Bobbie know to expect construction soon, but it was the scent of Toujours Moi that captured her attention. Bobbie turned to embrace Grace. "Exactly how perfect is he?"

"So perfect that I want Bobby to meet him."

"What? Why?"

"Because he needs a boyfriend that's not a truck, and unless I'm way off the mark—"

Bobbie laughed so hard she almost choked. She couldn't wait to tell Boy Bobby that Grace was matchmaking for him.

After she drove Grace to work, she picked him up and they brought breakfast from Miz Maggie's back to the apartment. Bobbie told him about the contractor and how much Grace liked him, and she showed him Grace's sketches for the kitchen remodel and he whistled appreciatively.

"Wow," he said studying the sketches, then looking at the

kitchen. Bobbie could see him imagining the remodel. "Grace really is quite amazing."

"She thinks you're kinda special, too. So special, in fact, that she intends to get more information about the handsome contractor Mr. Grimes—that's his name, by the way, David Grimes—from her dear friend Eileen." She shared the description of the contractor, adding, "And she and Eileen are plotting how to introduce you two because she thinks you need a boyfriend that isn't a truck."

Bobby's mouth hung open in shock until he found some words. "Mr. Grimes sounds like he can definitely, um, do the job better than some," he said. And at the look Bobbie gave him, he explained that Myrtle and Thelma had arranged for him to have dinner with a friend of theirs. "Did they tell you about it?"

Bobbie shook her head. She wondered if Grace knew; if she did, she'd said nothing about it. "So, I take it that you and—what was his name, by the way?"

"I don't even remember. That's how completely and utterly uninteresting the man was. He couldn't, or wouldn't, talk about anything, and it was never clear to me whether it was because he didn't know anything about anything or because he wasn't interested in anything, and believe me I tried, Bobbie. I talked about Lincoln University and Korea and being in the Army. I even talked about East St. Louis. And when I asked if he was familiar with any of these places, he had the same one-word answer: No." Bobby's look of wildly exaggerated exasperation was funny, but Bobbie didn't laugh because she could see the hurt it hid.

"Can you believe he didn't know where the Savoy Ballroom is? Or Smalls? And this is his hometown. At least he said it was. Can you imagine someone from London not knowing where that damn clock is? Or the damn palace?"

Bobbie was trying not to laugh and not succeeding. "Did Myrt and Thelma say how they knew this fellow? Is he a medical type?"

"If he is, he must work only with the dead. The man would bore a hole."

Now Bobbie did laugh. "You're a funny man, Bobby Mason," she told him as she showed him the letter she planned to deliver to Mme. Stephanie St. Clair later that day. All the funny left his face.

"It is, of course, a masterful letter."

"I sense a *but*."

"But you don't leave the woman any run-and-hide room. She either has to agree to see you or tell you to go jump in the Hudson River."

"Yes," Bobbie replied.

"Well, I predict she'll see you. Everything I've heard about her—she doesn't run or hide, and her behavior is always correct. Whatever she decides, she'll write you the same kind of letter you wrote her, probably on the same kind of paper."

"I hope you're right. I'd dearly love to have her and her, um, employees dealing with the store owners, leaving the college students safely out of it. Besides, I've heard that she feels obligated to help the people who've made her rich and I want to know if it's true."

"I just hope she's not too deeply retired to get involved."

"Bobby, please tell me what is happening with your job." Bobbie's sudden change of subject didn't rattle him as she suspected it might. He just sighed and tried not to look sad.

"It seems you were right to be worried. Technically, I no longer have a job, but Mr. Greeneway is dragging his feet finding my replacement."

"If he doesn't want to replace you, why don't you have a job?"

"Because he doesn't own the building. He's just the super, and the people who do own the building agree with a lot of the residents who don't think a Negro should be the assistant super, especially since I also live in the building, the only Negro to do so. Mr. Greeneway has argued, so far successfully, that a

US Military Veteran should have the job. But—" He shrugged, having no more to say on the subject, and in truth there was nothing he could say.

Bobbie couldn't speak. Nothing she could say would make him feel any better, and she didn't want to let fly all her anger and rage because it would fall onto him. But she could do one potentially useful thing: she could ask Eileen to ask her husband if he knew any apartment building managers who needed an assistant super.

Bobbie dropped him off then went to deliver Mme. St. Clair's letter since she lived just a few blocks away. She parked in front of the building and ran up to the front door. The doorman was about to shoo her away until he saw the letter in her hand and the intended recipient. He readily accepted it. She thanked him, hurried back to the car, and quickly drove to Grace's office building, where she left the car in the garage, and took a taxi home.

The morning's heavy snow had tapered to flurries but was still driven by a fierce wind. Bobbie huddled into her coat in the taxi's backseat where the heat never reached. She hadn't been home very long when Mr. Turner called to give her the phone number for Williams the contractor, and to thank her again for selling him "that beautiful Buick!"

He had refused to believe that he did her a favor by taking it off her hands, so she didn't tell him again. She thanked him and called the contractor who readily agreed to meet with her.

Meeting Bobbie outside the Slow Drag building, William Williams was a fireplug of a man: short, stocky, and, Bobbie guessed, anyone who misjudged him as a fat man made that mistake but once. He wore a heavy overcoat and thick-soled boots, a pork pie hat, and no earmuffs or gloves. Topping off the vision Bobbie marveled at were the thickest glasses Bobbie had ever seen.

Williams spoke and moved quickly.

"Thank you for meeting me, Mr. Williams. My name is Bobbie Hilliard—"

"Hilliard!" he exclaimed. "That's the name of the man who owned this building and had the original work done." He peered at Bobbie through his thick lenses. "I truly am very sorry what happened to your people, Miss Hilliard. Damn shame. You the daughter, then?"

"Thank you, Mr. Williams. Yes, it was, and yes I am."

He peered at her a few seconds more through the thick lenses, then smiled. "You do resemble your ma a lot. She was a very beautiful woman, and a very nice one."

Bobbie returned his smile, changing the subject before tears came. "I never knew what this building looked like before your construction. What I'd like to know is what's above the nightclub floor, and whether the garage still exists? Does your blueprint show these things?"

Williams' smile turned into a grin. "I don't even need to open this," he said, tapping the rolled-up paper under his arm. "There's a full two-bedroom apartment with a kitchen and bathroom on the top floor, and the garage is still right where it was under the building." And yes, he answered before she asked, he could make both accessible. She asked for an estimate and withdrew the Hilliard Inc. checkbook from her pocket, writing him a check that widened his eyes.

"Pretty sure I'm coming back, aren't you?" he said, with a grin.

"I'm pretty sure you'd better," she replied to the man, who was still laughing as he walked away.

Bobbie watched him until he turned the corner, then walked in the opposite direction, hailed a taxi, and went home to find Grace and Eileen drinking champagne, eating popcorn, and listening to Carmen McRae records. They cackled like teenagers.

"If you say that I'll deny it," Grace proclaimed through a guffaw.

"She'll never believe it anyway," Eileen retorted. "She thinks you're perfect."

"She is perfect, Eileen, but I'd dearly love to hear what my Gracie will deny."

Grace sprung to her feet, rushing to embrace Bobbie. "For the record, I'm denying any and everything Eileen might ever tell you about my medical school and residency days."

Bobbie peered over Grace's head at Eileen and asked, "Are you open to bribes?" and the two old friends laughed uproariously. So loudly, they didn't hear the knock at the kitchen door or see Bobbie go to answer it. She was surprised to see Boy Bobby.

"Grace wanted to see me," he said warily. "Did you tell—"

"Haven't said a word. I just got here, so I'm in the dark, too."

Grace came toward them, arms outstretched, and, embracing them both, she led them into the living room. "Bobby, please meet my friend, Eileen McKinley—"

Bobby remembered hearing about her, "the gorgeous one with the husband." Eileen quickly stood and embraced him, shocking him silly. "Oh my goodness yes. He is perfection," she said, already thinking of the matchmaking she was planning.

"I've been called many things, but perfection was never one of them," Bobby said, "and it's a pleasure to meet you, Miss McKinley." *And you're even more gorgeous up close and in person!*

Eileen held his hand between both of hers and smiled at him. "Actually it's Mrs. but my friends don't hold that against me. Isn't that right, Bobbie?"

"How could anyone hold anything against you and the ever-wonderful Dr. Scott?" Bobbie said, sharing a look with Grace, who winked at her as she led Eileen to the front door. "Goodbye Mrs. McKinley," Bobbie said with emphasis on the Mrs. "Please give my regards and a big hug to Joyce."

Bobby sat down hard on the sofa. "She's a doctor, too?" he asked.

"The PhD kind. She teaches at City College. If you run into her on campus you'll know her—brilliance pours off her in waves," Grace said. "Our Bobby has something to tell you, Gracie," Bobbie said, sitting on the floor at their feet.

Grace listened to Bobby about the job situation. There was nothing to be said that would make a difference. So the three of them sat in silence for a long while, their proximity to each other their comfort. Grace finally spoke: "Would you like to stay here with us tonight, Bobby?"

"Of course, I'd much rather sleep where I am surrounded by people who love me than where I am surrounded by hate. And threats. But I'm not letting a bunch of—"

"Threats?" Bobbie and Grace exclaimed in horrified unison. It took him several moments to calm and convince them that he really was safe, that it was only one resident of the building who'd actually made a threat against him, though quite a few complained to the management company about having to live in a building with a Colored janitor.

"I won't be threatened, so this janitor is going home, for as long as it is my home."

After Bobby's departure, they ate a dinner of scrambled eggs, sliced tomatoes, and cheese toast, but they couldn't stop talking about Bobby and worrying about him. Yes, he was strong and intelligent and resourceful, but he was a Harlem novice still learning about the city in every sense of the word. How and where would he find a new job and a place to live—immediately?

"Maybe you could ask Eileen's husband if he knows of a building in immediate need of an assistant super?"

"I'll call him right away. But suppose the job doesn't come with an apartment?"

"I might have a solution," Bobbie said slowly, and when Grace's only response was a raised eyebrow, Bobbie told about her meeting with William Williams at the Slow Drag premises and the plan for a subsequent meeting to see inside the building, half of which had been unused since her parents' death.

"And what makes now the time to . . . what are you thinking to do, Bobbie?" Grace asked.

Bobbie took a deep breath. She looked a little sad but mostly her face showed the excitement of the kitchen remodeling news. "I inherited several pieces of property and quite a lot of money from my parents, all of which I ignored until the lawyers stepped in and said I had some decisions to make. Some of them were easy," Bobbie said, "like keeping this apartment, the two next door, and one of the downstairs units, the Slow Drag building, and the house on the Cape."

"You have a house on the Cape?"

"Yes, my love, *we* do," Bobbie said. "In Oak Bluffs."

"I married an heiress! First vacation of my life, here I come."

"Can I stop talking about this now?" Bobbie asked plaintively.

"Most assuredly not," Grace replied. "But if you must, for now you can jump to the part that has to do with Boy Bobby."

Bobbie sighed, explaining that her father had bought the building housing The Slow Drag because he planned to open a piano bar on the second floor, the current site of The Slow Drag, and a studio for Eleanor Hilliard on the top floor. "The studio was originally two bedrooms opened into a huge space that had a kitchen and a bathroom. I saw it once. Haven't seen it since. But I'm thinking that all it needs is a good cleaning, perhaps new kitchen and bathroom fixtures—"

"And it could be home for Bobby Mason?"

"That's what I'm hoping," Bobbie replied.

"You'll see it today?"

"Tomorrow or the next day—Mr. Williams will call me."

"Please take Bobby with you. He shouldn't have to spend another minute wondering what will happen to him," Grace said. "He deserves better."

"Yes, he does."

"One more question?" Grace asked. "Where did you get the idea for The Slow Drag? It's such a wonderfully secure place for women like us to be ourselves, drink good whiskey, and listen to good music. And dance with sexy women bartenders."

"One of the lawyers told me I was almost obligated to make use of the liquor license issued to my parents. He said liquor licenses were very difficult to obtain, especially for Negroes, much like taxi medallions Both are mob controlled and we're not mob favorites," Bobbie said, "except when making music is involved."

"Do you think—?"

"I think my father knew many different kinds of people and did business with them here and in Europe. I know he was not a saint or an angel, but I also know—I believe—he did what he did to take care of his family."

"And you're like him in that regard, Bobbie, my love. You take care of people."

"I just want to find a way to help as many people as possible, in as many ways as possible. I wish I could take care of people the way you do, Gracie."

"I want you to always do what you do, Bobbie, the way you do it, and I want you to always be who you are, and to always follow what you believe to be the right path."

"Even if you don't always like my path?"

Grace understood immediately what Bobbie referred to. "Listen, Bobbie, I know you did what you did to Von because of what she did to me. You were taking care of your family, which makes me proud."

CHAPTER SEVEN

Bobby joined Bobbie and a concrete block of a man in the middle of a short street he hadn't known existed, between 137th and 138th Streets. She introduced him to Mr. William Williams, and the bones in Bobby's hand wanted to cry when Williams shook it. They stood in front of a nondescript building that wouldn't have been noticeable if not for the heavy wooden door that stood open, revealing an equally sturdy though decorative metal gate which Williams unlocked with a key. Bobby stood aside for Bobbie to enter but she gave a formal bow and said, "After you, Boy Bobby." Playing along, he curtsied and entered, and Williams pushed a button. The lift slowly but smoothly rose. When it stopped, the door opened with the same deliberate smoothness.

"Wow, what is this place?"

"It was to be my mother's studio, but it's been empty for three years. It's yours if you want it."

Bobby stared at her. Then he took a few steps into the wide expanse of the room and spoke slowly, quietly. "How can I accept this generosity from you—again? But how can I refuse it when I need it—again?" Looking at her he continued. "I am so very grateful for you, Bobbie, for the person that you are. But I'm also very afraid that you'll get tired of coming to my rescue, and that would damage if not destroy our friendship. I couldn't bear that."

Bobbie grabbed his hand and squeezed it. "We see our association so very differently, Bobby. I know I could call you at any time of the day or night and you would come, no matter what. I know you would lay down your life for Grace Hannon because that's what I would do. I know for certain you are that kind of friend to me, that you will always be that kind of friend to me."

She moved to stand in front of him, to force his eyes to meet hers. "I offer you this apartment because I have it and because you need it. Please tell Mr. Williams how you'd like things to be because I'm guessing that, unlike my mother, you'd appreciate a wall or a door. Or two."

She gave his hand another squeeze and headed for the door.

"Will you be home this evening?" Bobby asked.

Bobbie nodded. "Grace even promised to quit early and head home to get some much needed sleep and wait for me to bring dinner."

"Why don't I pick up dinner and meet you there? What time is good?"

"The time you arrive with dinner."

Bobbie was having lunch with Larry McKinley in The Grill at the Hotel Theresa, a meeting he'd requested following several meetings he'd already had with the Black Mask people.

"What do you want with me if you've already talked to them?" Bobbie asked. She had thought— and hoped—that she was off the hook for helping to make Black Mask a reality. She should have known better. And anyway, she had something else she wanted to talk about. "So tell me about the new man in your life, the one who is 'The One.'"

Larry lit up like a little kid on Christmas morning. "His name is Ben Jones, and we were at Rutgers at the same time, but he was on an academic scholarship and I was on a football scholarship and never the twain did meet."

"And now that the twain have met?"

"He's been offered a full professorship at City College. I arranged for him to meet one Dr. Joyce Ann Scott and they've established a good rapport."

"Is he aware of your . . . connection . . . to Dr. Scott?"

Larry shook his head and frowned. "I'm not sure what to tell him, or when to tell him. I'm thinking he needs to know whether City College is a place he'd like to work, and Joyce is the person to help him with that. I'm not sure what else he needs to know. Right now anyway."

"Where is he teaching now?"

"Lincoln, in Pennsylvania."

Bobbie inhaled deeply. Sometimes the size and scope of the world narrowed so quickly and so sharply it was breathtaking. Could Boy Bobby know Professor Ben Jones? Aware that Larry was watching her, she said, "Such a large, small world. I have a dear friend who attended Lincoln for two years before joining the Army, planning to use his VA benefits to complete his degree at City College."

"He's the fella Grace called me about," he said. "When was he in the Army? Was he in Korea?"

Bobbie nodded and told Larry the story of Bobby and Jerome and the Korean War, their plans to move to New York, and Bobby's decision to live their plan even if Jerome could not.

"Let me guess: he's still waiting on the VA," Larry said bitterly. "I don't know a single Negro soldier who's been able to collect his VA benefits. Makes me damn glad I ignored my parents and stayed out of the military."

"He's written and visited Congressman Powell's office—"

Larry snorted and waved dismissively in the direction of

Powell's 125th Street office. "The great man has much more to do down there in Washington than worry about what we're doing up here in Harlem."

"I really hope that's not true," Bobbie said, not wanting to think that two of her dearest friends could find their dreams of higher education derailed for very different reasons.

"Tell me about him," Larry asked, and she told him about Bobby Mason, including the story of how they met, and when Larry stopped laughing, he asked Bobbie to have him call. "I'll be very happy to put Mr. Mason to work. His experience working in a building of that size, working for a property management company of that size—he has knowledge and expertise that my company needs, Bobbie. I will pay him well and I will treat him well—he's practically family, after all."

"But if he wants to finish school—"

"He will have my full support and encouragement—that's a promise." He looked at his watch and quickly stood up, apologizing for the hasty exit. "Please have Mr. Mason call me." And he was gone. Bobbie had another cup of coffee and reviewed the notes she'd taken and what she'd promised Larry she would do. She drained her cup, stood up, and headed for the lobby, stopping at the phone booths to call Grace.

"She's not here, Bobbie, and I don't know when she'll return," a harried Myrt said, and explained that a woman who was not a patient staggered into the office forty-five minutes ago, hemorrhaging blood like a broken water pump, the victim of a back-alley abortion gone wrong. Friends brought her to Grace, operating under the erroneous belief that a "real" doctor could fix what the abortionist had destroyed. Myrt called for an ambulance and Grace rode with the woman to the hospital. "At least she can receive some kind of care," Myrt said, "even if, as I think is the case, it will be too little, too late. Grace is a genius but she's not a magician."

"Oh God, Myrt, I'm sorry! That's awful. Anything I can do?"

"Can you make Harlem an easier place for Colored women to live?"

"If I had that power, it would have happened ages ago," Bobbie replied, sounding as sad as Myrt sounded angry.

"Can she reach you when she returns?"

"Hmmm, I suppose I'll be at home." And that's where she was when Grace called two hours later. "Is that woman all right, Grace?"

"Too much damage done and too much blood lost. Even if she'd lived, her insides would have been useless for the rest of her life. Goddammit, if abortion can't be made legal, then at least men should be prevented from being back-alley practitioners. They know little and care less about how women are constructed and function."

"Do you want me to come to you?"

"No, I'll come to you. I closed the office and sent everyone home. They were completely rattled, especially poor Mrs. Butler. She's not trained to see things like that. Hell, I wasn't trained to see things like that. I'll come home."

When Bobbie exited the phone booth, she was too focused on buttoning her coat and wrapping her scarf securely around her neck to realize she was being watched from within the coat check room. Concealed behind and within several left-over coats, Von Thompkins seethed, hatred burning within her like molten lava. She was still sore and bruised from the beating Bobbie Hilliard had inflicted, and she likely never again would see properly from the eye Bobbie punched. She didn't know when or where or how it would happen, but she would kill Bobbie Hilliard. She promised herself that. Then she'd kill that damn Grace Hannon.

Boy Bobby was at Grace and Bobbie's home with food when

Grace awoke from an all-too-brief nap. "However did I manage to live so long and be so productive without you and Bobby in my life? Not that it really matters because I have you both now, never to be deprived again." Grace beamed at them.

In addition to bringing dinner Bobby also had overseen the delivery of the new kitchen appliances: The refrigerator was in the pantry, the dishwasher was adjacent to the newly installed sink, and the stove was across from the new food preparation island. "The electrician and plumber will be here in the morning to get everything wired and connected," he told them.

"You make one heck of a good construction supervisor," Grace said. "I'm glad David was able to reach you and you were available to be here."

"Available is my new middle name. Now that I have a place to live I told Mr. G to go ahead and hire my replacement."

"But what about all your things?" Bobbie asked.

"Mr. Williams said he'd have my new place ready by the end of the day tomorrow. Ennyday and Benny will help me move. I'm all packed and ready, and to tell the truth, it will be a relief to get out of there before there's any more trouble."

"What trouble?" Grace and Bobbie asked with alarm.

He gave a sad head shake and shoulder shrug. "I was so glad to have a job and a place to live I guess I let myself believe all was right with the world. I should have known better," he said, more sad than bitter. "I was ready to move back into the drag queens' rooming house until you all gave me a safe haven above the finest dyke bar in Harlem. Now I just need to find gainful employment."

"I think I can be helpful in that regard," Bobbie said.

"And you can explain how while we eat," Grace said, herding them and the bags of food into the newly constructed dining room where the new table was the only furniture. They sat on the old chairs, with bath towels as tablecloths—everything else was in storage waiting for the new kitchen to be ready. However, the lack of proper plates, cutlery, linen, and glassware did not diminish the vigor with which the meal was attacked, especially by Dr. Grace. "All my favorites, Bobby, bless you, including grape Nehi soda."

"I'll trade you an orange for a grape," Bobbie said, eyeing the bottles of Nehi beverages on the table, three each of orange, grape, and strawberry.

"Done," Grace said, most agreeably.

They ate in comfortable silence for a while, enjoying, as they always did, the food prepared by Miz Maggie who considered them family. None of them had eaten since breakfast. Boy Bobby pried the cap from a bottle of strawberry Nehi and passed the opener to Girl Bobbie who opened both an orange and a grape. She extended both to Grace who didn't hesitate before selecting the orange. Bobbie blew her a kiss and took a huge swallow of the grape, emitting an indecorous burp after. "Pardon me," she said in mock horror.

"And now that you feel so much better, perhaps you'd care to explain how you can help in my hunt for gainful employment?"

"I met today with Larry McKinley—Grace you know about this," she said, and Grace nodded. "Bobby, Larry is Eileen's husband and a principal in what is probably the largest Negro real estate and property management business—not only in Harlem, but in New York City. He was most interested to know that you worked for Westside and he wants to meet you ASAP. Actually, he wants to hire you—"

"He said that? He wants to hire me?"

"His exact words were, 'I'll be very happy to put Mr. Mason to work,' and he meant it."

"So I take it you liked him, despite your misgivings?" Grace said.

Bobbie nodded. "Well, it is an odd situation with him as Eileen's husband. But you're right—he really is a very nice fella—though I still have guilty feelings about liking him."

"Why?" Bobby asked. "I'm prepared to like him quite a lot."

"It feels like I'm being disloyal to Joyce. After all, he *is* married to Eileen."

Boy Bobby's face fell. "Oh yeah. Right."

"It took a while, but Joyce likes him quite a lot, too," Grace said. "Yes, it's odd, but it works for them. For Joyce and Eileen."

"How is that possible when he's literally in bed every night with the woman she loves?" Boy Bobby was aghast.

"He most certainly is not," Grace said emphatically, and explained that though the McKinleys shared a house and two children, they did not share a bed. "Larry has always known that Eileen loves Joyce and that she married him only because she wanted children—two of them and only two. It worked out well."

"Does this mean that Eileen's mother has finally accepted Joyce—"

"Oh God no! She just wants to see her grandchildren on a regular basis, and Larry made it very clear that she'd never see them if she didn't leave Joyce and Eileen alone."

"I'm ready to go to work for this man sight unseen," Bobby said.

"And he's not bad to look at," Girl Bobbie said, "It seems he's finally found 'The One,'" and she told them that story. "So now, Mr. Mason, we just need to find 'The One' for you.

"I'm actually having warm fuzzy feelings about Mr. Williams, especially if he has my place ready tomorrow." He laughed the loudest and longest of all, in his case truly laughing to keep from crying tears of joy at the news that Larry McKinley was ready to hire him. A job and a place to live on the same day—just like it had happened before.

Bobbie's phone rang very early the next morning. "Yes, hello?"

was followed by, "Good morning, Madame St. Clair. Thank you for calling." She almost laughed out loud at Grace's expression even as she listened to Stephanie St. Clair ask—demand, really—that Bobbie explain the reason for her letter.

She didn't hesitate to answer the woman's demand: "A little more than a week ago a woman was thrown down the steps of the 135th Street station by a man who was angry that she was reading and sharing a flyer advocating the boycott of a market at 134th and Broadway. That market sells spoiled milk and juice, rotten vegetables and fruit, and bug-infested flour and meal. Most, if not all, of the markets on Broadway and Seventh Avenue are guilty of the same, and few of the residents can afford to travel outside the neighborhood to shop for better quality food." When silence on the other end of the phone indicated that she had the great lady's full attention, Bobbie explained in detail everything that led to her letter, especially the treatment of older Negro women by the shopkeepers.

"I thought to come to you, Madame St. Clair, because you have men in your employ more qualified than old women or college students to show the shopkeepers the error of their ways." She held the receiver out so Grace and Bobby could hear Madame St. Clair's appreciative cackle. Then the great lady asked, "The woman thrown down the subway steps—how is she?"

"Still hospitalized. She was gravely injured, and she lost the child she carried—" Again Bobbie held the phone receiver out so Grace and Bobby could hear the torrent of angry French that lasted for several seconds. Oh, right, they remembered, she was a native of one of the French-speaking Caribbean islands.

When the Queen of Harlem calmed herself, she told Bobbie she no longer had men in her employ because she no longer operated a business that required them. "But I know many men willing and able to show these shopkeepers the error of their ways, and I will see to it, Miss Hilliard. Now, tell me, please, how I can pay the hospital bill for that poor woman? What is her name?"

"Her hospital bill is paid, Madame St. Clair, thank you, but the doctor bill accrues daily. Dr. Grace Hannon is a Negro woman doctor who cares for any woman who needs her help, and most of them are not able to pay. Yet not one of them is ever refused medical treatment and her office waiting room is always full."

Bobbie spelled Grace's name, gave her office address and telephone number, thanked Madame St. Clair for her care and concern for her community, and hung up the telephone.

Grace and Bobby stared at her, open-mouthed. Finally, Bobby said, "I'd forgotten you wrote to her."

"I never knew you wrote to her," Grace said, "just as I never knew you paid Mrs. Smith's hospital bill. I love you to distraction, Bobbie Hilliard. Now I must go to work, but we will discuss these things later." And she was gone.

"What a woman," Boy Bobby enthused.

"You have no idea."

"Maybe some idea," he said with a comically lewd smirk, adding that he had to leave, too, to pick up Ennyday and Benny to help him move. "I'll see you later, yes?"

She nodded. "I'll be here. Don't forget to call the phone company, and don't forget to call Larry McKinley."

"I'll be calling Mr. McKinley first thing while I still have a phone to call from."

"He may be able to pull some strings and get your new phone in quickly," Bobbie said, and asked him to call her from his new phone the moment it was installed. He hugged her and hurried away. She locked the door behind him and poured water into the pot to brew coffee, but a knock on the door interrupted her. Did Bobby forget something? She quickly unlocked and opened the door to find general contractor David Grimes and two men, both of them strangers to her, both carrying toolboxes.

"Good morning, Mr. Grimes. The kitchen is beautiful!"

"Good morning to you and I'm glad you like it. However, and I intend no disrespect, I'm anxiously awaiting those words from Dr. Hannon."

"As well you should," Bobbie replied with a smile as she stepped aside to allow the three of them to enter, "but I think I can tell you with confidence that you have nothing to worry about."

"Consider me out of your way," Bobbie said, heading for the piano. She hadn't played in several days and missed it. She'd barely launched into the "Tarantella in A Minor" when the phone rang. Expecting Grace or Bobby, she was surprised to hear Eileen asking if she could come over. "Of course. There's no popcorn or champagne because Mr. Grimes is here with the plumber and the electrician, but there is no shortage of Carmen McRae."

"As long as there's bourbon and whatever else you put in a Manhattan."

"Always," Bobbie said, "but there's no ice."

"I'm at Joyce's so I'll be there shortly—with ice cubes."

And she was. She gave Bobbie a quick hug and headed for the kitchen. "Oh how wonderful! Grace's description didn't do it justice. Hello, Mr. Grimes. This is beautiful."

"Afternoon, Mrs. McKinley, and thank you."

She sat down at the bar and watched Bobbie make the Manhattan. "You're not joining me?"

"Not until I've accomplished more of Grace's To Do list. And since it's highly unlikely that I'll ever do anything in that kitchen except brew pots of coffee, I can at least make it ready, which doesn't mean I'll let you drink alone." She placed the Manhattan on a napkin, watched Eileen take an appreciative sip, poured herself two fingers of bourbon, added two ice cubes, restacked the albums already on the record player, and led them to the sofa.

"I've really enjoyed spending time with Larry. Grace is

right—he really is a very nice fella."

"He is that," Eileen said. "He's singing your praises as well, and congratulating Joyce and me for bringing you and Grace together. But I told him you brought yourselves together."

"It was mostly Grace—"

Eileen laughed. "That's not how I heard it. In fact, Grace said—"

"Never mind what Grace said."

"Good," Eileen said with a smug grin, "because I want to talk about you."

"Whatever it is, I didn't do it."

Eileen smiled and patted her shoulder as if Bobbie were one of her children. "I can definitely see Grace's influence. Now, to see how far it extends."

"Uh oh."

"Larry wants you on the Black Mask Board, but I want you to run the whole thing." Bobbie shook her head 'no' before Eileen finished the sentence. "Which part?"

"Both of 'em, Eileen. Board members should be people like Larry and Grace—pillars of their professions and in the community, and I'm not either of those things. And the person who runs the school should be an academic with experience managing teachers as well as students. Somebody like Dr. Joyce Scott."

Eileen's huge smile was full of love. "She would be perfect, but she's already said no, and she's given us a few names to consider. Which brings me back to the board—"

"Not only am I really not qualified, Eileen, but, well, I might not have time."

Eileen gave her a long questioning, speculative look. "I know you know you'll have to explain that, Bobbie. Please and thank you." Now she grinned like one of her children. "Proof of my good upbringing, my mother notwithstanding."

"How is Millicent?"

"She hasn't changed, speaking of things we won't be

discussing. So, other than teaching piano and beginning voice at Black Mask, whenever that happens, what else is claiming your time?"

"I have this idea, Eileen. I want to do something to help Grace help her patients."

"You have my full attention."

"Many of Grace's patients are from Down South, and Grace is the first doctor many have ever seen, and the first Negro woman doctor any of them have ever seen. Grace is glad they come, but she is overwhelmed, and it's the non-medical that is really worrying her."

"The non-medical? I don't understand." Eileen looked confused.

"I want to make it possible for Grace to give every patient sanitary napkins and belts, bars of soap, deodorant sticks, and vitamins. I want to do this, Eileen, but I haven't yet figured out how to make it happen."

"What does Grace say?"

"I haven't told her yet, because there's nothing to tell, Eileen—"

"Of course there's something to tell, Bobbie. What you just told me is one of the most beautiful things I've ever heard—"

"But it's just an idea, Eileen. How do we make it more than that; how do we turn it into a reality? And how soon can we make it happen?"

"Black Mask is just an idea and we're making that happen, and that's how ideas become reality, *we* becoming the operative principle."

Bobbie grinned at Eileen and gave her a huge hug. "And it's all because of a two-letter word: *we*. We need a wholesale source, a place to purchase everything at a good wholesale price. Then we need a warehouse, a place to store it all—"

"Larry's people can handle those two things. What else, Bobbie?"

"Somebody to run the warehouse, to manage the giveaways. Not every Negro woman in Harlem is Dr. Hannon's patient, and when those who aren't learn of the giveaways the office will be swamped, and Grace and her nurses can't handle that," Bobbie answered.

"You must tell Grace all of this, Bobbie," Eileen said, "and then you can tell her that I'm presenting the info and the idea to the sorority, along with the suggestion that our chapter purchase the pads and belts and vitamins, and a request that Larry and some of his real estate pals give us a garage once a month to hold our giveaways."

"You said 'our' giveaways," Bobbie said to Eileen, "so you'll be pleased to know that I've committed to attending sorority meetings regularly. Since I am a Soror, after all."

Eileen gave her a conspiratorial look, leaned in close, and said, "How long did it take for your right butt cheek to heal?"

Bobbie's face morphed from shocked to conspiratorial glee. "Grace told you about the butt cheek tattoos?!"

Elieen had a good laugh, and Bobbie eventually joined in. What else could she do? Eileen hugged her and confided that she and Joyce had always been a bit jealous and had always wished to have tattoos of their own. Did Bobbie know how to get in touch with the Soror responsible?

"It's been a while but maybe. Does Grace know you want a butt cheek tattoo?" Either the question or the way Bobbie phrased it sent Eileen into another fit of laughter. And yes, not only did Grace know but she encouraged it. She just didn't know anymore how to find the Soror who managed to get so many of her sisters to expose their buttocks to a stranger. Changing the subject, Eileen said, "If you won't serve on the board, it would be very helpful if you could recommend a few appropriate candidates."

"A few! Where am I supposed to find a 'few' candidates for the board?"

"Friends of your parents—artists one and all." Bobbie let that thought roam around her brain. Either of her parents would have been perfect. "What about Dorothy West? She was wonderful at the Christmas fundraiser," Eileen said.

"Yes, she was, and she'd be perfect. How often will the board meet?" When Eileen shrugged, Bobbie said it was important to know because Dorothy West lived full-time in Oak Bluffs and rarely came into the City. "Get me some copies of the Statement of Purpose. Do you know Pauli Murray and Lois Jones Pierre-Noel? Billy Strayhorn?"

"I will get you several copies of the Statement of Purpose. Such an interesting life, being raised by artists." Eileen stood up, saying she should leave so she'd be home when the children arrived from school.

"Are they as wonderful as ever?" Bobbie asked.

"They are pure perfection," said Eileen, her voice full of love and pride. She looked at Bobbie. "I've never told you this, but I always envied how your mother loved you and Eric, and I always wished my mother had loved me the same way."

Bobbie was totally taken aback. "How, exactly, did my mother love us, Eileen?"

"Completely and totally and with pride and admiration and respect. She treated you like people, even little Eric. She didn't baby him, she just loved him the same way she loved you."

Bobbie was speechless. Though she'd never heard anyone describe Eleanor Hilliard's love for her children, everything Eileen said was absolutely true. Bobbie and Eric were Eleanor's raison d'être. Bobbie nodded understanding.

"That is exactly how you love yours, and they will always cherish the feeling, Eileen. As much as I miss her—and I always will—it is the knowledge of her love that kept me going in those darkest days."

"And then you met Grace."

"And then I met Grace."

"You are qualified, by the way, to administer the school and not just teach in it, *Dr.* Hilliard."

Literally shocked speechless, Bobbie did not reply immediately. Finally she managed, "Does Grace know?"

"She told me, and she's waiting for you to tell her. But why do you keep it a secret?"

All the strength and energy she had put into forgetting about it, into consigning the PhD in Music Composition awarded to Eleanor Roberta Hilliard to a dark and locked place, was eradicated in an instant. She didn't talk about it because she didn't deserve it. Surely they could understand that. When she raised her eyes to meet Eileen's, she found love and compassion and pride. She hugged her tightly and they headed for the door.

"What you're doing for Grace and for the women of Harlem is truly wonderful, and please consider me a worker bee in whatever form the project takes. I'll be right there." Bobbie stopped walking, and so did Eileen, who had to turn and come back a few steps. "Bobbie?"

"Grace said I should tell you and Joyce why I left St. Philips, so this is why. The Reverend Father said I should take comfort in the fact that the murder of my family was God's will."

Eileen drew in a deep breath. She clutched Bobbie's arm with one hand and her own stomach with the other. She opened her mouth, but no words emerged. She shook her head, then continued her walk to the front door where she hugged Bobbie again, very tightly, and left.

"Miss Hilliard?"

She looked up to see David Grimes beckoning to her, and she hurried to cross the wide expanse of the living and dining rooms to the kitchen. "Yes, Mr. Grimes?"

Stephanie St. Clair stood outside the door and read the name

263

etched in gold leaf:

N. GRACE HANNON, MD

And below it:

The Practice of Obstetrics and Gynecology

Much more impressive than the Dr. G. Hannon on the directory in the lobby. She opened the door to the office, and a dozen pairs of eyes looked up. Most looked away or back down. Those that didn't widened in recognition.

"Queenie! That's Queenie, y'all!"

"Madame Queen!"

"Good morning, everyone," Stephanie St. Clair said, walking over to the counter where Mrs. Butler, the office manager, rose to greet her. "Good morning, Madame St. Clair, and welcome. How may I help you?"

"I know I don't have an appointment, and I'd like to make one if I may, but I'd also like to give this to Dr. Hannon." And she held up a flowered cloth bag. At the same moment the hallway door opened.

"Mrs. Taylor, please. Mrs. Susie Taylor," Nurse Gertrude Johnson said, reading from her clipboard. She looked up from the clipboard she held, looking for Susie Taylor. Then she recognized Stephanie St. Clair, and her mouth froze in a comic *O*. But before she could speak again Grace materialized behind her.

"Good morning, everyone."

"Good morning Dr. Hannon," came the reply, followed by "Look who's here! Queenie's here, Dr. Hannon!"

"I see," Grace said, followed by, *"Bonjour, Madame St. Clair. Comment allez-vous?"* Grace asked her patients to please forgive her for a moment while she spoke with Madame St. Clair, and she led the woman out of the waiting room and down the hall to her office.

"*S'il vous plaît, pardonnez-moi, Madame le Docteur. Je suis désolée!*" Madame St. Clair hurried to apologize before Grace could speak but Grace silenced her. She didn't have time for pleasantries or formalities.

"It is I who must apologize, Madame St. Clair, for I cannot spend time with you as much as I'd like to. You've seen my waiting room."

Indeed she had. Just as Miss Hilliard had described it—so many Colored women, many of them poor women, in need of so much help. And beautiful Colored nurses and Madame le Docteur the most beautiful, all of them dressed in perfectly starched white, there to help. Stephanie St. Clair did not know Miss Hilliard so she could not call her a liar, but she could not believe what she said without proof. And now she had it and more. Dr. Grace Hannon in her starched white coat, her name written in script above the pocket, two pens inside the pocket. "I will be sitting in your waiting room as soon as I can schedule an appointment, Dr. Hannon. In the meantime, please accept this," and she offered Grace the flowered cloth bag.

Grace looked inside. The bag was full of money. "What is this? I cannot accept it." It was one thing for Bobbie to give her a bag full of money, quite another for a perfect stranger to do so, and she shoved the bag back toward Stephanie St. Clair.

"I spoke with a Miss Eleanor Hilliard this morning—Bobbie Hilliard—you know who she is?"

"I do," Grace said, "and I'm certain that she didn't tell you to give me a bag of money."

"No. She did not. But she did tell me that you provide medical care for the Negro women of Harlem whether they can afford the care or not. She said you do not refuse anyone care."

"That is correct, but—"

"Then please use the money for the care of those who

265

have no money—for medicine, to pay the nurses, for heat and electricity—for whatever you may need it for." She extended her hand and Grace took it. "I have not visited a doctor in a very long time because I have never known of a Negro woman doctor—only men doctors and they are all animals, Colored and white." She smiled, which made her attractive face beautiful. "I just hope I'm not too old to see the doctor."

Grace returned the smile, assuring her one was never too old to see the doctor, and she escorted the great lady back to the waiting room where she asked Mrs. Butler to please schedule an appointment. She thanked Madame St. Clair for her visit and returned to the examination rooms after putting the bag of money safely out of sight if not out of her mind.

The women in the waiting room paid vocal homage to Stephanie St. Clair, the Queen of Harlem, and Queenie thoroughly enjoyed the adulation. She thought she'd been forgotten in her neighborhood by her people, and it pleased her to know that was not the case.

Before the end of the day, Grace received another surprise visit. There were three patients remaining in the waiting room when Myrt all but ran into her office. She wasn't carrying a patient chart, and she had an unusual expression that Grace did not recognize. "What is it, Myrt? Is something wrong?"

"There's a young couple in the waiting room who say they put you in a taxicab the night you were, the night you escaped from Von—"

Grace was on her feet and into the waiting room before Myrt finished speaking. Grace remembered the young couple and had often wondered how she could contact them. They hadn't introduced themselves that night. They had only asked if she needed help, summoned a taxi, and put her in it, telling the driver "The lady is a doctor, and she'll tell you where to go."

"I am so very glad to see you," she said to them, leading them to her office. She apologized to the waiting patients, saying she'd be right with them. In her office, she told the young couple "I have wondered so many times how I could find you and thank you. You will never know what a wonderful thing you did for me that night. What are your names?"

"We are Buddy and Naomi Joiner," the young man said, and Grace realized that they were not much more than children. She'd bet her salary that neither of them had seen their twentieth birthday.

"I'm very pleased to meet you, Mr. and Mrs. Joiner," Grace said, shaking their hands. "And I owe you both a huge debt of gratitude." They blushed and ducked their heads like the children they were, giving her a chance to study them, albeit briefly, but what she saw raised red flags. "Is something wrong? Is there a problem, something I can help with?"

The two young people looked at Grace with a mixture of emotions, and Naomi began to cry. Buddy put his arm around her and looked at Grace. "We got married in secret, didn't tell nobody. Naomi is living with her folks, me with mine. Then her friend, Annie, spilled the beans and Naomi's daddy put her out."

"How old are you two?" Grace asked.

"Naomi is sixteen and I'm seventeen," Buddy replied proudly, and Grace thought but didn't ask, who in the hell would marry these children without their parents' knowledge? She continued the conversation, seeking to find out.

Bobbie crossed off the last item on Gracie's To Do List and looked all around the kitchen.

The phone rang and she hurried to answer it. It was Joyce telling her how truly sorry she was about the dumb-as-hell remark the rector had made about the death of her family. "He'd better be glad I'm not God because I'd make him sorry he ever said anything so damn stupid."

Bobbie thanked her, then asked about Eileen. "She was truly rattled when she left me, and I was worried about her."

"She was still rattled when I got home, and she couldn't stop crying," Joyce said, overriding Bobbie's apology and offering her own. "We wanted to know why you stopped coming to church and you told us. We are so very sorry, Bobbie, that you had to endure that extra pain added to what already was too much to bear."

Bobbie thanked her, then changed the subject to a more pleasant one, asking about their children, EJ and Scottie. "Elaine promised that we could see them soon. Please, let's make that happen."

As soon as Bobbie hung up the phone it rang again. "I'm on my way to you, love. Meet me in the garage?" said Grace.

"Give me time to shower—"

"Do you really need to shower to go see Boy Bobby's new home?"

"Yes, I do, since I spent the day slaving in the kitchen as directed by my woman." She hung up listening to Grace chuckle and hurried into and out of the shower. Grace was just driving into the garage when she got there, and she spread her arms in welcome. Grace got out of the car and stepped into Bobbie's arms. "Whatever I did to deserve that, I'll be happy to do it again." Bobbie held her tightly before releasing her. Grace walked around to the passenger door, opened it, and got in, and Bobbie was happy to drive.

"So, slaving away at some woman's direction?" Grace said.

"Not just *some* woman, *the* woman, *my* woman, and you should see her kitchen! It is a true work of art. All it needs is some food."

"We will shop for food tomorrow, my love. Lots and lots of food." Then Grace picked up the flowered cloth bag from the seat and, as Bobbie stopped the car at a traffic light, she opened the bag and said, "This should prove helpful in that endeavor."

Bobbie glanced down into the bag, did a perfect comic double-take, and pulled the car over to the curb. She looked the unspoken question at Grace.

"Madame St. Clair visited this morning to see for herself whether you were telling the truth. The waiting room was full, and at least half the women recognized her. They afforded her the recognition appropriately due royalty, and, Bobbie, there truly is something regal about the woman. The money is to pay the bills of any woman who needs financial assistance, to pay the staff and the rent and the electricity, and to take care of any other needs I may have. And if I need more money, I have but to ask."

Bobbie was stunned. "How much is here?" Grace shrugged. Then she saw Boy Bobby, outside waiting to direct them to the garage on the back side of the Slow Drag building that had been bricked up. Inside waiting for them—the best spaghetti and meatballs they'd ever tasted.

"My grandma's recipe," Boy Bobby said proudly. "And when I told her I was making them for you, she made me promise to tell her how you liked them."

"They really are the best meatballs I've ever tasted, but you did not get this meat in this neighborhood," Grace said darkly, and he shook his head.

"Larry took me to Queens to shop."

"Speaking of which," Bobbie said, tossing the bag of cash to him. "Madame St. Clair visited Dr. Hannon this morning, and was so impressed by what she saw—"

"Why didn't I know that you wrote to her?" Dr. Hannon asked gently.

"Because I forgot about it, Grace, honestly, I did. And if I'm honest, I didn't really expect a reply. There were so many other things to think about that I didn't think at all about whether Madame Stephanie St. Clair would answer my letter." She stood up, leaned down to hug Grace and kiss both cheeks, and then stacked the empty plates to take to the sink. To Boy Bobby she said, "Why don't you count the money while I wash the dishes?"

"Why don't you make Manhattans first, then wash the dishes?"

The new bar was fully and impressively stocked. "Your new place is wonderful. Are you sure you just moved in here?" Grace said. "Your decorating skills are first rate. The stove and fridge are perfect. I have an affinity for white kitchen appliances. They don't get in the way of creative decorating."

"They got in the way of something! You should see the dents in the backs of them. Larry took me to this wholesale place in Queens. I paid practically nothing, and the guy delivered them in an hour."

"Sounds like you and your boss—"

"He truly is a very nice man," Bobby said. "He warned me that he intends to work my ass off—his words—and I assured him that I was ready, willing, and able to be worked as hard as need be. They've got four buildings, and they've never really had a super in any of them."

"So you'll be the super in one of them?"

Boy Bobby grinned. "I'm the super in all of them until I hire guys to do what I did in my old building. Then I supervise the four of them and kinda manage all four buildings—"

"But that's an impossible amount of work," Grace protested.

"It won't be once I get a handle on it—"

"But *four* buildings, Bobby. How many apartments, how many people—"

He hurried across the room to hug and reassure her. "My four buildings combined won't have as many units as the one Westside building I was responsible for. The problem I'll have is that they haven't ever been properly maintained or managed, so there's a lot to do, and the residents may not welcome the new guy and his new rules and regulations."

"Uh oh," Bobbie said darkly, giving him a double Manhattan. "Not sure I like the sound of that."

"Beats the hell outta being shot at by North Koreans."

"Well. Since you put it like that—"

"And I feel like I'm doing something useful, working for a Negro real estate and property management company, helping to make sure that our people have clean, decent places to live." He didn't need to add, *unlike all those buildings owned by people who live on Staten Island or in New Jersey and who never make repairs or provide heat and water but continue to raise rents.* "And anyway, since I don't need to sleep—"

Bobbie quickly washed the dishes, cleaned the kitchen, brewed a pot of coffee, and heated up the apple pie while Boy Bobby counted the Queen's money. Bobbie served coffee and pie after stacks of cash were shifted out of the way, and she joined the others at the table.

"How much?" she asked.

"Don't have a final tally yet. I stopped counting at three thousand—"

"But enough for me to give everyone a raise?" Grace asked.

"Easily," Boy Bobby answered.

"Including yourself?" Bobbie asked, and at the look Grace gave her, said, "When was the last time you took your full salary from the practice, Grace? Honest answer, please."

Grace gave a sheepish half smile and said, "I honestly don't know. But thanks to you—and the Queen of Harlem—I can now count myself among the gainfully employed."

Boy Bobby raised his coffee cup to toast Grace. "Here's to us, Dr. Hannon, in the ranks of the gainfully employed."

Then Grace's smile faded a bit and she looked at Boy Bobby. "May I ask you something about your buildings?"

"Of course you may. What is it, Grace?"

Bobbie and Bobby were silent when she finished telling them about Naomi and Buddy. Then they both had questions, the first and most pressing one being whether the marriage of such young people was legal, and Grace explained that it was,

271

with parental consent.

"Then who kicked them out if their parents consented to the marriage?" Bobbie asked.

"Naomi's mother consented, her father didn't. He didn't even know about the marriage, and when he found out he put both mother and daughter out."

"Where's the mother?" Bobbie asked.

"I asked the same question, and Buddy said the mother could return but not the daughter if she stayed married to him, and Naomi said she wanted to remain married to Buddy."

"I can find a place for them, and some work, too," Bobby said. "Where are they now?"

Grace hesitated then said, "At Myrt and Thelma's—"

Boy Bobby reached across the table, grabbed the phone, and dialed. "I'm coming to get those kids in a little while, Myrt," he said, adding "in an hour or so." Then he took Grace's hands. "I'm sure Naomi and Buddy are good people, Grace—after all, they rescued you, no questions asked— but we don't know them."

"I agree. And a married couple needs their own place," Bobbie said.

"And I'm sure young Buddy would appreciate being gainfully employed. I sure as hell do."

He kissed Grace's hand, then picked up the wrapped package Bobbie had placed on the table. He tore open the paper and when he saw what he held he began to weep. It was a painting by Eleanor Roberts Hilliard of four-year-old Eric, beautiful and laughing and happy. He wept harder, and Bobbie and Grace hurried to hold him. He finally grabbed napkins and wiped his face and blew his nose. "I will have it framed and I will hang it over my bed. When I get a bed."

He studied the painting, running his finger over the *ER Hilliard* signature in the bottom right corner. He hugged the painting, and kissed it before hugging and kissing Grace and Bobbie, but because his eyes remained full of tears, he missed the look they were sharing with each other.

"You don't have a bed?" Grace asked.

"Is that why the bedroom door is closed?" Bobbie asked.

"It's an empty room," Bobby said through a sniffle, "Nothing to see on a housewarming tour." Then he looked closely at them. "Why do you ask?"

"You know we're getting new bedroom furniture," Grace said.

"It's being delivered sometime tomorrow afternoon," said Bobbie.

People unfamiliar with Harlem, such as Bobby when he first arrived, thought it a huge place with a huge population, but in reality it was more like a village, kind of like the part of lower Manhattan that was called The Village. Everything in Harlem was pushed close together, including the many thousands of people who called the place home. What was good about that was that none of the friends lived very far from each other (except for the McKinley mansion in Queens) so they got home from Boy Bobby's in no time.

Bobbie opened the trunk of the Caddy and grabbed Grace's medical bag, then grabbed Grace's arm with the other hand, and quick-stepped them to the elevator as it had turned sharply colder. Bobbie unlocked their door and waited for Grace to enter the kitchen and turn on the light. The expression of stunned delight on her face was proof that she had indeed forgotten that her kitchen was open for business. She walked all around looking at everything, touching, opening every drawer and cabinet. Her gaze fell upon the To Do list she'd given Bobbie and she stared at it, traced the line drawn through every item. Then she looked at Bobbie. "You really did slave all day for your woman."

"Truth be told, I enjoyed every minute of it. I expect you'll want to do some rearranging and reorganizing, but your kitchen, Grace my love, really is quite wonderful."

"And so are you, Bobbie Hilliard," Grace said, opening the freezer compartment of the refrigerator. She laughed her appreciation at the full ice bucket, which she gave to Bobbie, saying that she would meet her in the living room after she changed her clothes.

Bobbie had the drinks made, the fire lit, and Carmen McRae on the phonograph when Grace hurried in wearing a pair of Bobbie's flannel pajamas and thick socks. She snuggled next to Bobbie and sipped her drink. "Delicious, as always," she said, "as are you, my wonderful one. I can't believe that you got everything put away."

"I just followed your instructions. Piece of cake."

"And then there's all that *you* do, Bobbie Hilliard, all the things you keep to yourself. Like paying the hospital bill for Mrs. Smith, like writing to Stephanie St. Clair, like working on a plan to supply sanitary pads and belts and vitamins free to the poor women of Harlem." Tears ran down her face. "Wonderful, beautiful things, Bobbie, and you do them for me. Yes they will help others, but you do these things for me and I am so very grateful to you and for you."

"I take it Eileen called you."

"Of course she did. Did you think she wouldn't?"

"Do you two tell each other everything?"

"Not quite everything," Grace replied with a sly, wicked grin.

A few hours later they were awakened by pounding on the kitchen door. "What the hell?" Bobbie mumbled, stepping into the flannel pajamas so hastily removed by Grace only a little while ago. "What?!" Bobbie snarled at the door.

"It's me! Open the door." Bobbie unlocked and threw open

the door to admit Boy Bobby. "Whatever is the matter?"

"The Queen's men are wreaking havoc on two of the markets—throwing everything off the shelves and on to the floor, pouring out all the milk and juice, opening bags of sugar and flour and cornmeal and pouring it into the milk and juice. People are standing out on the sidewalk and cheering. And one of the Queen's men is beating the crap out of one of the store owners. People say he's the one who ordered Mrs. Smith thrown down the subway stairs."

"Have the police arrived?" Grace asked.

"Not when I left," Bobby replied, out of breath.

"Then make certain not to be anywhere in the vicinity when they do show up," Grace said. "And make certain to let the young people know to stay well away."

"But what about the Queen's men?" Bobbie asked, but Grace cut her off.

"You can rest assured that anyone who worked for Madame St. Clair has enough sense not to be present when the police arrive." Then she looked hard at Bobbie. "And don't you even think about going out there, Eleanor Roberta Hilliard, and I mean that."

"Oh shit," Boy Bobby muttered. "When somebody calls you all of your names, you know they mean business."

"I don't know all of your names, Robert Mason, but I expect you to go directly home, steering clear of all the activity."

"Robert Henry Mason the Third, and I will take the long way directly home."

The Tricolore Market owner sat spread-eagle on the floor, in the middle of spoiled, rotten, stinking, bug-infested food, solid and liquid. He wept, begging the tall, white-haired Colored man who had broken both his kneecaps, to please stop beating him with his cane. Why the hell was this old nigger in his store beating on him?

"Where is the man who threw that woman down the subway steps? You said you called him."

"I did call him, told him to get over here right away. He said he was coming—"

"He better get his ass here, soon."

"He got nothing to do with this store! What you want with him?"

"I'm gonna throw his ass off the Verrazzano Bridge."

A similar scene played out ten blocks away at 150th and Broadway where another of Queen's old soldiers was acquainting the owner of the market there, in an up-close and personal way, with the smell and feel of rotten produce, juice, milk, and bug-infested flour, cornmeal, cereal and grits. He, too, used a cane to help make his points.

"I got no money to buy more food! The peoples, they don't buy."

"They don't buy 'cause the food is rotten! Are you crazy or what?"

"I'm poor, too, just like your peoples."

"My people don't sell you rotten food, now clean it up or board it up."

Broadway was busy, as usual, though both vehicular and foot traffic were heavier than usual because people had heard about the shopkeepers taken to task for selling rotten food. A vehicle slowed as it approached a market, and three men inside stared.

"Look at 'em," the man in the passenger seat snarled. "Fuckin' niggers! They got no bizness bein' here! They oughta go back where they come from!" The man pointed two guns out of the window and fired rapidly. With so many people bunched together on the sidewalk his bullets found targets, screams began, and the men watched for three or four seconds, enjoying the mayhem and misery. The driver turned back to the street to find a tall Negro standing directly in front of the car. He, too, had two guns, pointed at the men in the car.

The Negro quickly fired four shots, two from each gun, two into the face of the passenger and two into the face of the driver, the windshield spraying bloody glass shards. Then the shooter hurried to the sidewalk before the now driverless vehicle could run him over. He quickly dropped the guns into an overflowing trash bin, knowing they most likely would not be found any time soon if ever. Then he melted into the crowd, just another Negro on the street.

The car with the two dead men in front traveled erratically until several men intervened. One opened the driver's door and grabbed the steering wheel, turning it hard toward the curb, while another opened the passenger door, threw the dead shooter out, leaned in, and turned the key off. The man in the back seat opened his door, got out of the car, and tried to run but he didn't get far.

Sirens pierced the air as some people scattered while others did not. They stood silent and still, waiting for the police, bracing themselves for what they knew would happen: the police would see dead white men in a car, not dead Negroes on the sidewalk. The police would not notice, at least not immediately, that they were surrounded by a crowd of living, and angry, Negroes.

CHAPTER EIGHT

"Dr. Hannon," Grace said, answering the phone in the middle of the early morning ring, as usual, then giving it a strange look. The phone rang again, and Grace replaced the receiver, turned over, and muttered to Bobbie that she should go answer her telephone.

"Why?" Bobbie muttered, whining.

"Because it's ringing, Bobbie," Grace said, as the phone rang again—Bobbie's phone on a table in the living room.

Cursing, though still whining, Bobbie tumbled out of bed, stumbled into the living room, and grabbed up the receiver, but before she could speak, she heard the buzz of the dial tone. Whoever was calling had hung up. She sat there staring at the buzzing receiver. Awake now, she wondered who would call her this early on Saturday morning only to hang up before she could answer? She shivered, hung up the phone, and hurried back to the warmth of Grace and the bed.

The next time her phone rang she was awake. This time it was Joyce wondering if it was okay to come over. Bobbie told her to hurry because Grace was making cheese, mushroom, and spinach omelets and fresh baked rolls. Joyce hurried. She knocked on the kitchen door just as Boy Bobby was getting a bottle of champagne from the refrigerator. He held it aloft: "Fresh pitcher of mimosas just for you, Dr. Scott!"

"Wow!" Joyce said, but she was talking about the kitchen, and Grace stopped chopping onions and mushrooms long enough to accept the accolades.

"Eileen gets at least partial credit," she said, hugging Joyce, and asking where her family was.

"It's Eileen's father's birthday so she and Larry and the children are over there helping him celebrate. Needless to say, I'd much rather be here. This kitchen truly is amazing."

"Come see the official and formal dining room."

Bobbie and Jack, tasked with folding napkins and setting the table, stopped to welcome Joyce. Bobbie gave her a big hug as Jack stared in wide-eyed surprise before exclaiming, "Dr. Scott!"

Joyce was completely taken aback and rendered speechless for a few seconds. She looked closely at Jack. "You were one of my students, and a very good one as I recall. And then you disappeared. Please remind me of your name," she said, extending her hand.

"Jacqueline Jackson," Jack replied, shaking her former professor's hand.

"I never knew Joyce taught you!" Bobbie exclaimed.

"And I never knew what happened to Miss Jackson," Joyce said.

Jack looked at her friends. "Can I tell her?"

"It's your life and your story," Grace said.

So Jack told Joyce what happened, why she dropped out of graduate school without notice. "I lived in misery for more than a year, and it was Bobbie who made my life even a little bit bearable. My parents wanted to help, but they didn't have the money. Bobbie did and she bought me a car because I couldn't walk, and then she met Grace and that's when everything changed."

Grace hurried to the kitchen saying, "I had no idea Jack had

279

been a student of yours."

Joyce smiled a bit. "No way for you to know, though I do wish I'd known what happened to her." Then her smile widened. "But even if I had known, I couldn't have delivered her into the hands of Dr. Grace Hannon, miracle worker."

"Grace made the miracle, make no mistake, and Harlem Hospital may never be the same!"

Bobbie poured everyone a mimosa, then took a glass to Grace in the kitchen and asked to be put to work. In the dining room, Jack Jackson provided as close to an eyewitness account as they were likely to get about the events of the previous night.

"Do you think he was one of the Queen's men?" That's the one thing everyone wanted to know but Jack did not have a factual answer. "Though it wouldn't surprise me if she had men stationed in the area, just in case."

"Just in case what?" Grace asked. "Could she really predict that some . . ."

"She really knows those hoodlums and how they operate." Jack had found the word that Grace was searching for. "I'm really glad you contacted Madame Queen," Jack said to Bobbie, "and I'm really glad she still cares about what happens in Harlem, especially to poor people."

"So you think she sent the first men, the ones who—" Boy Bobby began.

"I know she did because I know those men. Both of them worked for her for years. They were her top—well, you know. The two were top lieutenants in Madame Queen's numbers-running operation and known as enforcers. They kept everything and everyone running smoothly, and that meant keeping close watch on the runners and the money."

"I heard people say the men last night were old men," Bobby said, "but the ones this morning were younger."

"And when and where did you hear that, Robert Henry Mason the Third?" Grace asked.

"This morning, not last night. I walked up and down the block before coming here, talking to and listening to what people were saying—that the two old men last night used their walking canes to try and beat some of the meanness out of those two shopkeepers, and the younger ones this morning used their fists."

"I wonder if the results will be the same," Joyce mused.

"I think if people can buy fresh food they won't care if it was old men's walking canes or young men's fists that showed the shopkeepers the light," Grace said. "I am concerned, though, that Madame St. Clair doesn't bear the brunt and take the blame."

"So how do you know all this, Jack?" Bobby asked.

"Because Madame Queen's people, at her direction, took special care of the children who took education seriously, especially if those children, like me, were tasked with getting to and from school on their own because their parents worked two or more jobs." Jack thought back to her young self, protected by men other people considered gangsters.

"Do you think these men had families, children of their own?" Joyce asked. "Is that why they guarded children?"

"They guarded us because Queen told them to," Jack said matter-of-factly, as if everyone knew that people did what Queen told them to do. "These two old men, before they were old, also bravely battled Dutch Schultz's thugs when they attempted to take over Queen's Harlem numbers operation. They were wounded, but they managed to kill several of Schultz's men. They went to prison because Colored men didn't kill white men, not even if it was a case of criminals killing criminals. But they didn't stay long because Queen had dirt on cops and judges and lawyers, and it was good dirt, the kind involving prostitutes and photographers."

"How in the world do you know these things?" Joyce asked, looking astounded. She got a wide grin from Jack, along with the explanation that she had two cousins who worked in one of the Queen's houses.

"They weren't really whorehouses," Jack said, waving away the looks of disbelief. "The women didn't really have sex with the men. They just played the game, acted as if they would, got the men undressed and in compromising positions, and photographs were taken, and, well, you can imagine the rest."

Boy Bobby was curious. "There had to be a bounty on her head, to say nothing of what the power players would do to the—ah—women and photographers when they caught them."

Now Jack was laughing, explaining that her cousins, on the Queen's orders, had packed up and left town ahead of the arrest warrants bearing their names, as did the other participants in the scheme. The Queen herself, however, did not escape and did not try to escape. "She spent time in prison, I don't know exactly when or how much time, but she knew it wasn't as much as it could have been because she'd been amassing dirt on the city's VIPs for years. Not only did the Queen know where bodies were buried, she knew who buried them."

That statement halted all conversation. They all thought the same thing. Not only could a Negro have that kind of power over the white men who controlled all aspects of New York City life, but a Negro woman could. And did.

Being keenly aware they were lucky to be with their friends at a time like this, Bobbie and Boy Bobby went to clean up the kitchen while Joyce put more logs on the fire and then joined Grace and Jack on the sofa.

"Will you return to complete your master's, Jack?" Joyce asked.

"Yes," Jack nodded. "Eventually. But not immediately. I need to work and earn some money. And I need to get back in touch with myself. Before . . . before what happened to me, I knew who I was and what I wanted. I don't know those things anymore. Not like I did before."

Grace held out an arm and Jack quickly snuggled into

it. "You are still yourself, Jack. Perhaps a different version of yourself, but you remain Jacqueline Marie Jackson, and you are as brilliant as you ever were."

"Perhaps even more so," Joyce suggested, and at Jack's look of surprise she elaborated. "People often are altered and changed by trauma and, as a result, view the world differently. You still know that education is important, Jack, and before what happened to you, you knew what you wanted to do with your education. Perhaps now you will want to do something different with it."

Jack nodded slowly with a speculative look at Joyce Scott. "Maybe I can do what you do, Dr. Scott. Maybe I can teach students how to teach our children instead of teaching them myself."

"And if you ever decide to write, a biography of Madame Stephanie St. Clair, the Queen of Harlem, certainly would be a bestseller," Joyce said.

"I know I'd buy a copy," said Grace.

"I'd buy one for every one of our sorority sisters," Joyce added, and Grace pretended to look scandalized before laughing uproariously as she described the likely reaction of several of the more staid, upright, and straitlaced members.

In the kitchen cleaning up, Bobby asked, "What happened to Grace when Jack was talking about her cousins?"

"I'm not certain but she has two older siblings, a sister and a brother, whom she hasn't seen for many years. She doesn't know where they live, and they don't keep in touch. There are no photographs of them, she doesn't even remember what they looked like, and her parents will not discuss them. It's as if they never existed."

"Do you think—?"

"I think I'm going to ask." She did ask Grace about her siblings as soon as all the brunch guests left, and Grace shared a memory so long forgotten that she actually pinched herself to confirm reality.

"Ow, that hurt, which means I think the discussion about Madame St. Clair's, uh, houses may have opened some of my closed and tightly padlocked internal doors."

"Does that mean you know something about those houses, Grace?"

"I think my brother and sister worked there, and all hell broke loose because my parents found out." She frowned and tapped her forehead as if to dislodge a memory. "The three of them were yelling at each other and it woke me up. It was the middle of the night, and my mother was screaming about their clothes, of all things."

"Where do you two get the money for clothes like this? And where do you go every night until all hours? And what do you do? Why can't you tell us?" Edith Hannon, both hands on her narrow hips, demanded of her two eldest at top volume, never having realized that they had stopped listening to her hollering years ago.

"We've already told you," her son said, his voice a thick mixture of boredom and sleep. "We work in a private club. She's a hostess, I'm a maitre d'. We earn good money and we're expected to spend some of it on clothes—we have to dress well if we want to keep our jobs."

"I know who you work for and I know what you do. Private club my ass! You work for that snooty black bitch who calls herself a Queen. Nothing but a numbers runner and hustler!"

"I don't know why I didn't remember any of this until I heard Jack talking about the private clubs Stephanie St. Clair operated." She looked at Bobbie. "Why didn't I remember, Bobbie?"

"Maybe because it's painful, and the mind can be very helpful in that regard—protecting us from painful events," Bobbie said.

"And why can I so clearly see their clothes but not their faces? She wore a magnificent gold gown and his tuxedo fit him like a glove but I don't remember their faces. Or their names." She was crying now, hard, ragged tears and sobs and Bobbie held her, knowing only too well how that kind of pain felt.

Swiping away her tears, Grace managed a wan grin when she remembered that the elder siblings had promised to gift their parents elegant clothes like their own, and the parents alternated between fury and a bizarre expectation that soon a fancy dress and suit would arrive for them when it was clear that the elder siblings had left without a word. "They actually expected those packages, Bobbie. But after almost a year they gave up. And that's when they stopped talking about them or thinking about them. They even rented out their rooms. When I said I thought one of those rooms could be mine they said it could if I could afford it."

She dropped her head to her chest, then slowly moved it from side to side. "I thought I'd hear from them, too—a letter, not clothes. I thought they cared about me, cared what happened to me. But I didn't wait as long as my parents. After a few weeks I knew I'd never hear from them. I got several tutoring jobs on campus, rented a room for less than my parents wanted to charge me for my old room, and never returned home to live." She jumped to her feet, crossed to the bar, poured three fingers of bourbon into a tumbler, and came back to sit next to Bobbie on the sofa.

"Will you ever see or talk to your parents, Gracie?"

Grace heaved a deep sigh. "I wish I didn't have to but I know that I will."

"If you ever want or need me to go with you, you know that I will."

"It would give me a great and perverse pleasure to introduce you as the person who gives me furs and diamonds and cashmere and watch the confusion on their faces as they first try to imagine why you would do such a thing, and then wonder how they could entice such gifts from you."

Bobbie sipped the bourbon and welcomed the burn. "Please let's not visit any time soon."

"Perhaps let's forget about them and you take me to bed because you're who loves me."

"Excellent idea, oh brilliant one." Bobbie stood up, extended her hand, pulled Grace to her feet, and walked them to the bedroom. En route Bobbie whispered that just maybe it was possible that she loved Grace more than all their friends combined.

Monday morning's ringing phone didn't come as early as the previous day, but it was Bobbie's phone that rang while she was making coffee. It was Larry McKinley.

"'Morning, Bobbie. Sorry to call so early, but can we meet today?"

"Of course, Larry, is everything all right? Eileen? The children? Joyce?"

He was startled. "I'm so sorry, Bobbie! I certainly didn't intend to worry you. They are quite all right if you discount Eileen's dark mutterings about consigning her parents to the depths of the Hudson River attached to concrete blocks."

"Then we must keep her and Grace away from each other for a while; otherwise, two sets of parents will be wearing cinder-block booties on the Hudson riverbed."

When he stopped laughing, he asked if she'd meet him for lunch at the Theresa Grill. They agreed on a time and she hung up, taking Grace a cup of coffee. "That was Larry—we're having lunch at the Theresa. I can drive you to work."

"Thank you, my love, but I'm really quite all right. You helped me restore my equilibrium." Grace had wept last night the way Bobbie had wept at the murders of her parents and brother. Was it different, Bobbie wondered, having one's parents obliterated, and learning that one's very much alive parents did not love you?

After Grace left, Bobbie called Eileen. "It's Bobbie and I'm waking you up. I'm so sorry, Eileen. I'll call you later—"

"Not a problem and don't you dare hang up, Bobbie Hilliard. It's not often that I find myself alone so I take full advantage when the opportunity presents itself and I go to sleep. No wife, no husband, no children, no noise. I'm in heaven!"

"And you miss every second you're deprived of their noisy presence."

"Can't live without it, truth be told," Eileen said,

"We missed you yesterday. An interesting time was had by all," Bobbie said. "I'm sure Joyce told you part of it, but here's the part she doesn't know, and I'm telling you just a little so you're not gobsmacked when Grace tells you all of it." When Bobbie finished telling her the story about Grace's parents and siblings, Eileen was very quiet for a long time.

"Is she all right?" Eileen finally asked.

"She was better this morning, but she was also in Dr. Grace Hannon mode, worried about something at work. I'll know for certain when she gets home." Then Bobbie asked, "Is Joyce all right after her surprise meeting with Jack Jackson?"

Eileen gave a hearty laugh. "If you could have seen her face when she told me. She waited until the children were asleep, then said she almost peed on your sofa!"

"But she was so cool and composed," Bobbie said. "She was

the perfect Dr. Scott to her former student, and she had Jack wrapped around her little finger."

"She's been known to have the same effect on me when she does the professorial thing. And when I call her Dr. Scott . . ."

"Is she worried that Jack might compromise her on campus?"

"Good heavens no," Eileen said. "She said she wished all her students had the same level of respect for her that Jack does. I think she was just shocked to have encountered a student in a social setting in which both were revealed to be women who loved women." Then Eileen changed the subject, wanting to talk more about Madame Queen and the Harlem in which she flourished. "Did you know about the policy banks and the private clubs when you were growing up?" she asked Bobbie.

"Most certainly not. You know how protective my parents were where Eric and I were concerned, though I'm sure they probably knew everything there was to know about everything that happened in Harlem. I wouldn't be surprised if my father had visited one of the Queen's, whatever they were, more than once."

"Mine were overprotective to the point of ridiculousness, and if my father had ever set foot into such a place, guilt would have driven him to confess to my mother."

"Speaking of whom—" Bobbie began but Eileen cut her off.

"I'd rather not. Get Larry to tell you."

"Do you know why we're having lunch? He sounded, well, not very upbeat or excited."

"He's not and he'll tell you everything. Please have Grace call me when she gets home."

They were all assembled at Grace's office. "Thanks, all of you, for coming in early to hear the good news I have to share." All of the women who worked for Dr. Grace Hannon, including the two newest nurses, revered her and would have come to work in the middle of the night instead of a mere hour early if she'd asked, including Mable Harris, the bookkeeper, who only came in once at the end of each month.

"The first good news," Grace said, "is that, thanks to the generosity of Madame Stephanie St. Clair, everyone gets a raise." Instead of the cheers and applause that she expected, the announcement was met with a confused, stunned silence. Finally, Myrt spoke.

"Dr. Hannon, how does Stephanie St. Clair know about you?"

Not at all what Grace expected. How much then, to share? She would, of course, tell Myrt all of it—when it was a conversation between friends. But this was Dr. Hannon and her employees. "My good friend, Bobbie Hilliard, in conversation with Madame St. Clair about a number of Harlem-based issues, mentioned this medical practice—the fact that a Negro woman doctor provided medical care to any Negro woman who needed it regardless of her ability to pay. Madame St. Clair came to see whether that was true. When she discovered that it was—"

"She paid the fee for every woman in the waiting room that morning," said Mrs. B. "And she left enough money to pay every outstanding balance on the books. For the first time since I've worked for Dr. Hannon we are operating in the black."

Now came the cheers and the applause and the hugs for Grace, but silence descended again when they opened the envelopes Mrs. B gave each of them. Enclosed was a paper bearing the amount of each woman's new salary, and fifty dollars in cash—a thank you from Grace for the always excellent care they provided each and every woman who came seeking their help. And now, thanks to Madame St. Clair, that care could be provided without having to worry how they would afford it. Grace pretended not to see Myrt wipe away tears. She had doubled her salary, and the nurse deserved every penny.

"The next thing I want to tell you," Grace said, "is that we soon will have the additional office space we so very much need. Our good fortune, however, comes because our next-door neighbor, Dr. Fred Allen, lost his long battle with leukemia, and that space is now available. With thanks again to Madame St. Clair, we not only can afford the space but we can afford to remodel it to suit our needs. Myrt, if you and Mrs. B will put your heads together and—"

"I'm sorry to interrupt you, Dr. Hannon, but exactly how much money did Mrs. St. Clair give you?" This from Gertrude Johnson, the new nurse. "And isn't she some kind of criminal? Do we really want her money?"

Grace smiled at the young nurse without parting her lips, and Gertrude was the only one in the room not to read the danger looming. "You didn't grow up here in Harlem, did you, Nurse?"

"No, Ma'am, I'm from Newark. I came here to go to nursing school, first at Harlem Hospital, and then at Columbia, where Nurse Lewis was one of my teachers."

"Then I urge you to spend some time with Nurse Lewis and Mrs. B and Miss Harris learning a bit of Harlem history and Madame St. Clair's role in it. And as for how much money she gave me? A hell of a lot. She can afford it and I need it."

"I'm going to say this, and Dr. Hannon, I beg your forgiveness, but all of you need to know that Dr. Grace Hannon has not taken her full salary from this practice for seven months—"

"That's enough, Mable!"

"I'm sorry, Dr. Hannon, but it's not. They need to know that they got paid their full salary because you didn't, and that Madame St. Clair's generosity will allow us to begin to make a real difference in the lives of so many of our women, including Dr. Hannon, who can now take her full salary." Mable Harris's apologetic look was almost sufficient apology, but the look that Grace sent her was something just short of forgiveness.

Now Grace spoke. "I don't want any of you to ever worry about me. I am all right. In fact, I'm rather better than all right. I just want you to continue your very fine work with and for our patients—and one day soon Stephanie St. Clair will be one of them, right, Mrs. B?" To close the meeting she said, "I'd just like to add, for those of you who are aware of the events in two markets on Broadway known for selling rotten food, it was Madame St. Clair who sent the cease-and-desist message." And with that she stood up and went to her office, followed by Myrt, as Mrs. B opened the door to admit the women who were waiting.

"I don't know how to thank you, Grace."

"I don't know how I would have made it without you, Myrt, so I'm the one who owes you the thanks—for keeping both me and the office functioning during some very difficult times. You're a brilliant nurse and a stellar friend." Myrt embraced her, then stepped quickly away to resume the professional distance between them. She wiped her tears again and headed for the door and to manage the patient care. "How's Thelma?" Grace asked in a quick whisper.

Myrt turned briefly, shook her head, and left. Grace had no time to understand the negative head shake when asked about Nurse Thelma Cooper.

Bobbie left home early for her meeting with Larry McKinley, so she'd have time to walk along Broadway for a look at the two markets that were prepared either to change their modus operandi or to shut down. And she wasn't the only interested observer. Even from half a block away she could tell the crowd was sizable, along with a heavy police presence. Although they were well back from the crowd of spectators, if they decided to do more than stand and watch, they'd have the crowd penned in.

Not liking the look of that, Bobbie crossed the street and walked west, over to Seventh Avenue, where she'd walk to the Theresa. She spied Bobby in the battered green truck with *McKinley Property Management* written on the side. He didn't see her because he appeared to be in a very serious conversation with the two people in the front seat with him. She saw a taxi with its light on and stepped into the street to hail it.

The taxi stopped in front of the Theresa, Bobbie paid the cabbie, and before she could close the door, another woman immediately got in. Bobbie stood looking up at the elegant building. Her parents had dined regularly at The Penthouse, often in the company of musician friends of her father, occasionally in the company of visual artist friends of her mother, but always in the presence of storied and notable and famous Negroes.

"Thanks for meeting me on short notice, Bobbie," Larry said, spying her.

"Happy to oblige, Larry, though I confess to being a little bit worried about why."

His smile evaporated. "Me, too, truth be told." He led them inside and followed the hostess to a table. The waitress arrived immediately with menus. With a questioning look at Bobbie, he ordered them both cappuccinos, and they studied the menu while they waited for the waitress. Then they both ordered Waldorf chicken salad and French fries, and as they ate Larry told her there was good news to report.

"Thanks to you and your Black Mask report, we now have a full Board of Directors with the addition of Dorothy West, Billy Strayhorn, and Pauli Murray, all of whom cited your mother, and you by extension, as the reason for their positive response. Take a look," and he gave her the full list of names. She wondered why he was watching her read until she saw "N. Grace Hannon, PhD, MD."

"With a board like that we really must deliver," Bobbie managed through a laugh, adding in a near whisper, "She didn't say a word."

"She wanted to surprise you," Larry said, "and it seems she succeeded."

"Indeed she did, but you're still wearing a funny look. Please hurry and drop the other shoe."

"The board has agreed that you should be an ex officio member, Dr. Hilliard."

Bobbie dissolved into laughter. "I think I've been had, and I never saw it coming. Smooth as a Parisian silk scarf you are, Mr. McKinley." He quickly erased a tiny smirk and produced a notebook and pen from his briefcase.

She gave him a rueful, raised hands surrender, and asked in her sweetest voice what more she could do for Black Mask.

"Well, since you mention it, perhaps you could begin planning the annual Christmas fundraising gala?"

She shook her head in feigned dismay and asked if he could recommend a good jeweler. "How good? What are you looking for?"

"Something special for Grace. That kind of good."

He took a pen and a small leather pad from his inside jacket pocket, wrote quickly, tore out the small piece of paper, gave it to her, and said, "Be sure to tell him that I sent you and you'll get the friends and family deal." He looked at his watch, said he was about to be late for a meeting with Bobby, stood up quickly, gave her a quick hug, and practically ran from the room.

Bobby was waiting for him on the sidewalk in front of one of the four buildings his company owned, which he had yet to "whip into shape." The proof was evident. The front door was propped open with multiple people wandering in and out, and despite the placement of large metal drums with "Place Trash Here" painted on the sides, trash littered the sidewalk and yard. He walked forward to meet Larry.

"How much leeway do I have—"

"All of it!" Larry snapped.

"Good," Bobby said, and strode to the front door of the building, picked up the brick that was holding the door open, closed the door, making sure it locked, and returned to Larry, who was picking up the trash on the sidewalk and putting it into the metal drums. Bobby joined in.

"Mr. Mason, Mr. McKinley!" Both men quickly straightened up and looked around to see who was calling them. Larry frowned, not recognizing the young man hurrying toward them, a heavy stick in his hand. Bobby, on the other hand, relaxed, smiled, and held out his hand.

"How're you doing, Buddy?" he asked, shaking the young man's hand and reminding Larry who he was. "What have you got there?" Bobby asked, pointing to the stick.

Buddy held it up to show the thick, sharply pointed spike in the end of the stick. "My uncle let me borrow it. He works for the Parks and Recreation Department, and they use these to pick up trash. I got stuck by a needle yesterday picking up out here—"

"I'll have one of these made for you immediately, Buddy," Bobby said through gritted teeth, "And I hope this won't be an issue or a problem for too much longer."

"I appreciate that, Mr. Mason, 'cause I like working here, but some people make it hard for me to keep it clean."

"Just keep doing your job, Buddy, and know that I see and appreciate it. By the way, how is Naomi?" Bobby asked.

"She's doing good, Mr. Mason. She's got a part-time job cleaning up in a beauty salon over on Seventh Avenue."

"That's good, Buddy, but don't you all forget about going back to school. I'd like to see both of you finish high school."

"Don't you worry 'bout that, Mr. Mason!" the boy said, smiling.

Grace and Myrt reviewed charts. It was the end of the day and they were exhausted, but it had been a very good day and they were in good spirits. Until the last chart.

"She already knows something is very wrong," Myrt said, clutching the chart to her chest.

"I doubt she has any idea how very wrong," Grace said sadly, "and I don't look forward to telling her. We'll do all the requisite tests and get the second, even third opinions, but I'll have to tell her and make sure she understands that at this point surgery will not help."

"You do know, of course, that she's the third patient to come to us from him," Myrt said, her teeth clenched at the reference to a popular and well-known male Ob-Gyn.

Grace nodded, anger flashing in her eyes. "I expect he sends them to us—"

"When he knows they're dying, the bastard." Myrt was as angry as Grace. "I wish we could get all his patients while they're still healthy, so we can teach them good health habits."

"I pray for the day when there are more women Ob-Gyns, Negro women Ob-Gyns. There will always be women who will choose male doctors, but when they know they have choices, perhaps they will make different choices. I do wonder why a man who obviously has no regard for women would choose a practice where all of his patients would be women. Anyway, let's wrap it up so you can get home to Thelma, and Myrt, please tell me that she's all right."

"She's totally exhausted, Grace, and threatening to quit her job."

Grace was speechless. She was under the impression that Thelma was pleased with her job as head surgical nurse to the team of Crawford and Jennings, two of the hospital's top surgeons. She knew that they held her in very high regard. "Thelma is that unhappy?

"She says working for The Boys is fine, but they loan her to other surgeons so she never knows who she will be scrubbing in with, or when—very early morning or very late at night or on Saturday or Sunday if there's an emergency. And not all of the surgeons are nice men. In fact some of them are real nasty crackers. And she won't put up with that, so she's quitting."

Grace stood up, telling Myrt to ask Thelma not to quit yet and that she'd be in touch in the morning.

First thing the next morning, Grace called Thelma. "You didn't quit yet, did you, Thelma?"

"No, I said I didn't feel well yesterday and left early."

"Good. Call in sick today, then call Dr. Sarah Giles who runs the Columbia School of Nursing. I just spoke with her. Go see her today and if she offers you a job you're interested in, accept it. Then submit your letter of resignation when you can cite your new employment. Your being on the teaching staff at Columbia University Hospital's Department of Nursing will really wow them. But tell The Boys first, in person."

"Should I tell them the truth?"

"That's up to you."

Bobbie had her jacket collar pulled up and her cap pulled down low against the cold drizzle that had been coming down for the last hour. She'd seen enough of what was happening on Broadway to satisfy herself that Madame Queen's men had made the point that needed to be made. One market was open under new management and all items for sale were new and fresh while the other was closed permanently. Collateral response was swift as well, as every store of every kind and description had either been cleaned up or was in the process of being cleaned up—floors swept and mopped and front windows washed. Signs were spruced up or replaced, and a few announced: Under New Management.

She was ready to go home. Smiling, she reached her hand inside her jacket, into the inside pocket, and caressed the box that held the ring she'd bought for Grace, who she knew would love it. She was certain of that, though she knew Grace, being Grace, would initially insist that it was too extravagant. But she would put it on and there it would remain.

She'd been having trouble reaching Boy Bobby. He'd not been in his McKinley Property Management office all day, which wasn't surprising since he now was responsible for the maintenance and management of so much. She had briefly asked Larry how Bobby was doing as they left the Theresa and he'd grinned like she'd asked about one of his children, so Bobby was doing all right. She'd call him at home tonight. If she ever got home. Taxis zoomed past, none of them empty. She touched the ring again, put her head down, increased her walking speed, and headed for home, surprised and delighted to find Grace already there.

"You are soaked," she said, pulling Bobbie's sodden bomber jacket off her shoulders and heading into the backdoor hallway with it.

"Wait," Bobbie said, grabbing the jacket from her and reaching into the inside pocket.

"And what exactly is that?" Grace asked.

"You're spoiling my moment, Dr. Hannon," Bobbie said, giving Grace the box. She watched her open it, saw the shock on her face, followed by amazement, then wonderment. And then came the tears.

"Oh Bobbie, oh my goodness. This is exquisite. But why? What's it for?"

"It's for you, my love. Because you have enhanced and improved my life and our home, and I wasn't even aware they

297

needed enhancing and improving. Another reason for the ring: your penetrating wisdom in all things. Perhaps you'd like to put it on?"

Grace removed the ring from the box while smiling and muttering "penetrating wisdom." She gave the box to Bobbie, then held the ring up to the light, watching the diamonds sparkle. She gave the ring to Bobbie and held out both of her hands. "Where? You choose—left hand or right hand?" Bobbie took Grace's right hand and slipped the ring on the ring finger. "A perfect fit," she said. What she didn't say was with a ring like this there certainly would be questions, but on the left hand there likely would be more than mere questions, and ones that Grace most likely could not or would not truthfully answer. "Is that all right?"

"Yes, Bobbie, it's all right," she said, stepping into her arms, weeping. She reached for the box of tissues on the counter and wiped her eyes, then asked if Bobbie was hungry. They ate a good dinner and shared the events of the day, and even though Grace talked, her eyes never left the column of diamonds encircling her right ring finger.

"I'm very happy for Myrt and Thelma," Bobbie said. "They deserve to be able to slow down and enjoy their lives and not have to work themselves to exhaustion all the time."

"Living room or bedroom?" Bobbie asked when the drinks were made.

"Is that a serious question?" Grace replied. They were in the bedroom three hours later when they were jolted awake by the insistent ringing of the kitchen doorbell, accompanied by pounding on the door.

"What the hell?" Bobbie muttered, sitting on the side of the bed, pulling on her pajama bottoms and sliding her feet into slippers. She stood and headed to the kitchen while pulling a T-shirt over her head. "Yes, who is it?" she called out, switching on the light at the door. She heard Bobby's voice and swung open the door. He tumbled into her embrace, bleeding profusely as his weight pulled them both down to the floor. "Grace!" Bobbie yelled. "Come quickly! Bobby is badly hurt and bleeding all over the place!"

Grace hurriedly pulled on a pair of Bobbie's flannel pajama bottoms and a T-shirt over her head. She ran first for her medical bag and then skidded to a stop in the kitchen.

Bobbie sat on the floor cradling sweet Boy Bobby's bloody torso in her lap. Dr. Hannon took over. She knelt down and took Boy Bobby's head in her hands, feeling all over. No wounds. She then inspected his neck and was about to investigate his torso when she realized he was wearing a dress. Then she knew what must have happened.

She stood quickly, grabbed a pair of shears from a rack, and bent over Bobby, slicing the dress away from his body and the tape that held his penis unnaturally pinned against his body. There was what appeared to be a bullet hole in his shoulder, and a possible knife wound on his arm. "I'll pull him up, Bobbie, and you lever yourself beneath him, pushing and pulling him to his feet. And be careful not to slip in all the blood and fall. Robert Henry Mason the Third, do you hear me?"

His eyes fluttered open, then shut, then open, and his lips moved. No words came out but he heard her. He knew where he was, knew he was safe. He tried to speak again, but the words were little more than an unintelligible croak.

"Was Queen Esther with you?" Bobbie asked, and Boy Bobby's eyes filled with tears. "Is she hurt?"

"Stabbed," he managed to croak.

"Is she alive?" Bobbie asked. "Where is she?"

"Can we get him to bed first so I can look at his wounds." An order, not a request, by a doctor. She said to her patient, "The dress notwithstanding, we cannot carry you, my friend. You'll have to walk." And he did, very slowly, arms across their shoulders, down the hallway and into the guest bedroom.

"Lots of light, Bobbie, please," Dr. Hannon said, pulling the stethoscope from her medical bag and listening to him breathe, back and front, at the top and in the middle. She looked closely at his injuries, pushing and prodding them until they began to bleed, and he began to whimper. She asked Bobbie to please see how far her phone cord would stretch, almost to the door. Grace stepped into the hall and called Myrt and Thelma.

"I am so very sorry but I need you. Boy Bobby has been badly injured—shot and stabbed—and he's bleeding rather profusely. If you could come and bring whatever you have at home. Don't take the time to go to the office."

Bobbie took the phone. "Park in the front, not in the garage, please, and I'll explain when you get here." She went to Boy Bobby and knelt beside the bed. "Are the police involved? Are they looking for you?"

He opened his eyes. "They don't know who I am, but one of 'em maybe saw my truck. I was driving away probably too fast." A black-and-purple pickup that currently was parked in her garage. "Who else is hurt? You and Queen Esther and who else?" Bobbie asked.

It took him a long time to answer and even then he didn't look at her. "Two people are probably dead and I probably killed one of 'em." Grace flinched but didn't speak. Bobbie did.

"Killed him how?"

"With the pistol he shot me with. I took it from him and showed him how to use it, compliments of Uncle Sam," Bobby said, managing a slight grin.

"That's not the least bit funny, Robert Mason," Grace said, adding, "though he knew enough to place this in your shoulder." She held up forceps that held a bloody bullet, and Bobby groaned and passed out.

Myrt and Thelma arrived and went to assist. Bobbie stood up, leaned in to whisper to Grace that she was going to call Larry, and left.

Larry sounded wide awake when he answered, but then so did Grace no matter what time her phone rang. Still, Bobbie apologized for waking him before telling him why and saying she'd really appreciate his advice and assistance. He said he was on his way. Bobbie told Grace, then hurried into the kitchen to stuff the pile of bloody clothes into a bag and brew a pot of coffee. A trail of blood led down the hall to the makeshift surgery. Bobbie got another bag and a roll of paper towels and cleaned the floor. She had two bags full of bloody mess to take to the receptacle in the garage when the doorbell rang. Confirming through the peephole it was Larry, she opened the door.

"Thank you for coming." He followed her through the living and dining rooms into the kitchen where she pointed to the coffee and some cups. "Help yourself. I'll be right back," she said, holding the bags aloft. She rushed out the kitchen door and down the steps to the garage and the trash bins where, sure as shit, there was the black-and-purple pickup. She dumped the trash, then found the keys in the ashtray.

Back in the kitchen, she quickly told Larry everything she knew about how and why Bobby came to be bleeding on the kitchen floor, and how Grace and her nurses came to be performing surgery in the guest bedroom. Larry listened and drank two cups of coffee before he said, "The cops don't know who he is, but they do know that his truck was present, is that right?" Bobbie nodded. "And that truck is in your garage." It was a statement not a question, but Bobbie nodded again. "We absolutely must install a gate at the entrance to your garage."

"We'll pay for it. When?"

They hadn't heard Grace arrive. "Is he okay?" Larry and Bobbie asked as Larry gave her his stool at the counter. Myrt and Thelma entered and nodded. Before anyone could say or ask anything Thelma said, "A hot shower and back to bed," taking Myrt by the hand and walking her to the front door where they slipped their shoes on.

"I can't thank you enough," Grace said. "I couldn't have done it without you."

"You don't ever have to do without us," Myrt said. "See you tomorrow and consider yourself warned. I may have to fire our new nurse if she keeps wondering what all we're doing with Madame St. Clair's money," and they were gone.

Grace squeezed her eyes shut. Office drama she could do without. "Come see him before he's asleep," she said to Bobbie and Larry. "He's got just enough morphine in him so the pain won't keep him awake. As for how he is, he's lucky he's not dead."

Bobby was propped on a pile of pillows, his left shoulder and chest covered in gauze and tape. His eyes fluttered open and widened at the sight of his boss, and he tried to sit up. Grace eased him back down with a gentle but meaningful push. "My best friends are really angry with me," he said to Larry.

"I don't think any of us have said that to you," Bobbie told him.

"You don't have to say it. I see it in your eyes when you look at me: you, Grace, Thelma, and Myrt. You think I did a really stupid thing, but they've killed two of us now and nobody has done a damn thing about it."

"Killed what two, Bobby? When?"

"Miz Maggie's nephew—"

"Came out of his coma a couple of weeks ago I thought," Bobbie said.

"And he had a brain seizure and died four days ago because he never recovered from the beating. They kicked the shit out of his head."

"Oh God, "Bobbie muttered.

Bobby went on, "Then, the very next day, one of Queen Esther's good friends was killed in the same place, over by the river, in the same way: beaten bloody and unconscious, dress pulled all the way up to make it clear that this person wasn't a woman. Queen Esther called the police, but they said the victim was breaking the law, being what she was and doing what she was doing. Queen and her best friend said they were going to make somebody pay. I begged them not to go, but they told me to go back to my good job and my nice life and leave them alone; they could take care of themselves." He closed his eyes, shook his head, and said, "I just couldn't let them go alone into an alley near the river to confront men who made a habit of murdering drag queens and who treated it as a sport."

"But why go there?" Larry asked. "Aren't there bars, night clubs, restaurants they can go to?"

"And who'll take them, Larry? You? Me? Godammit!" he yelled. "They want sex, like we all do. But they want it with real men—"

"Men who hate them for who and what they are," Bobbie said gently and quietly, "and who kill them rather than fuck them. And we're not angry with you, dear friend; we're frightened for you, for what could happen to you. For what did happen to you this night."

"I was damn near killed because I helped a friend avenge a wrong is what happened to me, and I had to help because no one else would because no one believes we deserve to be protected. So we have to get our own payback." He started to cry as Grace got a syringe and a vial of medication from her bag. She drew some of the medicine into the syringe, tapped it, and injected the drug into the vein in the bend of Boy Bobby's good arm. He was asleep within seconds. "He'll sleep the rest of the night," she said, but the look she gave Bobbie meant she had something to say. Bobbie waited. "If the police know about his truck—"

Walking into the living room, Bobbie said, "I'll move it, Grace."

"Cover it with a tarp and put it behind the garbage bins," Larry said. "Unless someone saw him drive into this garage, they don't know where to look, and they don't know who he is. I'll have someone here tomorrow about the gate."

303

"Thank you," Grace said. She kissed Bobbie, saying she was taking a shower and going to bed.

"Everyone should have such a good friend," Larry said.

"Speaking of which, I doubt he'll be at work tomorrow," Bobbie said, remembering that Larry was more than just a good friend, "but I'm not brave enough to ask Grace about it until she's had some more sleep."

Larry grinned at her. "Not a problem. I already can't do without him. I just want him to heal. And if you're going to be here with him tomorrow, maybe I can come by?"

Grace's third morning patient was a woman in her third month of pregnancy who was experiencing heavy vaginal bleeding, pelvic pain that traveled up to her shoulder, and such dizziness that she'd fainted. A neighbor had brought her to the doctor, and just in time, Grace said. Myrt called an ambulance and Grace rode with her, monitoring her blood pressure all the way to the hospital. The ER attending physician hurried over to her.

"Ectopic pregnancy I believe," Grace told him. "With way too much bleeding and pain."

"You go get gowned and gloved and I'll have her sent up."

"Thank you," Grace said, shaking his hand and hurrying to the elevator. When she was prepped for surgery, Grace went to talk with the patient, to explain what she thought the problem was and what she planned to do about it. The woman, a thirty-year-old mother of three who looked forty looked almost relieved when Grace said surgery involved removal of the tube in which the fetus was growing.

"Take both of 'em, Dr. Hannon!" Taken aback, Grace asked the woman to repeat herself, and she did: "Take both tubes. I don't want no more children. Three is enough. Since you have to take one of the tubes, take the other one, too. Please."

Bobbie made sure that Boy Bobby was steady on his feet before she left him in the bathroom on his own, but she stood in the hallway just in case while he washed his face and brushed his teeth and did whatever else he could do with one hand and arm. She hadn't realized last night that Grace had taped the injured arm to his chest to keep it immobile. He leaned heavily against the door frame to keep his balance. Whatever drugs Grace had given him helped him sleep but left him woozy this morning.

"That smells so good I feel better already," Bobby said, as Bobbie gingerly walked him to the kitchen, got him straddling a stool and resting the elbow of his taped arm on the countertop. She fixed him a cup of coffee and a plate of buttered toast. He'd probably had no food since yesterday afternoon. She opened the refrigerator to see what was there when the doorbell rang.

"I hope you guys are hungry!" Larry said. "Miz Maggie tried to give me enough food for ten or twelve people—all of 'em linebackers!" He put the bags of food on the counter and walked over to Boy Bobby and gave him the once-over. "You sure look a hell of a lot better than you did last night," he said, and poured himself a cup of coffee.

"You saw me last night?" he asked. "Grace. I remember Grace. And Myrt and Thelma. Oh, I've got to call and find out how Queen is." He tried to stand up too quickly, and if Larry and Bobbie hadn't caught him he'd have crashed to the floor. "Bobbie, a phone, please." She pulled her phone as far as it would stretch, dialed the number he recited, and passed him the receiver. Then she and Larry grabbed the bags of food and retreated to the dining room.

"Did Miz Maggie mention her nephew?" she asked Larry. "Or say anything about last night?"

Larry shook his head. "I didn't get the sense that she was

aware of anything. I don't think she knows that people are committed to avenging her nephew's death," he said, then frowned. "I did think it odd that she gave me three times more than I ordered and charged me half of what I owed, so maybe she does know."

Still a bit weak and woozy but not nearly as disconnected as he seemed just a bit ago, Bobby returned to a seat. "Queen Esther is injured, but not as badly as I thought. She's safe, and she'll be all right. The boarding house might not be, though. The cops raided it early this morning, and they left really pissed off because they found no evidence that anybody there had anything to do with what happened in that alley—not a single drop of blood, not a single bandage. And nobody would talk to them. Wouldn't answer a single question except to say 'I don't know what you're talking about.' I will have to move my truck, though. Cops asked who it belonged to."

"Unless they know to look in this garage—" Larry began.

"And they don't," Boy Bobby insisted.

"Then you have nothing to worry about. It's under a tarp behind the trash bins. And it's possible that the measurements for the gate have already been made. I'll find out when I get to the office," Larry said. "Now eat, please. I have something to discuss with Bobbie."

"I'll be with you as soon as I call Jack."

"Call her for what?" Boy Bobby asked, eyes wide.

"You can't possibly believe that I could know you were injured and not tell her! Now eat, please."

Her call to Jack was quick as she knew it would be, and ended with her saying, "Use the front door. I'll explain later." And she joined Larry in the living room.

"Before we talk, Bobbie, tell me: did you get to the jeweler?"

"Follow me," Bobbie said, dashing to the bedroom.

She opened Grace's jewelry box and carefully lifted out the box containing the ring, opened it, and gently passed it to Larry.

"Holy smokes, Bobbie. I've never seen anything so beautiful." Then he frowned. "Doesn't Grace like it?"

"She loves it," Bobbie replied, returning the ring to the jewelry box.

"Then why isn't she wearing it? Too elegant for the office?"

Bobbie told him about the nurse and her insistence on knowing how much money Grace had received from Stephanie St. Clair and what she planned to do with the money.

Larry huffed and muttered darkly about what he'd like to do to "Nurse Whateverthefuck."

"Hmmm, Larry, do you know where Grace can purchase things wholesale—things like bars of soap, women's vitamins, sanitary napkins and belts, in large quantities? She wants to give them to all of her patients, just one of the things Nurse Whateverthefuck questions where the money to pay for it comes from."

Larry thought for a moment then said, "I maybe know a fella who knows a fella."

"It's the next best thing to removing both tubes so she's happy with that, yes?" Myrt said, and Grace nodded. She'd explained to the patient that she could not ethically remove a healthy fallopian tube, but that she could close or block it, preventing sperm from getting through. "You'll see her tonight?"

"I will," Grace said to Myrt. "And I've added a daily vitamin to her medicine list, which I'm sure will raise eyebrows and which I'll have to explain to the hospital nursing staff."

"I've already had to explain it to Miss Priss—three times. I can't take much more of her, Grace. I really do understand how she might be surprised by how we do things here. Even some of the patients are surprised by how we do things here. But they understand why we've started giving them the vitamins, probably because most of them have children and understand the importance. Priss, however, doesn't understand—that or any damn thing else."

Grace sighed, pulled an office chair closer, and lifted her legs onto it. Then she kicked off her shoes and sighed again. "Is our part-timer qualified for full-time work?" she asked Myrt.

"I think she has the knowledge, but she doesn't yet have the experience that Priss does. In all honesty, Miss Priss is a really good nurse. She's just a royal pain in the ass."

"I'll explain about the vitamins. Is she still going on about Madame Queen and the money?"

"Oh yeah! Now it's about the vitamins and the sanitary pads and belts. How can we afford to give these things to *every* woman for free? And where are we getting them? Why can't we be told how much money—"

Grace reached across her desk for the phone. She punched the button that gave her Mrs. B and asked who was still in the office. "Please send her to see me," Grace said, and hung up the phone, none too gently.

A brisk knock and Nurse Gertrude Johnson entered. "You wanted to see me, Dr. Hannon?"

"Come in and have a seat and tell me why you continue to ask questions about the money given to us by Stephanie St. Clair?"

"It wasn't given to us; it was given to you—"

"It was given to the medical practice of Dr. Grace Hannon to benefit the staff and patients of this medical practice. What part of that do you fail to understand?"

"Why can't we know how much money she gave us?"

"Because you're the only one who wants to know and because it's none of your business," Grace said.

"I just want to be sure that we're not doing anything illegal or immoral—"

Grace picked up the phone and called Mrs. B. To the

new nurse she said, "You're uncomfortable working here and I'm uncomfortable having you work here—" The door opened and Mrs. B. came in. "Nurse Johnson is leaving us as of this moment. Please do the necessary paperwork and prepare her final paycheck to include a week's severance pay and mail it to her."

Nurse Gertrude Johnson began to stutter, then to whimper. "My job . . . you can't take my job . . . I need my job. Please don't take my job."

"If you spent more time doing your job and less time focusing on matters that are my job and none of your business, you'd still have a job," Grace snapped in a rare display of the anger they knew she was capable of but which she very rarely displayed. "Mrs. B, please do Nurse Johnson's paperwork, get any keys or garage cards she has, and lock the door behind her."

"Dr. Hannon, please!"

"Please what, Nurse?"

"Please don't fire me!"

"Why? Because you said please?"

"Because I need my job!"

"And I need people I can trust working for me and I don't trust you, Nurse, because you apparently don't trust me. Good day."

She nodded to Mrs. B who took the young nurse by the arm to lead her out of Dr. Hannon's office, just as Nurse Thelma Cooper approached the door in her full formal uniform, complete with all her pins and badges. Nurse Priss almost fainted: her replacement already had arrived.

Grace hadn't seen Thelma in her cap and cape in a long time, and it truly was an impressive sight. She got to her bare feet to welcome her friend, whom she was almost certain was soon to be an instructor in the Columbia University School of Nursing. Both Grace and Myrt waited for the office door to close, and Myrt locked it. Then they both looked at Thelma and waited for her to deliver the news—which she did by swirling her cape and doing a cha-cha step. Then she grabbed Myrt and danced her around the office as Grace chanted "one, two, cha, cha, cha!" Thelma released Myrt and grabbed Grace, but she didn't dance her; she just hugged her tightly.

"They have to check all my references, but I'm as good as hired!" She grew serious. "I did talk with The Boys this morning and while they said they regretted that I was leaving, they hugged and thanked me and gave me their good wishes. Which I hope will translate into strong, positive references."

"I don't think you have anything to worry about," Grace said, returning to her chair with her legs elevated on the adjacent chair.

With an arm still around Myrt, Thelma pointed to the door. "Was that—?"

Myrt nodded. "Grace even tried not to fire her, but you know I keep wondering what's wrong with her, and I think she must be in one of those religious groups that spouts lots of moralistic do's and don'ts but is short on explanations. Then impressionable members like Priss don't really understand any of it, usually because the one spouting all the nonsense doesn't understand it either. And those who really want to do right get it all wrong."

"And end up getting themselves fired," Thelma said, as a knock sounded at the door. "Oh, Lord, is she back?"

"I certainly hope not!" Myrt said, opening the door to Bobbie.

"What a lovely surprise!" Grace jumped to her feet, meeting Bobbie for a long embrace. Bobbie looked at Thelma. "I don't know whether to salute or genuflect."

"Both," Thelma said without hesitation, and Bobbie delivered. Then she straightened and gave Thelma a head-to-toe scrutiny.

"They should put you in a position of power and authority so the young nurses will see how to comport themselves," Bobbie said, this time with a deep bow. Then she held aloft a gold bag neither of the others realized she was holding. She placed it on the edge of Grace's desk and removed three items—two long boxes of equal size and Grace's ring box, all of them the same gold color. She gave each of the long boxes to Myrt and Thelma, and she gave Grace her ring box.

Though Grace didn't know exactly what was happening, she played along. "Myrt, you and Thelma open yours first," and they gasped when they did: each box held a watch and a bracelet.

"White gold and yellow gold—you choose," Bobbie said, and they switched boxes, Myrt taking the yellow gold set.

"Bobbie, what . . . why . . ." they sputtered in pleased amazement.

"To thank you both for being such good friends to Grace, for being such brilliant nurses and healers, to congratulate you, Thelma, on what I hope will be a wonderful and rewarding new opportunity." They were both weeping and hugging Bobbie, then both tried on their new jewelry, requiring assistance from Grace and Bobbie.

"Grace, I'm guessing that's not a bracelet and a watch," Thelma said pointing to the ring box. "Are you going to open it or just stand there looking at it?" Grace opened the box and repeated her previous response to seeing the ring. She hugged Bobbie and wept, then gave the ring to Bobbie and held out her hands. Bobbie placed the ring on the right ring finger. Thelma and Myrt took turns holding Grace's hand and staring at the ring, turning it around and around on Grace's finger.

"I don't care what hand it's on, I think you two just got married," Myrt said, and the newlyweds beamed at her. Then Grace, still holding Bobbie's hand, returned to her chair and put her legs up. Bobbie took one look at the swollen ankles and lifted the legs, sat in the chair, put the feet in her lap, and began to massage them. Grace sighed happily.

"Can we go home now?"

"You can," Grace said, "but I need to check on a patient in the hospital. And by the way—"

"Jack's got him well in hand," Bobbie said laughing, and regaled them with Boy Bobby's many attempts to get around the behavioral rules and regs Grace had set for him. Finally tired of the game, Jack had threatened to call his grandmother and tell her that he was seriously injured—shot *and* stabbed—and that he was wearing a dress when it happened. Out in public. The four of them had a good laugh and congratulated Jack Jackson in absentia on her skillful management of the situation. "He's still worried that we're angry with him," Bobbie said, "though I told him that we were not angry but worried that something exactly like this would happen, and that next time he might not be as lucky."

"I appreciate your words, Bobbie, but I am angry. I'm damned angry!" Grace withdrew her feet from Bobbie's massaging hands and dropped them onto the floor. "We—none of us—have the right to put ourselves in harm's way when the people who love us will be left to mourn us." She stood up and paced back and forth as the three women who knew and loved her best watched. "I know that he was avenging his friend. I respect that and I applaud him for it and I'm proud to have such a loyal friend. But I don't need—or want—a dead loyal friend."

Bobbie reached out to Grace and grabbed her hand, halting her pacing mid-step, pulling her into her lap, and wrapping her arms around her. They sat together like that, quietly, until Bobbie said, "I no longer try to imagine a time when we won't be hated—either because we're Colored or because we're women or because we love other women—or, in our case, for all three. Nothing we can do about them or their hate. But there are things we can do to protect ourselves from it—"

"Like what? Please tell me," Thelma said, bitterness dripping, "Because if I never again have to see a maimed, disfigured Jack

Jackson or a shot-and-stabbed Bobby Mason, it'll be too soon."

"Like the things I do to keep the cops away from The Slow Drag, the three primary ones being not to allow ofay women to enter, not to allow Negro women to hang outside—either in line to get in or just to hang around laughing and talking—and the payment of healthy bribes to two police lieutenants to keep patrol cops away. I'm not naive or crazy: I'm certain the cops know the club exists, but I won't give them any reason to think too deeply about it or to come inside to inspect."

"Out of sight, out of mind?" Myrt said.

"Something like that," Bobbie answered. "But I will shut it down if I ever have reason to think the cops have us on their radar screen. I will get rid of the whiskey, I will sell the jukebox, and I will take my liquor license off the wall, lock the doors, and leave." Grace stirred in her lap. "Besides which," Bobbie said, "the place has done more than enough for me: it gave me my Grace, and it pays my bills."

Grace turned to face her, kissed her, and stood up. "I have to go to work."

"And I have to go get some food—"

"What? Why?" Grace asked with a disbelieving look.

"Because unless you want me to cook dinner for you—"

"Bobbie, my love, there's a freezer full of cooked meat and a larder full of vegetables."

"Really?" a surprised Bobbie said. "In that case—"

"In that case we're inviting ourselves to dinner," Myrt said.

"Right," Thelma said. "Grace, what should we take from the freezer and the larder?"

CHAPTER NINE

Nurse Thelma Cooper, all dressed up in formal wear yesterday, was in her regular nurse's uniform this morning, filling in until a permanent new hire could be found, or until her new job began. Thanks to long years of experience, Thelma knew how Grace's office functioned, the office staff knew her, and many of the patients remembered her, so the place ran smoothly all day, which was good because Dr. Hannon was gone for most of the day. As always, Grace delighted in the delivery of healthy babies, and she had two of them that day. She also had two long and difficult surgeries—one for a young woman who had once been horribly and cruelly sterilized and who was shocked and devastated to learn she would never bear a child. After this day, Grace sought the comfort of home, where her friends awaited her arrival, and she could feel the comfort of love all around her.

"Bird bath only, Grace's orders," Myrt said in the tone of voice that must be taught in nursing school, along with the look that accompanied it.

"But I stink," Bobby wailed. "I need a shower!"

"Pits, privates, face, and neck. Period, end of discussion," Myrt said, ending the discussion.

"Grace said there would be hell to pay if you get those wounds wet," Thelma said.

Boy Bobby heaved a heavy sigh, sat down, and let the nurses unbutton and remove his shirt. Meanwhile, Queen Esther watched intently from the other side of the room as the nurses carefully cut away the bandages, then just as carefully examined the two wounds on Bobby's shoulder and chest. They gently lifted the arm up and down and he winced. Then they tried a gentle rotation, and he howled. Bobbie hurried to comfort him. Myrt and Thelma gave him a sympathetic but meaningful look though they didn't say anything. They didn't need to. "Bird bath and no heavy lifting," he said, saluting them with his good arm.

"Would you like for us to look at your arm, Miss Queen?" Myrt asked.

"Yes. Yes I would!" Queen Esther stood quickly, wobbled, then sat back down. Hard. Myrt and Thelma hurried over to her and were shocked and troubled by the dirty bandage on her arm and the odor emanating from it.

"Before you do your budgie imitation, Mr. Mason, we need to take Miss Queen into the bathroom to remove her bandage," Thelma said.

"Can I help?" Bobbie asked. And she followed as the nurses led their patient into the bathroom and cut away Queen Esther's dirty bandage.

"Who dressed your wound?" Thelma asked.

"A doctor by the name of Augustus—don't know if that's his first name or his last. He calls hisself a doctor but I don't b'lieve he is one. But he's the only one we can go to when we need care. No other doctor—no real one—will even let us in the door."

She looked at her festering arm. "Don't look like Bobby Mason's, and we got hurt the same night. His already look to be healing. I guess that's the diff'rence between having a real doctor

315

and a quack."

Thelma and Myrt poured antiseptic over and into the wound, and Queen Esther flinched but made no sound. "We need to clean it, Miss Queen, and it will hurt," Myrt said, "but it is infected and—"

"You do what you have to do, Nurse. I appreciate it, I truly do." And though she still made no sound, the old queen's knees buckled, but Bobbie was there to catch her and keep her upright as the nurses finished their work. Queen Esther gently touched the clean new bandage and thanked Nurse Myrt and Nurse Thelma profusely.

"A friend of Bobby Mason's is a friend of ours," Myrt said, "and we take care of our friends, who may sometimes become patients."

"I don't mean to be rude, Miss Queen," Thelma said, "but when did you last eat? And where do you live? Will you be able to keep the wound clean and dry?"

The old queen sighed and closed her eyes. "I think I ate something a coupla days ago but since I don't really live nowhere—"

"Can you please explain that, Miss Queen?" Myrt said in a calm yet demanding voice.

"I been stayin' in the storeroom of the cleaning company I work for 'cause the cops still watchin' the boarding house, the bastards. And no, I cain't promise to keep this nice bandage clean and dry 'cause I got to work, don't I? And that means I'm up to my elbows in soapy water all the time."

Now Bobbie focused on Queen's attire: she wore a faded green coverall with worn patches on both knees, and the sleeves were cut out of both arms just above the elbows. A floral cloth or scarf was tied around her head and knotted in the front, and her red lipstick was but a memory. "I know why you asked and I know you didn't mean no harm, Nurse, but right now I just cain't do no better than what I'm doin'. I wish I could."

Bobbie looked at Esther and said, "I need someone I can trust to supervise the cleaning crew in my bar every Monday. I try to keep an eye on them, but I need to spend most of my time in the office on receipts and inventory, trying to make sense of numbers that don't add up."

"Your staff stealing from you, Miss Bobbie?"

"Yes, I think so," Bobbie said slowly.

"What?" Boy Bobby erupted. "You never told me that. Jack never told me that." Then he calmed and looked closely at her. "Does Grace know?"

Bobbie shook her head. "And you won't tell her, nor will you say anything to Jack. I have no proof, and I won't make accusations based on suspicions."

"Mr. Mason has told me all about The Slow Drag, especially the part about how no males allowed, ever. But Wednesday through Saturday, right? Who refills the stock and empties the cash registers?" Queen Esther asked.

"My two managers."

"And nobody else?"

Bobbie started to shake her head, then stopped herself. She couldn't swear to that. There was a lot she couldn't swear to these days. "You've worked in a bar, Miss Queen, that much is clear."

"When I was younger. The bar business is young people's business, and you look to be young enough to do it," Queen said, giving Bobbie an up-and-down perusal that contained appreciation and approval.

"But I don't want to do it anymore. Not four nights a week."

Queen Esther grinned at her. "What I hear 'bout Dr. Grace, I don't blame you. You don't leave a woman like that at home by herself every night."

"I certainly don't," Bobbie said. "But the bigger question is do you want to supervise my cleaning crew on Mondays?"

Queen Esther nodded. "Yes, ma'am, I do. At least until I can get back to my regular work full-time."

317

"I'll pay you $50 to supervise the cleaning crew: make certain they really clean the place, out front and behind the bar. Really clean it, ceiling to floor."

Queen stuck out her hand and Bobbie shook it. Then she asked if Bobbie would get her a new pair of coveralls and some work boots. "I want to look like I can show them how to really clean if I need to—and I can, too. Been cleaning up behind somebody or other since I could hold a mop and a broom."

"What color?" Bobbie asked.

"Red. To match my lipstick."

Boy Bobby went into the bathroom for his bird bath while Thelma poured two cans of chicken noodle soup into a pot and Myrt made two cheese sandwiches. While Queen Esther gratefully ate the food prepared for her, Myrt and Thelma applied medication and fresh bandages to a quasi-clean Boy Bobby's wounds.

The more time Queen Esther spent in the company of these people the more she wished she had friends like Bobby Mason's. Then she gave herself a figurative slap. Two professional nurses had cleaned the infection out of the slash on her arm, poured what seemed like a gallon of medicine into it, and wrapped it with clean bandages. Then they fed her more food than she'd had at one time in maybe ever. Then she got a job earning more in one day than she did in a week, and she didn't even have to get filthy to earn it. These people already treated her better than any friends she had and she just met them. Maybe she didn't know how to be grateful because she'd never had anything to be grateful for. The thought all but knocked her on her ass. "What time do you want me to be there Monday morning, Miss Bobbie?"

"Eight thirty, Miss Queen, and I'll leave your work clothes with Bobby as soon as I get them. Is that all right?"

"If it's all right with Bobby?" And when he nodded, she said, "All right then. I should go."

At that moment the phone rang and Bobby answered it. "Doing really well, Larry, thanks. My favorite nurses are here now. They've cleaned the wounds and changed the bandages, and I'm cleared for work but no heavy lifting or Grace will kill me. Then she'll kill you."

Myrt, Thelma, Bobbie, and Queen Esther moved toward the front door. "Thank you, all of you, for being so kind to me," Queen said. "I thought Mason was stretching the truth when he talked about y'all. I didn't b'lieve people could be so nice, 'specially to somebody they didn't even know. Now I see he spoke nothin' but the truth."

"It's very easy to be nice to Bobby Mason," Bobbie said smiling. "He's a very special fellow."

"Ain't nothin' special about me and you been nothin' but nice to me, so I think it's just the kind of people you are," Queen Esther said.

Everyone put on a coat or a jacket except Queen Esther, who seemed not to have one. As always spring was playing hide and seek with New Yorkers—warm and sunny today and maybe tomorrow, cold and wet the next three days—and they adhered to the "better safe than sorry" dictum. But a warm breeze met them when they opened the door, no jackets needed. "I'm going back to my rooming house tonight," Queen Esther said.

"I thought the place was being watched by the police," Bobbie said.

"I'll go after the midnight shift clocks out, and I'll go in the basement door. I doubt they even know about the basement door."

"I used to live there, and I don't know about the basement door," Bobby said.

"You wouldn't unless you were turning tricks outta that door."

"Oh. Well, that explains it," Bobby said. "Can you get in? And why take the risk, Queen?"

"I need to get myself cleaned up to go to work just like you do. And anyway, I think the flatfoots are 'bout ready to give up thinking anybody in our house knows anything 'bout who whipped them grocery store people."

"You really must keep that wound clean and dry, Miss Queen," Myrt said in the heavy silence that followed. "Another infection could really be dangerous."

"I can keep it dry, I promise."

Thelma opened her medical bag, removed the roll of adhesive tape, and wrapped another layer around Queen's damaged and bandaged arm. Bobbie said she'd deliver Queen's work clothes to Bobby's as soon as she could, and they all left. Bobby locked the door behind them and followed Bobbie and the nurses to the garage while Queen Esther hurried away in the opposite direction.

Bobbie was unpacking the food when Grace entered the back door looking more depleted than Bobbie had ever seen her. Bobbie hurried over and took her coat, purse, and medical bag. She dumped everything on the counter and pulled Grace into a wordless embrace. They stood there, not speaking, just holding each other, until it seemed that Grace was ready to do— something. "Hot bath or hot shower?" Bobbie asked.

"Shower because it's faster and I'm weak with hunger."

While they ate, Bobbie described in detail the miracles wrought by two of the best nurses to wear the white uniform, and Grace worried, as Bobbie knew she would, about Queen Esther. "I have to keep reminding myself that despite the name she's given herself she's not a woman and I have nothing in my medical bag that can be useful to her health."

"She's not young, Grace, and after a catastrophic injury, nights sleeping on a storeroom floor, hiding from police, and insufficient food, the age shows in her face and on her body. Her legs gave way while Myrt and Thelma were cleaning her wound."

"If you can pay her enough so she doesn't have to return to that job, perhaps Larry has a room in one of his buildings she can afford, especially if she can do some light maintenance work or cleaning on the premises."

"Excellent idea, Gracie. He and I have a meeting tomorrow and I'll ask." Though she did have guilt pangs about not telling Grace that she suspected someone at The Slow Drag was a thief, she meant what she said earlier: she would not accuse based on suspicion. Anyway, she sensed that Grace was finally ready to talk.

"Two successful surgeries and two patients who, it seems, wish that I had failed. There are no post-surgical complications, but the failure to thrive seems a deliberate choice with both women."

"Why?" Bobbie asked, and Grace thought a moment, choosing her words carefully before answering.

"Because women too often blame themselves for things that go wrong with their bodies, and too often so do their men. In these cases, both husbands have one foot out the door. They are so full of blame for their wives for what befell them, as if they could have prevented it, but there is absolutely no sympathy for what the women have endured and are enduring—the pain and the humiliation. The men see themselves as the ones who've been wronged, the ones who are suffering. Useless piles of crap, both of them. They should take a lesson from Mr. Smith. That man, with a little help from me and The Boys, is the reason his wife is still alive after being kicked down a flight of subway stairs. He sat beside her bed, Bobbie, day and night—and yes, the night nurses let him stay with her—alternating between begging her to live and daring her to die. He told her he needed her, that he couldn't make it without her. He didn't blame her for getting herself thrown down the damn stairs."

"Do you remember what you said to me the night Boy Bobby slammed the door on that awful doctor's hand, Gracie?"

"That I could feel no sympathy for him even as I tried to imagine my life without the ability to use my right hand. Today would not have been possible. Yet I felt nothing for him. Yes, I remember."

"And I said that was because all your feelings were being used. You felt what Jack felt in that alley—the fear, the anger, the fury, and the pain. You felt what she felt as she lay there alone in the dark, wondering whether anyone would find her. You felt what she felt in the hospital, the place of healing, where she was abused and humiliated further. You felt all of that, Grace. Then you had your own fury to feel when you learned that the man responsible for so much of Jack's pain had returned to her hospital room—and for what purpose? If not for Bobby's intervention, what would he have done to Jack? My dear, wonderful Grace, your feelings were otherwise occupied. I know I didn't use those exact words, but that is the essence of what I said and what I meant."

Tears filled Grace's eyes, and she let them collect and fall. Bobbie continued to hold her hands and Grace did not attempt to free them. "So you believe that there are people who are undeserving of the sympathy of others?"

"Yes, I believe so," and Bobbie knew they both were thinking of Von Thompkins. "I also believe that you restored the possibility of life to two women today, Grace, but you are not responsible for how they choose to live those lives. Or even if they choose to live them. You are not responsible for the men they married or how those men treat them. You are one woman, Grace Hannon, who, despite all odds, strives to be of benefit to all women." She released Grace's hands and pressed tissues into them. Grace wiped her face and blew her nose.

"I'd like a drink, Bobbie. And please make it a double."

"Your wish is my command, Gracie my love."

Grace looked at the ring finger of her right hand and rotated the ring. "One of my patients looked at this ring and asked me how it felt to be loved so much."

"Did you respond?"

"I did. I told her that I give thanks every day that I am so loved."

Along with the thanks, she practiced good common sense and from then on, consigned the ring to the depths of her purse while at work. She didn't care if people wondered who gave her such obviously expensive jewelry, but she did care if anyone other than a silly nurse ever wondered whether patients were shortchanged because she bought herself an expensive ring, especially if that someone was Stephanie St. Clair, who was several minutes early for her appointment the following morning. Of course, she was welcomed as royalty in the waiting room, and the other patients looked surprised when she signed in with Mrs. B, then took a seat to await her appointment time.

Not only did she not receive special treatment, but she seemed not to expect any. Then, right on time, Nurse Myrtle Lewis opened the door and called for "Mrs. Stephanie St. Clair." Queenie gracefully rose to her feet and walked to Nurse Lewis. But first she turned back to the waiting room.

"I wish you all a good day, and good health," she said, and followed Myrt into the hall.

"Good morning, Madame St. Clair," Myrt said, leading the way to the exam room.

"Good morning to you, too, Nurse," Queenie said, and followed her into the exam room, where, at Myrt's request, she removed her dress, hat, shoes and stockings. She stepped onto the scale, then off, then stood erect as Myrt checked her height, and, using the foot stool Myrt provided, stepped up and sat on the exam table. Myrt took her temperature and blood pressure, then held her wrist and counted her pulse.

Grace knocked on the door, opening it to see her patient. *"Bonjour, Madame St. Clair. Comment allez-vous?"* They chatted in French for several seconds while Grace reviewed the chart. Putting the stethoscope to work, she listened to the woman's back and chest. She tested her reflexes. She examined her ear canals. Then she asked the woman to lie back. She pulled on rubber gloves, went to the end of the exam table, and prepared to conduct the pelvic exam until Myrt caught her eye and shook her head. The nurse pointed to Madame St. Clair's wrist and made a rapid thumbs-up gesture: the patient's pulse was racing. But why? She placed the stethoscope on her chest again and this time heard the sound of galloping horses. She stood beside her, took her hand, and squeezed gently.

"Je suis désolée," the obviously frightened woman whispered. "Please forgive me, Dr. Hannon. I am so sorry."

"There is nothing to forgive, Madame St. Clair, and if I have done something to frighten or offend you, then it is I who should apologize. Please tell me what has upset you?"

It took several moments but they finally understood that all of Madame St. Clair's pelvic exams had been done by men, and all were inappropriate, and most were painful. Grace sat her up while Myrt went to get her a glass of water and to tell Thelma what was happening. The woman wept for a while and Grace let her. Then Grace promised if she felt any pain or discomfort during the exam she should say "stop," and Grace would stop. Immediately. "But you must relax your abdomen and pelvic muscles. And your buttocks. Just relax your entire body." While Myrt breathed deeply with her, Grace conducted the pelvic exam. Myrt and Madame St. Clair were still breathing deeply, in and out, when Grace removed her rubber gloves.

"Tell me when you're going to do it," Madame St. Clair said quietly. "I am ready now."

"I have finished the pelvic exam," Grace said, "and I will now examine your breasts. Nurse Lewis can hold a mirror so that you can see what I'm doing."

"They always hurt me, the men did. They grabbed and squeezed and pulled the nipples. Hard, always so hard. Why, Dr. Hannon? Why do men treat women with such degradation?"

Grace didn't even attempt an answer. "Aside from being maybe a bit too thin, you appear to be in excellent health, Madame St. Clair, and I promise that everyone associated with the Hannon Obstetrics and Gynecology Practice will always treat you with dignity and respect."

"I do believe that to be the truth," Queenie said.

"However, I do think you could benefit from taking a daily vitamin and from gaining a few pounds. Do you eat regular meals, Madame St. Clair?"

And the legendary Madame Stephanie St. Clair of Harlem lowered her head as if taken to task by her mother. "No. No, I don't, Dr. Hannon."

"Is that because chewing is difficult? Because digestion is difficult? Is keeping food down a problem? Is proper elimination a problem? Please tell me, Madame, why don't you eat?"

She raised her head and met the doctor's gaze. "Because I cannot cook. I never learned, and I never learned because I did not care to learn. Now when I try—" She gave a hopeless shrug.

Was it possible that the Queen of Harlem didn't know about Miz Maggie's? Myrt was dialing the phone before Grace spoke the question and she handed her the receiver. "A very good morning to you, Miz Maggie."

"There's something vaguely familiar about this building," Bobbie said slowly, but she knew she'd never been here. Not counting the lobby, it was a five-story residential building, short for an

325

uptown New York City apartment building, but she thought as she scrutinized the brick and the detail and the windows and the beveled glass in the brass doors, it was designed to be a special one. So why did it look so dumpy? She was about to ask Larry when she remembered that the owner had walked away rather than rent to Negroes. But someone lived here as the building, though ill-kempt, was not vacant. "Why are we here?" Bobbie asked.

"Because I want your assessment of the property and its potential."

"You're the real estate magnate, so why do you need my assessment? What brought you here anyway?"

"The 'who' was Mr. Robert Mason, and he's responsible for my presence here. He has a bird's-eye view of this building from his bathroom window, and he saw some movement, so he came over to get a better look. The owner was locking the doors and affixing a 'For Sale, Good Terms' sign. He was driving the McKinley Property Management truck."

"How fast did you get here?" Bobbie asked, not attempting to conceal her amusement as Larry unlocked the building's door, with no "For Sale" sign in sight.

"After you see it and hear my plans, I want to know what you think." Larry led them to the elevator, pressed the call button, and the door opened immediately. They got in, and the door closed smoothly and silently. The car began an equally slow and smooth ascent.

"The elevator is new," Bobbie said.

"So are the heat, plumbing, and electrical systems."

"The most important and expensive fixes before—uh oh." Bobbie's voice and her face did a fast drop. "Let me guess. All of the apartment for rent ads were answered by Negroes, and their ability to afford the rent notwithstanding, he wasn't interested in having them as tenants. But he seems not to mind selling the building to you."

"Seems green is the universal language, and Mr. Mason arranged a verbal deal with the owner before I arrived," Larry explained. "It was such a good deal I wrote a check on the spot. It was Bobby's deal so he deserves the credit, which is why the company is now McKinley-Mason Property Development and Management."

"Wow, have you told him?"

"Not yet." The elevator doors slid silently open on the dimly lit fifth floor where they got out. "Come on, let me show you the place, and then let's go to the Theresa."

They toured the entire building, from the attic to the basement, talking, assessing, and evaluating the entire time. They continued on the taxi ride to the Theresa where the conversation stopped only long enough for them to eat. Larry finally said, "I really appreciate your insight, Bobbie. For a musician you know an awful lot about construction."

"All learned from my father the musician," Bobbie said, "and all learned from his father the carpenter." She reached into the inside pocket of her jacket, withdrew a folded piece of paper, and gave it to Larry. "In case you want a silent partner."

He unfolded a check and his eyes widened. "Bobbie?"

"You're a good man, Larry McKinley, and a good businessman."

He looked about to cry. "Don't you dare," Bobbie whispered, tossing her napkin toward him.

"All these years I've never had a partner, never wanted one, and in one day I have two. I don't want you to be silent, Bobbie. Please speak up as often as possible."

"In that case, I want to rent one of those large rooms downstairs. What were they used for?"

Larry shrugged. "Never used, I don't think, but they were supposed to be meeting rooms or social spaces for residents. You have thoughts or ideas?"

"One of them would be perfect for the Black Mask Adult

Literacy Program," she said. After several seconds of thought, he grinned.

"I can't wait to tell Elaine. She'll be overjoyed. That Adult Literacy is everyone's favorite idea."

"Glad to hear it," Bobbie said drily, adding, "and since it seems you're keeping my money, I'll have my lawyer call yours . . ." She stopped talking as her eyes widened in shock and surprise, tinged by fear. Bobby Mason was coming their way as fast as possible in the crowded restaurant, the maître d' hot on his heels. "Mr. McKinley, Miss Hilliard, I'm so sorry—"

"Whatever is the matter, Bobby?" Bobbie overrode the maître d's apology and grabbed Boy Bobby's arm, pulling him down into the booth while Larry stood and soothed the maître d', assuring him that everything was all right and that Mr. Mason would be joining them for lunch. If and when his breathing returned to normal.

"They stole all of Queen Esther's things! Everything she owned; she has nothing left!" He calmed down and explained that when Queen Esther went into hiding because the police were looking for her, the residents of the rooming house where she lived broke into her room and took everything. "They took her wigs and her clothes, her French lingerie, her makeup. They even took her bed, her chaise, and her lamps. She has nothing left but the dust bunnies on the floor."

"Where is she?" Bobbie asked.

"At my place, and she wants to call you, Bobbie, to thank you for the coveralls and work shoes you left for her, but to tell you she's sorry that she can't work for you because she has no way to clean herself, to make herself presentable. Those are her words." Boy Bobby looked so sad that Bobbie and Larry thought he was about to cry.

"Here's an idea," Larry said, suggesting that Queen Esther become the resident manager of their new building, living in the studio apartment at the end of the hall on the ground floor and responsible for maintenance of the building, much as Bobby himself had been when he worked for Westside.

For a long moment Boy Bobby did not reply. He didn't know what to think. He looked at Girl Bobbie and they held each other's eyes. Hers held no answer for him, only her assurance that she would support whatever he decided. He received a similar message when he shared a look with Larry. "Let's give it a try," he finally said, explaining that his decision was based on his not wanting Queen Esther to return to live in the storeroom where she worked.

He wanted her to have a safe, clean place to live where she could recover from her wounds. He wanted her to be able to help Bobbie at The Slow Drag. He wanted to be able to do for Queen Esther what Girl Bobbie had done for him. So they devised a plan to pick up Queen Esther and take her to get what she needed immediately.

Larry gave Boy Bobby the keys to the new building—their new building—saying he needed to return to the McKinley Properties office, but giving his permission to buy whatever was necessary within reason. Bobby had worked with him long enough to know that his boss was a very reasonable man.

Larry told Bobbie, "You two and the two greatest nurses in the world are expected at Eileen and Joyce's at six thirty this evening. And yes I know why, and no I'm not telling." He rushed away.

"What are Joyce and Eileen up to?" Bobby asked.

"No idea but you can rest assured that good food will be part of it, along with the two most adorable children on this earth. Now, Mr. Mason, about your friend Queen Esther."

"What a terrible violation," Myrt exclaimed. "People she thought were her friends violated her home and took everything—" She shook her head in disgust as she talked with Bobbie and Grace at Grace's office.

"While she was risking her life seeking payback for the murder of another friend." Thelma was thoroughly disgusted. "Not to mention keeping the cops away."

"I'll find some pretty sheets for the Murphy bed," Bobbie said.

"Since you'll be shopping anyway, my love," Grace said, kissing her cheek, "here's my list for tonight. I promised Eileen I'd get these things. If you'll be so kind as to fulfill my promise, I can remain here and finish my paperwork, which will make my nurses happy. And happy nurses make for a happy doctor and happy patients."

"Speaking of which, are you responsible for Madame St. Clair buying food for everyone in Harlem from Miz Maggie's today?" Bobbie asked. "That's all people were talking about on The Avenue."

"I told you she would," Myrt exclaimed. "I knew she would. I just knew it." And she told Bobbie how Grace had called Miz Maggie and ordered enough food for a dozen people and told her who it was for. Bobbie understood. Not only would Madame St. Clair have paid many times more than what she owed for the food, but Miz Maggie would have wanted everyone to know that the Queen of Harlem was still taking care of her part of town and her people.

"You women give new meaning to the concept of doing good in the world. I wish more people would follow your example," Bobbie said as she left Grace's office, adding that she'd see them later. Halfway to the elevator she stopped in her tracks, turned, and headed back to Grace. A quick tap on the door to her private office and Grace quickly opened it.

"Is something wrong, Bobbie?"

"Just something I forgot to tell you, something I did, and I didn't want you to hear it first from Eileen or Larry." She explained how she came to be a not-too-silent partner in the McKinley-Mason Real Estate Company.

Grace's eyes widened. "McKinley-Mason?!"

"You've made a new man of him, Bobbie, and we are most grateful," Eileen said by way of a greeting when she opened the front door that evening. She hugged and kissed her, then hugged and kissed Grace, and thanked her for allowing Bobbie to spend so much time with Larry. "He does everything Bobbie tells him to do," Eileen enthused, "which means he's no longer worrying Jo and me about what he should do or not do about some problem or issue."

"I also do everything Bobbie tells me to do," Grace said sweetly and wiggling the ring finger of her right hand where the circular column of sparkling diamonds reached almost to the knuckle. Bobbie guffawed, kissed the top of her head, and followed her into the living room where they were greeted by Larry and Boy Bobby. Before the door could close behind them, they were followed in by Myrt and Thelma.

"What is that heavenly scent?" Grace asked, following Eileen's hurried return to the kitchen. Widely known and respected for her culinary skills, she was putting the final glaze on a pork roast the size of a boulder before returning it to the oven. The two dear friends shared warm hugs, and Grace offered her assistance.

Bobbie entered bearing an armload of flowers, observed them, and said, barely above a whisper, "I could spend the entire evening in the kitchen watching my two favorite gorgeous women hard at work." Simultaneously the two gorgeous women in question stopped what they were doing and glared at her. "Or I could find vases for these flowers or do something else to help?"

331

"Glad to see you wasted no time getting her properly trained, Gracie," Eileen said drily.

"It was easy. She was most willing," Grace said smugly.

"Hey, I'm standing right here."

"So you are, Bobbie my love," Grace said with a sweet kiss as she told her where to find the vases and the shears for trimming the stems. Bobbie quickly and good-naturedly abandoned all pretense of injured feelings.

"Where are your wonderful offspring?" Bobbie asked Eileen.

"JoJo took them to the park. They were annoyingly underfoot and bouncing off the walls. I'm hoping that bouncing off the swings and sliding boards instead—"

Whatever Eileen was hoping proved inconsequential as her offspring erupted into the living room like engines in overdrive. Joyce couldn't keep hold, and they slipped through their father's grasp as if his hands were oiled. They spied Boy Bobby across the room at the bar mixing drinks for Myrt and Thelma and called out in unison, "Uncle Bobby! Uncle Bobby!" He scooped them both up and hugged them tightly until Joyce and Larry could corral them.

"Do you two know Nurse Lewis and Nurse Cooper?" he asked his children. They shook their heads but bestowed wide, happy grins on the two nurses, along with cheerful greetings. Then they spied Bobbie and Grace coming out of the kitchen and once again Larry wasn't strong enough to hold them.

"Auntie Bobbie," EJ cried, careening toward Bobbie, who bent low and scooped her up as if she were weightless.

"Auntie Grace!" Scottie barreled into Grace, almost knocking her over, but she recovered her balance and grabbed the little boy up into a big hug, kissing him enough times to send him into a fit of wiggly giggles.

"May I have everyone's attention please!" Larry called out, holding bottles of champagne up, one in each hand. "This is a celebration. Our closest family and friends are here to celebrate two of our own. Which two? Well, Mr. Robert Henry Mason the Third, welcome to the business now called 'The McKinley-Mason Real Estate Company!' I am very pleased to be able to call you my new partner.!" A loud and sustained explosion of cheering, clapping, and hugging and kissing left the new partner looking startled and a bit disbelieving.

Larry opened the champagne, and Bobbie passed glasses as he poured. Eileen opened a bottle of ginger ale, pouring it for EJ and Scottie. Then everyone raised a glass and shouted, "To Bobby Mason," followed by a chorus of "For he's a jolly good fellow, which nobody can deny." Wiping away tears, Bobby tried to speak but no words came, so he hugged Larry. Then Eileen, and on to Bobbie, Grace, Joyce, Myrt, and Thelma. Grace, who was still holding Scottie, passed him to Larry and called for everyone's attention. "My dearest friends and family, please show your love and pride for the first Negro nurse to teach full-time at the Columbia University School of Nursing: Nurse Thelma Cooper, BSN, RN, MSN!!"

The cheers and whistles were deafening. More champagne flowed, subsequent bottles were popped, and Boy Bobby and Thelma hugged each other.

The feast prepared by Eileen followed, accompanied by laughter, stories and love.

"Two more deserving people do not exist," Bobbie said on the short drive home.

"I agree wholeheartedly," Grace said.

"Well, we have more champagne at home, and a new garage gate."

"What a beautiful sight," Grace said as they drove up to it. "Can you make it open?"

Bobbie lowered the window, reached out to the pad on the garage wall, punched in four numbers, and the gate slid open allowing the car to slide in. Bobbie waited for the gate to slide shut before driving forward, explaining that the man who'd installed the gate said it was extra security—to make sure that no one followed the car into the garage. "And we'll never forget the code. It's your birthday. By the way, I didn't get a chance to tell you how much I love you in that outfit. How much I love you in any outfit."

"Would you please just unlock the door and let us inside?" Grace didn't want to allow the flirting to progress any further until they were at least in the kitchen with the door closed and locked behind them.

They both were enjoying exactly what came next when Bobbie's telephone rang, at eleven thirty. "Go answer your phone."

"Don't want to."

"Since no one ever calls you at this time of night," Grace said, "I think you should—"

"All right, all right." Bobbie ran into the next room. "Yes, hello? What is it?"

"Sorry to bother you, Bobbie, this is Myrt."

Grace was with her and safe, but Bobbie's heart skipped a beat anyway. "What is it, Myrt?"

"There are white women in The Drag, Bobbie. Lots of them. So many that we left. Jack told me to call you."

Bobbie didn't respond. She heard what Myrt said, but it didn't make sense. Ofays were not allowed in The Slow Drag. "Are you sure?"

Now it was Myrt's turn not to respond. If it were anyone else but Bobbie . . . "Yes, Bobbie, I'm positive. Would you like Thelma to tell you?"

"No. No, Myrt, I'm sorry. I guess I just can't . . . I don't know . . ."

Suddenly Grace was there, and she took the receiver from Bobbie. "Myrt? Is that you?"

Myrt explained with much greater detail. Grace thanked her, hung up, and looked at Bobbie who said, "I'm going. I've got to go see."

"I'm going with you."

"No, you're not. I don't want you in there. Things might get ugly."

"Then I won't go into the club, Bobbie, but I am driving you there. Go get dressed while I call Boy Bobby and ask him to open his garage door."

They were dressed and in the car in a matter of minutes, having not said a word. Bobbie didn't speak until she asked Grace to drive to a strip bar on Seventh Avenue at 126th. "The bouncer there is a friend, and I want her to go with me since I'll need to fire my own bouncer when I get to my own bar." She directed Grace to drop her and her new bouncer off at Bobby's garage and said she'd return as soon as she could.

The bouncer was six feet tall, weighed 200 pounds, and looked like the man everyone thought she was. She was good-natured about it—except for her name, which was Margaret Ann, which she absolutely refused to be called. Mack was the name she used. "What's going on in your place, Bobbie, and why do you need me?"

"You know I don't allow ofays in my bar."

"Everybody who knows you knows that," Mack replied.

"Somebody called me at home less than an hour ago to tell me that a dozen or more of them were in the place, and there's only one way that could have happened," Bobbie said.

"Through the front door, right past the bouncer," Mack said. "So how're we doing this?"

"I go in, you follow me, then lock the door. I'll send Verne, the current bouncer, up the steps ahead of me. If she resists, you can help her along. When we reach the top, I'll turn on all the lights, turn off the music, and order everyone out except the staff. There might be, probably will be, some pushing and shoving, and you can keep pushing and shoving everybody right down the steps and out of the door. Of course, nobody gets in.

I'll let you know when everyone is out; then you can lock the door. I'll turn out the lights in the stairwell and you can hang the 'Closed' sign. Then you can come upstairs."

It went like clockwork. Bobbie, in black slacks, a black T-shirt, black socks, and black loafers looked imperious and impervious. She had the staff stand in the middle of the room and face her. She had her back against the bar, and she looked at each of them for several seconds. Except Jack. She couldn't look at Jack. How could Jack be complicit in this travesty of her trust and the love between them? "I don't know whether I will reopen this establishment but if I do, none of you will be employed here."

"Wait!"

"Hold on a minute!"

"But Bobbie!"

They all tried to speak at once. All except Jack, which was a good thing because Bobbie didn't want to hear it, and she shook her head at every attempt by anyone to speak. She pointed to the door. "Good-bye. I hope you all find someone to pay you as well as I paid you." Then Mack strode toward them, and they all moved quickly toward the exit. All except Verne, who walked toward Bobbie. "You should be the first one out," Bobbie said to her. "They got in here because you let them in. I don't want to hear anything from your mouth. Get out." And she turned toward the bar to prevent anyone from seeing the tears in her eyes.

Verne stomped away and down the stairs. There was the sound of some scuffling; then she heard Jack calling her and she hurried toward the stairs. "Bobbie, please talk to me! Please!" Jack implored. She struggled to control the sob deep in her throat. It tore at Bobbie's heart.

"Meet me at Boy Bobby's. Grace is there."

"Thank you, Bobbie," Jack said, and Mack opened the door for her, then closed and locked it behind her and came upstairs.

Bobbie stood in front of the bar. Mack didn't know her well enough to read the expression on her face, but she knew tears when she saw them. She also knew that everyone Bobbie employed was a friend and that firing her friends had to hurt.

"Thanks for your help, Mack." She held out a wad of folded bills, which Mack could tell at a glance, without unfolding them, was more than Bobbie had promised to pay, and she said so. Bobbie didn't say anything.

"If you decide to reopen this place, I'd be happy to be your bouncer," Mack said.

Bobbie turned to face her. "They were stealing from me, too, Mack." She shook her head. "I don't understand it, I really don't. I pay a good salary, much more than they'll earn anywhere else, which they'll soon learn."

"If you hire me, Bobbie, I won't let the Virgin Mary in the door if you don't want her in here, and I would die before I would steal from you, and I'd beat the shit out of anyone who tried."

Bobbie looked at the big woman, wiped her eyes, and grinned. "Do you think the Virgin Mary likes girls? Better still, do you think she can make a decent Manhattan?"

"I can teach her. I'm licensed. I was the only Colored woman in my class though they thought I was a man. Name on the certificate says Mack Ashton."

"If you know two more you'll vouch for, I'll reopen next week—if I still have a manager."

"When will you know that?" Mack asked.

"When I get downstairs," Bobbie replied. She turned out the lights upstairs and waited for Mack to get downstairs to unlock and open the door before turning off the lights on the stairs. She locked the door, then went out to find Grace, Jack and Boy Bobby waiting for her. Grace rushed into her arms and Bobbie held her close for a long moment. Keeping one arm around her, she introduced the three of them to Mack Ashton. Then she asked Bobby how best to prevent anyone from entering until all the locks were changed.

"Glue," he said, turning and going inside. "Be right back."

"Bobbie, I—" Jack began.

"Did you steal from me, Jack?"

"Oh, Bobbie, no! On my life, on Grace's life, I swear that I did not. I wasn't sure what the hell was going on until the ofays started to show up—"

"When was that, and why didn't you tell me, Jack?"

"Wednesday was the first time—four of them. Then half a dozen on Thursday. Then the whole bunch of 'em tonight. I saw Myrt and told her to call you."

"Let's talk tomorrow, Jack. Just the two of us."

Weeping, Jack hugged her, and Grace hugged them both. Then Grace said to Mack, "Shall we drop you back on Seventh Ave. or is there someplace else—?"

"Wherever you need to go, Mack," Bobbie said, still holding on to Grace and Jack.

"I think I'll walk awhile, enjoy the sights on The Avenue, stop somewhere for a bite to eat, maybe something to drink," Mack said, her hand wrapped around the wad of cash from Bobbie that said she didn't need to return—tonight or ever—to a job she disliked so intensely. "Grace, Jack, it was very nice to meet you both."

"I need a telephone number for you, please, Mack."

Nodding, Mack took a small notebook from her back pants pocket and a pencil from her front shirt pocket, wrote her number, tore out the page, and gave it to Bobbie. Then she bid them good night and ambled slowly but purposefully toward the lights and sights of Broadway, a good night about to get better. Bobby said he'd call Bobbie in the morning. He waited for her and Grace to get their car out of the garage before he closed and locked it; then he took Jack home with him. It was just a short drive home and Bobbie knew she needed to tell Grace everything so she wouldn't worry. Grace spoke first. "You know that Jack didn't betray you, Bobbie, don't you?"

"Yes, Grace. I think I do. I hope so. I don't know—"

"But I know, love. She did not betray you."

"It would kill me, I think, if she did."

"Yes, Bobbie, I know it would."

"They, the others, must have—what, Grace? Why didn't Jack tell me something was wrong?"

"Ask her tomorrow. She'll tell you."

"Did she tell you? Do you know, Grace?"

"What are you going to do about The Drag?"

Bobbie's half grin was almost its own answer, but she replied verbally anyway: "I opened it on my own terms, and I'll close it the same way. Having learned a very valuable lesson."

"Which is?" Grace asked.

Bobbie took a moment to formulate her thoughts. "I will always hire my friends if and when I can, but I will never again expect friends to care as much about my business as I do. When we're at work, we'll work, and when we're not at work we'll discuss the weather, or debate who's the most gorgeous— Dorothy Dandridge or Lena Horne. These are the rules I'll operate my business by and I'll put it in writing if necessary."

"I know which one I think is the most gorgeous," Grace said.

"Me, too," Bobbie said, first squeezing Grace's hand, then bringing it up to kiss. "May I monopolize your time Saturday from about 9:30 a.m. to 2:30 p.m., after which I will happily join you on your Saturday shopping rounds—if, of course, you'd like me to."

"Consider it done—all of it." Whatever Bobbie had planned certainly was all right with her, but first Grace had an errand of her own to accomplish, and Friday's unexpectedly light patient schedule made it possible for her to visit Larry's jeweler in the East Sixties. She was greeted formally by a couple behind the display case. However, the man suddenly smiled and hurried from behind the counter.

"A pleasure to see you, Dr. Hannon." When his beaming glance traveled to the ring finger on her right hand, she understood why he knew who she was. She returned his greeting and placed a piece of heavy vellum on the counter, displaying sketched interlocking *H*s. Before she could explain further the woman, who had been silently observing, turned and hurried into the back room, was gone a few seconds, and hurried back, a velvet tray of wide gold bands in each hand. She placed the trays on the counter in front of Grace who didn't reach out to touch until she saw the ring she wanted: the only one that wasn't circular but not square, either. The edges were smooth, and its lack of thickness made it appear almost delicate. She lifted it from its place in the tray and was surprised that even with a delicate appearance it was heavy. It was beautiful and it was the one.

"This exact design?" the woman asked, pointing to Grace's sketch, and she nodded.

"And a stone?" the man asked. Surprised, Grace pondered a moment, then shook her head. She hadn't considered a stone but thought the ring would be better without one. She wrote a check for the deposit, received a receipt with a date, thanked the couple, and left. Bobbie's birthday present.

CHAPTER TEN

Benny Williams was Bobby Mason's first hire after Larry McKinley first hired him, and if he had three or four like Benny, Bobby's job would rarely feel like work. Benny was so enthusiastic that Bobby often had to tell him to calm down and slow down. The boy had never been late for work. In fact, he usually was ten or fifteen minutes early as he was this morning, waiting for Bobby at the front door. Queen Esther needed to take lessons from the boy, or she'd be looking for a job. Bobby gave up ringing the bell and pounding on her door and hurried across the lobby to the front of the building to what was now called the Adult Literacy Classrooms. He carried the tools and equipment Benny would need and got him set up and ready to work. Then he hurried back across the lobby to Queen Esther's apartment. He would pound on the door until she opened it and he didn't care how angry she would be. Too many people had done too many good things for him in his seven months in Harlem for him to allow her to spoil it.

"What th' hell is wrong wit you, boy," she snarled at him as she swung the door open. Her eyes were barely open, and the odor of cheap whiskey emanated from her every pore.

"You were due to start work over an hour ago," he said,

forcing her eyes to meet his.

"I had just barely got home then," she said, wobbling and weaving and finally leaning into the door frame. Her eyelids flickered as if she would fall asleep standing there.

"And what has that to do with the price of rice in China?" Bobby said dryly.

"Say what?" She forced her eyes open.

"Get dressed, Queen, and let's get to work."

She shook her head and started to close the door, but he pushed back. She stumbled back into the room, barely remaining upright. She shook her head again. "I'll be ready to start about noon time."

"If you're not out here dressed and ready to work in about five minutes, Queen, about noon time is when I want your apartment cleaned out. Unless you can pay the rent."

Now he had her full attention, and a range of emotions played across her face: shock, anger, disbelief, and finally fear. "I don't have nowhere to go. You know that, boy. Just like you know I can't pay no rent."

"What was the arrangement when you moved in here?" Boy Bobby asked calmly, and now there were but two emotions across her face: resignation and acceptance.

"I'll get dressed and be out in a minute," she said, and she was as good as her word. She wore the khaki coverall Bobby had given her, and she'd ironed it and starched the collar so that it stood up. She had washed and ironed her floral head scarf, and she had found red shoelaces for the work boots Bobby had supplied—the red matching her lipstick, nail polish, and the flowers in her scarf.

"You look gorgeous," Bobby said and meant it.

"I look like shit," Queen Esther muttered and meant that was how she felt.

"If you insist," Bobby replied. He explained their tasks for the day: they would first polish all the brass until it gleamed, then wash all the glass until it squeaked. "I wish we had time to strip all the wood, but we don't, so we'll polish it, and we'll wash the walls—here and on the second floor—until we can paint them." He looked all around the lobby and shrugged. "We'll paint the interiors of the vacant apartments on both floors, and install new fixtures, so we can get them rented immediately, but we'll paint yours first since you're already in it. I'll help you get started."

Bobby and Queen Esther worked nonstop the next two and a half days and when they finished, the first-floor lobby was pristine, as was the front of the building. When Queen complained that being a resident manager seemed like more work than she wanted to do, Bobby said that when they finished getting everything squared away and added a coat of spit and polish, not only would she love the job, but she would love living where the job was and be proud that she did. And he was right about almost everything.

She had needed to ask him what getting squared away meant, whether he really expected her to spit on something to clean it, and what kind of polish? He laughed and told her that was Army slang for making one's environment perfect. Then he'd asked, "Don't you know any fellas who were in the military?" She hadn't liked his tone of voice, but she'd replied, "Oh, yeah, I knew a few." Then she'd looked him up and down and added, "But they didn't look like you, and they weren't called fellas, and there ain't a lot of squarin' away or spittin' and polishin' in the stockade where the *fellas* I know spent most of their time."

Queen got over the desire to be out dancing and drinking until sunup because she finally allowed herself to admit how important it had become to be up taking care of her building first thing in the morning, beginning with sweeping the sidewalk in front of the building and washing the glass in the front door until it sparkled. This was her building, and as often happened when a person who'd never owned anything came into possession of something special, she guarded and protected it with the fierceness of a new mother.

When, on the following Monday morning, she at last was able to change from her McKinley-Mason khaki coverall into her red Slow Drag coverall and meet Bobbie Hilliard for her second job, she felt the same sense of ownership. "You look wonderful, Queen," Bobbie said, unlocking the door to let them into the building, relocking it, and leading them upstairs to the bar. She switched on the lights—all of them—and lit the place up. Queen looked all around, nodding her approval and claiming it. She'd been in a lot of bars, but this one was special.

"I wish we had a place this nice. I know this joint is jumpin' on those nights when it's open! I hope you don't have to shut it down, Miss Bobbie."

"So do I, Queen," Bobbie said, and she meant it, just as she meant that she would certainly keep it closed if that became necessary. She had gone to the apartment building to tell Queen in person that The Slow Drag was closed, and why, and the place had been closed and empty since that awful night. This Monday was the beginning of a new day.

Queen was behind the bar, looking beneath the shelves, even beneath the sink. "You got lights back here?" she asked, and Bobbie turned them on. After several seconds Queen let go a raucous cackle of glee and placed almost a dozen paper bags on the bar top.

"What's all that?" Bobbie asked.

"A few hundred of your dollars," Queen replied as she pushed open the cash register. Bobbie watched, wondering, as Queen lifted out the tray, put it on the counter, and began scooping dollar bills from the bottom of the drawer. "You might wanna kill them lights before the cleaning people—or anybody else—gets here."

"Who else do you think might come?" Bobbie asked.

"Whoever left these bags of money and tried to hide this

cash," Queen said, explaining that they would want to remove the money before anyone could find it, but Boy Bobby had changed all the locks that night. It was well known that the place was cleaned on Monday, but this was the first Monday since the night Bobbie closed the place that the cleaners had come in. She switched off the lights behind the bar just as the cleaners knocked on the door. She ran downstairs to admit them, and by the time they were all upstairs Queen Esther was seated on a bar stool, legs crossed, freshening her lipstick. She wore Bobbie's horn-rimmed glasses with clear lenses, and she cradled a large paper bag in her lap, which she gave to Bobbie before she turned her attention to the cleaning crew. "Good morning, ladies," she said. "My name is Esther Jones."

"I bet that ain't what your ma named you," one of the cleaners snarled as the others laughed.

"She named me Chester, but didn't nobody ever confuse her with somebody smart," Queen retorted without missing a beat, and all the cleaners cackled. They belonged to Queen Esther from that moment on. She walked around the room with them, explaining how she liked things done, asking who had a task she especially hated doing, who had one she especially enjoyed doing, who was afraid of heights, who had a bad back or bad knees or rheumatism. She had every woman's full attention, including Bobbie, Mack, and Jack, whom she hadn't been aware were in the room. "You need me, Miss Bobbie?" she called out.

"Just for one moment, Miss Esther, if you don't mind."

"You tall girls take these mops, climb up on a table, and start cleaning the ceiling, and for Christ's sake don't fall 'cause I can't catch you!" When the laughter died down, she told the short girls to get started behind the bar. "The rest of you breathe easy till I get back." And she hurried over to Bobbie who was at the door with Mack and Jack.

"You just earned yourself a big raise, Miss Queen," Bobbie said with true admiration.

"Why, Miss Bobbie? 'Cause I talked to people like they was human beings? I always said if I ever got to be the boss I would treat people decent. A cleaning lady is still a lady."

"You're absolutely correct," Bobbie said. She introduced Jack and Mack to Queen Esther and laughed when Queen asked how she told them apart—the nearly six-foot-tall Mack and the just over five-foot-tall Jack. "We'll be in the office downstairs. You may hear people trying to get in but they can't because all the locks were changed. They'll knock on the doors, beat on them, then they'll call out, but ignore all of it. They don't work here anymore, and everyone who should be here is here. I'm having lunch delivered. Ask your crew, please, if they're all right with burgers, fries, and soda?"

"Yes'm Miss Bobbie, we definitely all right with that!" somebody called out.

"'Specially if we can get two of them burgers and lots of them fries," somebody else added.

The work went smoothly and quickly after that, both upstairs and downstairs. The cleaners liked Queen and she liked them. After lunchtime and all the work, it was decided that The Drag might reopen the next week, cleaner than it had been since the early days. Bobbie gave Queen one of the bags of cash and told her to pay the cleaning crew whatever she thought they deserved. Then she led Jack and Mack behind the bar.

"Queen Esther found these stashed back here," Bobbie told them and showed them the bags of cash that Queen had found, and she told them that she expected to find missing liquor when she conducted a thorough inventory. "If Justine and Verne were stealing cash, which I find very hard to believe, I suppose I'd better prepare myself to believe they'd steal the booze, too."

"I'll help with that, Bobbie," Jack said. "If you want me to."

"And those'll be the last bags of cash you will ever find back here," Mack said.

"We all ready to go," Queen Esther said, leading her

cleaning crew to the front of the room and toward the steps. Bobbie walked toward them.

"Everything looks absolutely wonderful," Bobbie said honestly. "Thank you, Queen, and thank you, ladies. Same time next week?"

"We'll be here, won't we, ladies?" Esther asked, and received a rousing "Yes, ma'am!" Before anyone could say or do anything else a loud pounding on the door grabbed their attention, and Mack turned and ran down the stairs.

"It's Verne!" she called up to Bobbie, and Bobbie followed her down the steps, but the door remained closed and locked.

"I need to talk to you," Verne called out but Bobbie shook her head. "Please!" Bobbie kept shaking her head and waving Verne away, and after a few moments she stomped off.

"Miss Queen, you and your ladies can come on down," Mack called out, and the cleaning crew clambered down the stairs, thanking Bobbie and bidding everyone good evening.

"Thank you, Miss Bobbie," Queen Esther said, returning the paper bag. "They were very happy with what I paid 'em."

"And what did you pay yourself?" Bobbie asked.

Queen looked confused. "You already told me what I was gon' earn," she said, "and I didn't take not one dollar more."

"Then I'm telling you to double what I originally told you," Bobbie said. "And get enough to take a taxi home. You deserve to ride after what you accomplished today, my treat." Queen thanked Bobbie, wished them all a good evening, and left. When she got home, which was a very short taxi ride, she took a hot shower (being careful not to get the newly applied bandage on her arm wet), ate a good dinner, drank two glasses of wine, and went to bed. Time was she'd be getting dressed to go out now, but that was a time when she had no reason to get up before noon the following day. This was a different time. And a very different place. She slept better than she ever had even when she was a baby.

She found that she liked waking up without a headache and a hangover, and she found that she also liked having a percolator pot and making fresh coffee every morning, and being able to sit at a table, listen to the radio, and look at *Ebony* and *Jet* magazines. They were all old ones that Bobbie Hilliard gave her, and Queen had told her the truth: that it didn't matter if they were old because she was just looking at the pictures because she couldn't read very much. But that didn't matter. She was sitting in her own kitchen, surrounded by her own things, and for the first time in her life feeling safe.

In a newly washed and ironed McKinley-Mason coverall, Queen Esther was already cleaning the lobby of her building when the early birds left for their jobs. "Good morning, Miss Jones," they said, one after the other, and she returned the greeting, calling each of them by name. She wasn't really sure how old she was because she'd been lying about her age for so long, but she did know that in all the years of her life people had never said "Good morning, Miss Jones" to her, and she liked it.

She swept then damp-mopped the second-floor hallway and down the steps, swept the lobby again and emptied the trash cans. Then her favorite task of every day: polishing the mailbox after the mailman left. She loved to see the large brass rectangle on the wall sparkle and shine. She had just finished and given a final wipe with the cloth when the front door opened and her least favorite resident, mailbox key in hand, came toward her.

"Afternoon, Mr. Bailey." He ignored her, dropping his cigarette on the floor and grinding it out with his shoe. He opened his mailbox, grabbed the contents, closed and locked the box, then dropped the mail he did not want on the floor and turned toward the elevator. It took but a moment for her to find her voice. "Hey, asshole, get back here and clean up your mess! This ain't no ashtray or trash can, you nasty pig!"

The elevator door opened, but Bailey turned in a rage and barreled toward Queen. She stood her ground, hands on her narrow hips, eyes narrow slits. "What did you call me, you ugly freak of nature?" he snarled.

"You heard me; now pick up your trash."

"How about you suck my dick!" He unzipped his pants and exposed himself, and Queen beat a hasty retreat. He laughed and called her ugly names as she ran to her apartment.

She slammed the door and grabbed the phone. "Bobby, please! You got to get over here right now, please!"

"I'm on my way," he said, without asking her a single question. It was serious, whatever it was, because she was terrified. So frightened her voice was quivering. Queen Esther—who hadn't been frightened that night in the alley when they both were shot and stabbed and left for dead—was terrified. He couldn't imagine it now, so he just drove, being thankful that she was so close. He parked the truck on the sidewalk in front of the building, ran in across the lobby to her door, and pounded. She opened it immediately, pulled him inside, and started talking. She was talking too fast, and he wasn't following. He got her to slow down, to tell him everything from the beginning. Then she grabbed his hand and pulled him across the lobby to the mailbox and pointed to the cigarette butt and mail. "Stay here, I'll be right back," he said, and ran to the stairs and up them two at a time. She heard him pound on the door.

"What the hell—" she heard Bailey begin.

"Get your ass down those stairs!" She had never really heard Bobby angry. She only thought she had. She heard scuffling, then tumbling, and she saw Bailey grabbing the staircase railing with both hands just in time to keep himself from hitting the bottom hard. Bobby was right there.

"Get over to the mailbox and clean up your mess and be quick about it, you low-class piece of shit." If Bailey thought he could take his time, he was sorely mistaken. Bobby was on his heels, pushing and shoving until he stumbled and almost fell at Queen's feet. He reached out for purchase, but she sidestepped his grasping fingers. Bobby grabbed his shirt collar and kept him on his feet. He repeated the command: "Pick up your mess and do it now." Bailey bent down to pick up the cigarette butt and the discarded mail and put it in the trash can that was there and visible for everyone to see. "Get the ashes, too," Bobby barked, imitating his old drill sergeant.

Bailey faced Bobby with an ugly sneer, but at the glare he met in Bobby's eyes he bit back whatever he wanted to say, grabbed an envelope from the trash can and tore it in half, then used one side to sweep the ashes into the other and returned it to the trash. "Satisfied?"

"One more thing," Bobby said. "You expose yourself again and I'll call the police—and I hate the police—but I'll call 'em. I'll tell the cops you're a child molester who runs around exposing himself. Or maybe I'll just put the word out to the men in the neighborhood. Let them have their way with you."

Bailey's throat was so dry he choked on his own spit. "You . . . you can't do that!"

"It's my building and I can do anything I want to, and I'll do whatever I have to do to keep my employees safe. Now let me know that you understand."

Bailey gulped and tried a couple of times to swallow. "Yeah," he growled. "Anything else I can do for you?" he asked, sarcasm dripping, but it was wasted on Bobby who laughed at him. He turned and stalked away and instead of waiting for the elevator he ran up the flight of stairs. Queen Esther's breathing returned to normal.

"Thank you, Bobby. I didn't know what else to do," she said. "It ain't like I never seen a dick before, but when it belongs to somebody who hates me and wants to hurt me—"

"You did exactly what you should have done, Queen. You don't get paid to put up with shit like that. You get paid to do exactly what you're doing—and you're doing an excellent job. We've heard from several people who've stopped by the office to pay their rent. They've said how much they appreciate living in a building that is so beautifully maintained, and they all mentioned you by name."

Queen Esther was speechless. Tears came to her eyes. "We got off to a bad start and I'm sorry for that, Bobby." She wiped her eyes. "I didn't know how to live but one way—the way I always lived, in a room with a hot plate and the bathroom down the hall. Ain't nobody ever respected or appreciated me. I like living like this," she said, opening her arms to embrace her home. "I want to stay here, to live like this *and* get a salary! And I don't want to be treated like I'm not even human by some pig bastard."

"I don't think you have to worry about Mr. Bailey, but just in case always keep a broom or a mop in your hand—something to use as a weapon—and don't be afraid to use it, knock the shit out of him if necessary. And Queen, I will always support you and stand by you. I really will put his ass out if he transgresses again."

"Does transgresses mean fucks up?" she asked.

Bobby was still laughing when he drove the short distance to the new building to see how work was progressing at the Literacy Center and was surprised—and pleased—to find Larry, Grace, Bobbie, and Eileen there, and of course they wanted to know why he was laughing so he told them. Then they all were giggling and repeating, "Transgresses means fucks up." And they all agreed that if the pig bastard fucked up again Bobby should let the neighborhood men deal with him.

"You two should come with me and meet Queen Esther," Bobbie said to Grace and Eileen.

"Oh, Queen Esther will love them," Boy Bobby chortled.

"You stop that," Girl Bobbie admonished him.

"You can explain that later," Grace said to her. "Right now, I need to get back to work." To Larry she said, "It is amazing how much work you've gotten done in this building—both of you," she said, including Boy Bobby. "The exterior and the lobby are most welcoming."

"I'm thinking to move Queen Esther over here, but I don't know how she'll take it. She loves 'her' building, and the residents love her, but if she were here, she could transform this lobby and I could concentrate on the exterior," Bobby said.

"What's so special about the lobby of Queen Esther's building?" Eileen asked.

"Oh, I must take you to see it," Bobbie said, adding, "and you'll fall in love with Miss Esther Jones."

"I need to get to work," Grace insisted.

"It won't take long, I promise," Bobbie said, grabbing her hand, and in a few short minutes they were parked in front of the McKinley-Mason building that Esther Jones managed.

"If it's this pretty inside," Eileen began as Bobbie rushed to open the front door, and both she and Grace exclaimed happily when they entered.

"How beautiful," they enthused.

"This is all Queen Esther—she keeps it this way. That's why she was so pissed off when some ignorant asshole transgressed."

"I don't blame her," Eileen said as Bobbie led them to the door in the far corner of the lobby. She lifted the knocker and let it fall and almost immediately the door opened to reveal a Queen Esther who looked as if she expected them.

"'Afternoon, Miss Bobbie, ladies," she said with a shy smile.

"Good afternoon to you, too, Miss Queen," Bobbie said. "I'd like for you to meet my dearest friends: Grace Hannon and Eileen McKinley."

Grace extended her hand. "A pleasure to meet you, Miss Jones. I've heard a lot about you."

"As have I," Eileen said, shaking hands with Queen Esther who had been rendered uncharacteristically speechless. "Bobby told us how you demolished the cretin on the second floor. Congratulations!"

Queen looked totally confused now. Bobbie stepped in. "You kicked that fool's ass, and he needed it. Bobby is very proud of

352

you, Queen, as he's telling everyone he knows."

Queen exhaled her relief. "That man is the only somebody who acts like that. All the other residents are real polite and treat me with respect. I just needed to remember that Big Maybelle song: 'One Monkey Don't Stop No Show.'

Bobbie, Grace, and Eileen laughed all the way to their cars, repeating "One Monkey Don't Stop No Show" every few steps, vowing to purchase the recording immediately. Bobbie helped Eileen into her car first with a kiss to the top of her head. Then she turned to Grace. She hugged her closely, kissed her gently, helped her into the car, and closed the door. "When are you going to tell me what we're doing on Saturday?" Grace asked before she drove away.

"On Saturday," Bobbie answered and waved goodbye. Then she turned to go back inside, but she stood for a moment, looking critically at the outside of the building—it looked wonderful! She opened the door and entered to find Queen Esther straining to pull a dolly. Bobbie hurried to help.

"Those are flowerpots, aren't they? Why so heavy? And where are you taking them?"

"To the front door, one on each side. And they got cement in the bottom so people don't steal 'em. Bobby said we can nail 'em to the floor, too." And before Bobbie could offer to help, Queen lifted one, and then the other, placing them on either side of the door. "They'll be real pretty when they got those tall, green, potted plants in 'em," Queen said proudly.

"Beautiful," Bobbie agreed.

"Can I ask you something that's none of my business?"

"You can ask," Bobbie said lightly.

"Both of those your women?"

"Good Lord no," Bobbie said with a laugh. "Grace Hannon keeps me fully and happily occupied every waking hour of every day. Eileen McKinley requires the same amount of time and attention—"

"So she got her own doctor?" Queen asked.

"Indeed she does; only hers is the academic kind," Bobbie answered, and at the expression on Queen Esther's face, she explained what kind of doctor Dr. Joyce Scott was.

"They are some seriously beautiful women," Queen said. "Mr. Mason said they the most beautiful in New York City, maybe even in the world."

"And he's absolutely correct," Bobbie said. "They also are the gentlest, kindest, most loving, most generous women in the world, and I'm proud that they are my friends."

Queen Esther harrumphed, leered, and said, "One of 'em is a lot more'n that."

"Yes, indeed she is," Bobbie said

It took several hours but Grace, her nurses, and her office manager finally succeeded in rearranging and rescheduling all their patients to allow for the office to be closed the following Thursday and Friday for construction of the new office space. Grace had hoped to close for only one day but both contractors—David Grimes and William Williams—said it couldn't be done in three days—Friday, Saturday, and Sunday. David Grimes was in the middle of a renovation that wouldn't finish for another week or ten days so William Williams, by default, won the bid, and Grace was just as satisfied. She loved her kitchen but both Bobbie and Bobby gave Williams full votes of confidence, and he was ready to get started. He wanted to begin on Wednesday after they closed the office for the day. He would, he said, make all the necessary arrangements with building management so they would have nothing to worry about.

"Mr. Williams? Can you bring us a safe?" Grace asked. "The kind that can only be opened by the person who knows the combination. We need to make certain that all of our patient files and records are secure."

"Yes, ma'am, Dr. Hannon, I will bring you a safe. The kind that not even dynamite can open." He also recommended a security door for the back entrance to the office, the one from the garage used by Grace and the nurses. "The door slams and locks itself, which means you got to get yourselves inside and outta the way fast." He also advised a similar door on the room where the supplies and medicines were kept.

He made more measurements in their soon-to-be-new office, and they returned to Grace's office to finalize plans for handling any emergencies that might arise when the office was closed. They finally agreed that the three of them—Grace and the two full-time RNs—should alternate being on-call for Thursday, Friday, and Saturday and that Grace would take Sunday on-call, and they would, of course, call Grace if any situation required a doctor. Then Grace began opening and unwrapping bags and parcels, and presenting the art that would hang on the walls of the new reception room. It was all paintings or photographs of Negro women and Negro children who were happy and joyful, smiling and playing. They were all ages, shapes and sizes, and all the images were of Harlem. There was even a photograph of nurses in starched whites standing outside Harlem Hospital as the snow was falling—the darkness of the women in stark contrast to their uniforms and the snow. The three nurses were momentarily speechless.

Then Leola Johnson, their new full-time nurse, laughed. "These are the most wonderful things I've ever seen," she said. "And that picture should hang inside the hospital, in the lobby." She had worked inside that hospital for more than ten years, most recently on the night shift where she was assigned after she contradicted the doctor who had sworn he did nothing to hurt or harm Jacqueline Marie Jackson. Nurse Johnson knew better and helped Dr. Hannon prove it. It was she who, on the night Jack was hospitalized, sounded the alarm when that same doctor who had butchered her attempted to enter Jack Jackson's room in violation of an order by the hospital administrator. Her warning resulted in Bobby Mason's throwing him out of Jack's room, throwing him down the stairs, and slamming the door on his right hand, ending his surgical career.

More than a few hospital employees had resented her actions, and she had had more than enough of their displays of resentment, so Grace Hannon was more than happy to hire her away from the hospital. Since patient care was Leola Johnson's raison d'être, she fit seamlessly into the flow of the office, bonding with nurses and the patients quickly and easily.

"Our office will be mistaken for a gallery or a studio when these are on the walls," Myrt said with happy pride.

"I hope the women will like them," Leola said, "and that they will know and understand that they hang on our walls because of the love and respect we have for them and their children."

"When do you plan to tell me where we're going?" Grace asked as Bobbie parked the car.

"We're here," Bobbie replied, coming around to open Grace's door. But Grace was already standing in the parking lot. Bobbie looked at her, admiring the view. Grace told her to stop it and to behave herself. "No fun in that," Bobbie said with a grin.

She took Grace's hand and led her out of the small lot to the sidewalk and into an adjacent building Grace had not noticed. It was a neat, clean, unobtrusive, red brick building with a wood double door that opened into a clean, quiet, well-lit lobby. There were no other people visible. Bobbie led them to the single elevator and pressed the button. The door opened immediately, they got on, and the door closed before a button was pressed.

"Bobbie," Grace began but Bobbie pressed the top button, and the box slid slowly and quietly up without stopping. When it stopped and the door opened, Grace was rendered speechless at what she saw: a large, light-filled room that she recognized as the studio of some kind of clothing designer. Patterns and sketches and images from the fashion magazines covered one wall. On three large tables there were bolts of fabric, and between the tables half a dozen mannequins, some partially draped with fabric, others bare. Opposite was a wall of mirrors with a platform in front, and at the far end of the room a long desk with lamps at either end and someone sitting in the middle. Someone who suddenly stood and hurried toward them. A small woman who initially appeared much too old to hurry but whose electric energy dispelled any notion of age.

"Bobbie, my dear, I was so glad to hear from you. And I do believe that you are almost as beautiful as your mother." And she wrapped Bobbie in a hug.

"Only almost, Julia?" Bobbie said softly.

"Your mother was one of a kind," Julia replied, holding Bobbie at arms' length and scrutinizing her carefully. "And so, it seems, are you. Beautiful, certainly, but also . . . quintessential." She released Bobbie and turned her gaze on Grace. "And you! Oh my goodness gracious." She walked around Grace, then backed away and studied her.

"This is Grace Hannon, Julia—"

"Yes, I know who Dr. Hannon is. She saved your mother's life. And her sanity."

"Julia—" Bobbie began.

"That's what she told me, Bobbie. Those were her words. And now I see that perhaps the very beautiful Grace Hannon has saved your life as well?"

Grace opened her mouth to speak but first Bobbie stopped her and then Julia stopped her by taking Grace's hand and leading her over to the platform facing the mirrors. She helped Grace step up, then stepped back and looked at her. Studied her. From every angle, front and back and both sides. She asked her to remove everything except her panties and shoes, and she studied her again.

"Would you like for me to leave, Grace?" Bobbie called out, and Grace shook her head. At the same time Julia reached into a cabinet, withdrew a camisole, and slipped it over Grace's head. She ran her hands over it, and then laughed.

"Look at this, Bobbie. Look how wonderful this is."

Bobbie hurried over to see what was so wonderful and, looking from Julia to Grace and back to Julia, asked, "What am I looking at, please?"

"Good thing I know how brilliant you are," Grace said, taking her hand and raising it to her breast. "Feel. The bra is sewn *into* the camisole; it is *part* of the garment."

"Now that is something special," Bobbie said, and meant it, bowing to Julia.

Julia accepted the praise though her expression didn't change; she knew how special the garment was, just as she knew that one day the fashion and clothing industries would come to the same realization. "We have beautiful and bountiful bosoms, and they are *not* pointy. We should not wear the commercial brassiere, and certainly not one with pointy cups." Julia returned her full attention to Grace. She opened a drawer beneath the platform where Grace stood and withdrew a nineteen-by-twenty-four sheet of heavy stock, an artists' pencil, and a tape measure, and she began to measure Grace from head to toe. She returned the tape measure and pencil to the drawer, smiled at Grace, hurried to the back of the room, and disappeared.

Bobbie and Grace looked at each other, but before either could speak Julia reappeared pulling two racks of clothes, stopping before Grace. "Ignore color and fabric," she told Grace. "Focus on the design of the garment, and if you like something give it to me." Grace liked a few somethings, and Julia's arms were full when Grace completed her review. Then Julia presented books of photographs and patterns, which Grace expertly perused, choosing several.

"You have a very well-developed sense of style and fashion, Dr. Hannon," Julia said.

"Please call me Grace, and I know what I like. I've never had the pleasure of working with a—what are you, Julia, for you are much more than a seamstress?"

The older woman smiled her pleasure at the compliment. "I am a designer, but I was forced to abandon that work because those I designed for didn't feel it necessary to pay a Negro woman what I charged for original designs. I worked on Broadway and in Hollywood for several years, but I decided I could be happy being a seamstress on my own terms. I had a few clients like Mrs. Hilliard who could afford my designs but . . ." She shrugged, not completing the sentence.

"I'm very glad Bobbie brought me to you."

"As am I," Julia said. Then she turned to Bobbie. "You may step up here and undress while Grace gets dressed."

"Oh, no!" Bobbie protested. "I'm not part of this—"

"Oh yes, you most certainly are, Bobbie Hilliard," Grace replied in the tone of voice that Bobbie had come to know meant that argument was futile. Bobbie stepped reluctantly onto the platform, sighed heavily, and began to undress. She stepped out of her shoes, then her slacks, and remembered to reach into the pocket for the money she had brought for Julia, who nodded her thanks. When Bobbie unbuttoned and removed her shirt Julia gave her a camisole and said, "At least you're not wearing a silly pointy thing, but yes, Bobbie, you must wear this."

"But I don't have bountiful bosoms, so I don't need that."

"But you do have nipples and yes, you DO need this." Bobbie stood still while Julia measured her the same way she'd measured Grace, and though Bobbie was certain such detailed measurements were not necessary, she kept the thought to herself.

"These are some designs I think would be perfect for

Bobbie," Grace said, fully dressed and carrying an armload of sketches, photographs, and patterns. Bobbie pretended not to have any interest in them because she didn't intend to wear any of them. Being measured was her way of humoring Grace—she'd be easier to get along with. But when she was dressed and sitting on the platform, she agreed to look at the designs, and she was sold. Julia was right. Grace had an unerring eye for fashion and design, and not just for herself. She looked at her watch.

"We need to go, or we'll be late. Julia, you and Grace decide for me, and I'll wear your decisions. I'll be swell and elegant and sexy and—"

"Please stop talking, Bobbie," Grace said, but she was laughing when she said it.

"Julia, may we leave the car in the parking lot for a while? We've got a reservation at the Theresa in the Grill and I don't want them to give it away."

"Of course you may. I'll call Robert and tell him you're on the way." She hugged Bobbie and thanked her for bringing Grace. Hugging Grace, she told her she'd call when she should come for her first fitting and was surprised when Grace pressed money into her hand. She whispered that Bobbie had already paid her. Grace whispered that she was paying for the clothes that Bobbie thought she didn't want. Julia held both their hands when she walked them to the door and showed them out.

They got a taxi almost immediately and entered the Grill at 12:30 on the dot.

"Miss Hilliard, Dr. Hannon, nice to see you both. Right this way, please." They followed the maitre d' to a corner booth that was secluded but also provided a fine view of the full and noisy room. They slid into the booth toward each other and glanced around the room, but Bobbie was more interested in the menu.

"You know I've never been here," Grace said, taking in the scenery.

"No, I did not know that," Bobbie said. "I just knew you'd

never been here with me and I wanted to correct that. Dinner in the penthouse dining room soon?"

Grace smiled, nodded, and opened her menu, then closed it. "Why don't you order for me? What are your favorites?"

Without hesitating Bobbie told her: the Waldorf chicken salad as a salad or a sandwich, and the sirloin burger with fries or onion rings. "Larry and I always get one or the other."

"Then let's get both and share. And I think I'll have a Campari and soda."

"Then so will I," Bobbie said as the waitress arrived to take their order. Surprisingly, Eileen and Joyce arrived also.

"Move over, we're joining you." The booth was easily large enough to accommodate the four of them. To make life easy for the waitress Joyce told her they'd have exactly what Bobbie and Grace were having. When Grace told them where they'd been, Eileen wanted to hear every detail. And when she heard about the camisole, she wanted to see it. Immediately. So off to the ladies room they went, holding on to each other and giggling like they were back in school as they always did when they were left to their own devices.

"Do they ever run out of things to talk and laugh about?" Bobbie wondered, and Joyce, who had years of experience observing the two best friends in their totally relaxed state, began to answer the question. Then she stopped talking and her face changed. Bobbie looked where Joyce was looking and surged to her feet. Grace and Eileen were stumbling toward them, Eileen's arm wrapped around Grace's shoulders.

"Grace, what is it?" Bobbie met them, wrapping her arms around both of them, joined almost immediately by Joyce.

"What happened, Eileen?" Joyce asked.

"Gracie?" Bobbie asked gently. "Talk to me, love, please. What is it?"

Grace said nothing so Eileen said, "She saw that Von Thompkins—"

361

"What?" Bobbie asked coldly. "Where?"

"Up front there," Eileen said, gesturing with her head, her arms still around Grace.

"I'll be right back," Bobbie said, turning toward the front of the Grill.

"Bobbie, no," Grace pleaded, grabbing her arm, but Bobbie freed herself and hurried away.

"Take care of Grace, please. I'll be right back." But no one at the maitre'd station at the front of the room knew who Von Thompkins was. Bobbie strode into the ladies' lounge, which was as packed as the Grill, but when she described Von, no one had seen "anyone who looks like that."

Bobbie looked in the coat check room, which was unlocked but unstaffed this time of year—dark and empty. She looked outside, up and down the block. She thought she would recognize Von Thompkins, even from the back if she saw her, but she didn't see anyone, so she breathlessly returned to Grace and Eileen and Joyce and their lunch, which was being delivered.

"Are you all right, love? Did she say anything to you?" Bobbie whispered to Grace.

Grace looked almost recovered. "I was just so startled, shocked to see her. I really had almost forgotten what she looked like, Bobbie, but when I saw her it all came back." She shuddered, then shook her head, shaking away all the disturbance. Then she smiled the beautiful, gentle smile that was Grace Hannon. "You can cut that sirloin burger and give me my half," she said to Bobbie," and lunch proceeded, a happy affair, good friends enjoying each other and some of the best food and drink in Harlem.

They all declined dessert in favor of a second Campari and soda, and talk turned to the fitting at Julia Loughlin's. Even Bobbie was enthusiastic about her new wardrobe-to-be.

"I've always wanted to be dressed by Julia Loughlin," Eileen said, "but your mother was the only person I knew who knew

Julia, and one couldn't get an appointment without a personal recommendation. She was that popular. Is she still?"

Bobbie shrugged and Grace said, "I wouldn't be surprised. She's a genius. You should see her original designs."

"I'd love to," Eileen said drily. "May I count on you for a referral?"

"We'll do better than that," Bobbie said. "We left the car up there and if you go with us to get it, we'll introduce you, and then we'll take you home."

"And then you'll take me shopping, as you promised?" Grace asked.

"Indeed I will," Bobbie replied.

Larry McKinley looked at Bobbie as if her nose had migrated up to her forehead. "Are you certain of this, Bobbie? I've known this man for more than ten years."

"That doesn't mean you know everything about him, Larry, any more than he knows everything about you."

"But you just called the man a pedophile."

"No, I did not, Larry," Bobbie hissed, careful not to raise her voice. "I asked if he was the kind of person who would keep hiring Von Thompkins despite her terrible reputation and if so, I suggested a possible reason for it. That's all." Bobbie grabbed his arm and held it tightly.

This man was her friend, and he didn't want to believe that a man he considered a friend could also be guilty of being a despicable pervert. "Please do not dismiss this out of hand." They were in the lobby of the building and they were practically whispering, but the intensity of their interaction made clear to passers-by that they were not idly chatting. Even Queen Esther looked at them and walked in the opposite direction.

"Can you please tell me how you know this information

363

about the Thompkins woman?" When Bobbie finished telling him, it was his turn to hold her arm, ultimately pulling her into an embrace. "I am so, so sorry, Bobbie. I knew that something terrible had happened to Grace, Eileen and Jo told me that much, but I didn't know exactly what that something was. Small wonder you didn't kill Thompkins on the spot."

"That would have messed up Grace's expensive rugs really badly."

Larry smiled sadly and promised to look at the men who ran the various departments of the Hotel Theresa. Then he looked closely at her. "You mentioned a personal matter you wanted to talk about?"

She reached into her satchel and withdrew two manila envelopes to give him. "I want to open the Oak Bluffs house—" He grabbed her into a tight hug before the words were out of her mouth and began dancing her around the lobby. Good thing only Queen Esther saw them. This time she walked over.

"You two look better than you did a few minutes ago," she said.

"Miss Jones, always good to see you, and to thank you for all you do for McKinley and Mason. Bobbie, I'll talk to you later," and Larry left them.

Queen Esther looked hard at Bobbie and Bobbie let her. Whatever was on her mind she'd speak it, and she did. "How do y'all trust each other like you do? Did you all grow up here in Harlem at the same time? Know each other in school or church?"

Bobbie shook her head. Only she and Larry McKinley were Harlem natives, she told Queen Esther, but his parents moved the family to Queens when he was in high school. Bobby Mason was from East St. Louis, and the others—Eileen, Joyce, and Grace—were born in Queens. Then Bobbie asked a question of her own: "Where are you from, Queen? Did you grow up here in Harlem?"

"I wish I had. I b'lieve it woulda been better than growing

up in the fuckin' Bronx!"

Bobbie took a breath and then asked. "I know The Bronx is a sizable place, but do you know, or did you ever hear of a Von Thompkins?"

Queen Esther looked at her the same way Larry had looked at her earlier—as if her nose had moved up to sit in the middle of her forehead. "How the hell does somebody like you know that low-down piece of dog shit?"

"What kind of person is she, Queen? Exactly what kind of person is she?"

Queen Esther shook her head back and forth. "The worst kind. The lowest of the low. Not the kind of person any decent somebody would want to know."

"Then why do you know her, Queen?"

Queen Esther first looked shocked, then smiled. "Thank you, Miss Bobbie. That's a very nice thing for you to say."

"You're a very nice person, Miss Queen, and a very decent person. So how do you happen to know somebody who is the lowest of the low?"

"We grew up in the same project, in the same building, and folks thought we were the same 'cause I liked boys and she liked girls. That's what they *thought*. They didn't *know* a damn thing." Queen called up the long-buried memory of her youth in a Bronx housing project where she grew up being taunted and abused because she didn't just like boys, she wasn't just a faggot, but she thought she was a girl. She should have been born a girl and she knew it. And the masculine Von Thompkins didn't really like girls—or boys. She didn't really like sex at all, and after she damn near killed three boys who attempted to rape her, as if their brutality could instill a desire for sex, she was left alone and moved away from the neighborhood where she grew up.

Though The Bronx was a very large area, the stories began to circulate, Queen Esther said. Von took in poor girls, fed and clothed them, made them pretty, and then sold them to men, and sometimes to women, for sex. Queen Esther told Bobbie she blackmailed the people she sold the girls to, which guaranteed that she always would have enough money to keep the girls looking good until they got too old for the people who liked to have sex with young children. She'd get rid of them and buy new young girls from parents too drunk or drugged to care and start the process all over again. "It seems," Queen Esther said, her mouth tightening as if she wanted to spit out something nasty, "that grown people who like having sex with children don't like the children to be too old."

Bobbie, too, felt the urge to throw up, but something about what she saw in Queen's eyes and on her face forced her to remain calm and in control.

"What is it, Queen? You look like there is something worse than what you've already told me, though I can't imagine what it could be."

"You know I think that I was born in the wrong body."

"Yes, I know that you should have been born a woman, Queen."

Queen blinked mascaraed lashes and nodded. "But my body played a real ugly trick and gave me this dick that I do not *ever* use except to pee. But I got it, which means I'm a man, and I know that, Miss Bobbie, and wishin' I didn't have the damn thing won't make it go away 'cause if so, it'd be long gone. And I'm sure there're some women wish they had dicks to give their woman, though you prob'ly ain't one of 'em. Am I right?"

"Yes, you are, on both counts, Queen," Bobbie said, and waited for whatever was coming next, and she was certain something else was coming.

Queen held her eyes and inhaled deeply, then said, "You ever heard about people who have both kinds of sex things down there?" And she pointed to her groin. "A little tiny dick and a pussy you can't hardly see? You ever heard of that kinda thing, Miss Bobbie?"

Bobbie nodded slowly. She'd heard of such things, but she had no real knowledge, although Grace would probably know, she thought. "Why do you ask, Queen?"

"'Cause whatever they call them kinda people, that's what Von Thompkins is. She's one of 'em."

Grace was stunned into a very long silence and Bobbie could do nothing but wait. And worry because Grace had wiped her face clear of all thought and emotion. Her drink sat untouched. Finally, she got up and went into her office. She stood before the wall of bookshelves, moving her hand along the book spines as her eyes scanned the titles. She withdrew a book and brought it back to the sofa where Bobbie waited.

"They're called hermaphrodites—people with both male and female genitalia. I've never seen a case and I don't know anyone who has." She passed the open book to Bobbie who read the section where Grace's finger pointed.

"That's not a lot of information," Bobbie said after she read the section Grace indicated.

"That's because there's not a lot of information on the subject. There are some studies, most of them in Europe, and there are clinics where parents take very young children for surgery to . . . correct . . . what they perceive the problem to be. Again, most such facilities are in Europe—"

Bobbie raised a hand. "Correct what they *perceive* the problem to be, Grace?"

Grace sighed and shook her head. "This is very far beyond any knowledge or understanding I possess, Bobbie. This is science, biology, genetics, whatever it is, maybe all of it, that the medical profession does not understand and can do nothing with, about, or for."

"Will that ever change, do you think?" Bobbie asked.

"Probably. There are doctors who are scientists and who do nothing but research and study and ask questions, and then seek to answer them. I can't imagine excising genitalia because a parent wanted a boy or a girl, but I don't mind telling you how thankful I am that I only have to deliver them, and not make decisions of that magnitude."

"So, you didn't know . . .?"

Grace shook her head. "I had no idea. It was clear almost immediately that Von Thompkins targeted me to hurt you, but she had absolutely no interest in having sex with me, for which I was and always will be profoundly grateful. The only thing I could think about was what a fool I was for believing the things she said about you, and how I planned to do whatever it took to make it up to you."

Grace shivered as she recalled that ugly time. "She hated you though I didn't know why, but I did know—I learned pretty quickly—that's when and why she hit me. Any mention of you infuriated her."

"She will keep well away from you if she knows what's good for her," Bobbie said, "I don't care how fucked up her biology is."

"But you know that she can't help that, Bobbie, yes?"

"I know that your compassionate nature is a large part of why I love you, Grace Hannon."

"Please tell me that you understand, Bobbie."

"I understand that Von Thompkins should stay away from you," Bobbie said, and she returned the book to the empty space on the shelf in Grace's office, Verne's words careening around in her memory: *You shoulda killed her when you had the chance.*

CHAPTER ELEVEN

Boy Bobby, Ennyday, and Buddy were unloading supplies from the bed of the Mckinley-Mason Real Estate pickup truck into a wheeled handcart at the back door of Building No. 4—Buddy's building. The young man and his even younger wife were doing well living on their own.

Buddy unlocked the door and held it open while Ennyday and Boy Bobby, with great effort, rolled the cart into the building, waited for Buddy to slam the door shut and make sure it locked, then helped them push it up a narrow incline into the basement of the building. "We'll do the lobby first, make it beautiful so that people will be glad to get home in the evening after a hard day at work."

"We're gonna paint it and put up a new light—" Buddy began, but Bobby stopped him.

"First we'll strip all the wood, remove years of accumulated grit and grime, outside and inside. This fixture will go outside and this one inside, in the lobby." He watched Buddy's face as he explained, watched as he saw the boy understand what was to happen, but more importantly, why it was to happen. When the boy nodded, Bobby quietly sighed his relief.

"When do we start, Mr. Mason?"

"Tomorrow, Buddy. Ennyday and Benny will be here at eight thirty to help, so wear your dirtiest clothes because stripping wood is filthy work. It's beautiful when it's finished, but getting there is extremely tiring and taxing. They'll bring all the necessary tools and other equipment with them."

Bobby bid the young man good afternoon and hurried out the door.

He hoped he wouldn't be too late for his dinner with Eileen and Joyce and the very handsome David Craig. As it happened, he and David arrived at the same time, almost thirty minutes late, because of traffic.

The food, of course, was excellent, prepared by Eileen, and the entertainment was equally superb because it was provided by EJ and Scottie, who crawled and climbed all over Uncle Bobby as if he were playground equipment. David was charmed and amused, which charmed and amused Bobby. Grace had told him that David was a little older, but Bobby didn't think that would be an issue—he was funny and charming.

When Joyce and Eileen took the children to be bathed and put to bed, he and David had time to talk a little about their backgrounds and to learn that both had stopped college, though for different reasons. Both were determined to finish: David, who had dropped out of Morehouse College in Atlanta after his sophomore year, had recently completed his BA in History at City College; Bobby, recently enrolled at City College, would complete his BA in Education when and as time permitted. "Don't worry about when," David told him. "Getting it done is what matters."

They exchanged addresses and telephone numbers and David, who had to be on a job at seven the next morning, prepared to leave, though he waited for Joyce and Eileen to return from putting the children to bed to thank them for what he called "a really great evening."

"Well?" Eileen pressed, looking closely at Bobby when

David was gone.

"Well, what?" Bobby replied.

"JoJo, would you please get Gracie on the phone—"

"He's wonderful!" Bobby exclaimed. "You were right. And EJ and Scottie like him so he must be something special."

"When will you two have your first date?" Joyce asked, and Bobby sighed. They were going to be worse than Bobbie and Grace.

On the way home Boy Bobby wondered the same thing. When would they have their first date, and who should make that first call? He'd only had one boyfriend—Jerome—and it was he who had made the first move. Should he wait for David? Could he ask Larry for advice? He was hanging up his slacks and shirt when the phone rang, and he looked at it as if the thing could tell him who was calling. Wouldn't that be a neat trick. He answered on the second ring and it was Ennyday. A very frightened Ennyday.

"Boy Bobby," he whispered, his voice quivering, "those boys who hurt our Jack, they're doing that to another girl in that same place. You got to go stop 'em."

It felt to Bobby like his ears relayed the words to his brain in slow motion. Then understanding. "You saw boys doing what, Ennyday? Hurting a girl? In that alley?"

"And she was crying, Boy Bobby. That girl was crying, and that drunk cop was there, too. Just sittin' on the ground lookin' at 'em."

"You go home, Ennyday, and you stay there, you hear me? Promise me you will run home as fast as you can and that you will stay there."

"I will, Boy Bobby, I promise."

Girl Bobbie answered her phone on the second ring and at the expression on her face as she listened to whoever was on the other end of the call, Grace hurried to her. "That was Bobby. Ennyday just called to say that a girl was being raped in the alley

371

where Jack . . . it may well be the same boys, Grace. And that damn drunk cop is still drunk and sitting there watching it all. I'm going to meet—"

"The hell you are!" The near whisper of Grace's voice belied the fear and anger it held.

"I must, Grace. I need to. And I can't let him go alone." She freed herself from Grace's grip and hurriedly dressed in Levis, a black T-shirt, black Converse high tops, and a No. 42 Brooklyn Dodgers cap. When she got to the back door Grace was there— in Bobbie's pajamas—car keys in hand.

"I'm driving you there," Grace said, and it was not a request.

"And then you're coming directly back home?"

"Yes—if you promise that you and Boy Bobby will come directly back here after you do whatever you're going to do." Bobbie nodded her acquiescence, and they hurried out the door to the garage. The gate began to lift as the car approached and Grace sped out without waiting for the gate to lower itself, not something they were in the habit of doing. The alley in question was twenty downtown blocks away and Grace made good time until the final two blocks. Bobbie opened the car door, hopped out, told Grace to hurry back home, told her she loved her, and started to run.

Bobby's truck was blocking the alley entrance, and his back was against the hood of the truck. He was swinging a heavy wooden stick or pole at two boys who were crouched low and inching toward him. Bobbie peered into the bed of the pickup and spied four wooden sticks like the one Boy Bobby held. She reached in and grabbed one, and swinging it, moved quickly toward the two boys, surprising them. She hit the closest one with her stick; he screamed and went down and writhed on the ground. Boy Bobby swung and dropped the third boy, and it was when he was down that Bobbie saw the girl on the ground. She was naked from the waist down, her long, black hair was spread out on the filthy alley ground, and she was weeping quietly.

Bobbie knelt beside her and took her hand. *"Nina, que es tu nombre? Por favor, digame."*

She began to cry loudly and scream in Spanish and Bobbie didn't understand a single word. French was Bobbie's language, not Spanish, and she felt totally helpless and useless. She wished now that Grace was here because the brutal damage to the girl's vaginal area was visible.

"Oh goddammit," she muttered to herself and turned to look for Bobby, finding him tying up the rapists. She helped him finish the job, then helped him lift and throw them into the bed of the truck. He grabbed a blanket from the storage box in the truck bed and walked toward the girl to cover her, but she began to scream and cry, so he gave the blanket to Bobbie. *"Por favor, Senorita; Por favor, por favor."* The girl quieted, looked at the blanket, understood what it was and what Bobbie wanted to do, nodded, and Bobbie covered her.

Then they both watched as Boy Bobby stalked over to the drunk cop propped against the alley wall, legs splayed out in front of him. Bobby first kicked him but got no response. He swung his stick hard on the man's legs and his eyes flew open, then his mouth, but no sound came out. Bobby didn't care. He hit him across the legs again, hard, and Bobbie knew that bones broke, knew that this drunk would not walk a beat in this neighborhood again, or in any other neighborhood in New York City. Then Boy Bobby picked up the not-quite-empty booze bottle, poured the remains over the drunk cop, and threw the bottle against the brick wall. Glass shards showered down. Other cops would find the stinking mess when they found him.

The silently weeping girl allowed Bobbie to wrap the blanket around her waist and legs, and she allowed Boy Bobby to carry her to the truck. "Should we sit her up or lay her down?" he asked and Bobbie shrugged. She had no idea. She wanted to call Grace for advice, but she knew Grace would come running and she didn't want that.

"Let's lay her down. I'll get in the back and you can put her head in my lap. But move the assholes out of the way first. I've got to get her to tell me where she lives."

Bobbie felt a tug on her arm and simultaneously heard the whispered words, "One Forty Street and Five Avenue." She looked down into the tear-and-blood-stained face of the girl whose mocha-brown eyes were wide open and staring at her.

The girl spoke English, thank heaven, and probably understood it, too. "What is your name, please, and where do you live? Where is your family?"

"I am Angela and *mi familia* is at One-Forty and Five Avenue."

"Bobby," she called out, "One-Fortieth and Fifth!" The truck started up and began to back out of the alley. Horns honked and Bobby honked back, continuing his backward motion until he could shift gears and move forward. He wanted to get Angela home as fast as she did, Bobbie thought, and then she had another thought. Even though he didn't know the girl's name yet, he knew he had to get her somewhere to be taken care of, and he for damn sure needed to get the three rapists out of his truck.

Angela tugged on Bobbie's arm again. "*Mi hermano* . . . my brother and his friends, they will be in the alley behind the building, from the One-Forty Street side," she said. Bobbie knocked on the window and when Boy Bobby stuck his head out, she relayed the instructions. It wasn't long before the big truck turned carefully into the mouth of the narrow alley. It was instantly met and surrounded by almost a dozen hostile young men speaking in rapid-fire Spanish. Bobbie had no idea what they were saying, but it wasn't "how are you" and "welcome to the neighborhood."

Angela struggled to sit up and began to call out in Spanish. Almost immediately the boys stopped their verbal assault and one of them stepped out of the crowd and approached the bed of the truck. "Angelina? Angelina!"

He was trying to open the gate of the truck. Then his eyes moved from his sister to the three bound rapists. "Rogelio!" Angela cried out. At the same time Bobbie spoke. "Your sister is badly injured and she needs help."

"Rogelio!" Angela called out again and continued with a torrent of Spanish. The tears returned and turned into sobs, and the girl pointed to the bound boys who now were conscious enough to realize they were in danger and were trying to sit up. Angela and her brother and a few of the other boys conversed in Spanish for a moment. Then Rogelio extended a hand to Boy Bobby and thanked him for helping his *hermanita*. He and Bobby released the locks on the truck gate, but before they could lift Angela out Bobbie intervened.

"Rogelio, please keep Angela wrapped in the blanket—"

"Why?"

"Listen to me, Rogelio, please. *Por favor*." She pointed to the rapists. "They hurt her. They hurt her very, very badly. They *raped* her, Rogelio. All of them did. Now take your sister to her mother, please. Take her now, Rogelio."

Bobbie watched the young man understand her words and saw the emotions that traveled across his face as he did. Then a torrent of rapid-fire Spanish flew from his mouth, and the hands of his compatriots grabbed the three bound boys from the truck bed and dragged them deep into the alley. Rogelio gently lifted his sister, and she wrapped her arms around his neck. When she was all the way out of the truck, Bobbie jumped down and wrapped the ends of the blanket around her legs, tying the ends tightly so that it would not come undone. As brother and sister made their way home, the sounds from deep within the alley suggested that those three boys would rape no more Colored girls in the alley between 135th Street and Seventh Avenue.

"What was she doing all the way over there?" Grace asked, a question Bobbie and Bobby had asked themselves more than once as they drove away from 140th and Fifth Avenue.

"Visiting a friend?" Bobbie said, and added, *"Quien sabes?"*

"What's that mean?" Boy Bobby asked.

"It means *who knows*," Grace said, adding, "and we most certainly never will. Please be sure to thank Ennyday. He must have been terrified to have witnessed such an ugly horror twice."

"I definitely will thank Ennyday, and also tell him how brave he is. How does one reward such a brave act?" Grace and Bobbie were pondering when Boy Bobby's face lit up: "I'll let him order whatever and as much as he wants from Miz Maggie and then I'll drive him home so he doesn't have to walk home carrying that many bags."

"He'll get enough food to feed his family for a week," Bobbie said. "He's a good boy, that Ennyday is."

"He certainly is that," Grace agreed. Then she said, "I'm going to call Jack and invite her to come eat ice cream with us, so you two can tell her about your night."

Jack listened without speaking as she ate two bowls of ice cream—the first with butterscotch syrup, the second with caramel. "I wish we could've been the ones who gave them what they had coming to them, but I don't suppose it really matters who delivered the message," Jack finally said in a voice devoid of emotion.

"Indeed it does matter," Grace insisted.

"Surely you're not thinking cops and courts," Jack queried, with plenty of emotion in her voice now.

Grace shook her head. "I know better than that. I'm just very glad that it wasn't my people who had to deliver the message, the justice."

"But it *was* your people, my love," Bobbie said to Grace, taking her hand, "because it was me and Boy Bobby who delivered the rapists to those who delivered—"

"The payback!" Jack interrupted. "Payback is a bitch, and that's on a day when she's on her best behavior."

"You've been spending too much time with Joyce Ann—sounds like something she'd say. And speaking of her eminence, how was dinner, Mr. Mason?"

"Dinner was excellent, I'm sure," Bobbie said. "What I want to know is how was Mr. Craig?"

Boy Bobby smiled widely. "What a man! But I need some help—"

"You swore that you would know exactly what to do when Mr. Right came along."

"I do know *exactly* what to do when it gets to that point, but how do I get it to that point? Do I call him first or wait for him to call me first?"

"I had to wait for Miss Hilliard to call me first—had to wait until Monday," Grace said.

"I didn't have a number for you, Dr. Hannon, nor did I know where you lived, though my good friend Jack Jackson did know where you lived—"

"Oh no, don't you try to pin that on me. Not my fault you waited until Monday to call, especially since you were drooling all over yourself when you put her in the car that Saturday night."

"Was she, now?" Grace asked with a wicked grin. "First I'm hearing about it."

Bobbie changed the subject. "If you exchanged numbers—"

"And addresses."

"Then I don't think it matters who calls first. Call him in the morning before he goes to work."

"He's due on site at 7 a.m., which reminds me! I'm meeting Larry first thing—and for us that's 8:30—to show him a warehouse off 156th near the river—Grace, Bobbie—to house the thousands of sanitary pads, belts, and vitamins he's getting wholesale, and where women can come to get them safely and privately. And I have a suggestion: call whatever happens in that building, however it happens, after Stephanie St. Clair."

Since Grace and Bobbie looked at him in wide-eyed speechless wonder, it fell to Jack to hug him tightly and kiss the top of his head and tell him how very wonderful he was.

Buddy Joiner met Queen Esther Jones at her building promptly at 7 a.m. and not one minute later, as she had told him. A stickler for being on time, Buddy was there when she opened the door to admit him. But first, he asked, could he look at the door, at the outside of the building, which looked to him like something he'd see on the East Side. She did better than just let him look at things; she let him watch her work: how she first swept the sidewalk free of every bit of trash and debris. Then how she polished the wood and brass of the door, and washed the glass until it shone. She repeated the process inside, in the lobby. She was greeted by the residents with their usual, "Good morning, Miss Jones," and she responded in her usual way with a "Good morning" and the resident's name.

"Will the people in my building call me Mr. Joiner?" Buddy asked.

"You will get respect, Mr. Joiner, when you earn respect," Queen answered.

"Miss Jones?" she heard from behind her, and turned to find Miss Ernestine Carr hobbling toward her, cane in one hand, omnipresent black patent purse in the other.

"Good morning, Miss Carr, and you know that I told you I'd bring the elevator to you if you called to let me know when you were ready to come downstairs."

"And I do appreciate it, Miss Jones, but I'm saving the special treatment for when I really need it, like when it rains and the rheumatism really acts up something awful. Don't worry, I'll call you then. But I do need a favor today if you don't mind." Miss Carr explained that she was expecting a package to be delivered, but didn't want it left on the floor in the way of people accessing their mailboxes.

"I'll be on the lookout for your package and take it into my apartment when it comes. Then I'll ride you both upstairs on the elevator," Queen replied and bid Miss Carr a good day.

"I wish my lobby was this pretty, Miss Jones," Buddy Joiner said, looking all around with appreciation. "And also this big."

"Your lobby can be as pretty as you make it, Mr. Joiner, no matter the size."

"I don't see how," he replied morosely.

"Would you like for me to visit your building and take a look?" And the young man's toothy grin was answer enough.

Later that afternoon when Bobby made his usual weekly visit, she told him about Buddy.

"He's a good kid. Works hard, learns fast, and is determined to make something of himself. Both of them are."

Queen frowned. "What both?"

"Buddy and his wife, Naomi—"

"Wife! How old is that boy? And he is a boy, Mr. Mason. I bet money he ain't yet seen twenty."

"He's seventeen and his wife is sixteen." For the first time in their association Bobby witnessed the Queen rendered speechless, though she recovered quickly.

"Do you help *everybody*, Mr. Mason?"

"Everybody I can, Queen."

"Why?"

He shrugged. "I suppose *because* I can. And because people helped me. And because so many of our people need help, and sometimes it's just a little bit of help, until they get on their feet. Then they can walk. Sometimes when a person can walk—"

"The feet that can walk can run," Queen finished.

"Queen, those of us who can help must help. Just like you're going over to Buddy's building to help him—because you can."

"And because somebody helped me. I ain't forgot that, not for one second, Mr. Bobby Mason, and I never will, not if I live to be a hundred years old."

Almost a dozen workmen swarmed over and around the warehouse on 156th Street as Bobbie, Grace, and Stephanie St. Clair observed, mesmerized: men scraping away old, flaking paint and painting new color; removing old windows and doors and hanging new ones, then painting them; creating rooms from open, empty space; and replacing and/or repairing the roof. Hammering and sawing and men shouting back and forth to each other, a cacophony of sound that was music to the ears of every person there. Bobby and Larry had moved men from several of their projects to the warehouse to get the repairs and renovation completed before the delivery of some 7,500 sanitary napkins and the arrival of a rainstorm the next day. Even if the rain came the delivery truck could drive into the loading dock and ensure a safe and dry delivery. Boy Bobby and Larry had invited the women to observe and had no idea of the tragedy that was only narrowly averted.

Bobbie and Grace arrived first, mere seconds ahead of Madame St. Clair, who arrived in a black Packard sedan driven by one of her employees who was helping her out of the car when Bobbie turned and saw them.

She immediately began to shake and cry and sank to the ground. Grace, unable to support her, and afraid that she was beginning to hyperventilate, sank down with her. Bobby and Larry, watching from a distance, knew immediately that something was wrong and began running toward the women.

Stephanie St. Clair, who had no idea what was wrong, stood looking at Bobbie and Grace, almost paralyzed by shock. Bobby went immediately to Bobbie and Grace while Larry went to Stephanie St. Clair to explain. Tears sprang to her eyes and she, too, began to breathe heavily. Larry put his arm around her, surprised to find that she was such a small woman. She directed her driver to take the Packard away quickly and come back for her with the Cadillac. "Back that damn thing out of here and do it quickly," she ordered, before whispering, "I should have made the connection and remembered: all those stories about Robert Hilliard and his family murdered by that ignorant ofay cop because they committed the crime of driving an expensive black Packard with New York license plates. It was thoroughly reported in the *Amsterdam News* at the time. I just didn't remember. That was Miss Hilliard's family. And I came here this morning in a black Packard sedan. What must she think of me?"

Though he had no idea what was happening, Larry's construction foreman ran toward them with several rolls of paper towels and a bucket of cold water. He was followed by two workmen carrying sawhorses and planks of wood from which they fashioned a bench of sorts, and Larry tried to get Madame St. Clair to sit down but she wanted to go to Bobbie. She did accept some of the wet paper towels to wipe her face. Grace was using a handful of the cold, wet towels to wipe Bobbie's face and control her breathing. Boy Bobby sat on the ground behind her, arms around her and supporting her. Grace whispered to her almost nonstop, which finally calmed her.

Then, as if conjured, Stephanie St. Clair was on the ground beside Bobbie, whispering to her in rapid-fire French, and weeping uncontrollably. Then Bobbie was comforting the older woman. Grace wrapped her arms around both women. Boy Bobby and Larry looked at each other. No words were necessary; their look said it all: if they lived another hundred years they would never understand women, but they knew without a doubt that women were the superior beings of the species.

The following day the delivery truck and the heavy rain arrived as promised but the rain did not deter Eileen, Joyce, and a half dozen of their sorority sisters who came to witness firsthand what their biggest project would involve. Later, when the trucks were unloaded and the supplies cataloged and shelved, Madame St. Clair approached Grace for a whispered conversation. "I'm selling the Packard immediately. If I'd known I'd have driven it into the river myself," she said. "I don't ever want Miss Hilliard to see it on the street. If only I had known—"

"But you didn't know, and when you found out you had the car removed. That's all you could have done under the circumstances," Grace assured the other woman, and Stephanie St. Clair heaved a sigh of relief, patted Grace's arm, and went to circulate among the other women, all of whom knew who she was and thanked her for her generosity to the women of Harlem. Boy Bobby had invited four of the young women, City College students, who were actively involved in the effort to clean up the markets on the Avenue, and they were bouncing around and hopping excitedly about like Eric would have. Girl Bobbie said as much to Boy Bobby. He watched them, nodded agreement, and swiped away the tears that filled his eyes before they fell.

"What should we call it?" one of the girls said.

"Why do we have to call it anything?" another girl said. "It's enough that it's here."

"We have to give it a name because it's so special."

"How about, 'The Madame St. Clair Harlem Negro Women's Center?'"

A long moment of silence, then cheers and applause with Madame St. Clair joining in.

"We need chairs and tables, a water cooler and paper cups and napkins, and some books and magazines and pencils and paper!" The girls were on a roll. Madame St. Clair met Larry's eyes and nodded, and he knew that she would pay for whatever was needed to make the warehouse look and feel like home to the women.

"But . . ." One of the girls tried in vain to talk over the dozen or so voices that were all talking at once. Finally, she yelled, "Hey, can everybody listen for a minute, please?" And all eyes turned to her. "What do we do when the males show up? And you know they will. Any time we get or do something for ourselves, here they come, and they'll want to take over and make it theirs." She was almost in tears. "We have to be able to have something good just for us."

"I'll take care of that," Madame St. Clair said into the silence, and all eyes were on her as she explained how she would take care of it: a woman who had worked for her many years ago, running one of her policy banks, was severely injured while preventing the gangster Dutch Schultz from robbing the place. "He liked to come with his Tommy gun and spray bullets all over to frighten and intimidate people, but Vickie wasn't the type to be frightened or intimidated, so she dropped down beneath her desk until he was done spraying bullets. Then, from beneath the desk, she pumped half a dozen bullets into him. He dropped the Tommy gun, and it began to fire on its own while it was on the floor. While Vickie was on the floor."

Madame Queen closed her eyes and shook her head as if to blow away the still vivid memory. "Bullets tore through her legs and she hasn't walked since. She sits in a wheelchair reading or looking out at the street, watching people come and go. I think she'd love it here taking care of the Negro women of Harlem."

"Why?" one of the young women asked.

"She's alone all day while her girlfriend is at work, her only company the .45 special in her lap, and she's still a crack shot. Being able to share and protect a place that's just for Negro women and girls will make her feel good and proud."

"Who in the hell is Dutch Schultz?" one of the young women whispered to her friend.

"An evil son of a bitch who needed shooting," another one replied, meaning every word.

"I'm still not real sure who Stephanie St. Clair is, but I definitely won't be making her mad."

"Do your homework, girl, or ask your mama. Stephanie St. Clair is the Queen of Harlem, and she's a living legend."

On the last Sunday in May, which was the next to last day in May, Grace surprised Bobbie with breakfast in bed. It was a light meal of cornflakes and milk and a big bowl of strawberries and, of course, coffee, because the big meal of the day was to be Bobbie's birthday feast at Eileen and Larry's home in Queens. A backyard barbecue! They both were looking forward to it because, in addition to sharing food with their closest friends, which was always a favored activity, the McKinley backyard surrounded a large swimming pool. Being able to swim *and* eat surrounded by those they loved the most—it couldn't get any better. It promised to be a perfect day. Then Grace reached into the drawer of her nightstand and withdrew an elegantly wrapped package, and the day got even better.

Bobbie stared at the ring. The gold shone. The interlocking *H*s etched into the surface seemed to reach out to her. The beveled edges dramatically softened the almost square shape of the ring. "It is magnificent, Grace."

"Do you think you'd like to put it on?" Grace asked, gentle humor enhancing the love in her voice, and Bobbie did what Grace herself had done when she received the gift of her ring from Bobbie: she extended her hands and looked the question. *Which hand?* Grace gently lifted the ring from the box and slid it onto the ring finger of Bobbie's right hand where it fit perfectly. Bobbie let her tears fall freely but did not take her eyes off the ring.

One evening, a week later, Bobbie was at the piano when the music changed, drastically and dramatically, from the pieces Grace generally heard in her home. Grace stopped writing the article she was submitting to the medical journal and looked across the room toward Bobbie, who seemed to be trying to remember the music. She stopped and started, stopped then resumed, until finally she found what she was searching for, and she played uninterrupted for several minutes with a passion Grace had never before witnessed. She closed her notebook and walked quietly into the living room where she sat out of Bobbie's sight. But it didn't matter because her eyes were closed. Tears streamed down her face, and Bobbie let them fall where they fell. The music shifted from slow and gentle to percussive and powerful. Grace was so mesmerized that for a moment she wasn't aware that the music had stopped. When she opened her eyes, Bobbie was looking at her.

"I've never heard anything like that, Bobbie. So masterful, so powerful! What is it called? Who is the composer?"

"It's called 'Melody of the Drums,' and I am the composer. This is the composition that earned me my Doctorate in Music Composition." Then, for the first time, she told Grace all of it, and Grace held her as she wept. Her parents shared a great aunt, a woman who was related to both of her parents and who was loved by both of them, and when she died they didn't hesitate to make arrangements to attend the funeral in Atlanta. But they were adamant that Bobbie remain in New York to defend her doctoral composition because both parents were convinced that she would succeed: her pianist and composer father who believed that "Melody of the Drums" was a true masterpiece, and her mother the painter who believed in the brilliance of her daughter in every area. So they had packed the car as little Eric cried and pleaded to be able to stay with Bobbie, and they drove away. The family lost to Bobbie forever.

Bobbie, deep in thought, walked away from Grace, but quickly returned to the circle of her arms. "I never don't think, Grace, about what their final moments must have been like. The terror they felt, and the rage. They knew they were about to die because some ignorant redneck didn't think niggers should be driving a white man's car. That's what he told his superiors—the reason he gave for killing them.

"I should have been there, Gracie, not here defending a thesis, a piece of music that has never been heard anywhere by anyone—"

"Except in your own living room, Dr. Bobbie Hilliard, by the woman who loves you above all else. And what could you have done had you been there with them except perish with them?"

"Why shouldn't I have perished with my family?"

"Because the family you have now—me and Boy Bobby and Jack and Myrt and Thelma and Joyce and Eileen and Larry and EJ and Scottie—would be without you, which would leave a hole too large to be filled. I cannot imagine my life without you, Bobbie, and I truly do wish that you didn't wish yourself dead." Bobbie held her tightly and kissed her deeply, a wordless apology. "Why now, my love?" Grace asked, wordless apology accepted. And after the briefest hesitation, Bobbie replied:

"Because I'm going to play it at the Black Mask Christmas Gala, and it's a good thing I have lots of time to practice. I'm a bit rusty. I haven't played it in more than three years."

CHAPTER TWELVE

Grace was more excited than she'd ever been. She was going on the first vacation of her life and about to spend seven days and nights in Oak Bluffs. Martha's Vineyard. Massachusetts. An island in the Atlantic Ocean. In the house Bobbie had inherited, the house she now owned with Bobbie. Her only worry was that she might wish to remain there.

"You are coming back, aren't you, Grace?" Myrt looked at her as if she could read her mind.

Grace gave her a grin followed by a shrug. "I've never, ever been relaxed, Myrt. Suppose I like it? Want to get used to it?"

"Then your house better have a room for me, too."

"I will always have room for you, my friend," Grace said, looking at her watch and getting quickly to her feet. "I've been summoned to a meeting with his Not So Royal Highness, and I don't want to be late."

"Why didn't you say you'd meet with him when you return?"

"Because I didn't want him on my mind while I'm enjoying my first vacation."

Myrt nodded. "Good thinking."

"Good to see you as always, Dr. Hannon. I appreciate your taking the time."

"It's good to see you as well. It's been a while, which I suppose is good news since it means I've not been in trouble." Grace laughed when she said it and though it took several seconds, so did the hospital administrator.

"Not only not in trouble, Dr. Hannon, but I hope you'll be pleased with the reason I've asked to see you. I'd like for you to become a full-time member of the medical staff of this hospital."

Grace was shocked. Stunned. Momentarily speechless. Was she really to be the first and only Negro woman physician on the staff of Harlem Hospital? She knew he was watching her so she finally managed a smile. "Does this honor come with the same salary, rights, and privileges the male doctors enjoy?"

In three seconds, the administrator's face registered shock, surprise, and humor, and he laughed. "Yes, indeed, Dr. Hannon, and I certainly know better by now than to extend such an offer without the proper and correct details."

She stood up and extended her hand. "Then you have my thanks and my acceptance. I'm on vacation next week. May we formalize things the following week?"

"Of course. Where are you off to?"

"Martha's Vineyard."

"Oh, that's wonderful! I love it there. Do you know people there, or will you be in one of those lovely inns or guest cottages?"

"We have a house there," Grace said, and exercised more self-control than she thought she possessed not to laugh at his reaction.

She slept most of the first two days. She awoke long enough to swim for hours in water so gentle and warm it was hard to believe that it was the Atlantic Ocean, and to eat seafood so fresh and delicious she wondered whether she'd ever again be able to eat ordinary fruit de mare. "I must apologize, Bobbie, my love. I didn't realize how utterly exhausted and depleted I was."

"No apology necessary, Gracie. I'm pleased to see you so relaxed."

"Are you all right being here? It's not too painful?"

"I'm wonderful, and I want to show you everything." And what sights there were. Walking, biking, boating, and, when necessary, driving—the exploration of the island was delightful beyond her every expectation.

"I could spend a month here," Grace said, imagining Myrt and Thelma and Eileen and Joyce and the children, and the boys, all being here with them later in the summer. "I see why Dorothy West lives here full-time."

"Don't forget that she wants to see us," Bobbie said.

"Then let's go see her tout suite. But first I have something to tell you."

Bobbie looked as shocked, and was as speechless as Grace herself had been when she shared the news of her new appointment and the attendant responsibilities. After hugs, kisses, and congratulations the ever-practical Bobbie said, "You know you'll have to hire another doctor and a third nurse."

CHAPTER THIRTEEN

The second annual Black Mask Cultural and Artistic Holiday Fundraiser was in full swing in the penthouse ballroom of the Hotel Theresa. Last year's event had been successful and well-attended, but what Eileen and Larry watched tonight exceeded their every expectation. They were raising a small fortune for the program, and Dr. Ernestine Miles, the executive director, was so happy she was speechless. She was walking around, smiling at everyone, shaking hands with or hugging those who knew who she was and accepting the congratulatory good wishes from people who were learning about Black Mask and its work. She was learning a few things as well. She was well acquainted with Lawrence McKinley, chairman of the Black Mask board, and board member Dr. Grace Hannon, and with Bobbie Hilliard and Eileen McKinley and Robert Mason and Esther Jones, but she had never seen them like this. Grace Hannon and Eileen McKinley and Bobbie Hilliard looked as if they had stepped from the pages of a fashion magazine, and in a way they had, for all three wore original Julia Loughlin creations. They were, to put it mildly, jaw-droppingly elegant. The tuxedos of Bobby Mason and Larry McKinley were the height of new fashion, and Miss Esther Jones, who took care of the building, looked nothing like a building caretaker. She looked right at home in the company of the others. And the program listed the woman she knew as Bobbie Hilliard as Dr. Eleanor Roberta Hilliard! What a night this would be.

The ballroom grew more crowded as more and more elegant people arrived. Dr. Miles was surprised at the number of whites in attendance, though she shouldn't have been given who the board members were, most of whom were recognizable only by their names on tags. Tonight, however, in a private gathering before the ball formally got underway, she had been formally introduced to the Black Mask Cultural and Artistic Center Board of Directors, and she came face to face with Dr. Pauli Murray, Billy Strayhorn, Dorothy West, Lois Jones Pierre-Noel, Ossie Davis and Ruby Dee, and Dr. Benjamin Jones. All of them had attended several of the concerts and performances by young people enrolled in Black Mask programs and had read and critiqued some of their writings and evaluated some of their artwork. All of them had attended the very special event the previous evening where several members of the adult literacy classes had bravely stood at the front of the room and read lessons from their textbooks—people who proudly proclaimed that prior to attending the adult literacy classes they could not read or write. One of those proud people was Miss Esther Jones, the caretaker of the building where the Black Mask Adult Literacy Program was housed.

The band started up to loud applause and cheering, and since Billy Strayhorn was part of the private board meeting, who was conducting the band? Everyone looked at Strayhorn, who was grinning widely. "That's the Duke, telling me to get myself to the bandstand and get to work." The crowd was ready no matter who the bandleader was. Couples danced with abandon, some exhibiting better footwork than others, but no one cared because everyone was having a good time. Except Bobbie Hilliard who was regretting committing herself to being the evening's principal entertainment. Wasn't it enough that Sarah Vaughan was singing? What did they need with her? Doctors Arthur Jennings and Oliver Crawford and the hospital administrator kept wanting to dance with Grace, but her hands were full trying to prevent Bobbie's mutiny. Besides, she knew full well that they were gobsmacked by her appearance and only wanted to get close to her. Bobbie felt the same way, and if she hadn't promised to be part of the damn program, she'd no doubt have her hands all over Grace, which would get her smacked so . . .

"You are absolutely stunning, Gracie," Bobbie managed to whisper. "You are, without a doubt, the most gorgeous woman in this room."

Grace looked all around. "I don't know about that, my love. Mrs. McKinley looks rather spectacular."

Bobbie stifled a giggle. "Did you see how Larry was looking at her?"

Grace stifled her own giggle. "I did, and I also saw how Dr. Jones was looking at Larry."

Bobbie returned her attention to Grace and reached out a hand to—Grace didn't know what she planned to do, but she gently slapped the hand away with a whispered, "Don't you dare."

Grace wore a strapless white gown that tightly hugged and caressed her body all the way down until it flared at the bottom where a crimson lining was visible. Diamond and ruby necklace, diamond and ruby earrings, hair piled atop her head, Bobbie's diamond ring on her right hand—no wonder the men of Harlem Hospital were beside themselves. Grace knew how she looked. She also knew that Boy Bobby was keeping a close watch on her hospital colleagues, making certain they didn't get too close, and their hands didn't wander.

Eileen's gown did a deep dive down into her cleavage even as it clung tightly to her back and shoulders and down her waist and hips to the floor. Julia called the color pomegranate but whatever it was, no one had ever seen anything like it. She wore Bobbie's diamond and ruby necklace, letting it fall all the way into the cleavage. Joyce was on the other side of the room with the children, deliberately staying well away from her, which Bobbie would have been doing if she hadn't needed Grace to keep her from fleeing.

Queen Esther, Myrt and Thelma, elegantly clad in evening gowns, watched the people—men and women alike—react to Grace and Eileen. "Those are some kinda beautiful women," Queen Esther said more than once.

"I think we look pretty good, too," Myrt sniffed.

Queen Esther grinned, took each one by the arm, and moved toward the stage. "I want to be in the front when Miss Bobbie plays."

Bobbie and Joyce were clad in black: Joyce in a high-necked, sleeveless, tight-fitting outfit with pants that hugged her narrow frame all the way down to her knees, where suddenly they flared. It was shot through with silver and looked like the night sky with sparkling stars. Bobbie, too, wore a one-piece with a tight-fitting, sleeveless top and wide-legged pants that moved with every step. A snugly fitted, beaded bolero jacket completed the ensemble. If Grace hadn't been so occupied with keeping Bobbie's hands off her, she'd have had her hands all over Bobbie.

Then it was time. Billy Strayhorn stilled the band, took up the microphone, and the audience moved toward him.

"Tonight is very special for me. I've known Bobbie Hilliard since she was a little girl. Her father, the great jazz pianist Robert Hilliard, was my friend and my teacher, and little Bobbie here was my student for a while. Then she passed me by, got better and better until there was nothing I could teach her. This composition has never before been performed in public. The one other time Bobbie played it was for the committee at Columbia University that awarded her the Doctor of Philosophy in Music Composition. This will be the first time the composition will be played with an orchestra. It is my honor and my pleasure to present Dr. Eleanor Roberta Hilliard."

Grace was crying so hard she couldn't applaud, but everyone else made enough noise that Bobbie was carried all the way to the stage, up the steps, and to the piano, where she and Billy Strayhorn hugged and whispered to each other. They were more than friends, as close as siblings, with that kind of love and respect for each other, which is why he was able to calm her by giving her his conducting baton and telling her to get to work.

Bobbie bowed to the band, then to Billy, returned his baton, and took her seat on the piano bench. She inhaled deeply, placed her hands above the keyboard, and lowered them as Billy raised his baton. Rhythmic, deep chords rose from the piano, then fell away. Rose again and fell away again. Bobbie Hilliard was in another place, a place inhabited by people like her, like her father, like her mother, like Billy Strayhorn and Duke Ellington, like Hazel Scott, like Dorothy West and Lois Jones Pierre-Noel: people who go deep within, to places that have no name, in search of the nameless gift that gives meaning to the life of the artist.

They played for a little more than an hour. Bobbie's piano slowed and quieted, the notes gentled and caressed by the timpani in the orchestra, then by the chords of the stand-up bass and the low, rich wail of an oboe. Bobbie's hands dropped away from the piano into her lap. She stood up and faced a silent, crowded room. Then all hell broke loose—screaming and whistling and shouting, foot-stomping, hand-clapping—and it went on for a long while as Bobbie finally realized, with Billy Strayhorn's encouragement, that she should be taking bows.

She turned and bowed to Billy and to the orchestra. As one, the men stood and bowed to her. She and Billy hugged each other; then she looked for Grace, who stood at the foot of the steps, arms wide open, tears streaming down her cheeks. And there was Boy Bobby and Eileen and Joyce and Larry and Myrt and Thelma and Queen Esther and Ben and David. And EJ and

Scottie.

Boy Bobby shouldered his way through the well-wishers to her side, put his arm around her, and moved her slowly but surely to Grace, who had been pushed aside. Not caring who saw or what they thought, Bobbie hugged her beloved Gracie tightly for a long moment, then released her because of course she cared who saw them and what they thought, especially the high-ranking personnel of Harlem Hospital. Because this was the Hotel Theresa, the food was as elegant as the crowd. And because Bobbie and Grace and the McKinleys and Joyce were well-known to the staff, trays of champagne and lobster thermidor were delivered to their table. They ate and drank while the band played, and the crowd swirled around them. Bobby placed himself strategically between Bobbie and Grace and began giggling before he managed a full sentence: "I can't wait to tell you in detail about all the tuxedoed gentlemen who recognized Queen Esther and almost suffered cardiac arrest." They had to control themselves because loud, uncontrolled guffaws from elegant ladies most definitely was not acceptable behavior.

"Was Queen aware of being noticed?" Grace managed to ask between giggles.

"Oh, indeed she was." Bobby grinned at the thought. "To call her expression smug would be to do her a major disservice."

People kept stopping by the table to congratulate Bobbie on her piano composition, and more than a few more stopped to compliment Grace and Eileen on their gowns. And they all danced—Boy Bobby, Ben, Larry, and David alternated partnering all the women and they loved every minute of it. Finally, things began to wind down and guests began to take their leave, creating long lines at the coat checks but Bobby, Ben and David, coat check tickets in hand, braved the line.

The crowd milled about on the sidewalk outside the hotel. What an evening it had been. Dancing to an orchestra conducted by Billy Strayhorn with a guest appearance by Duke Ellington, and the piano concerto by Eleanor Hilliard. Vocals by Billy Eckstine and Sarah Vaughan. And the faces in the crowd: Lena Horne, Sidney Poitier, Ruby Dee and Ossie Davis, Hazel Scott and Adam Clayton Powell Jr., Jackie Robinson, and Diana Sands. Limousines had quickly carried away the rich and famous, and the merely rich (of which there were quite a few), and though the queue for taxis was long, the crowd that hunched together for protection against the frigid temperatures was still talking about the wonderful event they had just experienced. Many people stopped to commend Bobbie as they passed by—Dr. Hilliard they called her because she was listed in the program as Dr. Eleanor Roberta Hilliard.

"Tell me again why we're standing out here shivering and freezing to death?" Eileen demanded to know through chattering teeth, the full-length mink having no warming effect, no doubt due to the fact that her gown was open to her waist.

"We're waiting for David and Ben and Queen Esther to bring the cars—" Boy Bobby began when Jack said, pointing toward the street, "There they are, and not a moment too soon!"

"Hey bitch, you ain't goin' nowhere!" The screamed words reverberated in the darkness. The evil hatred of the words sounded brittle, like the cracking ice on the Hudson in deep winter. They all looked for its source, emerging from the shadows on 124th Street beside the ivory exterior of the Theresa, and two of them recognized the danger immediately.

"That's Von Thompkins!" Grace shouted.

"She's got a gun!" Boy Bobby yelled as Von raised her arm and pointed.

Bobbie pushed Grace aside and strode forward toward the threat that was Von Thompkins just as the gun fired. Grace stumbled and fell to the ground, and Bobbie spun around and fell to the ground beside her. Boy Bobby ran toward Von Thompkins as she ran down 124th Street beside the Theresa Hotel and toward Seventh Avenue. Everyone else stood statue-still, almost literally frozen; then yells and screams split the air with everyone running to the two figures on the icy sidewalk: Bobbie and Grace, and one of them was bleeding.

"Bobbie!" Grace screamed. "Oh Bobbie no! She shot Bobbie!" Grace sobbed, trying her best to kneel beside Bobbie but the elegant, form-fitting gown prevented it.

Grace, struggling for control, saw Bobbie sitting up, a nurse on either side of her, and she kept trying to free herself from the arms that contained her so that she could go to Bobbie. But until Myrt and Thelma could assess the damage they would have to keep Grace away from her.

"Come and get in the car, Grace, out of the cold," Jack said.

"Not until I see Bobbie!"

Boy Bobby ran back toward them. "I lost her, goddammit! She must have run into the hotel."

"She ran to the train," Queen Esther said. "She's going up to The Bronx where she always goes when she gets her dumbass self into real trouble 'cause she's safe up there. Don't nobody who ain't lived up there know their way around. But I know my way around The Bronx. I know where Von Thompkins lives and where she hangs out."

"Then let's go get her ass!" Boy Bobby exclaimed.

Then, against all attempts to prevent it, Bobbie Hilliard pushed herself into a standing position. "I'm ready," she said, grabbing and holding tightly to Boy Bobby's arm.

"No, Bobbie!" Grace screamed. "You can't! Please don't, Bobbie—"

"It's time she was stopped, Grace. I can't live in peace if I know she could appear at any time and kill you. I will not allow that to happen."

Larry hurried over to them. "Bobby, Esther, what are you doing? You can't—"

"We have to, Larry. We have to stop her before she kills Grace."

"She almost killed you, Bobbie," Larry said, trying to take her arm, but she pulled away from him.

"Don't you understand, Larry, that I can't live without her?"

"And do you think she can live without you? You're bleeding."

"Please take care of her until I get back, Larry. You and Eileen and Jo and Thelma and Myrt: please take care of her until I get back."

"Suppose you don't get back?" Larry asked.

"She'll get back, Mr. McKinley, I promise you," Queen Esther said.

"If I have to kill that crazy, evil fool myself," Boy Bobby said through clenched teeth, "Bobbie will be back in a little while." He was damned if he was going to let a piece of shit like Von Thompkins harm the woman he thought of as a sister. As long as Von Thompkins could roam free Grace Hannon was not safe, and if anything ever happened to Grace, Bobbie would surely die. After what had happened to her parents and brother, to lose Grace would be more than she could bear. She almost certainly would die.

"I'll drive," Queen Esther said, "'cause I know where we're going. I know exactly where that lowlife goes to hide."

The Bronx was right next door to Harlem, and it didn't take very long to get there. Harlem had its share of run-down and impoverished buildings but nothing like this. Block after block, street after street, building after building—high rise or low rise—half of the windows were broken out and many of the others boarded up. Many of the buildings were newly constructed, but it was cheap, ugly construction, and Bobby would wager that the interior was ugly as well. The same often was true in Harlem, as if the Housing Department bosses didn't believe that poor people wanted or deserved an attractive place to live. Who the hell wanted to live with cinder block living and dining room walls?

"Where are we?" Girl Bobbie whispered, and the weakness of her voice frightened him.

"Somewhere in The Bronx," Boy Bobby replied, and tightened his hold on her. "I don't know exactly where—-" They were approaching a street sign. "East Twenty-Fifth Street, and I saw a sign with an arrow pointing to the Cross Bronx Expressway, whatever that is."

Queen Esther said, "Von Thompkins grew up in this building and moved out when she was about nineteen or twenty, but her mama stayed here, and when the mama died Von kept the apartment. Not many people who live here now know her, and nobody who knows her now is aware of this place. This is where she comes to hide from whatever bad shit she's gotten herself into."

Queen Esther parked the truck, extinguished the lights, and scrutinized the activity on the block. Nobody was paying attention to an old black pickup even though it did have a new paint job. Boy Bobby scrutinized the building, at least what he could see of it. "Can she see us coming?"

Esther shook her head. "Her unit is in the back. She won't know we're there until we knock on the door."

"We won't be knocking," Bobbie said. "What kind of tools do you have in this truck?"

"I've got a sledgehammer, but I don't think that's the way to do this, Bobbie," he said. "Don't forget she's got a pistol, and a sledgehammer pounding at her door could make her start shooting through it."

"He's right, Miss Bobbie. I'll knock and call out to her at the same time, tell her it's Miz Lillie at the door. That was her ma's name, and she'll open it right quick."

And she did, with the snarl Bobbie recognized all too well. "Who the fuck—" Von began but Boy Bobby shoved the door into her so hard he knocked her backward into the sofa and she lost her balance, falling to the floor. The pistol flew out of her grip when she hit the floor. Queen Esther grabbed it and backed up toward Bobby.

"You still are one ugly piece of shit, Devonta Thompkins," Queen Esther snarled.

Von got quickly to her feet, staring evil daggers at the three interlopers in her tiny, cramped living room. "Do I know you?"

"Esther Jones," Queen said, and Von roared with nasty laughter.

"If it ain't faggoty fairy Chester Jones," Von said, looking Queen up and down, and she was quite a beautiful sight, still in the gown she'd worn earlier. "You look like you come up in the world, Chester."

"You don't, Devonta. You still look like a ugly, sorry leech who lives off other people."

Von's eyes narrowed but she didn't speak. She turned her hostile glare on Bobbie, and surprise creased her face. She looked Bobbie up and down, taking in the elegance of her clothing, and seeing the blood pooling at Bobbie's feet, she laughed. "You look like you'll bleed to death before goddam Grace sees you again."

"Somebody hit her, please," Bobbie said, and Queen Esther slapped Von so hard Boy Bobby's teeth rattled. Von staggered but managed to keep from falling. "Do you even know why you hate Grace Hannon, or are you just evil and insane?" Bobbie asked.

"I don't hate your tight-assed doctor bitch, I hate your rich ass. Think your money makes you better than everybody else. You got your mansion up on Strivers Row, but you kept that apartment in the Theresa. Never took one of them girls to where you live, just like you never spent the night in that apartment with one of 'em. You just fuck 'em and leave 'em and rush back to your mansion. Then you meet the doctor—that's somebody who's good enough for you, right? Driving her white Cadillac and wearing her fancy clothes. Wonder how she'll like living in your mansion all by her lonesome? I wanted to kill her to bring you down low, but if you bleed to death, she'll be brought low, and that'll be all right with me." Von looked at the growing puddle of blood at Bobbie's feet and laughed, then suddenly lunged toward Queen Esther, reaching for the hand holding the pistol. Queen sidestepped her, raised the gun, and fired twice, both bullets hitting Von Thompkins in the chest.

Queen dropped the weapon into her coat pocket, saying, "Give me your belt, please, Mr. Mason, and your tie. We got to stop Miss Bobbie from bleeding. We can't let that piece of shit be right." They tied two tourniquets on Bobbie's arm—one at the shoulder, the other lower—and pulled them so tightly that Bobbie gasped and almost fainted. They practically carried her out to the truck.

Bobby opened the storage box in the bed of the truck and took out all the blankets and tarps. He spread them out, making a pallet, and climbed into the truck bed. He grabbed Bobbie under her arms as Queen lifted her legs, and they got her onto the pallet and covered her. Then Bobby sat down and put her head in his lap. With his back resting against the storage box he extended his legs, one on either side of her, to keep her secure and perhaps to add a bit of warmth. It felt at least fifteen degrees colder than it had before they entered Von's apartment.

"Drive like hell down to Harlem Hospital," Boy Bobby said, and Queen did, praying the whole way that no flashing red-and-blue cop lights would force her to stop and explain anything.

They screeched into the Harlem Hospital Emergency Room entrance, Queen Esther flashing the lights and blowing the horn. Four people ran out—three of them ER personnel with a stretcher. Larry McKinley was the fourth. All of them helped to get Bobbie out of the truck bed and onto the stretcher, and they took off running, shouting instructions and information as they went and gathering a crowd of medical personnel to assist.

"The surgeons are standing by," Larry said, "and Thelma will be assisting. Bobby, please go tell Grace that Bobbie is all right, that she's on her way to surgery. And make sure she sees that you're telling the truth—that Bobbie is alive—"

"She lost a lot of blood, Larry." Bobby closed his eyes at the memory of all the blood.

"Is she alive, Bobby?" When he nodded, Larry said, "Then they'll keep her that way." And when Bobby ran toward and into the elevator Larry looked at Queen. "Thank you, Miss Jones. For everything."

"Y'all are my family, Mr. McKinley, the only family I got, and family looks out for each other."

"And Von Thompkins—"

"Dr. Hannon and nobody else in this family will ever have to worry about Von Thompkins again."

Eileen saw Bobby the moment he stepped off the elevator and ran to throw herself at him. He held her and whispered that Grace would forever be safe from Von Thompkins, then walked with her toward Grace who was struggling to stand. He pulled her up and into an embrace. She was weeping uncontrollably.

"Bobbie's on her way to surgery, Grace, I promise. She's all right—"

"How, Bobby? How is she all right when she was bleeding—"

Myrt ran toward them holding a mask and gown. "Come on, Gracie! Thelma told me The Boys said to bring you upstairs."

"Thelma is in the surgical suite with The Boys?" Grace stopped crying. She was going to see Bobbie who was alive and who was going to be all right? She hugged and kissed Boy Bobby and Eileen, and let Myrt lead her to the elevator. She was going to see Bobbie. Then she stopped suddenly. Grace turned to face Boy Bobby and looked the question at him. She didn't have to say the name. He gave her two thumbs up, and she hurried into the elevator where Myrt was waiting for her. The elevator door slid closed, and she was en route to Bobbie.

"She lost an awful lot of blood" was the first thing Dr.

Arthur Jennings said several hours later when he joined her in the doctors' lounge. "But thanks to her overall excellent health she will survive that." Grace looked from him to his surgical partner, Dr. Oliver Crawford, then to the orthopedic specialist Dr. James Gordon, and they all wore the same affirmative facial expression. It meant that Bobbie was going to be all right.

"Whichever of your friends kept that arm pinned close to her side did a very good thing," the orthopedic surgeon said. "We repaired some tendon and ligament damage in the shoulder that will heal over time, but the damn bullet nicked the scapula. It is repaired and will heal, though it will take some time."

"And will full range of motion be restored?" Grace asked.

James Gordon gave a tentative nod. "Much depends on the kind of patient she will be."

Grace groaned. "Effort will be required, but she will not want to lose any degree of function in that arm so she will follow orders."

"Yes, it would be a true tragedy if her talent was lost to the world," Oliver Crawford said.

Grace sat beside Bobbie's bed watching her sleep and breathe, and eyeing with unease the complicated arrangement of weights and pulleys and ropes that kept her shoulder in the position James Gordon believed would restore normal use to it. Bobbie would have a fit. Grace knew it, and if Myrt and Thelma had seen it, which they most likely had, they knew it, too. Anyone familiar with Eleanor Roberta Hilliard knew what her reaction and response would be to the traction apparatus.

"What in the merry mother fuck." The words were whispered, but Grace was jolted awake as if they'd been yelled. She stood as close to Bobbie's bed as she could get and took her free hand, holding and kissing it.

"Bobbie my love," she whispered into Bobbie's ear. "I'm here, Bobbie."

Bobbie's eyes fluttered open and shut, then focused. "Gracie, is that you? What is this thing? And why in bloody hell does it hurt so much. Oh Gracie, it hurts so much. Please make it stop!" Tears rolled down her cheeks. Grace pressed the call button, and the nurse arrived as quickly as if she'd been standing outside the door.

"Hello, Dr. Hannon. Is our patient awake?"

"In and out, but very much aware of the pain. What can she have?"

"I'll be right back," she said, and hurried from the room to prepare the syringe with medication she would inject into Bobbie and which would return her to a place where she would not be aware of the pain—at least for several hours, during which everyone visited: Boy Bobby, Jack, Queen Esther, Myrt and Thelma, Joyce, Eileen, and Larry, and EJ, who started to cry as soon as she saw Auntie Bobbie in the hospital bed with the huge, scary-looking thing attached to her shoulder.

Grace held the girl and let her cry, then promised her that Bobbie would get better. "It will take a little while, EJ, because she was badly injured—"

"That person shot her with a gun, Auntie Grace. Why?"

Grace was shaking her head. "We don't always know why people sometimes do things that hurt other people. We just know that our Bobbie will be back to her old self very soon."

The little girl looked straight into her eyes. "Do you promise, Dr. Hannon?"

"Yes, Miss McKinley, I do promise." EJ giggled through her tears and hugged Grace. Then Larry picked her up and held her over the bed so she could kiss Bobbie. They left before anyone could see the child who most definitely was not allowed to be in the hospital.

"I know you're staying all night," Jack said. "I'll stay with you."

"Who's minding the store?" Grace asked, meaning The Slow Drag, and Jack grinned wickedly.

"Mack is so much more than just a bouncer. And I trust her, Grace. I'll go in Monday early and do all the paperwork while Queen and her crew get the place cleaned up for the week. We won't let Bobbie down, I promise."

"I know you won't, Jack, and it never crossed my mind that you would."

"I'll be returning to school in the new year, with Joyce's advice and assistance."

"I am so happy for you, and so very proud of you, Jack. You will be a fine educator."

It was Christmastime and everybody's favorite season. Even the weather got in the spirit. Every day it snowed a bit. Not enough to make a mess and interfere with people's lives, but just enough to herald and celebrate the season. Shopping was done, trees were bought and decorated, and menus were discussed over and over until they were finalized. Bobby's mother and grandmother arrived. He was so happy and excited he bounced all around like an intoxicated ball until Larry sent him home. Before that happened they took Queen Esther a tree and boxes of decorations, along with presents to go beneath it. They had seen how excited she was at decorating the tree for the lobby and had asked when she planned to put up her own tree. Sadness had crossed her face.

Bobbie and Grace were hosting the Christmas Eve gathering to which everyone was invited, and for the first time Bobby would be coupled with David Craig and Larry with Ben Jones in the presence of their friends. Also for the first time, some parents would join in: Bobby's mother and grandmother, Thelma and Myrt's mothers, and Jack's parents. Grace's parents and Eileen's parents had not been invited. But before any of the evening's festivities could be enjoyed, Bobbie insisted that everyone come to the garage to see her Christmas present from Grace.

"Well, if it's in the garage, it must be a car, isn't that right?" queried Bobby's grandmother, and no one contradicted her. Neither did anyone need to ask which car was the present from Grace to Bobbie because no one had ever seen anything like it: a brand-new, first-of-its-kind Ford Thunderbird. White with red interior to match Grace's Cadillac.

"And since you can't possibly drive it with your arm taped to your body, I'll be happy to drive you anywhere you need to go," Boy Bobby volunteered.

"Oh, you're too kind," Girl Bobbie responded.

"But Grace," Eileen said in a near wail. "Only two people can fit in at one time. How can Bobbie possibly take Joyce *and* me to anywhere at the same time?"

"Bobbie, dear?" Grace said with raised eyebrows, and the laughter carried them all back to the party upstairs.

Grace and Bobbie had hired a caterer and what an enjoyable evening it was. The festivities went on well into the early hours of Christmas Day—after EJ and Scottie were put to bed in the guest room and the caterers and bartenders had cleaned up and said good-night. The copious amounts of leftover food overflowed the stove and counters in the kitchen, and the copious amount of leftover booze (including champagne) lined the floor behind the bar and filled an entire shelf in the refrigerator, guaranteeing that the revelers would not go hungry or thirsty no matter how long or late their celebration lasted. And it lasted until nearly dawn.

Christmas Day and Christmas dinner were private affairs, everyone in their own homes with their closest loved ones, which left Queen Esther on her own. She didn't really mind. Lately she'd been doing a lot of thinking and feeling a lot of things—an unfamiliar combination for her. After she cleaned the outside of the building—sweeping the sidewalk, washing the glass front door, and polishing the wood and brass door handles—she swept and mopped the lobby and polished the wood and the brass. Then there was nothing for her to do.

Bobbie and Grace had told her to take as much food as she wanted and a whole bottle of bourbon. The little Christmas tree Bobby and Larry had brought her and which she loaded with colored lights and ornaments shone as brightly in her apartment as the huge one in the lobby. The first Christmas tree she'd ever had in her entire life! And the presents from the two of them, and from Grace and Bobbie, were the nicest, most thoughtful gifts she'd ever received from anyone. Also, she was learning to read and write at her age, whatever that was. "A person is never too old to learn, Queen," Bobbie had told her, and she was right. People she hadn't known a year ago now were friends and family while people she'd known for more than two decades were . . . what?

Try as she might, and as hard as she wished, she just could not get over the fact that people she once had considered her best friends and family had stolen everything she owned while she was in hiding from the police, cut, shot, and bleeding. How could such a thing have happened? Why had it happened? All the time they had spent together, all the laughter and tears, joy and pain, they had shared—was it all meaningless? Shallow at best, empty at worst? How was it possible that people she just met could care more for her than people she'd known and lived with for years? The pain of it was worse than the pain of the attack in the alley that had almost cost her her life. She could have died in that alley, probably should have. More than once she wished she had, for then she would not have known that her best friends had broken into her room and stolen all of her worldly possessions.

Not bothering to tie the usual floral scarf on her head, she pulled a red knit cap down low over her ears and wrapped a red wool scarf around her neck. She donned the heavy woolen overcoat she had purchased at a secondhand store on Seventh Avenue. She almost hadn't bought the coat, thinking it too masculine looking, but its warmth overcame that consideration. It also had a deep inside pocket into which she dropped the gun and three cans of lighter fluid. She turned off and unplugged the Christmas tree but left the small table lamp burning. She closed and locked her apartment door, crossed the empty lobby, and stepped out into the cold, clear Christmas Day air.

She got a downtown taxi almost immediately and in no time it seemed, the driver was stopping in front of the building on 111th Street she once called home. She paid the fare and left a sizable Merry Christmas tip. She stood on the sidewalk looking up at the building and tried to remember how long she'd lived here. Too long, she thought. "What a fuckin' dump!" She walked closer and stood looking up at it. Had it always looked like this? And if so, why hadn't she realized how run-down it was, and in what an almost dangerous state of disrepair: mortar cracked or missing from around most of the windows and the door; cracked and missing windowpanes, cardboard replacements looking like so many black eyes. She backed away from the building, stepping into the street to see the roof, aware that she was hoping not to see what she did see: damaged and missing tiles. "No wonder it was always so damn cold or so damn hot in there."

Esther walked farther away from the building as if she could unsee what she'd just seen—or perhaps trip over, the reasons she never been able to. She remembered that she had always been cold or hot when she lived here, that the roof had always leaked, that the basement had always flooded. But why was she remembering it now, standing outside the dump she once called home, on a frigid and snowy Christmas morning? Because before now she hadn't known any better—because she'd never lived any other way. She had never known or imagined that she could live as she lived now, and the change in her life was because the residents of this building had broken into her room and stolen

408

everything she possessed. She had had nothing and nowhere to live, and she came here this morning for her payback.

She was here to burn this building to the ground, killing all the drunk snoring queens in their beds, and to put two bullets into her own brain.

"I oughta wake 'em up and thank 'em," Esther said aloud, "but drunk as they are, not only wouldn't they hear me, they prob'ly wouldn't recognize me, 'cause like Devonta said, I look like I've come up in the world."

She walked to the corner to hail a taxi, realizing that she indeed had changed since she lived in the drag queens' hotel. She had learned a lot, including how to read and write, and her new friends told her that learning lasted a lifetime. And though she didn't know it until just now, there was more than one way to exact payback for harm done: Look like you've come up in the world.

ACKNOWLEDGMENTS

This book pays homage to the Creatives of the Harlem Renaissance: The writers, musicians and singers, dancers, actors, painters, and teachers—and those who supported, appreciated and championed them. Because they were, we are, and Harlem remains vibrant.

ABOUT THE AUTHOR

PENNY MICKELBURY is a trailblazing author and an award-winning playwright. She is a two-time Lambda Literary Award finalist, was a writer in residence at Hedgebrook Women Writers Retreat, and is a recipient of the Audre Lorde Estate Grant. Before focusing on literary pursuits, Penny was a pioneering newspaper, radio, and television reporter based primarily in Washington, DC, wrote journalistic nonfiction, and was a frequent contributor to such publications as *Black Issues Book Review*, Africana.com, and the *Washington Blade*. In 2019 she joined the other members of the *Washington Post's* Metro Seven as an inductee into the National Association of Black Journalists Hall of Fame.

Bywater Books believes that all people have the right to read or not read what they want—and that we are all entitled to make those choices ourselves. But to ensure these freedoms, books and information must remain accessible. Any effort to eliminate or restrict these rights stands in opposition to freedom of choice. Please join us by opposing book bans and censorship of the LGBTQ+ and BIPOC communities.

At Bywater Books, we are all stories.

For more information about Bywater Books, our authors, and our titles, please visit our website.

https://bywaterbooks.com